“I owe you life

The formality of Daffyd

“And if I refuse?” The words spilled out before I could censor them.

“I cannot accept your refusal,” he said so quietly that I wasn’t sure even Tucker heard. “You hold my debt and I must serve you.”

“Daffyd, I can’t—” I shut my eyes and crossed my arms across my chest, ignoring his outstretched hands. I knew what I was supposed to do. I’d seen it countless times in my mother’s cousin’s court: A debt acknowledgment required I take Daffyd’s hands and accept his offering.

I tried to make sure the words came out right. “Cousin, I acknowledge the debt and grant you freedom. You may return to your home, to Wales.”

Daffyd got a very distinctly amused look on his face. If I didn’t know better, I’d have thought he was smirking at me.

“My liege,” he said and sank to one knee. “I thank you for my freedom and I choose to stay.” He bowed his head, his long silver hair parting to bare the nape of his neck, the locks on either side of his face brushing the tile floor.

He’d bared his neck. I didn’t know if this was a Sidhe thing, but it was definitely a wolf thing and a Clan thing. When pledging service to one’s liege, the bared neck signified submission and acknowledgment of the other’s dominance.

“Damn it, Daffyd.” I pulled on his hands and he stood, a smile still dancing around his mouth and eyes. “You played me.”

***Blood Kin* is also available as an eBook**

Turn the page for rave reviews of Maria Lima . . .

Praise for Maria Lima's Blood Lines series

BLOOD BARGAIN

"Maria Lima captures the essence of urban fantasy, mystery, and romantic elements in *Blood Bargain*."

—SF Site

"Part of what makes this series so interesting is that Lima uses well-known tropes of the fantasy genre, yet gives them enough of a spin to make them recognizable to readers but keep them wondering if things will play out as expected."

—SFRevu

"Urban fantasy fans are going to love this—especially the Kelly clan, an extended family of supernaturals living within human society. . . . A strong tale that fans of Kelly Armstrong and Kim Harrison will want to read."

—Worlds of Wonders

"I couldn't put it down. Maria Lima's second Blood Lines novel is even better than the first, a fun and sometimes poignant paranormal treat."

—Fantasy Literature

"Grabs you from the start and keeps you turning pages until you solve the mystery. . . . I certainly will be watching for more books by Maria Lima."

—Fresh Fiction

"Ms. Lima spins a suspenseful tale and packs it with paranormal elements that will hold the reader's attention to the end . . . fast-moving."

—Darque Reviews

MATTERS OF THE BLOOD

"An absolutely spectacular addition to the paranormal landscape. . . . A classy, teasing tale riddled with intrigue and paranormal bliss."

—BookFetish

"Dark, seductive, and bitingly humorous. . . ."

—Heartstring

"A complex plot with the requisite twists and turns of a mystery, the passion of a paranormal romance, and the unearthly elements of urban fantasy."

—SF Site

"A great page-turner. . . . "

—The Bookshelf Reviews

"An excellent book, readable and gripping with varied characters. . . . "

—Curled Up With a Good Book (5 stars)

"A brilliant tale of supernatural power, revenge, and the excitement of newfound love."

—Darque Reviews

"Refreshing . . . I loved the story's vividly drawn rural-Texas setting."

—Fantasy Literature (4 stars)

"Another kick-ass heroine enters the paranormal arena in Lima's bloodthirsty whodunit. Feisty Keira narrates with a biting sense of humor. . . ."

—*Romantic Times* (4 stars)

"A superb paranormal whodunit with a touch of romance and with plenty of interwoven subplots . . . but the center holding this superb tale together is the likable Keira, who makes the abnormal seem so normal."

—Alternative Worlds

Don't miss the first two exciting adventures in the Blood Lines series by Maria Lima!

Matters of the Blood

Blood Bargain

BLOOD KIN

MARIA LIMA

POCKET BOOKS
New York London Toronto Sydney

Pocket Books
A Division of Simon & Schuster, Inc.
1230 Avenue of the Americas
New York, NY 10020

This Juno Books/Pocket Books paperback edition November 2009

JUNO BOOKS and colophon are trademarks of Wildside Press LLC used under license by Simon & Schuster, Inc., the publisher of this work.

POCKET and colophon are registered trademarks of Simon & Schuster, Inc.

For information about special discounts for bulk purchases, please contact Simon & Schuster Special Sales at 1-866-506-1949 or business@simonandschuster.com.

The Simon & Schuster Speakers Bureau can bring authors to your live event. For more information or to book an event contact the Simon & Schuster Speakers Bureau at 1-866-248-3049 or visit our website at www.simonspeakers.com.

Designed by Julie Adams
Cover design by Laywan Kwan
Cover photograph by Glowimages/Getty Images

Manufactured in the United States of America

10 9 8 7 6 5 4 3 2 1

ISBN 978-1-4391-5676-6
ISBN 978-1-4391-6673-4 (ebook)

Third time's a charm and this time, this book is for
my patient and supportive parents,
Yolanda and Sandy Bodine, neither of whom bear
any resemblance to the parental or other authority
units in this story.

ACKNOWLEDGMENTS

The village continues to grow as the wonderful people around me continue to help.

Merci bien a tous mes amis et mes aides. Diolch yn fawr iawn.

As always and with much love, Carla Coupe, the best beta ever. Without your input, I'm absolutely less.

To my sister, Laura, who lives up to her librarian training and eagle eyes. Thanks for your fabulous support.

To Tanya Kennedy-Luminati, for her insights and suggestions.

Thanks to Pam Thomson and Sylvia Tremblay for all their Canadian input.

Any mistakes about Canada or Vancouver are strictly my bad . . . please forgive.

To all my family for indulging me on the Vancouver trip and letting me squeeze in research while we were there.

A special thanks to Lillian Butler, who first wrote the line about Texas weather in her blog, and to Amber of Amberkatze's blog for pointing me in the right direction for Welsh language help.

Kudos to the lovely people of Canada and especially the city of Vancouver and the province of British Columbia. You all could not have been kinder, more helpful, or more amazing. I will state categorically that I fell in love with the city, the province, and the country.

BLOOD KIN

PRELUDE

The Beginning

*S*OUNDS OF BELLS *and laughter ride on the wind, punctuating feeling, lifting senses, accenting actions with melody.*

I shouldn't be able to hear it, underground as I am in a place blasted out of limestone, a refuge from all the events of yesterday, from the sun that most assuredly blazes outside.

Whispers of love intertwine with the music, kisses on skin, the touch of hand, lips, a lock of hair sliding across my breast, everything magnified, the intensity so much, so more.

My own hair cascades down my back. I feel everything: touch, scent, sound, taste, sight merge into one feeling, one being, one—

The music of the air surrounds us, envelops us, makes us part of its completion.

I gasp as we all reach our crescendo—me, my lover and the melody—all together as if choreographed.

It is gone.

I want to weep for the joy of it.

I want to weep for the loss of it.

CHAPTER ONE

I SUMMONED A DEMON ONCE. At least at the time, that's what I'd thought it was. I could probably chalk up both the summoning and my hesitation about its result to the fact that I'd been drinking and smoking a wee bit—okay, a lot—of something not quite so legal. One thing for sure: the damned beast had smelled rotten, like it'd been rolling in a thousand dead skunks or a few not-so-fresh corpses.

In my world, demons were nothing more than tangible evil.

And right now, evil was about to raise its stinking, ugly-ass head again—in the form of my former lover, Gideon.

Don't get me wrong. I'm not talking metaphorical he-done-me-wrongness or a badass boy who turned his back on my loving redemption. Gideon was neither the heartbreaking villain of a country-and-western song nor the hero of a romance novel gone amok. No, Gideon was evil. He had chosen the darkside. His power lay in darkness. He could speak to the shadows, call the shades.

I'd been in love with him and trusting and he'd convinced me to drop all my barriers, to open my naive self to him completely so we could truly be "one." I fell for it like an egg from a tall hen.

When I touched his soul, what I saw and felt inside him scared me so badly I ran from London all the way back to Texas.

But Gideon was also family. Not closely related, but

all Clan were cousins, aunts, uncles, all connected. Clan blood begat Clan blood. He was blood kin.

So when Aunt Isabel showed up declaring she needed my help because Gideon was dying, that I had to leave immediately for the family compound in British Columbia—I knew I had to go.

Of course Gideon wasn't the only reason I had to skedaddle to Vancouver. I'd also Changed yesterday, and not solely the capital-C Clan Change we all undergo when we come into our true Talent. I had to be special. I'd become the Kelly heir—yeah, *that* one, the one who only came along every so many blah-blah generations, etc. The one who didn't have only a single Talent, but got the whole supernatural shebang, all the Talents from astromancy to weather witching. Not something I'd ever imagined, nor wanted. Leave it to me, Keira Kelly, to be genetically unique . . . or maybe a genetic freak.

The previous couple of days had been insane in other ways, too—missing people, the one person I'd found that I could truly be myself with in a coma, my best and oldest human friend nearly raped and murdered . . .

The craziness had turned downright depressing, though. Said best friend, Bea, wouldn't even speak to me on the phone.

After yet another failed speed dial, I slammed the phone Bea would not answer shut and shoved it in the pocket of my backpack. A yelp came from behind me as I tossed the pack aside.

"Ay, watch it!" Bea's nephew, Noe, a gangly just-turned-eighteen-year-old loped into my living room, avoiding the pack, which had landed next to him.

"Damn. Sorry, Noe. I didn't hear you come in."

"No prob. I didn't exactly knock," he answered.

I kept my back to him as I tried to compose myself. Had Bea sent him to talk to me? To tell me to stop bugging her? I just wanted to explain to her why I'd done what I'd done. Why sentencing a man to death at the hands of a Sidhe instead of turning him over to proper human authorities had been my only choice. Noe knew none of this, however, only that his aunt and I were in the midst of some sort of disagreement.

"So, packing, huh?" Noe said as he settled onto a nearby chair. "You gonna keep calling Bea?"

I nodded and fiddled with the fastenings on a rolling suitcase I'd pulled out of the hall closet. Most of my clothes were at Adam's, but some of the cooler weather gear that I expected to need for my unexpected and unwanted trip to Canada were still at my house. The temperatures would most likely be mild, but I'd probably need warmer outer gear for nighttime.

"How'd you know I've been calling her?" I managed to say after a moment.

"You've only been calling the house and the café over and over for the past few hours," he said, leaving off the obvious "duh."

I rubbed my eyes, trying to avoid the tears that threatened. Thirty years and I still had no clue how to handle a fight with my best friend . . . and this one was a doozy. Less of a fight, really, and more of a complete dissonance in moral systems.

"You're heading to Canada?" Noe prodded.

"How'd you hear that?"

"I listened to the messages you left on the answering machine," he said.

"Yeah, of course you did," I muttered and put aside a pile of receipts and other detritus that I'd dug out of my duffle bag. Last time I'd used this, Adam and I had gone on a trip to a fancy vampire hotel.

"You stopping by the house first?"

Noe tried to make the question sound casual, but failed miserably. Sorry, kid, I thought, you're too damn young to dissemble. Ignoring him for the moment, I turned to search through the center drawer of a small chest I used for storage. It was a pretty cool item, picked up at a craft show last spring. The vendor claimed it was some sort of antique Asian-style chest. I didn't care about its provenance and had bought it because it was unusual. Instead of hiding it away in my bedroom, I'd installed it in my living room, its washed-out red paint and metal accents complementing my other furniture.

"Damn it, where the hell's . . . there you are." I slid three passports out of the back of the top center drawer, found the red one and tucked it into a travel wallet, which I then placed inside the front pocket of my backpack. Nothing like doing busywork, pretending I needed to be more prepared, even though at this point, I was as ready as I'd ever be. No need for packing much as I had plenty of clothes at the family homestead. I wasn't planning to take more than this small duffle bag and my carry-on backpack, private plane or not.

I liked to travel light. Besides, if I really needed anything while I was there, it was a good excuse to take a day or two trip to Vancouver.

"All those different passports yours?"

"What—oh, yeah," I said, trying to keep my brain on what I was doing. Did I want to stop by their house? Bea was there, sure. No doubt getting some much-needed rest and recuperating from what happened last night . . . well, early this morning.

"Didn't know you could have so many. You a spy?"

I stared at the boy, all six-foot-something of him sprawled across an armchair, body spare and rangy, whipcord lean in the way that only teenagers can be. "Spy?"

"Thought only spies had more than one passport."

I laughed despite my mood. "Only in the movies," I said. "I'm a citizen of the UK by birth, U.S. by family and Canada, well . . . I'm not really sure about that one, but I've had all three since I was a kid. Since I'm going to Canada, I'm going to travel on my Canadian passport."

"Huh. That's kind of cool." He threw a long leg over the arm of the chair and started to swing it, his natural nervous energy needing some sort of outlet. One hand toyed with the pull on the reading lamp.

"So what's up, Noe? You need something?" I tried to keep it light, keep my voice from breaking. I managed, but just barely.

"I came by because I didn't want her to . . . you know . . . she's—" Noe shrugged in that boneless way teenagers do. "I came by to tell you Tia told me to come see you and tell you that she's gonna talk to her."

Despite the run-on sentence and lack of pronoun attribution, I didn't have a problem parsing his message. "Yeah, thanks," I said roughly and turned away.

"You ready, sis?" My brother Tucker stuck his head through the door, one hand on the frame as he leaned in.

"Yeah." I picked up my backpack and slung it over my shoulder, trying to avoid looking at Noe. He'd done a good thing, coming out here to talk to me. Bea was the de facto matriarch of her small family, despite the fact she was about my age. Even her elderly aunt, Tia Petra, and uncle, Tio Richard, bowed to Bea's need to lead. She ran the house as well as she ran the café.

Bea and I had been friends for most of our lives. She'd been my first real friend, human and more accepting of my oddities than anyone outside my family. This estrangement was killing me.

"You leaving now?" Noe asked. "Without talking to Bea?"

Tucker started to say something, but I held up a hand. "We'll actually be here until tomorrow. Tucker's here to take me out to the ranch where we're spending the night."

"We were *supposed* to be leaving now," Tucker added. "But the pilot's delayed because of weather and can't get here until sometime tomorrow."

Noe stood up, brightening. "So you can come by, then, now that you have time?"

Surely Bea wouldn't turn me away in person, would she? "I'll be there in a while," I said.

"You got someone to take care of the house while you're gone?"

"We do if you're willing," Tucker answered for me as he picked up my larger duffle and hoisted it over his shoulder. "It'd be a big help if you could stop by every once in a while."

"Oh, cool. You mean me. Sure." Noe beamed. He was a good kid, mostly. Just a teenager with few prospects and very little money. He attended school part-time at the University of Texas at San Antonio and worked part-time at Bea's café, but there were few other legal ways to make ready cash around Rio Seco.

Tucker grinned at the boy's enthusiasm. "Excellent." My brother dug out his wallet and slipped Noe some bills. "Thanks, kiddo. You'll save me some worry."

"You know when you're coming back?"

Not a clue, I wanted to say, but didn't really want to go

into all the reasons I was leaving so suddenly. "I'm not sure exactly," I said, "but I'll call, I promise."

I damned well intended to come back as soon as I could, but so much was up in the air, I couldn't predict anything right now.

Noe nodded and in an unexpected move, he wrapped his arms around me in a hug. "I'll tell Tia." With that, I took one last look at the house that I'd sort of called home for the past couple of years and walked away.

I TRIED to swallow but, despite having gulped down sixteen ounces of water before I stepped out of my Land Rover, my mouth was as dry as the Llano Estacado. Bea knew I was here in front of her small limestone house. The Rover had a distinctive engine sound, one we'd laughed about in the past. "You can't ever sneak up on someone, *chica*," she'd teased.

My hand clenched, fist tight. Damn it. Knock already, Keira Kelly.

The brown wooden door opened before I had a chance.

I cleared my throat, still unsure of what to say, but it was only Noe. "Hey," I said, a lame attempt at being casual. I failed as utterly as he had two hours earlier at my house. I'd gone with Tucker to the ranch, dropped him and my bags off and returned to town to try to mend fences.

"Tia says that Bea says she needs some space." He looked down at the metal strip across the threshold, his toe worrying at a bent corner. One hand was propped up on the door frame, the other stuck in the pocket of his loose-fitting jeans, waistband riding dangerously low on his hips, the top two inches of white cotton boxer topping the denim. A skinny bare chest showed evidence of a recent workout. Tia Petra probably had Noe doing some heavy lifting at the café this morning. It was nearly three, the time I used to stop by my best friend's restaurant for a coffee, breakfast taco and a quick gabfest . . . just another afternoon in the life of Keira Kelly.

But all that had changed with Adam's arrival, Marty's death and now . . . oh, so much had changed now after Bea's near murder only two nights ago.

"Space?" I repeated the word like a badly trained parrot. "She does know I'm leaving for a while?"

The boy nodded; a more miserable expression hadn't yet been invented. Noe was eager to please, still a bit of a teen slacker, yet always there to help the family out. "She said she'll talk to you when you get back." He toed the metal strip again, one bare toe running a line across the ridges. He looked up at me finally. "You are coming back, right?"

I nodded, too full of questions, pleas, emotions I couldn't elucidate blocking my voice.

"'Kay, then." Noe nodded back at me. "She'll be here. You know she's still—" He blushed, a teen boy's embarrassment at girly stuff overwhelming his attempt to be the man of the house.

"Yeah, she's still my best friend," I said, my voice finally working. "Tell her, no matter what happens, I'll come back." I looked at him, Bea's amanuensis, the person who would report back to her. "Tell her. I *will* be back." I turned away, my eyes blurring. "I'll call her."

The door shut behind me and I climbed into the front seat of my car.

CHAPTER TWO

BOUDOIR IT WASN'T, but the bedroom met my needs. Underground, dark, cool and comfortable, suiting my nature completely. A king-size bed dominated the room; twin nightstands, each with a matching lamp, flanked it. There were no windows in the walls to let light in: a perfect setting for a vampire king . . . and me, his, uh, consort.

"You are leaving, then."

"Yes, regretfully."

Adam kissed the top of my head and ran a hand down my arm. We lay on his bed—exhausted, satiated and content.

I'd gone back to the Wild Moon after my attempt to talk to Bea, reaching Adam's house as day turned to dusk. We'd been up for hours, laughing, talking, making love, reconnecting in ways that I'd forgotten one could. It had been so long and I was oh, so grateful. And by long, I didn't mean the scant few weeks that Adam and I had been having issues, but long as in years—to the time before Gideon frightened me so much with his foray into the dark that I'd run back to my family. I'd never let myself go again, until Adam, but until now, he'd been reluctant to take all I had to give, all I offered. Too damn bad that our new state of reconciliation would be so short-lived. Going away now had not been on my agenda.

"Is she that frightening to you, this great-great-grandmother of yours?" He lay on his side, head propped up on a hand, black hair draping gracefully across his pillow. His scent filled the room, now just nutmeg and vanilla. I reveled in my enhanced senses, so happy that a scent and a touch could be so evocative, yet not trigger any disturbing visions or memories. What a difference a day . . . and a Change makes.

I stretched, then turned to face him, tired, but in such a good way.

In less than twelve hours, I would go . . . west, to British Columbia, to my blood family and away from my lover. I didn't want to, especially since Adam and I had just begun soothing and smoothing after some rough times, but considering I was now the—joy of joys—Kelly heir and duty calling and all . . .

"Gigi's not frightening so much as . . ." I sat up and wrapped my arms around my knees. How could I phrase how I felt about my great-great-granny, aka the Clan matriarch? "The last time I saw her, slightly more than two years ago, she—"

"She hurt you."

I lay my head on my knees and looked at Adam. So gorgeous, my vampire lover, so self-assured, competent. Nearly dying the real death hadn't fazed him . . . at least on the outside. Ever the confident king.

"Hurt? I suppose you could call it that," I said. "Mostly, I was angry." I took a deep breath and let it out in an equally deep sigh. Digging up emotional memories wasn't the way I wanted to spend the rest of my time with Adam, but he deserved answers. I was trying to let myself be open with him, not only as a lover, but someone who actually loves, trusts.

"Gigi's edict came while I was in London," I said.

"With Gideon." Adam said this calmly, without emotion.

Gideon was the man I'd been with when I'd first met Adam more than ten years ago at a soiree that was more boring than not. We'd flirted and laughed, but had never pursued anything more. On my part, it had mostly been because I'd thought Adam human—and I'd quit dating humans by then. He'd been the ultimate gentleman and, because I had a partner, he'd stayed on his side of the line.

I chewed my bottom lip, then continued. "After what happened, when he went darkside, all I wanted to do was come home. But home wasn't where I left it. The family had moved to Canada and I didn't want to go there. I stuck here, babysitting Marty, and you know how well that turned out." With Marty murdered, I didn't bother to say aloud. Not a topic I cared to think about too much and besides, Adam had been there for all of it. I'd failed in my one and only focus. Some caretaker I was.

"Did she ever explain to you why she was packing up the family?"

Adam wasn't fooled. It wasn't about coming back or moving or Marty, but about Gigi being Gigi—acting as queen bee of the Kelly Clan and expecting us to hop when she said "frog." We did, because that's who we were: in essence, her minions and her family. She was our Clan chief and her word is, was and would always be law as long as she remained in her hereditary office. If I had anything to say about it, that would be for a very, very long time.

"Never. She simply told me that if I was stubborn enough to stay behind, then I'd have to accept the consequences."

"What's going to happen now?" Adam's words held a mix of curiosity and concern. We'd never really discussed the possibility of me becoming the heir, nor much about specifics of the Change, other than that once it happened, I'd settle into my primary Talent. I'd expected to become a shapeshifter, like my six elder brothers and my father or, perhaps, a healer, like my aunts. This? So not on my agenda . . . at all.

As to what was ahead of me? No bloody clue.

Sure, I knew about our rules of succession and what it meant to be the heir in the same way an American knows about the British Royals—that is, what one sees on TV or in books or in the news. Ours was more than legend, but a story, nonetheless, something a Clan member learns about in our own home-school classes and stories told by others. History, not reality. Something that happened to someone else, in a time and place long ago and far away. Despite the fact that my own branch of the Clan produced the last heir, Minerva Kelly—somewhat affectionately known as Gigi to my generation (thanks to my inability to say "Minerva" as a child)—the stories were no more real to me than any other family tales. Gigi became the heir centuries ago, and had ruled the Clan for nearly that length of time. Frankly, she was a fact of my existence and I had never asked about the transition from the former Clan chief to her. It never occurred to me that I would need to know. Now, I did. Problem was, no one had any answers but Gigi herself.

Between my newfound position and my Aunt Isabel's information that Gideon was dying, I had to leave.

"What time will the pilot be here?"

"She's flying into San Antonio International, to the private aircraft terminal. Supposed to be there around six-thirty or so in the evening." I took a deep breath. "I'll need to head out around four o'clock so I can be on time to meet her."

Adam kissed my shoulder. "I will miss you."

I looked into his eyes, their clear green troubled with the words he wouldn't say. His fear echoed mine. We were both afraid now that I was heir, I'd be required to stay with the Clan chief and not return.

"I will come back," I promised, echoing my earlier words to Noe. "I swear to you. Whatever happens with Gigi, I will figure something out and come back." I leaned over and kissed him, a light peck that became deeper. This was what I wanted.

"You know, you could come with me." I murmured the words against his mouth, reluctant to let go of our connection.

He cupped my chin in his hand and stroked my cheek with his thumb. "Will you take your brother with you?"

I leaned into the touch, nipping at his thumb. "Yes. Tucker came here to watch over me," I said. "He wants to come back with me."

"And Niko?" Adam asked, referring to Tucker's lover and Adam's own second-in-command of the vampire tribe.

"I don't know," I replied. "Tucker was going to ask him. For my part, he's free to come, if you can spare him. It's a private plane. Plenty of room. Easy enough to leave after dark. Vancouver's only a few hours flight." A possibility crossed my mind. "Adam, you should *both* come."

"Vancouver? I thought you said your family was north of there."

"Yes, but we need to stop there first. Customs. After that, it's just a short trip north. There's a private airstrip. So come. The place is huge, plenty of accommodations. Gigi won't bite."

I mentally crossed my fingers at the last. I knew what I was doing—trying to bring reinforcements. Adam, Niko and Tucker. Three on my side. Not that I knew sides would be taken, but anything could happen around Gigi, and often did. My goal was to get there and take care of business, where business meant Gideon's incipient death first and figuring out my heirship duties second. Then it meant offering Gigi a deal of some sort for her to let me come back to Texas for a few decades or so, until I was technically of age, say fifty or sixty. Then, I'd return to the family fold. After all, I'd changed at thirty-seven; I wouldn't even be thirty-eight for a few more months. Normally, the Change didn't come until our fifth or sixth decade. I hoped, because of that, I could buy some time. This thing—*relationship*—with Adam was practically brand-new. I wanted to know what it could become.

Adam answered me with another deep kiss. Everything else left my head as I let myself respond. Before we could get much further, my phone went off.

I smiled at Adam ruefully. "Just a moment and hold that thought," I said and reached across him.

"Isabel?" I answered my cell phone, wondering why my aunt was calling so soon. She'd taken a commercial flight back to Vancouver earlier today—a sort of advance guard. By this time, she should have been on the road to the family enclave.

"Keira, sweetheart," she nearly gushed at me. "You are well?"

I moved away from Adam and sat up, puzzled. "As well as I was say, oh . . ." I looked at the clock. "Seven hours ago, when you left. What's up?"

"Well, I wanted to be sure to contact you before the phone signal got crazy."

"Contact me about what?" Phone signal? What was she going on about? Granted, the road going north from Vancouver went through mountains and such, but most phones did okay for at least most of the trip.

"Well, honey, I'm not actually sure of the details yet,

but Minerva left a voice mail for me whilst I was on board the plane. Told me to tell you to stay in Texas for a day or two longer."

"Stay? What's going on, aunt? Why on earth didn't Gigi call me directly? It's not like she doesn't have my number." In more ways than one, I thought.

"Sweetie, I have no idea. All the message said was that she wanted me to tell you to hang tight and that the pilot would ring and let you know when it's time."

Adam looked at me in concern. I was sure I was throwing off all sorts of anxiety vibes. This was extremely odd. "So I should stay here? What about Gideon? If he needs to be—"

"I'm sure Minerva wouldn't ask you to stay if Gideon was any less than stable," Isabel answered. "Look, honey, I'm sorry I don't know what's happening. I've been trying to phone Minerva but the signal here is pretty erratic. I'm going to try again now that I seem to be in a place where the phone is working. I'll ring you back if I get through. If you don't hear from me right away, don't worry. We'll get this sorted and someone will let you know—"

The call cut off. I looked at my phone—still connected. "Isabel?"

Nothing. Damn it. She must have lost the signal.

"I heard most of that," Adam said. "Any thoughts?" Thank goodness for preternatural hearing. Saved me from recapping the conversation.

"None whatsoever," I said as I flipped the phone closed and stashed it back on the nightstand. "Typical freaking Kelly MO—it's odd, but hey, that's the way we do things sometimes; first it's all rush, rush, then hurry up and wait."

"Shouldn't you call?"

"I suppose so," I said. Getting it from the horse's mouth

and all that. I dialed the main number at the enclave. Gigi didn't have a cell phone as far as I knew. After several rings, the line switched over to voice mail.

"This is Keira, calling for Gigi and trying to figure out what's going on. Please let her know I called." I snapped shut my phone.

"Is that normal?" Adam asked.

"Voice mail, you mean?"

He nodded. "I have someone answering our main line clock round."

"There's often someone answering the phone at the enclave during standard business hours, but it's after eight p.m. there. I'm sure they're just letting voice mail get it. I'll try Dad."

Once again, I got voice mail and left a message.

"Do you think something's happened?"

"I doubt it. I think Gigi's message to Isabel would have been more intense if there'd been something wrong. I think it's just the Kelly usual. My family's not the best in the world at being connected with the modern technologies. Dad's been known to go weeks without checking his messages. Usually Rhys or Ianto or one of the others makes him do it."

"And so about your Gideon?"

"Not mine," I grumbled and moved closer to Adam. "Hasn't been in a long time." I snuggled into Adam's embrace. "I'm sure he must have stabilized. There's no way Gigi would have delayed me if he were truly dying."

"Do you think that Isabel was exaggerating?"

"You mean earlier, when she said he was dying?"

"Yes, could that be the case?"

"I don't think so," I responded. "Isabel isn't one to exaggerate. I think she was passing along information from Jane, who may have done. Remember, Isabel was on walkabout, hadn't been home in a while. She never actually saw Gideon."

"You don't think this 'Gideon is dying' scenario was concocted by your Gigi, do you?"

"It's unlikely. Gigi may be a lot of things, but as far as I know, she's never felt the need to make something up. She's our matriarch. If she wanted me to come back that drastically, she'd have issued a command."

"Would you have gone?"

I thought about it a moment. Would I have? When I'd returned to Texas with my emotions in shreds, I'd balked at leaving the only place I'd known as a refuge. I'd argued with Gigi and she'd eventually relented. She hadn't insisted, nor even come close to commanding that I join them. She'd only suggested that it was in my best interests to do so.

"Yes, I would," I answered. "The reason I'm going now is because even if he's stable, Gideon's situation could change at any moment. I was and still am an Escort, Adam. If it's his time, I could be needed."

"To help him die." It wasn't a question. Adam was perfectly aware of what my duties as an Escort once were . . . to help family members pass through to death.

"I'll help him die if that's his choice, but that's not the only reason I'd go. Gigi's my leader, and ultimately . . ." I smiled as I tried to explain my point of view, even though Adam more than likely understood, being a leader himself. "Honestly, Adam, to her, my decision to stay behind in Rio Seco when they all left was nothing more than a silly adolescent rebellion. Don't forget, in her eyes, I'm only just past childhood. Now that I've Changed, I'm technically an adult, but still with a lot of learning to go. I've inherited all the abilities of the Kellys, but have no freaking idea how to use any of them. The only good thing about all of this is that I don't anticipate having any unexpected visions or episodes like I experienced pre-Change. No, I don't think Gigi or anyone concocted a story about Gideon dying to entice me home. They all know what's happened by now, at least the ones at the enclave do, and they absolutely expect me home soon. It wouldn't occur to them that I wouldn't come home—all recent Changelings do so they can work with a mentor to learn to use their new Talent." I gave him a quick kiss. "Something's off about this, but I'm happy to have a while longer here." Another quick kiss. "With you and—" I shut my eyes a moment.

"Bea," Adam said in a whisper. He kissed my eyelids. "You want another chance to make amends."

"Yes," I whispered back. "We've been friends for thirty years. I don't know where to even start, but I have to try."

CHAPTER THREE

A FEW HOURS LATER, misery had been replaced with sheer joy as I ran—for the first time in my short-by-family-standards life—on four legs in the bright sunshine of a Texas day, wolf fur rippling in the breeze. This, *this* was part of what I'd just inherited, this freedom and elation, the pure brilliance of ability. No wonder my brothers loved it so much. I hadn't known what I was missing.

I turned to look at the wolf loping along next to me, in all his red, furry glory, mouth open in what only could be called a shit-eating grin. C'mon then. I jerked my muzzle in the direction of the small copse of oak trees across the clearing, and nudged my brother's flank with my own furry nose. With a sharp yip he bit playfully at my pale fur and took off running. I followed, barely a few paces behind, soon to catch up.

Being a wolf was so *easy.*

Tucker and I had agreed this would be my first foray into the realm of the Changed, to learn to shift. He could teach me to be wolf: to run, to hunt, to simply exist in the moment. Existing in the moment wasn't something I'd been able to do a lot of lately . . . or, well, ever. Since our departure had been delayed and we had time, I figured I might as well learn how to use at least one of my Talents. Since Tucker was a shapeshifter, he could mentor me. Eventually, I'd have to find other teachers for other Talents, but for now, I could learn to be a wolf and *run.*

The oppressive heat wave that had marked most of the last few weeks was gone in the blustery blow of a blue norther, a wave of chill wind that had sent the temperatures plummeting not two hours ago, leaving behind near winter conditions—despite the fact that it was March in the Hill Country and, ostensibly, spring. Just yesterday we'd been sweating in the shade; right now, I'd be surprised if the mercury hit forty. Texas weather: giving a whole new meaning to the term bipolar.

Tucker howled in delight as his nose crossed the imaginary finish line a hair before mine. He capered like a cub, teasing and nipping as he entreated me to play some more. It had been a long time since I'd seen my brother so carefree and happy.

A sharp sensation at the end of my tail made me whirl, ready to jump on my brother. I stopped and let out a sound that was part growl, part wolf for "what the hell?" Tucker had obviously bitten at my tail, but was now shifting back to human. I had no idea why. We were comfortable enough in wolf shape, but in human form, we'd freeze out here. Taking an early afternoon while all the vampires slept to wander the Wild Moon, we'd gone exploring the area around the main ranch. I wasn't sure exactly where we'd ended up, but I knew we were at least a good half-hour lupine run from where we'd left our clothes.

"You make a beautiful wolf, cousin." The melodic tones came from behind me. Daffyd ap Geraint, cousin to me on my mother's side and Seelie Sidhe, stood next to a gnarled oak, his silver hair and flowing robes at odds with the rustic beauty of the Hill Country land. His companion, Gary Pursell, stood beside him. Although Gary was also clad in the flowing white robes of the

Sidhe, he could never be mistaken for anything other than what he was: human.

I chuffed, disconcerted that I'd neither heard them, nor scented their arrival. Torn between remaining wolf and shifting back to my human shape, I scooted next to Tucker, who stood with his arms crossed over his chest, formidable at six foot four, despite his nakedness. Tucker acknowledged the two with a nod.

"Tucker, I presume?" Daffyd's expression remained neutral. "You have a look of your sire about you."

"You know my father." Tucker's voice was as neutral as Daffyd's, not a question, but a statement. I wasn't sure what Daffyd meant, since our father was a tiny Pict of a man, dark-skinned and dark-haired with black eyes, who barely came to Tucker's shoulder. Not a one of my brothers resembled Dad. I'd always figured they'd taken after their various and very different mothers.

"I do," replied Daffyd with amusement. "Your father had the same mien when we negotiated with him and Branwen."

Branwen? My mother? I shook my head, having had enough of not being able to speak. Shivering and concentrating, I forced my body back into human shape, all the while my lizard brain protesting, as it was still enjoying being wolf.

"Fuck me, it's freaking cold," I muttered as I wrapped my arms around my nude self.

Tucker chuckled. "You should've stayed wolf, Keira."

"I should have," I retorted, "but then I couldn't speak."

"Try a warming spell." My brother smirked. "After all, you are—"

"The bloody Kelly heir, yeah, whatever," I snapped back and closed my eyes to concentrate. I muttered a few words and immediately felt better. Warming spells. I'd learned the words years and years ago, as a child sitting on my Aunt Jane's lap as she'd made me chant the small spells, one after another: warming, cooling, breeze, quiet, a whole list of others. Rote learning so eventually I could at least do those, even if I didn't become a spellcaster when I Changed. I'd always figured that Jane had been trying to distract me with kindness because, underneath it all, she was worried that I'd be different, have no magick, just like my mother's people, the Sidhe, said. I guess I'd fooled them all.

I shifted my posture, still uncomfortable, even though I was warming up. Most of my Clan was as comfortable in skin as clothing, but I'd been raised among humans and still wasn't quite at ease with my nudity. Plus, although Daffyd was technically family, I'd met him only a few days before when I'd discovered him in a cave where he'd lived for years, having been sent to keep an eye on me. Unlike my own babysitting of Marty, Daffyd had watched over me all too well.

"Me, too, please," Tucker said, shivering. His posture was relaxed, but he had goose bumps on his skin.

"You can't?" I was surprised.

He shook his head. "The ability vanished when I Changed."

I nodded and muttered the warming spell in his direction.

Daffyd spoke up. "I'd heard that sometimes you can keep the smaller abilities when you Change."

Both Tucker and I looked at him. He was right. After Changing, most of us inherited one major Talent, but often kept a few of the more homely charms and hexes learned as children. Warming was one of them—not that I personally was limited now. As heir, I had access to all the Clan Talents. Tucker was a shapeshifter, but I didn't really know much about what else he could do.

"You seem to know a great deal about us," Tucker said, back in his belligerent stance.

"May I approach?" Daffyd held his hands out from his body. A gesture of peace? Perhaps.

Tucker said nothing. I knew my brother well enough to know he was letting me take the lead here. It wasn't because I was heir, either, but because—in some sort of twisty way—Daffyd belonged to me now. I'd given him a life, thus saving Daffyd's own. I was responsible for my Sidhe cousin and he felt he owed me fealty.

I couldn't hate Daffyd, even after what he'd done to Adam. He hadn't realized, hadn't known that the power, the energy he'd been living on was draining my vampire lover into a coma, and nearly absolute, never-come-back-from-it death. When I'd asked Daffyd to stop, he had—to his own detriment. Without the energy, he'd fade and become nothing—in effect, he'd die, and his human companion would die along with him. He'd accepted that fact with aplomb and because I'd asked him. Maybe that's why I let him take Pete Garza.

"You look well, cousin," I ventured.

Daffyd inclined his head slightly. "Thank you, Keira. I am still strong and will remain so for several decades now, thanks to you."

Gary smiled at Daffyd's response.

"Yeah, well." What was I expected to say in this kind of situation? Gee, glad I could send a man to his death so you could live, even though said man was a murderous asshole?

"I came to look for you," Daffyd said. "We saw the both of you playing and running."

Gary stepped forward. "I—we've—been walking around a bit, now that we can," he said. "Since your vampires sleep in the day, we've taken advantage of that. It's nice, you know, being out." He looked around at the scrub brush and live oaks. Not much to look at but still, outside was outside and when you'd been imprisoned in a cave for about a decade . . .

"Thank you, by the way." He looked at both of us.

"No need to thank us," Tucker answered before I could.

"Yes, there is," Daffyd cut in. "Keira, I did come looking for you," he repeated. "I wanted to present my services."

"Your w-what?" I stuttered, shivering as an icy blast of wind cut through my humble warming spell. "Damn it, that was—look, it's ridiculous to stand out here in the cold. You obviously want to talk to me about something. Let's go back to the ranch, go inside the house and talk."

Tucker gave me a quizzical look. I ignored it and shot him a determined glance of my own. I knew what he was thinking. Bringing Daffyd back to Adam's house when he'd been the one to nearly cost Adam his life might not be such a brilliant idea. Maybe not, but I didn't want to keep standing around here, naked and cold. I wanted to be on my own turf, clothed and in control.

"Daffyd. Gary. If you'll come to the house?" I motioned vaguely in the direction of the main ranch complex . . . I thought. My sense of direction as a wolf didn't seem to be any better than it was as a person.

Daffyd and Gary exchanged a silent communication similar to Tucker's and mine. In this case, Daffyd was the determined one.

"We will come."

INTERLUDE

The Musician

*T*HE CITY IS MORE *than he'd bargained for, much more. He'd been used to something less frantic, more like Cardiff or Swansea. For some reason, he'd expected Vancouver to be less of a modern city. Didn't know where he'd gotten that impression. Perhaps the thought that Canada was sparsely populated overall lent itself to the idea. He supposes, as in many places, the population congregates in the coastal cities. Vancouver seems to be no exception.*

Two young women brush by him, animatedly chatting about some sort of exhibit at the art museum. An elderly man smiles at the girls, sharing his enjoyment of their youth with his own companion. Three middle-aged citizens in loose clothing practice some sort of flowing movement exercise in a small patch of grass.

So many of the people here seem to be relative newcomers to Canada—from Singapore, Japan, Saudi Arabia, exotic places he'd never been to, nor ever cared to see, each person speaking a language so musical in all its diphthongs and syncope, yet so sheerly foreign. *Very different from his quiet homeland, where most people tended to look the same and come from similar backgrounds, despite the fact that only a few at home spoke his ancient language and the taste of the Old Tongue was but memory for most. The stories of his homeland are all the same; the music, centuries old. He wonders how many wonderful kinds of music there are to discover here. He scowls as he remembers. His task here is not to gather music. This is simply a short interlude before he moves on. The one for whom he waits has not yet arrived. He has at least a day or two to spend in the city.*

Nearly everyone speaks English here, the main difference being the range of accents. He needs to remember that and not slip into his own language; too easy to do so when one comes from a land of dual tongues, like here. Although in his own country, the signs were not written in two languages as they were here, in both English and French. He'd been worried he wouldn't fit in, but there are so many different kinds of people here, some even look like him—tall, rangy, long hair, pale skin, light eyes, wearing leather, boots and carrying musical instruments.

He supposes that music festivals in the New World aren't much different than eisteddfods *or the random* ceilidhs *in his country. Musicians tend to look alike all over the world. Some are better dressed—the concert pianists, the orchestral types—but those solitary musicians who carry their instruments with them—whether string or wind or simply voice—often march to the beat of a different dressmaker. He'd seen them for years, looking as though they were wearing the clothes of the old ones: flowing shirts, trousers tucked into laced-up leather boots, men's hair long and as beautiful as the women's. He doesn't know if this was vanity, or simply a way to remember what once was; to conjure the power of the old bards in a world that has lost its connection. It doesn't really matter, though, as long as he manages to blend in with the crowd.*

However uncomfortable he feels around so many people, it is good that he has a few extra days here, before going further north. A music festival gives him the opportunity to once again practice his talents, be part of what made him. He can endure the crowding for a few days. After all, even at home he wasn't as isolated as some of the others of his kin.

"Hey, there, you." The raspy voice cuts into his thoughts. He looks up to see two men—well, boys really, they couldn't have forty-five years between them. One stands near to his height and is square built. Worker, he thinks. Someone who builds with his hands. A quick inspection of the boy's fingers confirms his supposition. Cuts and calluses map the skin, thicker on the pads of the fingers and palms. This one is no stranger to hard work. The other boy's skin barely covers his bones, stretched tight, near emaciation, the yellowed dryness of his flesh indicative of some disease. Malnutrition, perhaps? The whites of the boy's eyes remain clear, though—no sign of jaundice.

Both boys sport dusty denim pants and jackets over worn and filthy cotton T-shirts, tears and half-mended holes marking the clothing as likely to be their entire wardrobe. Neither boy looks to be dressed well enough against the late afternoon chill. It is March, and the weather has stayed mild, as it always does in this part of Canada. Nevertheless, the breeze brings whispered reminders that winter is barely past and tonight promises to be wet and cold. He wonders if the boys are tramps; those that call the outdoors home. What is the word again? The musician searches his memory. It is a word often used in news articles, in stories broadcast on televisions he has watched in different store windows during his travels. Homeless, that is the word. People who have no permanent dwelling but live in parks, in alleys, under bridges, using paper and twine for tents and carting their belongings about in wheeled trolleys, often stolen. In his day, in his world, these would be the Travelling Folk: restless wanderers who never settle, roaming lands in caravans, bringing their families and all their belongings with them. These two boys don't have any belongings with them, just themselves. Perhaps they are merely boys needing some help.

"You here for that?" The skinnier short one spits the words out, along with a globule of phlegm. The other one, taller by only a few centimeters, elbows the first.

"Dude, stop spitting. You don't want—"

Skinny's dark eyes narrow at Tall. "And who died and made you a Mountie, eh?" He pulls out a crumpled pack of cigarettes from his jacket pocket. "I'll do what I want." Skinny turns back to the musician and repeats the question. "You here for that?" This time, he points to a paper notice tacked on to a display board next to the park bench.

"The folk music festival?" asks the musician after perusing the sign, reading the printed words. It advertises the same event he'd read of at the visitors center mere hours ago. "Yndw." *He nods his assent, never noticing that his answer is in his home tongue. "You as well?"*

"Nah, we're helping to provide that what you need," put in Skinny. He takes a huge lungful of smoke from the now-lit cigarette and lets it back out, his mouth working oddly. To do what exactly? A wobbly ring forms finally and the musician smiles at the boy's demeanor. Some things truly are global. He recalls a certain afternoon with his da and elder brother, learning to load, tamp and light a pipe.

"And what would that be, exactly?" he asks the boy, his smile reflecting his amusement.

The tall one darts a few glances around them. The musician smiles again. There is no one nearby, no one within earshot. The two old men had moved on. Perhaps boarding a bus, perhaps walking away. He'd not noticed. On the far side of the path, the three middle-agers still move slowly in their ritual patterns, each of them absorbed in the poses, paying no attention to anyone else.

He'd been sitting on this bench for about twenty minutes, attempting to discern how to find lodgings from a small paper map of the city. Earlier, one of the musicians he'd encountered on a bus had mentioned something about a hostel at the corner of Burnaby and Thurlow, but he is having trouble locating it.

"You not from around here, eh?" Skinny tosses the cigarette down onto the ground and crushes it with the tip of a worn trainer. The canvas of the shoe had once been white, guesses the musician. Now, it is as gray as the circles under the boy's eyes.

"I came to visit—it is not important," the musician says as he recalls his duty. "I am attempting to find lodging. I must admit, I am a bit lost. The city . . ." He lets his words trail off. No need to explain how confusing he finds the streets, the traffic, the lights, the signs. So much information. So little understanding. He isn't sure of the rules here. The words are English, a language he reads, but so few things makes sense. He should have taken his kin's advice and gone directly north to his ultimate destination, but on the way here, he'd heard about the music festival. The travel to this place had been such a hardship. Without some sort of respite, he is afraid he'd not last.

Skinny inches closer and opens his jacket. One narrow

hand dips into a pocket, flashes a small bag containing something white and tucks it back into his pocket again. "If that don't suit ya," he says with a smirk, "I can get other stuff. Let me know. They all know me around here." His thin chest puffs up in pride. "Just ask for Jack."

The musician narrows his eyes and shakes his head at the boy. Always the same. No matter the place or the time. There is always someone who wants to sell happiness in a bottle, or pill, or powder. True ecstasy comes in the music for him. No amount of spirits, nor any other substance, can ever take its place.

"I thank you for the kind offering, Jack, but I must decline. I would, however, be indebted to you if you could help me find lodging."

Skinny Jack wrinkles his nose at the musician's formal words, cocking his head, his face blank as if processing the meaning. The other boy nudges him and whispers loudly enough to be heard by the musician, "Dude, he means he don't want any and he need a place to crash."

"I know that, Daniel." Jack smacks his friend on the arm and turns a fresh grin on the musician. "How about we show you a good place to crash, then? How much is that worth?"

The musician nods. "I accept your offer and I will be happy to pay you for your assistance."

"Ten dollars?" ventures Jack.

Ten. Which bill was that? The musician is still not familiar enough with the currency here. He rummages in his pack, moves aside his flute case and finds a small roll of paper money. There isn't much there. He may be new here, but is no fool. Most of his money is tucked away in the flute case and in other hidden places. This is simply show money. In case he gets—what is that word?—mugged.

He doesn't think most thieves will care about a musical instrument; besides, there are other precautions in place. If he can display a small amount of money that can be lost without too much damage, that is all for the better.

"What's that in there . . . that music case thing?" Daniel asks.

"A flute. I play."

"You performing then?" Daniel persists, his curiosity seeming genuine.

"Perhaps." The musician pulls a purple bill from the roll, verifying the number on the face of it. "If you help me find lodging, this is yours. If you help me find a place to eat, I shall buy you a meal." He looks the boys over and thinks they could use more than one meal. However, he is only willing to spend a small amount of time with them. They promise they will be helpful, but he begins to feel nauseated around them and regretful of his uncharacteristic generosity. Something feels odd about the two. It may simply be their hunger, so obviously reflected in their eyes, their demeanor, the sheer need underlying their offer of help. Or perhaps it is only his own discomfort. A meal, a rest and a return to the site when the music began will do him quite well.

He will do a good deed, feed them and they can help him find lodgings. Once he'd done so, as he'd had to do with everything—everyone—else, he must let them go. It is not his place to rescue them. For that matter, he is not here to rescue anyone—except himself, perhaps. He nods to the boys, who step a few paces away to confer.

Jack pulls on Daniel's jacket and whispers furiously in the other boy's ear. The musician does not strain to overhear, nor does he interrupt their discourse. They must make this decision on their own. Daniel seems to be arguing with Jack, not violently. His hands make choppy motions as he shakes his head in a no. Jack leans closer and puts his hand on Daniel's shoulder. Clever boy, that. If he survives the street, he can be successful. The boy knows negotiation and persuasion. With those traits, he can rise above his current status. The musician smiles to himself. With those traits, if young Jack were to return home with him, he'd rise even further. It isn't an option, however.

After a few more moments, Jack and Daniel approach him.

"If you want to save money . . ." Jack begins. Ah, then, the boy had fallen for the deception. He obviously thinks the musician has little cash. "There's a place we all crash. It's up a few blocks, over on West Hastings. You got a bedroll, yeah?" Jack motions to the musician's pack where a bedroll is lashed to the bottom.

The musician nods. It isn't the best of accommodations to be sure, but he's had worse and if he "crashes" in this impromptu place, he can avoid the issue of showing an identity card. He'd been able to pass so far, but his luck can only hold so long before something happens. He wants to avoid using other means as much as possible. Who knew who else might be in this city? Too many people to tell.

"I'd be happy to," he says, bowing to Jack and Daniel. "Now, if you can lead me to someplace we may have our repast . . ."

Jack scrunches up his face again. Daniel pulls him in the direction of the main street. "Food, Jack, he's going to buy us supper."

Jack happily darts forward. "There's a café over up the street, not far away. They don't mind if we go in there, long as we have money."

"And that we do," says the musician, who picks up his

pack and follows the boys as they scamper ahead of him. This may work out. Two guides, native to and familiar with the city. Perhaps he can employ them for the next day or two, whilst he is still here. He plans on staying for the festival, which runs for two days, then perhaps one additional day before he moves on. Lost in his thoughts, he never hears the boys whispering about the flute case.

CHAPTER FOUR

It didn't take us long to return to the main complex. Tucker and I reassumed wolf form and trotted back to where we'd left our clothes. We retrieved our clothes and dressed. Daffyd and Gary met us at the main gate. I didn't ask if they'd walked or been whisked there by Sidhe magic.

The Wild Moon was as quiet as always in late afternoon. With a couple of hours until sunset, all the vampires were either sleeping or holed up in their lightproof rooms, doing whatever the heck they did during the day. There wasn't a soul around, not even John, the human day manager, or any of his family.

"After you," I murmured as we reached Adam's house. Daffyd studied me for a moment. He knew exactly what I was doing. He and Gary climbed the porch steps and waited for me at the front door. Tucker brought up the rear. I stepped in front of them and opened the door. "You are welcome," I said as I motioned them inside.

"I accept your hospitality." Daffyd nodded solemnly, the formal words acknowledging his place.

There, that was settled. Hospitality offered and accepted. Now, we could speak together knowing that neither of us would attack the other—literally. Unless, of course, Daffyd was a fan of the way the Thane of Cawdor and his lady treated their royal guest Duncan in the Scottish play. I stopped that thought before it went any further.

"Please, have a seat." I gestured to the living room as I walked into the kitchen, intent on brewing a pot of coffee and unsure whether to offer refreshments to the pair. I knew the Sidhe ate. I'd spent the first seven years of my life watching them enjoy their food, drink, sex, dances, parties—all things I got little of. (Well, the food and drink, that is. I'd been all of seven when my father came to my rescue.) My mother's family treated me as the proverbial redheaded stepchild: unwanted, unloved and uncared for. It wasn't until my father had fetched me from the Sidhe and brought me to the Kellys that I learned what family could be like: smothering, irritating, annoying, but yes, loving and caring.

"Coffee? Tea?" Tucker asked as he ushered Daffyd and Gary to the living room. "Or wait, can you eat up here?"

A musical sound filled the air, notes of birdsong and water twisted through harp strings, a melody so gorgeous all you wanted to do was lose yourself in it. Startled, I nearly dropped the coffeepot. I hadn't heard Sidhe laughter in decades. It both charmed and utterly repelled me.

"Bloody hell, cousin," I muttered. "Warn a girl next time."

"Damnation," Tucker exclaimed. "That was your laughter?"

Daffyd smiled. "I'd forgotten how these past years," he said. "I must thank you again for bringing it back to me."

Tucker shook his head and joined me in the kitchen. "Make that a strong pot," he said.

I filled the carafe with water and loaded the coffeemaker. "If you prefer tea, Daffyd," I said, "I've got several blends."

"Either will do well," Daffyd answered. "Tucker, in answer to your question, it's not like Faery in reverse up here. Your food and drink will not bind us to Above."

Tucker ducked his head in embarrassment as Daffyd chuckled.

"I'll get the accoutrements, shall I?" Tucker rummaged in one of the rustic wood cabinets and pulled out mugs. I busied myself with the rest of the coffee fixings. Neither of us was wholly comfortable going in there and sitting with the two by ourselves. I knew why I wasn't. I couldn't fathom why Tucker wasn't. He was a 1,200-plus-year-old Viking Berserker. Why on earth was he nervous around a Sidhe and a human companion?

"So tell me, cousin," I said as I brought the refreshments into the living room. Daffyd and Gary were both seated on the dark purple couch. Daffyd, languid and looking like he belonged there, almost part of the stylish furniture, elegant as only a Sidhe could be, the light from the watered silk Victorian lamps flattering his features. Gary, less comfortable, sat more to the edge of the couch, his hands folded on his knees, the very picture of a schoolboy awaiting his fate at the headmaster's office.

I set the tray with full mugs in front of them on the low coffee table. "How exactly did you recognize us out there? It's not like I looked at all the same as usual."

No kidding. I'd been surprised when Tucker guided me through my first change, in the privacy of the bedroom he and Niko shared. We'd done it last night, after Adam and Niko had gone to Adam's office to review the final purchase paperwork for the Pursell ranch. I'd stripped off my clothes and knelt in front of a full-length cheval mirror, alongside my brother. Tucker then crouched down on his hands and knees.

"Watch and feel, Keira," he'd said. "Put your hand on my side and feel."

I'd known what he meant. Feel, as in "with touch and with *all* my senses." I'd dropped my automatic defense shields and reached out. With a shimmer and a shimmy, the man who was my brother became a gorgeous red-furred beast. I'd taken a deep breath and turned the sensation deep inside. It was as if I were reworking my bones, my skin, my self. I'd called to the wolf I found within me and she answered with a wiggle of tail and flash of fur; then, suddenly, I'd had four legs, white fur and—although just as much of a wolf as he—looked nothing like my brother. We'd practiced moving around, walking first, letting me get used to seeing things differently and without color, adapting to greatly enhanced senses of smell and hearing. Then he'd shown me how to revert back to human. Tiring at first, but oh, so much fun.

Daffyd reached for a mug of coffee, stirred in some cream and sugar. I held back a giggle as I watched him load the sugar into the hot beverage. There really was something extremely surreal about all of this: a real faery "prince" loading his java with carbs.

"I'd seen him"—Daffyd nodded in Tucker's direction—"before. Many years ago, when you were just a child. From there, it was only a matter of realizing that it was you with him and not one of your other brothers. So you've come into your power then?"

"You *know* about that?" I sputtered, trying to keep my coffee from spilling.

Daffyd looked puzzled. "Of course I do," he said. "It was one of the reasons we came to watch you."

I set down my mug on a side table and sat in one of the armchairs. Tucker joined me, one hip propped on the wide arm, his own coffee just as carefully placed on the table. He was in full protector mode.

"I don't get it," I said. "You people . . . my mother's people . . . didn't want me because I had no magick. Why then—?"

"I knew there was something about you," Daffyd said. "Something my own sire did not—or would not—see. I knew I must come. When I did I brought with me those who would join me." Daffyd took a sip of coffee and closed his eyes. I wasn't sure if he was enjoying the taste or remembering that all the Sidhe he'd brought with him some thirty years ago had faded, the faery equivalent of the final death, leaving only him.

Daffyd set the mug down next to mine and leaned in my direction. "Cousin Keira," he began, then shook his head. "No," he corrected, "my liege—"

I stood up and walked back into the kitchen. "No," I said. "You do *not* get to call me that." I opened a cupboard and pretended to look for something, trying to get my temper under control. Damn it. I hated this.

Daffyd remained silent for a few moments. I kept my head stuck in the cupboard. Ostrich? Yeah, exactly. Why did this bother me so much? I'd grown up knowing the heir was as much a leader as the current Clan chief. But the fact remained that I'd also been educated in a local human school system, full of democracy and the conviction that all men are created equal. Even the more socially stratified world of university in England had reinforced the theory. To me, Clan hierarchies were a fact of life, but one that barely applied to me. Didn't make a lot of sense, but until the Change, a Clan member was still a child and not subject to many responsibilities, so I'd pretty much ignored all that. I was immersed enough in modern Western thought to feel uncomfortable about this liege business and I'd be damned if I'd accept it from someone who was not only not Clan, but of a line of folk who all but exposed me to the elements because they saw me as a useless child with no magick. Despite my heritage on my mother's side, I was unwilling to step into any leadership role there.

Daffyd's voice was quiet and thoughtful. "I apologize, Keira. I know you do not like to be reminded of . . ." He stopped and then started again. I pulled my head out of the cupboard and turned around, remaining in the kitchen. I could see him fine from where I stood.

"Keira," he continued. "I came to find you because I know you are soon leaving. No," he said firmly. "I know you're going to ask how I know. Please permit me to finish."

I swallowed my words and motioned for him to continue.

"You are both my liege and hold my debt," he said. He looked directly at me, his gray eyes mirror to my own. I was the only one in my immediate bloodline with eyes that color. Tucker's were the clear blue of spring skies. Rhys and Ianto, the twins, shared a lovely hazel green. The rest of my brothers had brown eyes like our dad. I'd inherited the looks of my mother's family. Tall, rangy, thick black hair, skin just this side of vampire pale and gray eyes that sometimes shone silver if the moon was right.

I shook my head at Daffyd's words, unwilling to accept what he was saying. Tucker and Gary both remained quiet. Daffyd rose from the couch and approached me. He looked so odd in the kitchen, all flowing robes and Sidhe shine among stainless steel appliances and digital readouts. Two of my worlds, colliding. My cousin held his hands out and dropped his head into a bow. "Your mother is heir to the queen of the Seelie court, for that alone I am subject to you, but I also owe you life debt, Keira Kelly." The formality of his words chilled me.

"And if I refuse?" The words spilled out before I could censor them.

He raised his head. I stared into his eyes, seeing nothing more than sincerity and strength of will. "I cannot accept your refusal," he said so quietly that I wasn't sure that even Tucker heard. "You hold my debt and I must serve you."

"Daffyd, I can't—" I shut my eyes and crossed my arms across my chest, ignoring his outstretched hands. I knew what I was supposed to do. I'd seen it countless times in my mother's cousin's court, burned into my memory as I watched from the sidelines. A debt acknowledgment required I take Daffyd's hands and accept his offering.

How could I become responsible for someone else when I'd been so bloody *bad* at responsibility? I'd failed Marty miserably. I'd let Bea get kidnapped by a psycho killer. I'd gotten involved with Adam Walker, only to have him end up in a coma and almost die because of me. Didn't Daffyd know I wasn't safe? He'd be better off going back to—wait, that was it.

I opened my eyes, reached out and took his hands. He brightened. "Daffyd ap Geraint. Cousin." I spoke slowly, trying to make sure the words came out right. "I acknowledge the debt and grant you freedom. You may return to your home, to Wales." There. That's the ticket, I thought.

Daffyd's hand tightened around mine and he got a very distinctly amused look on his face. If I didn't know better, I'd have thought he was smirking at me.

"My liege," he said and sank to one knee. Appalled, I tried to pull him back up and failed. He was stronger than I was. "I accept my debt to you and willingly enter your service. I thank you for my freedom and I choose to stay."

He bowed his head, his long silver hair parting to bare the nape of his neck, the locks on either side of his face brushing the Saltillo tile floor.

Oh, for fuck's sake. He'd bared his neck. I didn't know if this was a Sidhe thing, but it was definitely a wolf thing, and a Clan thing. When pledging service to one's liege, the bared neck signified submission and acknowledgment of the other's dominance.

"Damn it, Daffyd." I pulled on his hands and he allowed me to let go. He stood and faced me, hands clasped in front of him, a smile still dancing around his mouth and eyes. "You played me."

"Indeed?" He laid a hand on my arm. "For that, I apologize, cousin," he said. "I appreciate the freedom. You do not know how much it means to me."

"Then why don't you take that freedom and go back to Wales? It's not like I'm going to be around here anyway," I said. "I've got a plane coming for me soon."

"You're going to your Kelly family," Daffyd said.

"Yes."

"Then I shall come with you." He nodded decisively and went back into the living room to sit next to Gary on the couch. Gary grinned at Daffyd. Tucker, who was supposed to be on my side, echoed Gary's grin.

"You're what?" I stomped into the living room, hands on my hips. "You cannot be serious. Why on earth would you want to come to British Columbia and see the very person who imprisoned you?"

"That's not known to be true," Daffyd answered. "You, yourself, do not know that it was Minerva who closed off the cave."

"No, but I would damned well bet on it." I flung myself into the chair. Tucker patted me on the head and I pushed off his hand. Damn it, I wasn't a ten-year-old, even if I was acting like one.

"Is Gary coming, too?" Tucker asked, looking over at the still-grinning man.

Gary's smile vanished. He looked at Tucker, then back at Daffyd, who nodded slightly. "I'm going to my dad," Gary said softly. "It's time he knew."

"But doesn't that mean . . . ?" I couldn't finish my thought aloud.

"Yeah, I'll die." Gary looked me in the eye. "I know it's not necessarily something you or your people would choose," he added, "but I'm human. Daffyd has given me years I'd never have had otherwise. I want to go spend the rest of the time I have left with my father. He's suffered enough."

He's caused a hell of a lot more suffering than he'd suffered himself, I thought. Gary's father, Judge Carl Pursell, spent years turning the other way when his foreman Pete Garza took illegal workers to the Sidhe. The Sidhe needed energy; the Judge got to know that Gary was safe with them and not dying of leukemia. Death for life. The way of nature perhaps, but this had been murder. The victims had not gone willingly. Neither had Pete.

"I know, Keira," Gary said. "He's not a good man. But he's my father and it's time to mend fences. I want to spend the rest of my life with family."

"It's your choice."

What else could I do? It wasn't as if I could bring the Judge to justice in a human court. I figure he could atone by taking care of Gary for the rest of Gary's life—however short that might be.

"So you're coming with us, then," I said to Daffyd, suddenly making up my mind.

"I am," he said.

"All righty, then." I looked at my brother, who'd kept uncharacteristically silent throughout all of this. "What?" I spat out as he laughed.

"Nothing," he said. "You're the boss." He leaned over and patted my head again. "I wonder what Adam's going to say about all of this."

I threw up my hands. I had no bloody idea.

CHAPTER FIVE

"YOU'RE SERIOUSLY *NOT* coming with me? But I thought . . ."

Adam's expression didn't change as he processed my umpteenth version of the same question in the last hour. He stood, surrounded by the lush elegance of his neo-Renaissance office, next to his dark mahogany desk, one hand on a stack of papers, the other tucked in his trouser pocket. He seemed at ease, relaxed and absolutely worry-free. But over these past few months, especially in light of what had so recently happened, it was easy for me to read behind the pose.

"I cannot." His voice remained calm and even. "It is extremely tempting, Keira, but I simply must stay here."

"That's what you keep saying," I said. "Stuff to do, paperwork, blah blah whatever." I got out of the tapestry-upholstered chair I'd been lounging in and stepped closer. He didn't waver. Not even a millimeter. "Adam, it's only for a few days." I crossed my fingers at this assumption. "Surely this place can run without you for a week or so."

What I didn't repeat was my initial run at this where I'd pulled out the guilt trip; the "Hey, you almost died the real death there, buddy, and I saved your undead ass, so you totally owe me" bit, which was the unadulterated truth, but pretty hard to use as leverage since I (or, rather, one of my family) was kind of responsible for having put him in the coma-near-true-death thing in the first place. Adam would never even have been in Texas Hill Country to begin with, let alone in a coma, if it hadn't been for me. So, dip your mug into the guilt cauldron and take a huge chug, Keira Kelly, this one's totally on you.

"The ranch can run without me. Perhaps you are correct in that regard." Adam abandoned his nonchalant attitude and went behind his desk to sit at his chair. "Tell me this, however: Is my going along with you necessary? As necessary as remaining here and demonstrating that I am well, whole and can still lead?" He didn't mention the fact that Daffyd was coming with me. I'd told him earlier and he'd just raised an eyebrow and nodded. Daffyd and Gary had both left the house before Adam woke. Tucker had gone back to Niko's. After some very much needed private time with Adam, I'd gone with him to his office and broached the subject there—neutral ground, sort of.

I sat back down, defeated. He was right; damn him and the logic he rode in on. No matter how much I wanted him to be with me on this bedamned trip, his staying here and making sure his people knew he was still king overruled my wishes. Despite our so-called modern ways living in twenty-first century civilization, some things are best left to tradition. Hell, even the Queen of England needs to sometimes put on a show . . . and as far as I knew, the Brits seemed to be a hell of a lot more forgiving of their monarch's foibles than a pack of vampires would be their master's shortcomings, however tame they might seem. At least Adam's actions weren't splashed across the front pages of every issue of the weekly tabloids.

"Maybe I'll just stay here," I said brightly. "That could

work. What would happen if I didn't hop a plane and obey Gigi? Besides, if she wants me, she can bloody well come to me. I can play Mohammed just as easily as my great-great-granny can." Mohammed had only had a mountain come to him. That had probably been easier than budging Minerva Kelly.

"And what about Gideon?" Adam raised an eyebrow at me. Damn it, I hated when he raised that eyebrow.

"Yes, well," I grumbled. I knew very well that once our pilot arrived, I'd have to leave, but damn it, I was cranky. Too much had happened in the past few days and all I was asking was some support from the person who kept telling me he loved me.

Adam started to say something, but then kept his mouth closed. Probably a good idea, because I kept right on talking. "Niko's coming with me, right?"

Adam ignored my abrupt segue and answered me. "He's not me, but . . ."

"Yeah, I definitely know that," I said, smiling back at him. "But he'll help run interference."

"And act as emissary of sorts," Adam said.

Emissary. More like a shoulder to lean on when family shit spread across the fan, which I expected no later than five or so minutes after I hit ground zero at Kelly Clan Central and announced my intention of returning to Texas. It totally might be a futile attempt, but I was hoping that Gigi would behave in front of company. Niko and Daffyd both equaled company. Not Clan, but a representative of a fairly powerful vampire king—his second-in-command—plus my Sidhe family member. Not to mention Niko and my brother Tucker were about as much an item as two people could get without uttering wedding vows or entering into an official civil union. In my humble observation, my shapeshifting Viking berserker brother Tucker, after twelve centuries of liaising, coupling, enjoying and otherwise having a great deal of fun, had fallen in love . . . with a capital and most definite L. I wasn't sure he'd realized it yet, but I knew that before Gigi would even say boo to me once we got to the Clan home, she'd say something to Tucker.

Not that my brother prided himself on being footloose and fancy-free; it was merely the way things happened over his long years. Kind of like how I'd first noticed a tall dark-haired guy on the fringes of various parties during my time in London; a man who had then shown up a few years later in my small redneck corner of Texas, having bought a ranch to house him and his tribe while giving himself a chance to woo me. Too bad the wooing ended up taking place while I was trying to solve my cousin's murder. But hey, things like that seemed to be the way my rather twisted life path was heading, so why the hell not? Him turning out to be a vampire: pure perfection since I never dated humans—anymore.

Both our phones rang at the same time. Adam headed to his desk and I walked out to the reception area so as not to bother him.

"Hello?" I said, not recognizing the number in the display.

"Keira Kelly?" a cheery woman's voice asked.

I cringed. I hated when a caller referred to me by my full name. Always figured it was someone who didn't know me. "Who's calling, please?" I asked, keeping my voice neutral. If it was a sales call, I could pretend I was someone else.

"It's your pilot," she said. "I'm headed your way and will be at the airport within the hour."

I checked the clock on the wall above the aquarium. "We'll have some company," I said. "Need to leave after sunset. Is that doable?"

"Absolutely," she chirped.

Egads, she was bound to be one of those bright-eyed and bushy-tailed young things whose constant perkiness made me want to hurt them. I bet she even woke up in a cheerful mood. She might be old enough to be my grandmother, but definitely sounded like a cheerleader type—a Texas cheerleader type—with perfect white teeth, twinkling eyes and bouncy hair.

"Great," I muttered. "We'll meet you at the airport. I'll give you a ring when we pull out."

"Cool beans," she said and disconnected the call.

I folded up my phone and put it back in my pocket.

"When do you leave, then?" Adam came through the office door to join me.

"Whenever we decide. The pilot's on her way. She'll be at the San Antonio airport soon and I imagine she'll cheerfully wait until we get there—no sense coming all this way to leave without us." I shrugged. "We can head out of here close to dusk. The back of Tucker's panel van is closed off so Niko can be shielded from the sun. It'll only take about two and a half hours to get to the airport."

"Makes sense." Adam walked over to the large aquarium against the side wall, picked up a can of fish food and tapped a few flakes into the tank. "Keira," he began. He gazed at me with a serious look on his face. "Are you going to stop by Bea's before you fly out?"

I'd told him yesterday about my encounter with Noe and how Bea hadn't returned my calls. I stared down at the floor. "No," I replied. "I . . . I don't know what to do,

Adam. How to fix it." Sheer single-mindedness hadn't accomplished anything. I'd called several more times, left shorter and shorter voice mails. The last call, I'd listened to the canned message and then hung up, completely out of ideas.

"I'd go over there, but I'm afraid that she'll—" That she'd still avoid me in person. At least, with leaving voice mail, part of me could pretend she was busy. I knew better, but it was a bit of a solace.

"Ah." He walked to where I stood and hugged me. I let myself relax into his strength, soaking up the power radiating from him. Ever since my Change, I could feel his energy so strongly. He'd been able to hide it before. Hell, I hadn't even known he was a vampire until we'd met up again. I didn't know if he still could shield from me, or if he just didn't bother now.

"I can't believe she won't speak to me," I mumbled into his shoulder. "We've never not spoken to each other." Not even during our insane teen years. Bea had been busy working at the family café, learning the ropes. I'd gotten a kick out of hanging there, belonging. Being a teen human is bad enough, but in Clan reckoning, I was still a young pup, so to speak. Barely out of nappies and really not very interesting. If it hadn't been for a combination of Bea, her family, my two aunts and my brother Tucker, I'd have grown up more of a basket case than I was. Now, part of my support structure was gone and I had no idea how to shore it up again.

"I'm sorry," Adam said and held me tighter. "She's been your friend for thirty years. I know how this hurts."

"Yeah." I tilted my head up and kissed him. "Thank you," I said, breathing the words against his lips.

Adam kissed me back, deepening it to something

just short of carnal, enough to remind me what I'd be missing in Canada. "She'll come round," he said after he pulled away. "Give her some time. It's only been a few days."

I nodded and turned to leave. Yeah, once she forgives me for sentencing a man to death.

INTERLUDE

John and Rodney

HE'D HEARD PEOPLE thought of them as folk singers, homeless to be sure, but he and Rodney always show up for the festivals, especially the ones that gather in Victory Square. The park's a few steps from their regular spot on West Hastings, a good place to hang out any day, but especially so when there's a music festival going on. The park isn't big, but it is always kept up nice by the city. John really likes it here. He spends most afternoons sitting on the side of the hill, on the grassy verge, listening to and watching people. Some days, he takes the Number 19 bus to Stanley Park and hangs there a few hours, but he always comes back here. It's smaller and cozier.

John especially enjoys watching the tourists. The Americans are usually easy to spot; they tend to be overloaded with backpacks, have those silly waist packs and often wear loud clothing. Some of them are very nice, though. There was a family group at the park last September, all gathered for a birthday celebration. They sat and listened to the music for more than an hour and tipped them a couple of twenties. When Rodney protested, one of the women smiled and thanked them for the joy of being able to relax and listen. "I have a very demanding job," she'd said. "It's not often I get to sit for a while and enjoy something as simple as music." She'd nodded then, to both Rodney and him. The family then left, off for dinner somewhere in Gastown.

The weather's been really mild lately, warmer than normal at twelve degrees. Easy days, more sunny than not, and easy to wait out the occasional rain. John likes the spring in Vancouver, so much better, so much warmer than where he grew up. The usual morning and afternoon drizzle don't bother him at all. Rodney hates the rain and John teases him a lot about it, since Rodney grew up here and should be used to it.

They both play instruments: John, the guitar, Rodney, a bodhrán. John chants more than sings the old songs, the ones from before. A scholar would recognize them as Child Ballads; John only knows that they're from when the first of his family came over, long time ago when the coureurs de bois *and the tribes still roamed free. His family. Didn't have much of that these days, but he remembers Mum talking about her great-grandda who sailed over from Scotland. "He were a bard," she'd say. "Sang for the queen." John kind of doubted that last, but the fact his great-great-grandda sang was true fact. John had found reams of scribbled-on paper in a box in the attic of the last house they'd lived in. At first, he thought the people who'd lived there before left the songs but one day, Mum found him reading and went to her room to cry. She'd come out after a while, wiping her eyes on the apron with the big red apples. "Those b'longed to yer great-great-grandda," she'd said. "You're named after him." And that was it. She'd never spoken of the songs again. John had scrimped together enough money to buy a secondhand guitar from old Pennyworth's and learned to play from a coverless set of Mel Bay books someone had tossed into the trash bin behind the music store. They'd been in Toronto then, but after they'd had to give up the house and start sleeping in the car, the winters got too cold to bear. Mum packed them up and drove to Vancouver—a long way, but Mum wanted to go as far as she could. John was thirteen then, full of piss and vinegar and angry at the world. He'd run away a year later and never looked back.*

The crowd continues to gather as he and Rodney tune up. They're not seated on the erstwhile stage, but over to the side, on the hill, where they like to practice together. They'd spread out an old raincoat as a tarp to sit on, since the grass was still wet from this morning's drizzle. Rodney grumps about the cold ground. John teases him again and pulls out a hat for tips.

"Heya, guys." One of the regulars nods to them as he stumps by, all rags and parcels, clean because he'd showered yesterday over at the Ramada. John likes the folk there; all of the workers were kind. In slow times, they'd often let one or two of the street folk come in and use the shower in one of the empty guest rooms, so long as they were in and out quick, before six A.M.

The hostel wasn't too bad of a place to stay, really cheap, but there wasn't any food and John never trusted the showers. Plus, lately, he'd heard tell of at least one guy found dead in his bed. Old guy, to be sure, but best to come in late, sleep with one eye open and leave as early as possible. Too many new people in town, too many drifters with one hand out for a handout and another in your pocket taking what little you had.

Sometimes, if John and Rodney were really lucky, the Ramada had leftovers from the breakfast the hotel offered guests. Rodney would go over on their behalf, stand at the back of the hotel and wait every morning around eleven. Most days, they'd get some toast and jam. Some days, they even got waffles or pancakes. Kind of rubbery, but it didn't really matter. Either way, it was nearly good as it could get, except for the days that they had some ready coin and could go over to Tim Hortons—the folks over at the Waterfront Centre were pretty nice—and shell out for a coffee and some Timbits.

A man passes them. A stranger to this place, John thinks, though he isn't sure why he knows this. The man's no more oddly dressed than anyone else here, from the ragtag people of the streets to the equally oddly dressed former and wannabe hippies: all long hair, ribbons and leather. The man wears knee-high leather boots laced up the center, like some sort of funky moccasin. He's not First Nations—can't be, not with pale blond hair, one braid down the left side of his face, the rest loose down his back and blowing in the gentle breeze. A small bell woven into the braid chimes as the breeze moves it. John nudges Rodney, who looks up and grimaces, grumpy to be distracted from his drum. "Looks like one o' them folksy hippie types," Rodney says and turns back to sliding his fingers across the drum's skin, as if to feel all the imperfections, the rough patches on the leather. He'd made the drum himself, learning how after hours and days spent in the library, both from books and online. He'd gotten the various bits and pieces from haunting a couple of Canadian Tire stores and connecting with a lumberman who helped find him the wood. Another person helped him find enough leather to finish it. Daisy-the-waitress, not to be confused with Daisy-with-long-hair, showed him a book she had on Celtic designs and Rodney painstakingly painted some of the knots on the wood of the drum.

John nods agreement. "Yeah, not from around here, I'd say." He watches as the man keeps walking, never looking at them, but going to sit at the edge of the crowd, his dark green trousers and flowing pirate shirt peeking from the folds of a cloak. John remembers a neighbor in Toronto who was in some sort of reenactment group. Dressed like that a lot. The guy in Toronto always looked kind of stupid, though, with his balding head and thick glasses. This guy . . . there is something about him . . .

The man pulls out a small silver object—a flute, maybe?—and sits polishing it with a cloth. John shrugs. Just another musician. He turns his attention back to his guitar and begins picking out "Tam Lin." Rodney picks up the beat only seconds later. The man looks over at them and nods, picks up his flute and joins in.

CHAPTER SIX

IT WASN'T EVERY DAY one could fly to Vancouver in a private plane piloted by a hound. Well, not exactly hound, but a dog at any rate. Tucker, Niko, Daffyd and I arrived at the San Antonio airport private plane terminal and it was dark enough for Niko to be able to be outside without harm.

Finding the plane was fairly easy. The person staffing the gate directed us to Hangar Ten. We trooped out with our bags and packs. It was a bit of a trek, but luckily, none of us carried much in the way of luggage or gear.

I'd asked Niko to provide clothes for Daffyd, as I didn't want to call too much attention to him. It was going to be difficult getting through customs in Vancouver with a Sidhe; the vampire, though, was evidently not going to be a problem. Niko had assured me his paperwork was in order. No doubt Adam had long since taken care of his vampires' legal documentation and since he and Adam had managed to get into the United States from England, I wasn't all that worried—it was a lot harder to come into this country than get out of it, even with the proper paperwork. Homeland Security—our tax dollars at work or whatever. If they only knew . . .

Daffyd, on the other hand, had nothing of the sort. When I asked him how he'd entered the country, he gave me that particularly Sidhe expressionless look—sort of like a fair-haired Spock, pointy ears and annoying attitude included. Then he'd told me he could cast a foolproof glamour, effectively hiding himself from human eyes.

A glamour wasn't necessary here at this airport, but the glowing, flowing, magick faery garb had to go. We were meeting our pilot at the hangar, but still needed to check in at the terminal. Bad enough I was traveling with three of the most gorgeous men in existence; having one of them wearing flowing robes would be too much.

My Sidhe cousin was now decked out in black jeans, a black shirt with silver tracings on the collar and cuffs and a pair of black Lucchese boots—half country singer, half Goth—only in Texas. Daffyd had pulled his hair back into a loose ponytail, fastening it with a silver clasp, taking to the clothes as if they were made for him. He'd managed to come across as something other than, well . . . *Other*—at least if his observer was a human. To me, he still felt Sidhe. Nothing could hide the sense of power that he emanated. Outwardly though, for the mundane world, he would do.

Once we reached the hangar, all we found was a tastefully appointed Learjet with "Kelly 2" painted on the side and a somewhat shaggy black dog wandering around. I'd been about to call the whole thing off and head back to the Wild Moon when the dog bounded up to me, licked my hand and enthusiastically wagged its tail.

Niko stepped back, barely repressing an automatic sign of the cross (right, this vampire had no problem with crosses) as the hound silently morphed into a redheaded woman of medium height, clothed only in her dignity. She tossed him a grin, then reached into a duffle bag that had been sitting next to the rollaway stairs. Daffyd never reacted.

She pulled out some clothing and gave us all the once-over. "I seriously want to ask which one of you is the Tin Man," she quipped. "A woman and three men, on a journey—"

"To see the Great and Powerful Oz," I muttered.

"If we are Dorothy and her companions," Niko said smoothly, "then you must be Toto?"

"Good one." The woman barked a laugh and pulled on a pair of jeans and a T-shirt. She nodded to me as if to congratulate me on my excellent taste. "He is a pretty one, dear cuz. Yours?"

"Mine," Tucker broke in, both pride and possession evident in his tone.

"Well, well, then, cousin. A coup. Bully for you." She turned to Daffyd, studying him. "This one is yours then?" I knew she meant me and by yours, she meant family. Even she could feel the resonance.

"Daffyd ap Geraint. I am Keira's cousin," Daffyd said quietly and inclined his head in a bow. "On her mother's side," he added unnecessarily.

Our pilot smiled and seemed to file this information away. She turned back to look at the group of us. "I was expecting one cousin and now have a whole tribe's worth. Nice. This ought to be fun."

Niko grinned, a hint of the rake I'd first met peeking through. With an elegant nod and slight bow, he addressed my cousin. "You have the advantage of me, ma'am."

"Liz Norton Kelly," she said, sticking out a hand in greeting. "Onyx, when I'm in dog form."

Niko raised it to his mouth and bowed over it. *"A votre service, madame."*

Liz tossed back her hair and let out a belly laugh. "Pretty *and* polite. Tucker, you dog."

"Wolf," my brother grumbled under his breath.

"So you choose," Liz said with a shrug. "I prefer *canis lupus familiaris*."

Niko regarded Tucker with a quizzical look, then turned back to Liz. "A choice, then? Is that the way of it?"

Tucker answered, "Always a choice, *cariad*. I prefer to become wolf than a cross between a border collie and golden retriever."

I could see Niko filing this factoid away. All six of my brothers turned out to be shapeshifters after their Change. Each and every one of them played wolf best. Some of the other shapeshifters in the family preferred other animals. I'd not thought much about it as when I'd been younger, I mostly stayed around my brothers and my healer aunts.

"Our pilot, I presume?" I cut in before this turned into a "whose pelt is prettier" argument.

"The one and only," she replied.

"So, Liz Norton Kelly," I said, "why the delay in coming to get us?"

"Weather, primarily. Couple of storms brewing north of the enclave. Then some sort of powwow or something." She fluttered her fingers dismissively. "I was in Vancouver for most of it, but Gigi told me to hang tight."

"Powwow? You know who?"

"Nope," she said. "Bunch of people in and out of there over the past week or so, but I didn't recognize any of them. Not that I would. I try to stay out of the politics."

"Probably safest." Tucker gave her a huge smile and opened his arms. "C'mere, you."

Liz merrily pounced on my brother, who enveloped her in a bear hug. She planted a huge kiss on my brother's smiling face. "It's definitely been too long, Cousin Wolf."

Tucker stepped back and patted her head, dropping a kiss on her hair. "That it has, Cousin Hound. How's the piloting biz?"

Liz laughed. *"Comme ci, comme ça,"* she answered. "Haven't had too many stunt piloting gigs lately."

"Stunt piloting?" I asked.

"Lots of movie studios up my way," Liz said. "I hire out to do stunt work sometimes. These days, though, I'm more or less our dear matriarch's beck-and-call girl."

"Aren't we all?" I mumbled. "Well, c'mon, then, children. If we're to do this thing, it best be done now."

"In a hurry, dear sister?" Tucker teased.

I climbed up the steps to the plane. "I just want to get this over with."

"Homeward bound, then," Liz said.

"To hell, more likely," I remarked as I ducked inside and tossed my backpack on a seat.

Tucker laughed as he and Niko followed me on board. Daffyd, still silent, brought up the rear.

Yeah, this was going to be a fun trip . . . not.

"ARE WE there yet?"

I rolled my head against the back of the plush leather, trying to ditch the sarcasm, but failing. I really didn't do boredom well. Whatever had possessed me to leave without packing a book or three? I suppose that I'd expected to pass the flight time talking to my brother and Niko.

I'd spent the last couple of hours alternately napping in my too-luxurious seat and trying to avoid staring at my brother and Niko canoodling directly across from me—well, not exactly canoodling. They were just sitting together and talking quietly; every once in a while, they'd share an easy touch, head lean, or just a simple smile between the two of them. It further demonstrated to me how much those two belonged together.

Daffyd sat in the back of the plane, quietly reading. It was as if he planned to be as much in the background as possible. I should probably use this time to talk to him, find out as much as I could about my mother, about that side of my family, but frankly, I didn't want to. There'd be enough time for that later. All I really wanted was to get this trip over with.

And there was a good possibility this was not the best time to chat with my faery cousin. He might be somewhat uncomfortable surrounded by all this steel. Steel is, of course, an alloy consisting mostly of iron. Iron and Sidhe were not a good mix. Luckily, because our family had been known to entertain the fey from time to time, most of our planes were coated inside with a special treatment; the chemistry was something that eluded me, but I knew it was brewed with a hefty dollop of magick. Faery folk could ride in the plane, but the ride would still be less than relaxing.

"Grumpy?" Tucker gave me a smirk.

"Just bored." I sighed.

"Any word from Isabel before we left?"

"Nothing. I tried calling a couple of times, but no answer. Couldn't get in touch with Gigi, either. Maybe she's too busy powwowing to pick up. Wonder what that's all about?"

"Who knows?" Tucker said with a lazy stretch. "I imagine if it involves you in any way, she'll be letting us know."

"That's what I'm afraid of," I muttered, then swung my feet up onto the seat and tucked them under me, reclining onto the comfortable arm. It had been so long since I'd last flown Air Kelly, I'd forgotten how incredibly luxurious it was to have a well-appointed aircraft all to oneself and carefully selected others. Liz was holed up in the cockpit, doing whatever she did to make the plane go.

"And your . . . Gideon, was it?" Niko said. "He is stable?"

I nodded and tried to hide my expression by taking a swig from my water bottle. Not mine. Not for a long time. "Stable enough," I replied and took another swig. "Isabel said she'd call if there was a change. No call means no change. I just wish I knew why the delay. First Isabel tells me that Gigi pulled her away from her trip—something done only in an emergency situation in our book—and had her come to Texas to fetch me *tout de suite* . . . then all sense of urgency disappears? Still bothers me. What if it's all some sort of trickery on her part to get me there and keep me?"

Tucker scooted forward and patted my knee. "It's not a trick, Keira," he said. "You know Isabel wouldn't do that."

"I wasn't talking about Isabel, bro—"

"Might I ask something?" Niko interrupted.

"Shoot," I said.

"You both"—he inclined his head at Tucker then nodded toward me—"have been attempting to phone your Clan leader over and over in the last few days. You, Keira, seem to be worried that things are not as they seem and there is some urgency on your part to contact her. I'm not sure I understand why. Surely she is not so vicious and cruel that you fear her?"

I wasn't sure whether to laugh or take him seriously. "She's not exactly the type to send the flying monkeys out after us," I said, continuing Liz's earlier analogy. "Not the Wicked Witch of the West, East or anywhere in between."

More like a really dainty dominatrix, my mind supplied. I shook off the unbidden imagery and continued. "She's strict, strong and very much used to getting her way," I said. I thought about it for a second, trying to formulate the words. "I think it's more that I tend to turn into a twelve-year-old girl around her," I continued. "She triggers all my guilt responses better than a Jewish mother at a bat mitzvah."

"You feel that her summons on the heels of your transformation followed by an inexplicable delay might have something to do with you?"

"Yeah," I said, reluctantly realizing as Niko spoke just how self-centered I'd been. "You know, Niko, you may have a point. I—we all—have been operating on the supposition that the delay had to do with me or Gideon. I tend to forget that my great-great-grandmother runs several multinational businesses and pretty much has the welfare and well-being of thousands of Clan members as her responsibility."

"Well, that wasn't exactly what I was—"

"Hey, kids, we're getting close to YVR." Liz's voice came over the speaker. "Buckle up and get your passports out. We should be pulling up to the customs station in about thirty minutes."

CHAPTER SEVEN

"PASSPORTS AND PAPERWORK, please," the customs agent asked. We'd landed on the appropriate runway and taxied over to the designated customs location. I hadn't been sure how this worked, having flown commercially for so long. It seemed fairly simple. Since Liz flew back and forth regularly, she was a member of CAN-PASS, a program for frequent flyers. She'd phoned ahead, gotten her instructions and now all we needed to do was wait until the customs agent reviewed our paperwork and passports. Easy as frozen pie in a microwave.

"How's it going, Ben?" Liz smiled at the agent and passed over a folder.

The tall dark-haired man smiled at my cousin. His blue eyes twinkled as he spoke. "Mighty fine, young Liz," Ben replied with a wink. "More family?" He nodded to us and flipped through the folder that contained Liz's papers and our passports.

"More?" Liz asked. She looked at me and I shrugged. How the hell should I know? I'd been in Texas for more than two years. I figured family came through Vancouver pretty regularly unless they were coming in from the east, where Toronto or Ontario would be a more logical customs checkpoint.

"Few of your folk came through here about a half hour ago," Ben said.

"Anyone I know?" Liz asked with a puzzled look on her

face. "Didn't realize any more family was heading home. I went down to Texas to pick up my cousins earlier today—quick turnaround."

Agent Ben shook his head and made some notations on the papers. "Can't say as I recognized them," he said. "Kellys, though. Came in the blue plane. Had at least one guest aboard." He handed Liz back some papers and then began stamping passports.

I shot a glance at Niko, who returned my questioning look with a serene bland one. I hadn't paid attention earlier when Liz had collected our passports and wondered what nationality he was supposed to be.

As soon as we'd touched down, Daffyd had, as promised, woven a do-not-notice glamour on himself. To a human, there were only four people on that plane.

"Keira Kelly," Ben the agent said and handed over my passport. "Welcome back to Canada, miss."

I smiled and took back my passport, tucking it into my backpack.

"Mr. Kelly, Mr. Marlowe."

"Marlowe?" I mouthed at Niko as he took his obviously Canadian passport from Ben.

Niko smirked and handed me the small red folder without saying a word.

As Ben stamped and returned Tucker's passport, I looked at Niko's.

"Nicholas Christofer Marlowe," I read and rolled my eyes. "Date of birth/*date de naissance*: 1979/26/02. Place of birth/*lieu de naissance*: Canterbury, UK." Oh great, delusions of poethood . . . or maybe he'd known the man himself and borrowed his name. I handed the passport back to Niko with another eye roll and a mouthed "please." He winked and tucked the passport into his jacket pocket. I had to give him props for amusement value, though.

"Everything's in order then," Ben said. "You can taxi down to the hangar."

"Oh, we're continuing on," Liz said. "Need to get on up to the homestead."

"Oh, dear," Ben said. "'Fraid you're going to have to change your plans, yeah?"

"What is it?" Liz asked. "Something wrong with the paperwork?"

"There's been a front blowing in up north, grounded most light craft for at least several hours, probably overnight. Unless you're in a hurry, I'd suggest staying in town tonight and then trying again in the morning."

"We could stay at the condo," I ventured. "Call Gigi and let her know."

Liz shrugged. "If the storm's big enough to ground a small jet," she said, "Gigi's probably well aware we're grounded, but yeah." She turned to Ben. "What's the forecast? We expecting it here?"

He shook his head. "Don't expect it to come this far south, but it's stalled up in the mountains and not a good one to fly into. Stay in town a day or two if you're not in a hurry. Do some shopping. Lots of sales on, I hear. My wife and the girls went up over to Robson Street last night and did a little damage to the pocketbook." He scribbled some more on the flight plan and handed it back to Liz. "There you are, Liz. You know where to go from here, eh?"

She nodded and took the flight plan back, stashing it back in the folder. "Thanks, Ben," she said. "Please give my regards to your wife for me, yeah?"

"Will do." He started to turn away, but then stopped.

"Hey, before I forget. You know that restaurant you like? Irish Heather? Heard it reopened last night after being closed for a while."

"Closed? They do great business and no way it was the health department. Why'd they shut down?" Liz asked

"Nothing to do with business. Some homeless guy was found dead in their old storefront."

"Jiminy," Liz said. "Poor Dan and Liss. They still own that old place, right?"

Ben thought a moment. "I believe they do," he replied. "Hope this doesn't hurt business."

"Do you know what happened?" Liz asked.

"Not yet," Ben said. "I know a couple of homeless folks have been found dead around there and up on West Hastings recently. They're being treated as suspicious deaths."

"Suspicious?" Tucker asked. "Something going on we should know about?"

Ben scratched his head. "I'm not so sure on my end, but I don't know that much, really. Just what I read in the papers, see on the news. Possibly malnutrition and exposure are the cause, but I heard one of the officers talking this morning that it may be a drugs case. Stuff like that gets involved, you never know what kind of folk show up in town." He shook his head and tucked his ballpoint pen into his shirt pocket. "Cheers, all."

At Ben's words, my jaw clenched. Great, suspicious deaths on the heels of arriving. Could it have anything to do with me or mine? Oh, dear powers that be, I certainly hoped not. Vancouver was a big city, right? Homeless people died all the time.

"Ta then, Ben, and thanks." Liz stepped back inside and gave the man a wave as he descended the steps. She waited until he was out of earshot before pulling up the stairs and shutting the door and turning to me.

"You okay?" she asked. "I could feel your tension even from outside."

"Yeah, I'm good," I said and rotated my head down and around to loosen up my neck muscles. "Hearing about suspicious deaths so few days after—"

Tucker rubbed the back of my neck. "It's a city, Keira," he said. "This sort of thing happens all the time."

"I know, I know," I said. "I just . . ." I sighed and rubbed my eyes. "Sorry, it's not exactly the first thing I wanted to hear on arrival."

"Not the first thing, actually," Liz said.

I gave her a puzzled look.

"What about the weather?"

"Oh, right, yeah," I said. "Damn. This just blows. I guess we're stuck here."

"Anyone want to try to call Gigi?" Tucker pulled his phone out and dangled it.

"I suppose I should try," I said and grabbed my own cell out of my pack. "Liz, can you punch up weather forecasts or anything? See what you can find out?"

"Yeah, I'll hit up satellite." She went back into the cockpit.

Tucker settled back into his own seat, throwing an arm around Niko, who seemed relaxed. Daffyd, once again, said nothing. What could be going on in his head? I suppose that in the grand scheme of life, a day or two delay was small potatoes to those who'd already lived centuries. Not that I wasn't okay with staying in Vancouver overnight. I loved this city as much as I loved London—plus, it didn't have the taint of my experience with Gideon as did the latter city.

The phone rang once at the other end, then cut off. I pulled it away from my ear and checked the display. "Huh," I said and pressed the end call button. "That was weird." I tried again, this time getting nothing but the fast busy signal. "I think we're hosed, gang," I said. "I bet the phone lines are down." I looked up toward the cockpit where Liz sat in the pilot's seat staring at a screen. She had her headphones on so I wasn't sure she'd heard me.

"Heya, Liz, anything?"

She didn't look up, but waved her arm in a "hang on" gesture.

After a couple of minutes, she took off the headset and returned to the main cabin. "Looks like we may be here for at least a couple of days," she said. "Ben was spot-on. A huge thunderstorm system hit the Coast Mountains and isn't expected to let up until tomorrow evening. I've put in a call to someone I know at a weather outpost. He'll text me if the forecast changes. In the meantime, I suggest you all head to the condo and settle in, after we call Minerva and tell—"

"Tried that," I interrupted. "Rang once and disconnected, then a fast busy."

"Damn," she said. "That's a pain. Those lines are usually pretty good, especially for the area, but a bad thunderstorm can knock them out quick."

"Why don't we all head out to get a bite to eat, then go on to the condo?" Tucker suggested.

"Sounds like a plan, bro."

"I'll taxi us over to our hangar," Liz said, "then you all can call a cab. My car's here, but I'm afraid we won't fit. I bought a smart car. It's great for me, but too tiny for our gang—only sits two. I'll head on over to my place and give you a ring tomorrow."

"You live here?" I asked. "In town, I mean."

"Over in Burnaby," she said. "Easier for when I hire out. Several of the film studios are there and it makes the drive faster if I don't have to deal with as much traffic." She grinned. "It's loads of fun. I like to keep an apartment close to the action."

"You should join us for dinner," I said. "My treat."

"I really need to get back home," she said. "Since I was supposed to bring you all up to the family tonight, it could be they're trying to get in touch with me. I should try to email. Even if the phones are down, maybe . . ."

"Perhaps we should try driving," Niko suggested. "Won't your family be worried?"

"Yeah, worried no doubt, but driving?" Liz shook her head. "Not with that weather system. Looks to be a wicked big storm and there are some mountain roads between here and there that are pretty treacherous. In good weather, it's a good ten- or twelve-hour drive and only about two-thirds of that on main highway. I'd not risk it with storms. You all go on and when I get home I'll email the homestead," she said. "You get settled in and let me know if you hear anything. I'll do the same."

"If they can't call, how likely is it that they're online?" I wondered aloud. "I could try to text them, but would they get it?"

"Not too likely, true, but I figure at least with email, they'll eventually get the message," Liz explained. "Keira, if it's okay with you, I should get moving. You folks can hail a cab from the terminal."

"Okay with *me*?" Why on earth was she asking me?

Liz looked confused. "You're kind of my boss, right now . . ."

"Excuse me?" Her boss?

"Keira, in case it's escaped you, you're the heir. For all intents and purposes, you speak with my liege's voice," Liz explained.

"I *so* do not," I exclaimed. "Oh no, I absolutely do not want this. I'm not your boss." Bad enough that Daffyd claimed me as his liege. I didn't want responsibility for anyone else. Didn't they know that people died under my watch? Not happening again, thanks very much.

"But you are." Liz said. "It's not a matter of if or wanting. It's a fact. You're the heir; the only one you answer to is Minerva. Not that I wouldn't argue with you if I thought you were doing something stupid." She beamed and for a moment, looked like a smaller, female version of my brother. I wondered briefly if Liz was a much closer cousin than I knew.

I tried to explain how I felt. "I'm not comfortable with this whole boss thing, Liz . . . and that includes you, too, Daffyd," I said, briefly turning my head toward the back of the plane. "Liz, you don't need to ask me if you can go to your own home. I'm not Gigi and don't plan to be ruling or leading anyone anytime soon. As far as I'm concerned, you go on and do whatever it is you need to do. I'm good with that."

She shrugged. "Thanks, but frankly, in my opinion, it wouldn't hurt to practice. You're going to need all the advantage you can get, Keira. Minerva's been at this a long time. You're not even four decades old yet. Much too soon for you to have this burden on you—from everything I know, you Changed way too early."

I did a double take. What was she saying? "What do you know? Are you telling me that early onset of Change isn't because I'm the heir?"

Liz shook her head, her red curls glinting in the lights

of the cabin. "I was probably not meant to hear, but I was out chasing a tennis ball the other day, in dog form. I don't think anyone saw me because I was around a corner."

"Gigi?"

"No, an uncle and aunt, I didn't recognize them. I think they were part of a group that arrived a few days ago from England, maybe? In any case, they were talking about how odd it was that you'd Changed so early. The aunt said that usually, the heir Changes later than normal, at the farther end of the range, about age sixty or seventy. They're older, more mature, you know, likely to handle it better."

"Say what?" "What are you saying?" Tucker and Niko spoke over each other. Daffyd remained silent, his gray eyes glittering. I couldn't parse the look on his face. Interest? Boredom?

"But, Isabel said . . ." I shook my head, trying to understand. My aunt had practically told me that the reason I Changed when I did was twofold: first, because I was the heir, and second, I'd triggered it because Adam had nearly killed me. Both things were necessary, or that's what I thought.

"That's what Isabel *told* us, sis," Tucker reminded me. "Could be dear Aunt Isabel was being more coy than forthcoming."

Niko perked up at this. "Your Aunt Isabel lied?"

Tucker shook his head. "Not lied so much as shaded the truth a little." He glanced at me. "Keira, I think she was trying to spare you."

"From what?" I exploded out of my seat and strode to the back of the jet, nearly tripped over Daffyd's foot, then whirled and came back to where Tucker and Niko sat. "I have had enough of this—from early onset Change, having to sentence a man to death by life-sucking, rescuing my boyfriend from a coma due to the life-sucker, who, by the way, happens to be my damned cousin on my mother's side. Then, said boyfriend practically sucks all my blood out, which triggers my Change and I find out I'm the bloody Kelly heir." I took a deep breath and let it out with a whoosh. "What the hell else do you think she could be sparing me from?"

"That, dear sister," replied Tucker in an infuriatingly calm voice, "is for her to know, and us to figure out."

I sank down into the plane seat and covered my face with my hands. I'd thought that I was freaking done with the secrets, with the hidden stuff. All I'd been expecting was some sort of confrontation as I not-so-calmly explained to my great-great-grandmother how I was absolutely not going to come quietly to BC to train as her heir. I just started to have a life and I wasn't ready to give it up. Now, it seemed that there was more going on than we knew.

"We'll find out," Niko said and reached over to pat my hand.

Surprised at the gesture, I resisted my immediate urge to pull away. Ever since Niko and Tucker had become more than just friends with benefits, Niko's attitude toward me had made a complete 180. From being a straight-up dickhead who'd looked me over as if I were a piece of luscious meat—or, I guess in his case, a goblet brimming with fresh blood—to treating me with respect and, now, with understanding and concern. How things changed in so short a time.

I liked it. He squeezed my hand and sat back. Huh. No shock, just a tingle of electric energy, nothing more than I'd feel if I was touching my brother or another close relative. I guess my shields must be stronger than I expected.

"Thanks, Niko." I smiled at him.

"You're very welcome," he replied and obviously meant it.

"If you're all ready to bust Gigi's chops, then go for it," Liz said. "Just give me warning before you do."

I managed a small laugh. "So you can watch—or hide?"

"I'm not sure yet," Liz said. "All right, kids, buckle up while we taxi, please. I need to get this puppy over to our hangar and then you all can head into town."

"I need a drink," I said, glancing at the clock mounted in the bulkhead. Only 9:35 P.M. local time. Blessed be the two-hour time change, I thought.

INTERLUDE

The Music

THE MUSIC SWELLS, power rising with it as it blankets the block. Aural fog creeps into crevices and cracks in wood, brick, mortar and stone. Melody wars with and entwines with harmony, like two lovers parrying, thrusting, wrapping around each other, oblivious to surroundings, their rising energy combining, making a whole much greater than the sum of its parts. No human notices consciously. Moods lift or wither, people smile or frown, depending on their sensitivity. Chords of atonality enter the melody, vibrate below the notes, discordance weaving the weft and warp of the song, twisting it, imbalance complementing the perfection of the top notes. The complex tune continues, filling the night air, carried on the slight breeze.

At the place where they sleep, the melody sneaks inside, touching flesh, skin, mind and thought, some feelings turning to love and beauty, others to hatred and fear. Dreams turn on a quarter note, a semiquaver, a vibrato unheard by any still living, by any mortal being.

In one bed, two men whisper, still awake, smiles turning to kisses and soft touches, careful not to wake the others sharing the space. In another bunk, an older man sighs and remembers his dead wife of thirty years, lost only three years past. Silent tears slip from his closed and unseeing eyes. Down the hall, Mary Rafferty whimpers at the memory of her daughter's firstborn, so small and fragile, so many weeks too soon.

Sam Jones shifts in his sleep, hand clutching the flat feather pillow, his swollen knuckles aching with tension. He runs in his sleep, dream body young once again, arthritis now only something read about in adverts. He follows the music, so eager to join, to sing again and pluck the strings of the guitar, as he once did. They'd come to hear him once more, the young, the beautiful, the women and men entranced by the sound he could coax from the polished wood and nylon strings.

A tall man stands at the rise of the small hill and beckons Sam closer. Such beauty, thinks Sam as he steps closer to the shining one. The man reaches out his hand. When Sam takes it, the music stops.

CHAPTER EIGHT

"Did you hear that?"

"What?" Tucker asked as he shifted in the front seat of the small cab. I'd been hoping for a van, but the dispatcher had said that he could only send one of the smaller sedans. We'd crammed into the cab and asked the driver to take us to Gastown, a popular tourist district and a great place to find a restaurant.

I thought we'd drop our bags off at the condo on the way to the restaurant, but Liz had insisted on going out of her way and taking the bags for us. Getting our four bags into her tiny car was almost as tight a squeeze as the four of us getting into the taxi, but we managed.

"Music, I think?" I strained to hear more clearly. Snatches of an almost familiar melody teased at the outside edge of my hearing.

Both my brother and Niko shook their heads.

"I hear it." Daffyd's voice was quiet, almost a whisper. "I hear it." There was a strange note in his voice. I was about to remark when the driver spoke up.

"Radio's not on, miss," the driver said. "Maybe it's a cell phone?"

"See, I'm not—there it is again," I said. "Can't you all hear it?" The soft melody sounded as if it were echoing from somewhere nearby. Except we were all stuffed into a cab and driving down Seymour, heading into downtown Vancouver. The music had to be inside the cab.

"I still can't hear it, but it's got to be a phone," Tucker muttered. "Not mine, though, I turned it off."

Niko didn't carry a cell phone with him, and I knew that wasn't my ringtone. Besides, I would've felt the vibration since my phone was in my jeans pocket.

"Could it be my iPod?" I'd stored it in my pack, in one of the inside pockets and my backpack was in the trunk. The melody had that quality of being faraway, as if bleeding through someone else's headphones. Except no one in the car had headphones and I really doubted that even if my iPod was on, the earbuds would be plugged in, which would be the only way we'd hear the music. Plus, despite everyone's enhanced hearing, I was pretty sure the ability to hear that small a sound over the noise of the car and from the trunk wasn't possible. "You really don't hear anything?"

"No, but even if you do, it's doubtful that it's your iPod," Tucker answered me. "No way we could hear that from inside the car. It's got to be someone's phone or something in here with the volume turned low." He gave the driver a look. I knew my brother was humoring me. Was this some sort of weird manifestation of my new Talents? I'd thought that after Change, I would have to actually have to do something to turn a Talent on, so to speak. No more wild and unpredictable abilities bleeding through. Hadn't Isabel practically said that in so many words?

The melody continued at the edge of my senses, teasing me like a stray and longed-for breeze at the height of a Texas summer. I knew this tune, but couldn't place it, only hearing enough to make me need to hear more. "Damn it," I said. "It's just there—so familiar . . ."

Our driver shot me a look in the rearview mirror, mumbled something in a language I didn't understand

and, with his right hand, fumbled inside the center console, rummaging among some papers. He pulled out a small folded cell phone. It was silent. With a practiced flip, he opened it, brandished the silent phone at my brother and me, then flipped it shut again. "See. Not this one," he said. "I don't have an iPod, either."

I started to protest that it wasn't a phone when the insistent buzz of my own cell caused the heretofore taciturn cab driver to scowl at me, his expression saying what he was only too polite to: see, it was you all the time. Except it wasn't. I'd flipped it to buzz mode when we'd boarded the cab, after one more try to reach my dad's number, then Adam's. Neither had answered. I'd left voice mail for both. One good thing about modern communications is that cell phone technology lets you leave messages, even if the signal wasn't getting through at the other end. I'd totally have called and left messages for Gigi, but she insisted on land lines at the enclave and no cell phones.

In order to reach into my right pocket, I had to practically lie across Niko, who was sitting between me and Daffyd, in what my brothers used to call the bitch seat. Tucker had chosen shotgun, as his long legs made it impossible for him to sit in the back of the environmentally friendly hybrid cab. Nice idea, but the damned vehicle was not meant for four fairly tall adults plus driver.

"Sorry," I mumbled to all the occupants of the car as I answered without looking at the display. I tabled the music discussion until later.

"Hiya, honey." My dad's warm voice rolled out of the speaker. "You touched down yet?"

"What the—" I pulled the phone away from my ear and stared at the display, verifying the number. "Dad?"

Tucker turned as best he could in the small front seat. "Dad?"

I nodded and returned to the call. "I thought the phone lines were down up there."

"Oh, right," he said. "I'm actually not at the homestead," he said. "Flew down to Seattle yesterday on an errand. Wanted to see if you'd arrived."

"We're all fine, Dad," I said. "Couldn't fly into the enclave because of the weather. We're headed to the condo."

"Yeah, storm's a bit of a doozy," he said. "Stormy here, too. Came up quicker than expected, frankly. Forecast called for it to blow in sometime tomorrow . . ." His voice trailed off. I strained to hear if we were still connected.

"You still there, Dad?"

"I'm here, sweetheart, sorry," he said. "Isabel's tugging on my arm."

Say what? "Isabel's there? I thought she went to the enclave."

Tucker was poking my arm and waving his hand. I slapped his wrist and concentrated on hearing my dad. The line crackled with static; between that and the reverberating hum of the car engine and the music I could still sense more than hear, I was having a hard time making out the words on the other side of the connection.

"She was. I asked her to come down with me. Wanted to—" The rest of his sentence got lost in a burst of static.

"I didn't hear that, Dad, what was it?"

"Never mind, honey, not important. Let me give Isabel the phone before she has a conniption."

"Wait, don't go yet," I said. "Gigi knows we're stranded here in Vancouver, right?"

He laughed. "She does, honey. She was going to call you but I guess the phones went. Your brother's there though, right?"

I looked at Tucker. "Yeah, he's with me."

"Oh, good then," Dad said. "I was hoping—"

More static and something that sounded like "Gigi told him . . . tell you . . ."

"Tell me what? How's Gideon?" I hurried to ask before we completely lost the connection.

"He's okay for now, Keira." Dad's voice went all somber. "He was in pretty bad shape for a while. We sent for you—"

Another blast of static then a female voice blared out of my phone's earpiece. "Keira, he's stable for now." Isabel must have grabbed the phone from my dad.

"So what happened, Aunt?"

"No one there knows," she said. "I tried to do some diagnostics, but he was in pretty bad shape magickally when I got there. Your father said he thinks the boy was trying something—"

"Again?" I said, letting the disgust through. Figured. Gideon was the magnetic poster boy for bad and very stupid shit. Limits? Yeah, he'd heard of them—enough to figure out how he was going to break them. This time, though, it sounded as if those limits broke him, instead.

Isabel let out a heavy sigh. "I know, dear," she said. "He's not . . . well, never mind that. I've managed to put him in a healing sleep. He'll be resting for now. Jane's watching over him while I'm gone."

"So, he's not dying?"

"Not anymore," Isabel said. "I'm not sure how to fix him yet, but we'll figure it out. How about you? You doing okay?"

"I'm fine," I said, wondering at the abrupt subject switch. "Why?"

The crackle static tinged Isabel's answer. Did she hesitate, or was it the signal? "Well, just wondering," she said.

"I'm fine. Is there any reason I shouldn't be?" Egads, *was* there something wrong with me? Was that why I was hearing the music and no one else was—oh wait, except for Daffyd.

"Yes, yes, indeed, that's right." I could almost hear Isabel nodding her head earnestly.

"Are you trying to tell me the—um—" I looked over at our taxi driver, who was deliberately staring straight ahead at the road. We were stopped at a traffic light. I recognized the street corner. We were only about a mile or two from our destination. "So my condition and my circumstances, should be different?" I meant different in style, not in amount of Talent—that part, I knew.

"Well, no, not exactly," Isabel said. "You're right, despite your many Talents now, your magick should be settled."

Okay, well, that meant the phantom music wasn't a symptom . . . maybe. "Isabel, what are you trying to say?" I asked.

"Nothing, nothing, dearie," she said. "No worries. Just—"

Oh for . . . "What is it, Isabel? You keep asking if I'm okay and now I'm freaking."

"Just be careful, sweetheart," she said. "You've not yet been trained and I was hoping to take a fuller look at you when you arrived, but this dratted weather . . . I'm stuck in Seattle for at least another day or so. Perhaps, though, it would be a good idea if you try to avoid using your Talents until I can check you out more thoroughly."

More thoroughly than what? Than the full body scan she did on me before she left Texas? What was she worried about?

"Aunt—" I began.

"Right then," Isabel cut in. "I need to run, sweetheart. The battery's beeping at me. Get some rest and I'll call you later when we get back to our hotel."

Rattled, I blurted out, "Am I going to be okay?"

"Oh, honey. Sorry for worrying you. I'm sure you will be," she said. "I'll see you soon. And if you get the chance to go the enclave before your father and I can get out of Seattle, go on. We'll meet you up there."

I closed my eyes and let out a deep sigh. "I'll do what I can, Aunt. It's not like I'm going to try to do anything beyond my normal capabilities anytime soon. I'm in the city. That would be a bit obvious, don't you think?" I hoped the cabbie didn't catch that.

"Well, yes," Isabel said. "Very well, then. Talk to your brother. Gigi's filled him in, so I'm sure as soon as she can, she'll send a pilot to you."

That totally didn't make sense. I looked over at Tucker, who shook his head. I was now completely lost in this conversation. As far as I knew—and from Tucker's expression, it seemed I was right—Gigi hadn't communicated with Tucker any more than she had communicated with me. And what was all this last minute worrying? Isabel had left Texas with a cheery outlook and glad I was so healthy. What the hell had happened in the last couple of days that I didn't know about? The other shoe dropped as I processed the last part of what Isabel had said.

"Send a pilot? We have a pilot. Liz is here in Burnaby. Why can't we—"

"Oh, I know, honey, but Gigi wants to send her personal plane for you. You know, as a gesture."

I sagged back against the seat and rolled my eyes.

Tucker whispered at me, "Say yes."

"Fine, Aunt," I said, tired of trying to figure all of this out. "Please give me a call when you all get to your hotel or whatever. I'll be on my cell or you can ring the condo." At which time, I thought, I was going to grill the shit out of both my aunt and my father. Something was most definitely up. Something that was ringing way weird.

A couple of short beeps interrupted and Isabel's voice faded in. ". . . soon, dear. Soon as we can."

The connection went dead. I closed my eyes and counted to ten before I said anything. "What was that about?" I asked Tucker. "I'm taking it that Gigi never contacted you."

"Not a peep," he said. "I think Dad and Isabel are smoking the crack."

A snort from the cabbie made me smile. As we turned onto another street, the driver stomped on his brakes and swerved hard as a small dog ran out into the road. I fell against Niko, who slid into the now empty seat next to him.

Daffyd had disappeared.

CHAPTER NINE

"WHAT THE—" Niko twisted in the seat and looked wildly around. "Where—"

"Driver, please pull over," Tucker said. The man looked at him, shrugged and did as he was asked.

"Did you see—" "Where did he go?" The three of us spoke over each other.

"Gentlemen, lady," the driver began. "What is the matter? Is someone ill?"

"Did you see?" I demanded.

The man twisted in his seat and stared at me, his expression clearly reflecting the fact that he thought me insane. "See what, miss? We did not hit the dog."

"No, the man, the other man."

"I'm sorry, miss. Sir?" He looked over at Tucker, who looked at the driver and then the backseat, then back at the driver. Tucker's eyes narrowed.

"You never saw him, did you?" Tucker asked the driver. "The third man in the car, the blond."

The driver now looked at each of us as if we'd gone way over the bend and were entering utter insanity. "There was no other man," he said. "Just you, the gentleman there"—he motioned toward Niko—"and the lady."

"How—" I shook my head, hoping to make this all make sense. "You didn't see the man sitting behind you? Tall, long blond hair, dressed in black? Got in with us at the airport."

The driver scowled at me. "No one was there. I did not know why this gentleman sat in the middle when there was space, but I do not question my fares."

"Okay, this is getting weirder by the second," I said. "Let's get out of here." I opened the car door and scooted out.

Tucker pulled out several bills after glancing at the meter, which read $26.00. "This should more than cover the fare," he said to the driver. "I apologize for any inconvenience we might have—"

"Fine, fine," the driver waved one hand at us as he tucked the bills into his pocket. "But . . ."

"We are leaving," Niko said and joined Tucker and me on the sidewalk.

The driver sped away, nearly running a red light half a block away.

"So now what?" I said, my hands on my hips. "Part of me wants to say that did not happen, but I'm not hallucinating . . . am I? Daffyd was here with us, right. On the plane, in the cab?"

Tucker turned slowly, scanning the area around us. We were already downtown, not too far from where we'd been going in the first place. Most of the buildings were commercial—combined office space and some restaurants, all of which served the daytime population. Nothing was open. We were at least eight or nine blocks from the major hotels.

"No sign of him," Tucker said finally. "No scent, no sound. It's as if . . ."

"As if he were never there," Niko finished. "But he was. I would swear on it. I would swear on my oath to Adam." I looked at Niko with a start. That was a blood oath he made to Adam and unbreakable.

"Can fey vanish like that, sis?" Tucker asked me. "I know so little about them."

I thought back to my short time among the Sidhe, the faery folk in Wales, my mother's kin. "I saw them walk through mirrors, reflective glass, a pool of water—to go from Underhill to Above, but never like that, never just poof, like—"

I started in shock as a thought occurred to me. Could Daffyd be a shade? I'd seen shades, or ghosts, plenty of times when I was working as an Escort. Once through the veil to the other side, most remained there, content in their choice. Occasionally, some would still be tied to this world, and their shades, reflections of their former selves, could appear on this side—but they'd never felt solid. I'd touched Daffyd, hadn't I? Besides, Tucker and Niko had seen him. So had Liz. Niko had even given the man clothing. He couldn't have been a ghost, not if the others had all seen and interacted with him. I was the one with the connection to the dead. I could perhaps understand with Niko, since he was dead himself, but Tucker? Nah. He'd never been sensitive to those who'd crossed over.

No, no, he wasn't—isn't, I insisted to myself. I *know* the dead. I know the feel of the dead, the sense, the pattern of energy.

"May I?" I asked as I reached toward Niko, my hand palm up, stopping it inches from his chest. Niko watched me in grave silence. I didn't even need to close my eyes to concentrate anymore as I'd had to before the Change. This close, with intent, I felt his essence, his soul, for the lack of a better word. The sense of the walking death magick that animated him and Adam and other vampires. Something not of human make, though they'd both been human before death. Niko's energy vibrated against my palm, green and cool and vibrant with infused life-from-death. "It's different," I said, amazed. "Different from Adam. Are you all this way, then?"

Niko studied me, pausing before speaking. "All different? I do not know," he said. "Never has anyone done such a thing to me."

"Did you feel it?" I wondered aloud. "Feel me sensing you?"

"Indeed," he said. "As if you touched inside me and plucked the strings of my soul."

"Poetic."

He nodded gravely. "It was . . . unusual . . . but not disturbing." He tilted his head. "Did you sense Adam this way?"

I shook my head. "Not exactly." I'd not really realized I could. I'd reached out to sense him, yes, but that was before. When he'd been in a coma and I'd still been unChanged. "It was different before. More a sense of energy, more diffuse." Adam had always felt grounded in deep rich colors and a sense of Other that he'd once kept so well hidden from me.

"Daffyd did not feel like this," I said firmly. "He was as alive as you or I, Tucker. Thing is . . ." I reached toward Niko again, refreshing my sense of his being. "There's something there," I said. "Some underlying . . . are you fey, Niko?" I asked in wonder as the sense of green energy merged with my own, striking a vibrant chord that reminded me of—

Niko's eyes widened and he stumbled back a step, visibly disturbed. "How . . . no, I was human," he said. "You know my past. Do . . . do not ask about them." I stared at him, all his confidence stripped away, his eyes wide in terror.

"The music," I exclaimed. "The music disappeared when Daffyd did. You, just now, Niko, you felt like . . . *of* the music. You feel—there's a vibration, almost a melody in your energy. Before, when you lived, were you fey?"

"What frightens you, *cariad*?" Tucker murmured as he wrapped his arms around Niko, who was visibly trembling. "Please, tell me."

"I don't want to remember," he whispered. "Do not make me—"

Oh bloody hell, what the . . . what on earth scared a man . . . a vampire whose very existence was the stuff children read about in delicious horror?

"They came when I was a child," Niko said, words broken with emotion, his hands clutching at Tucker's shirt, voice nearly muffled as he buried his face in my brother's shoulder. "I saw them."

My brother's hand cupped the back of Niko's head. "Hush, *cariad*, you're safe here." Tucker looked around and, noticing a bench, motioned for us to move there. "Come, let's sit," he said to Niko. The three of us sat, Niko in the center, still shaking.

"Once . . . it was before I was a nobleman's pet. I was a young child kept with other boys, with other orphans. One of my mates was taken one moonless night. He disappeared from his pallet, as if he'd never existed—in the dead of night, they came and took him. One of them saw me watching. He said nothing, but I'll never forget his eyes shining in the dark. In the morning, when they came to wake us, I saw what they'd done. In place of my mate, they'd left a twisted dead thing, a changeling, dark of countenance and sickly. It lived only a few hours. I saw it and noticed, but no one else did. The nurse, the adults, all thought it was the same boy, only suddenly taken ill. Orphans get sick, they die. They never knew. And I could do nothing. I couldn't help him, my friend."

Niko buried his face in his hands. "I'd forgotten," he said, his voice muffled. "I buried this memory. Forced it away. You made me remember—when you touched me . . ." He looked up at me, his voice accusing. "I never even discussed this with Adam . . . and he knows *everything* else about me, from the pleasures to the tortures I endured as the plaything of a rich lord of Elizabeth's court. I had to forget. I shut it away and closed that lock long ago. It was as if it had never existed." Niko's eyes looked haunted as he remembered his pain.

"When Adam first came, when I woke up after he rescued me, I . . . I thought he was one of them. One of the shining ones come to take me below, Underhill. I was so frightened. But then he showed me, explained how I'd been dying and he'd saved me by turning me. I wept for days with relief. I only ever told him that it was a frightening dream I'd had. He never knew it was truth. He told me that I'd be safe from Faery, as long as I was his."

"Shhh, *cariad*," whispered Tucker, bending over Niko, enfolding him in an embrace. "You are safe with me."

I stood and paced several steps away from the pair, shaking with the revelation that Niko, Adam's so-strong second-in-command, a vampire, could be brought to this—shivering like a frightened child, nearly choking trying to explain his fear to us. He'd regressed into a child's memory—something he'd long suppressed. Damn my mother's kin for this. They'd not only scarred me, but so many others. Sure, the Seelie court never admitted to stealing human children and leaving changelings in their places. That was the purview of the Unseelie—so they said. When I'd left—been rescued—I never looked back. Until now. Until my cousin, Daffyd ap Geraint—son to the Sidhe relative who told my mother I'd have been better off left out in the world above to die of exposure—had entered my life.

Had Daffyd tricked me? Could all Sidhe disappear like that? Teleport, disapparate—whatever the hell you wanted to call it. I'd never seen evidence of it, but I spent so much of my time hiding away from everyone Underhill that, for all I knew, they were shapeshifters, too. I knew there were lesser fey folk who had non-human shapes, but although they'd shared space at court, they weren't Sidhe, just other fey, other denizens of Faery. Some of them could flit about at will, but those were the wee folk, so far from human they never ventured Above anymore.

I stared across the quiet street at the silent concrete and glass retail-cum-office building. No one else was around but us at this time of night. Downtown Vancouver pretty much rolled up the sidewalks as soon as the offices that fed it closed for the evening. Stores and cafés both followed the standard office hour schedules, with the exception of the Tim Hortons restaurants spotting the landscape. We were still a few blocks from the more tourist-type areas, with late-opening restaurants and more people.

Niko's voice came from behind me. He'd stepped close, all signs of his emotional outburst now gone. "First he was there, then he wasn't. No sound, only displaced air and the lack of pressure on the side of my arm where he'd been seated." He came up beside me. "I apologize for—"

"No, don't worry about it," I said. "I know what they're like."

He nodded. "Tucker doesn't."

"No," I agreed. Tucker stood next to Niko, still hovering, concerned, but keeping silent.

"Daffyd being around us never set you off?"

"No," Niko replied. "He kept to himself during the flight. Then we were only in the taxi for a short time. He shielded well."

The three of us studied the street, staring at the storefront across from us as if it held answers. The only answer it could provide, though, was that Montblanc pens were on sale through Friday.

"Seriously, what the fuck?" I finally said. "What in all the thousand levels of all the hells is going on here?"

Both men regarded me in silence.

"I only wish I knew, sis," Tucker finally said. "I think we should ditch our dinner plans and go directly to the condo. We can always call for pizza or something. I'm sure there's got to be some liquor stocked there. Wouldn't be a Kelly house otherwise."

"No doubt," I said and inclined my head toward the right.

I had no fucking clue what was happening, where Daffyd vanished to or where he could possibly be now. But standing around with our heads up our collective behinds would accomplish absolutely nada. Time to regroup.

Tucker hailed another cab. This one was no bigger than the last, but there were only three of us to fit into it this time.

CHAPTER TEN

THE RIDE TO the condo was fairly short and very silent. The building was located in a cul-de-sac off Cordova, its approach via a private drive. No gate was needed, as the latest security devices were employed to keep the unwanted out. Sometimes I'd felt that the unwanted person was me. Luckily, the last couple of times I'd come here to visit, I hadn't had to deal with anyone other than a brother or two.

The driver dropped us off at the turnoff for the private drive.

The condo was a twelve-story glass and steel tower on the water. Its glass shone dark, a reflective coating hiding the interior from passersby.

We approached the building's entry and Tucker dug into a pocket and pulled out a plastic card key. He waved it in front of the sensor, then, more slowly, placed his open palm on the reader for a few seconds. A red light turned to green, then to yellow and remained flashing. Tucker scowled and tried the card swipe and palm placement again. Same result.

"I don't know why . . . Keira, you try." He handed me the card. I wiped it on my jeans, then repeated Tucker's actions. The moment my palm touched the sensor pad, a green light flashed, a click sounded and one of the double doors swung open in silent welcome.

"Guess you've got the touch, sis," Tucker said.

"Nice." Niko nodded at the door with an approving look. "Biometrics?"

"More like bio-magick," I said as I stepped through the door. On passing the threshold, I felt the whisper touch of energy shimmy through me as if I'd stepped through an invisible barrier—which I had, but the last time I'd done this, I hadn't felt a thing. The wards weren't meant to be felt. I hesitated a moment, then kept going. Someone must have boosted the energy recently or something. Either that or I was more sensitive now.

"Damnation," Niko exclaimed as he followed directly behind me. "Magick, indeed," he said, dropping his voice to a whisper as he shivered. Tucker followed him and the smoked-glass front door shut behind him.

Niko stopped walking and was looking around the place. There wasn't much to see, but what there was, was pretty impressive. The building's lobby was large, simply decorated in that understated yet extremely expensive way that fairly screamed loads of money. Simple leather-topped benches sat on either side of a bubbling stream, which was fed by a waterfall pouring from the rock wall. Tasteful plants lined the stream and the small pool.

A curved dark marble reception desk sat to our right, empty of staff, its brownish gold accents subtly reflecting the subdued recessed lighting. No clutter, nothing showy, only simple clean lines and emptiness as if the entire lobby was nothing more than a film set, a museum diorama waiting for its mannequins.

"Your family warded a private building?" Niko asked. "How's that work exactly? I would have supposed the building employed security guards and the usual keycard access or digital code. How do the other tenants get in?"

"We own the place," I said. "It's definitely warded nine ways to the next millennium and keyed only to family."

Niko stopped dead in his tracks and whirled around to stare at Tucker and me. "I thought you owned a condo," he said. "That's what you both kept calling it: condo, as in singular."

"We do." Tucker grinned. "One condo—and all the others, too. Mostly, when we refer to the condo specifically, we're talking about the penthouse. That's reserved for immediate family to use whenever—me, Keira, our brothers, Dad. The rest of the condos in the building are sometimes occupied by family or guests. I don't keep track since I'm no longer in town."

I strode over to the elevator and pushed the access button. "No one ever staffs the desk," I said, "because there doesn't need to be anyone there. No one outside of Kellys or our guests ever get issued keycards or access codes." I gestured with my hand. "As for preventing break-ins or vandalism? No need for security guards when the best in the business set those wards."

"Fairly strong wards—impressive," Niko said. "I haven't felt a barrier like that in a long time."

"You felt it?" Tucker asked. "That's odd."

"Odd how?" I scowled at him. "I felt it, too. I thought someone had upped the mojo or maybe I'm more sensitive now."

"I'd buy you being more sensitive," Tucker said. "But Niko? I don't think so." He frowned and looked back at the entrance. Two tinted glass doors, nothing special and certainly no visible sign of the magick that warded them. "I didn't feel a thing, as per usual."

The elevator doors swooshed open and we piled inside. I stabbed the top button. "Huh," I said. "Wonder what it means?" The doors closed silently and we began our ascent to the penthouse.

I PALMED the sensor at the entrance to the penthouse, a few steps from the elevator. The door opened to a scene right out of some home decorating show on HGTV Canada.

"What the bloody blazes are *you* doing here?" I demanded as Tucker, Niko and I walked into the wide entryway.

My brother Rhys stood on a small stepladder, hanging a black drape in front of one of the floor-to-ceiling windows that made up the outside wall of the main living area. He'd obviously been at this a while, as the rest of the windows were already draped. Liz, seemingly perfectly at home, stood next to him, another drape over her arm and holding up a hook in her right hand.

"Making the place lightproof," Rhys said, mumbling around a couple more hooks he held in his mouth. "Just a sec." He took the hook from Liz's hand, hung another section and then quickly finished the last panel. Hopping down to the floor, he gestured toward his handiwork. "Ta da! What do you think?"

I shook my head and went to the couch to sit down. This was more than I could handle in one day. "I wasn't talking to you, Rhys," I said. "Though, I wasn't expecting you here, either, but obviously, you being here is a heck of a lot more expected than you." I pointed to Liz, who plopped down on a nearby leather chair. "Didn't you go home?"

"I was on my way here to drop off the luggage and got a call from this one." She nodded towards Rhys. "He asked if we'd landed yet."

Rhys shrugged. "I needed help and figured if you all were heading this way, I'd wait until you showed up."

Made sense, I thought.

"I told him you were going to dinner, so I'd stay and help." Liz leaned back in the chair and stretched out her legs. "So where'd you go eat?" She looked us over and did a double take. "Hey, come to think on it, where's Daffyd?"

"Yeah, well . . . that's a bit of a story." I sat down on one of the low modern couches artfully arranged in a conversation pit. Niko sat down across from me, on another couch that was catty-corner to Liz's chair. Rhys kept fiddling with the curtains, like some sort of demented Welsh Martha Stewart.

"Daffyd kind of vanished," I said and explained what had happened, including the music I'd heard. I left out Niko's story. That was for him to share.

Liz blinked a few times then reached over to the small end table next to her, where an open bottle of Gastown Amber Ale sat on a stone coaster. She picked it up, took a long swig and regarded the three of us. "That's one hell of a story," she finally said. "What now?"

"If we weren't in the middle of Vancouver, I'd suggest my brothers shift into wolves and try to find him." If I weren't so damned new at it, I suppose I could shift myself.

"You mean to get his scent and track him?" Rhys asked as he gathered another curtain and tied it back. The view from these windows was beyond spectacular. The building overlooked the water and in the short distance, we could see the lights on the mountains. "Hold that, will you?" Rhys handed Tucker another curtain tie. Tucker complied, more patient than I would have been. "That's impossible, you know," Rhys continued.

"What do you mean?" I asked.

"They don't have scent."

"No scent, that's—" I stopped as my sense memory

kicked in. Niko: check; Tucker: always. Adam: check. Rhys: family. Liz: same. Daffyd . . . I cast my thoughts back to when we'd met, just a few days ago when I'd been down in the cave where he'd lived for the past thirty years. I remembered shine, light and music, but no scent particular to the man himself. Even Gary Pursell had one. Moving forward to earlier today, in the smaller space of the plane, the closer quarters of the cab. Our driver had smelled of earth, a hobbyist gardener most likely, a man who liked to be close to growing things. I even recalled the light citrus of his body wash, the slight bitterness of a long work day overlying it, a whiff of the oil/metal/cloth from the taxicab on his skin. But from Daffyd? Nothing, not a bloody damned thing. How could I have not noticed?

"That's fucking impossible," I said. "He is a living being. We all have a scent."

"He's Sidhe, Keira," Rhys said and fluffed the final drape, done with his task. "They are more not-human than we are. What you think of as scent isn't quite the same."

"Well, yes," Tucker said as he joined Niko on the couch. "That much is obvious, but I've never heard of them not having scent, nor the ability to disappear—other than—" He looked at me. "Hey, could he have cast a strong glamour and slipped out of the cab when we stopped?"

"No," Niko said. "You forget, I was sitting pressed against him. When the cab swerved, he was gone and I slid into the seat. He was definitely gone before we opened any of the doors."

"Do you think Daffyd came to Vancouver with you simply to lose himself in a city?" Liz asked. "Sidhe live from absorbing energy. Maybe he wanted to come somewhere there were plenty of humans and energy—"

"Well, hell," I said, "if he wanted a city, all he had to

do was travel southeast of the Wild Moon and lose himself in either Austin or San Antonio. Why on earth travel thousands of miles with us? He's either up to something nefarious or, for all we know, is simply wandering the streets of Vancouver. He seemed genuine enough when he asked to come, but damn it, he's Sidhe—"

"Seelie," Rhys interrupted.

"Seelie or no," I said, "as far as I'm concerned, they're no more to be trusted than the Unseelie Sidhe. The only difference between the two is that the Unseelie are a hell of a lot more honest and open about screwing you over—or for that matter, just screwing you."

Rhys and Tucker both laughed, knowing I was right.

"I thought he was different, but hell, I've known him all of a few days," I said. "Who knows if this isn't some twisted, long-term plot of my mother's tribe, or, hell, maybe even Gigi."

"Yeah, right," Tucker snorted and relaxed back into the soft leather cushion. "Our Clan chief is out there plotting with your mother's people. Don't you think she had enough of that when they negotiated your release to us?"

"Well, when you put it that way." I smiled. Tucker was right. None of us got along very well. Like the British Isles in the old days, we were many groups with many kings, but no single leader, no one ruler to unite us. I wasn't all that sure any of us wanted to *be* united. My own Clan, and I assumed that of the Sidhe, the vampires, the wers and all the others were probably perfectly happy as is. No one was looking for a modern-day Pendragon to wake and lead them.

I let myself relax into the softness of the chair. Rhys sat in a large armchair to my left, his long legs straight out and crossed at the ankles, mirroring Liz. Like his twin, Ianto,

Rhys was tall, but not as tall as Tucker, lean and lanky with that rawboned look peculiar to many Celts. He and his twin both wore their dark hair cropped short, unlike Tucker's long mane. In the spirit of Kelly casual, Rhys wore jeans and a T-shirt, the family uniform for those of us of the same generation—that is, my father's children. Even boring old Ciprian had long ago given up the more formal male attire and spent most of his life in jeans or sweats. Rhys looked as at home here in the penthouse as he did running around the Hill Country or in the forests of British Columbia.

The building had originally been built by Japanese investors who'd had to sell at a great loss when the Nikkei had bottomed out some years ago. My family picked up the entire building for pennies on the loonie. Ciprian, who was my eldest brother and our financial genius, heard about the sale and before Gigi could even say go, he'd snapped up the place, presenting her with a fait accompli and an amazing pied-a-terre in the middle of Vancouver's soon-to-be vibrant downtown area. Gigi had fallen in love with the building and immediately set her team to updating the structure, decorating the interior and setting the wards. This was one of several residences owned by our family, all due to Ciprian's rapacious perusal of industry publications. I was pretty sure that every time he bought property, he had an orgasm. To be fair, accounting and finance ran in his being and he was damned good at it. Over the centuries, he'd grown the family trust into a behemoth that kept gaining value. I knew that not a one of us—except Ciprian himself and maybe Gigi—had any idea of the full extent of the Kelly holdings. I didn't want to know, really, but I had a sneaking suspicion that lessons would be forthcoming.

Most of the condos in this building would sell for at least

two to four million in the current market, high luxury in the city of many luxurious residences bought with Singapore-based money. But the penthouse—oh, this was the jewel indeed. If it weren't for the fact that I'd made my Texas bed and would prefer to lie in it, the idea of moving to Canada would have been a whole lot less angst-ridden with this gem of an apartment to live in. The penthouse consisted of five en suite bedrooms, a half bath for guests and an open-plan living and dining area with a lovely rooftop garden. If I had to come live near family, I was calling dibs on this place. With a few modifications, Adam could live here, too. We'd have to keep up the blackout curtains permanently or modify the tinted glass somehow.

I looked over at Rhys. "Thanks for the efforts, bro," I said to Rhys. "All that glass would be pretty unhealthy for the undead among us."

In the morning, the place would be filled with sunlight. I recognized the type of drapes Rhys had hung on all the windows. Complete blackout, expensive and damn well worth it. With them drawn, Niko could have the freedom of the penthouse and not be cooped up in one of the baths . . . come to think of it, most of the bathrooms had windows, too, only not floor to ceiling. Good thing Rhys thought ahead.

Come to think on it . . . how the hell had he known we'd have a vampire in tow?

CHAPTER ELEVEN

"JUST HAPPENED TO HAVE those drapes on hand, Rhys? Or did you have to make a special trip? I can't imagine that you could get custom draperies in a couple of hours, even for a Kelly." None of the walls of windows in the penthouse were standard sizes. "How'd you know you needed them, anyway? I didn't call you and you're not prescient."

Rhys shrugged. "You never know what you're going to find on hand around here," he responded. "Sometimes it's caviar, sometimes it's blackout drapes." He looked at the three of us. "Dad called me. Told me you were coming and to get stuff ready."

"Oh, so you're the brother Isabel meant."

"Huh, what?"

"Isabel. When I talked to her and Dad on the phone. She said Gigi filled in my brother. I thought she was talking about Tucker."

"Oh, gotcha, yeah. Gigi said to get my ass to Vancouver and take care of things. Frankly, I was on the verge of some serious cabin fever," Rhys said. He ran a hand through his hair and sprawled out even more. "Gigi had us spit-polishing the place for the past several weeks. I was glad to get a break."

"So instead you come here and play Suzy Homemaker?" I asked. "What's Gigi doing anyway, getting ready for all those visitors?"

Rhys looked at me in surprise. "Visitors? Surely you jest, sister mine," he said. "Since when does Gigi ever put on the dog for mere visitors? Besides, I don't know anything about visitors."

"I thought . . ." I frowned, trying to remember what the customs agent had said. "Liz, refresh my memory, didn't Ben say something about Kellys in a blue plane arriving?"

"Oh yeah," she said. "Does sound like out-of-town cousins. There've been a few of them in and out over the past few days, but you know, Rhys meant the sprucing-up routine was for you. Our fearless leader had the entire in-residence gang running around like we were expecting royalty—oh—wait." She ducked her head and smiled. "I guess we kind of were."

I rolled my eyes and waved a hand in a bad imitation of Queen Elizabeth II. "Shall I practice the royal salute?"

Tucker burst out laughing. "I'm thinking your salute might be somewhat different, Keira." He began to raise a couple of fingers and Niko grabbed his hand.

"You people are children," he scolded. "Your leader goes to special pains to welcome you as her heir and you joke?"

"Niko, please," I said. "It's so ridiculous. I'm sorry, but I don't want any pomp and circumstance. I'd rather do this quietly." I'd rather not do this at all.

He nodded. "Perhaps you are correct," he said. "And I do not know if this is customary. I presume it is not, from your responses?"

Rhys and Tucker looked at each other. "I don't have any idea," Rhys said. "It's been too long. None of us were alive when Gigi took the throne, much less when she Changed."

Liz argued, "The customs might be lost in the mists of time, or whatever, but c'mon, it only makes sense. It's not like the Kelly heir is the firstborn or even pulls a sword out of a stone, eh? There's probably some sort of formal recognition."

"Yeah, like the baby princess in 'Sleeping Beauty,'" I said in a drawl. "We hold a big hoopla and someone will curse the honoree—me. That's all I need." I sat up straight. "Hell and damnation, do you think Gideon got cursed?" Could that have been what happened?

Tucker looked thoughtful. "I wouldn't be surprised. If he's still dabbling in the dark arts and pissed someone off . . ."

"And that someone . . . or someones . . . might have placed a curse on him," I finished for him.

"Well, yes."

"Now that's a thought not too far from probable reality," Rhys said. "I didn't see him, but . . ."

"A death curse?" Niko asked. "Is that possible with your people?"

"If you really, really mean it," I said. "Mostly, our people don't die until they're ready. Then, someone like me, an Escort, helps them cross—voluntarily. With the help of drugs and some spells, they leave behind their bodies and their spirits move on. A death curse is kind of like the same thing, but involuntary. It takes a great deal of power, an immense amount of evil intent and, frankly, some weakness on the part of the cursed. Gideon's not weak, though." Far from it, I thought, remembering. He'd always been stronger than me, power-wise. I'd been able to do the small homely things, work as an Escort, but that was it. Both of us were pre-Changed and our abilities were limited, but he'd been able to work stronger magicks than I had.

"He's arrogant," Tucker said. "Arrogance is its own kind of weakness."

Niko and Rhys agreed to Tucker's assessment with nods.

"I've not met the man," Niko said. "But I've found that to be true."

I nearly burst out laughing. When I'd first met him, a few short months ago, last October, Niko had been one of the most arrogant men I'd ever met. Granted, he'd mellowed, most especially after taking up with Tucker.

"I imagine we'll find out about Gideon when we get to the enclave," I said. "As for Daffyd, I'd feel better about it if we went back out . . . now . . . and looked for him. He was kind of under my care. I'd rather not give up on him without a search."

"I guess we could go out and take a look-see," Tucker said. "Besides, we still need to grab some food."

"Anyone else we know in town?" Tucker responded. "We could put out an alert."

"That's a good thought, Tucker," I said. Multiple Kellys equaled many different sets of eyes, ears, senses on the search.

Rhys shook his head. "I'm pretty much it, except for you all. Gigi called everyone local back to the enclave."

"Where do we start looking?" Liz asked. "Back where he vanished?"

"You were close to Gastown when he disappeared," Rhys said. "Couple of places doing the late-late dinner there these days so that would solve finding food. We could wander in that direction, keep an eye out, talk to some of the street folk. A Sidhe's bound to be pretty conspicuous."

"Except maybe this one," I said as I stood. "He's damned good at the glamour."

Rhys gave me a serious look. "Keira, do you have any other ideas as to what happened? If Daffyd left the car voluntarily?"

"Well, if he didn't, that puts a whole other spin on things." Could it have been some sort of summoning spell? As far as I knew, none of my own people could do anything of that caliber, but what I knew about Sidhe powers could fit onto the head of a pin and still have room for some dancing angels. "Is that possible, Rhys? Do you know?"

"Not really," he said. "Other than one or two visits by the courts years ago, I've not had any exposure to the Sidhe."

Niko had seen Sidhe at least once as a small child. Rhys had been around when the Courts came calling a couple of times. Tucker and Liz were even more clueless. I'd lived among them, was part Sidhe, but I knew nothing myself. Not exactly an expert search team for a missing fey. "Okay, I say we get out there, get food and, on the way, do some looking. Maybe we'll get lucky."

I crossed mental fingers at that final hope. Luck was kind of the last thing that had visited me lately . . . although I supposed some would call it that. Becoming the heir wasn't my idea of winning the lottery; in fact, it was the diametric opposite. I would have happily spent the balance of my many, many years as a shapeshifter, a healer, a weather witch . . . whatever. No responsibilities beyond that of my own household and life. A boring, but satisfying life. I'd found someone I could love, be happy with. Someone not human and who loved me back. That would have been more than enough for now.

Niko nodded at me, a look of approval on his face. "We have several hours until sunrise. We should all go search."

Liz stretched. "Rhys, what cars are below? Anything that'd fit the five of us?"

"Don't know. We'll have to go check."

"We should have something," I said. "At least we did last time I was here—which reminds me. Hey, Rhys, you know anything about a change in the wards? Tucker couldn't get the door to open and when we walked in, both Niko and I felt the barrier. That's never happened to me before."

Rhys ran a hand through his hair, brow furrowing as he thought. "Wow, that is weird," he said. "I know Gigi sent someone down some time ago. Damn, I can't remember exactly when, maybe six, eight months or so? I think she said something about doing some maintenance, so I guess it could have been that. I didn't notice anything, though. Liz?"

She shook her head. "Nope, not a thing," she said. "Door opened fine for me."

"Me, too," Rhys said. "Tucker, maybe you've got bad juju from hanging around the vampires." Rhys ducked as Tucker pitched a small throw pillow at him.

"If he's tainted, so'm I." I picked up the pillow, which had landed at my feet, and set it on the couch. "We've been around the same vampires the exact same length of time."

"I was kidding," Rhys laughed. "You're both Kellys; just because you hang out with other species, even supernatural ones, that's not exactly going to rub off."

"Well, it kind of can," Liz said.

The three of us looked at her with identical questioning expressions. "What do you mean, Liz?" Tucker asked. "I'm not following."

"There's a way to set a ward to sense these things."

"C'mon, Liz," Rhys protested. "That's an old wives' tale. You can't pick up auras or whatever from proximity."

Liz crossed her arms and scowled. "You can and I was an old wife for years, Rhys ap Huw Kelly. I may look like a sweet young thing, but you and I both know that I'm older than you are and have been around a hell of a lot more blocks in my time. I studied ward casting with Aunt Cat Lee when I spent time in Korea."

"How the hell does that work?" I asked, fascinated by this information. Had I picked up Adam's aura? Scent? What?

"That part, I'm not sure of," Liz said. "But I do know that couples—or families—who have been together a long time tend to pick up characteristics of the others. You know, like how humans who've been married a long time tend to start resembling each other?"

"Yeah." I answered, but both my brothers and Niko seemed to agree, too.

"We've only been together a few months," Tucker said. "Less than a year, in fact. Surely it can't be that quick—especially with our life spans."

"I'm not so sure it has anything to do with time, but with intensity," Liz explained. She gave us each a calculating look. I tried to see the three of us through her eyes. Niko and Tucker were practically joined at the hip. If I concentrated on the two of them, I could almost see the harmonies weaving them together. As for me, I resonated with the absence of my own vampire and was newly Changed, power throbbing just under the threshold of awareness, waiting to be used. Threaded among what twigged as "Kelly" was another band of energy, tinged dark purple, redolent of spice—dry and pungent—rich with the musky night.

"Damn, Liz," I said. "I can see what you mean. It's there, just under—" I reached toward Niko and Tucker, as if trying to touch the energy bands around them, so similar to my own uncompleted one. "Wow."

"Wow, indeed," Rhys said, his voice no longer playful. "When you concentrated, I sort of saw it, too. The energy. You're one hella powerful Changeling, Keira."

I let the concentration go, the energy disappearing back into thin air. Despite that, I still sensed it *there*, waiting. "Good genes?" I quipped, trying to make light of it.

How exactly did I feel about this raw power, now almost at my disposal? I knew I'd consciously been suppressing it since the Change, only letting loose when I'd shifted and some just now. I had a ginormous amount of potential sitting there, a powder keg waiting for the right spark, the right cue. Before I let any of this loose, I really wanted a way to leash it.

"So I guess Tucker's aura or whatever had a tad of Niko, and affected the sensor seeing him as Kelly?" I asked.

"Perhaps," Liz said. "It's quite possible. Especially"—she motioned toward Rhys—"if, like he said, the wards have recently been updated. If you want, I could try to sort the wards, see what I can find out. I can't guarantee anything. It's been too long since my last warding. I was never that good at it."

"No worries," Tucker said. "Good to know I'm not defective."

Niko scowled at him. "Never."

Tucker caressed Niko's cheek. "Happy you think so, *cariad*."

Rhys snorted. "No wonder your auras merged. Keira, shall we be off to look for your missing Sidhe? There're plenty of cars below. We won't fit in Liz's smart car, but I've got a Range Rover and there are the family vehicles . . ."

"We could walk." I stood. "It's not far."

Tucker looked at me quizzically. I picked up my backpack. "I want to walk."

"Seriously? Walk, you?"

I gave in to the temptation to smack my brother. "Yeah, seriously. It's not like I'm unfamiliar with the concept."

"You never seemed all that interested in being outdoors—"

"In Texas," I cut him off. "In the heat and the humidity and sweating, so not my thing. This is totally different." It was.

Oddly for me, my body ached with the need to walk, to stretch my muscles, be outside. Could it be from my brief foray into wolf world? To be completely honest, Tucker was right, I'd never been fond of the out-of-doors. My idea of a good time usually came accompanied by five stars . . . service, hotels, restaurants . . . or no stars, but involving snacks, a decent movie, a comfy couch and good company. Not so much into the woods and chigger bites thing. Except when I'd shifted; then I'd found nature glorious.

But even before I discovered the joys of the outdoors on four legs, I loved walking around Vancouver on two. It's a beautiful, clean city with little or none of the dirt and grime so common to many large U.S. cities. For that matter, to London, my other favorite haunt. "I wouldn't mind being around someone other than us," I admitted. "Even for a short while. Besides, easier to look around and talk to people if we're not in a car."

I'd been sequestered in small towns or among Clan for so long, it would be great to walk through anonymous crowds, through late-night tourists taking photos of Gassy Jack, of the steam clock, stopping to peer at store windows, being totally and utterly ignorant of those of us that walk among them: a couple of wolves, a hound, a bloodsucking fiend and me. Any and each of us enough to strike the worst of fears inside a human's soul. On the surface, though, only three men and two women, who looked no more harmless than a double date with benefits.

CHAPTER TWELVE

"THEY WATCH, YOU KNOW." The old man leaned closer, his voice dropping to a conspiratorial whisper. "I'd be careful, m'lady, if I was you." Like many of the others gathering, he was dressed in his homeless finest: an almost-new tweedy overcoat of some lightweight wool blend swung over his too-long rolled-up black cotton trousers. Natty yellow suspenders, worn but clean, held up the trousers and accented his brown cowboy-style shirt. Around his neck, he'd tied a scarlet cloth in some parody of an ascot. A toque sat atop his grizzled close-cut curls, the hat red as a Delicious. Scuffed shoes, once the pride of someone's three-piece ensemble, completed the man's attire. He'd obviously chosen his clothing with care, careful to tuck in what needed tucking and making sure that things more-or-less matched.

"They?" I asked in more than a little amusement. Our search for my missing cousin had landed us in the middle of a pre-dawn street people salute and memorial for a recently expired colleague. Around us, a few dozen of the homeless walked toward a small park known as Victory Square. From what I'd overheard, one of their own, an elderly man named Old Sam had died a couple of days ago. This was their way of paying their respects.

The old man nodded and placed a finger on the side of his nose. "They are here. Only them that is around us, they don't know so much. They look just like us."

Confused by his "thems" and "theys," I looked around me and saw nothing more unusual than a ragtag gathering of the area's homeless, each holding a candle stuck into some sort of homemade holder—a scene familiar to those who attend vigils or have seen them on TV. The atmosphere was familiar, too: respect was the same whether offered for those cut down in the prime of a memorable life or for ones like this, a man whose real name, unknown, would never be carved into a memorial stone. His vigil would never make the news; he'd never be remembered by any history outside of the stories told by these survivors.

Was my new toque-wearing friend a bit around the bend? Probably and, more than likely, somewhat moonstruck—if the "moon" was the same kind that could be combined with "shine." He didn't reek of the stuff, but there was a slight whiff of alcohol about him, perhaps taken as a token of remembrance for a lost comrade. Surprisingly, he seemed clean enough in other respects, as if he'd managed to find a place to shower and shave. Another sign of high regard for a lost associate . . .

I shook my head. I was getting ridiculously maudlin, letting too much of the crowd's emotion seep in. I reinforced my shields, but not before something at the edge of my senses shimmered—

"What the bloody hell was that?" I blurted out.

"You saw the light?" The old man poked me in the side with his free hand and cackled in glee. "I knew it. I knew you were royalty," he said.

"I'm sure you have no idea what you're saying." I stepped away from him, all sorts of alarm bells ringing in my head. How in Hades could he know anything like that about me? I looked about as far from royalty as he did. Besides, the likelihood of this stranger knowing anything about me or my family was about as much as me having a wild, passionate affair with the homeless old geezer.

"Oh no, I know," he said and, once again, laid a finger to the side of his nose. I finally twigged—Paul Newman and Robert Redford used the signal in the movie *The Sting*. "I see them because I was touched once . . ." the man continued. "You see them because you can."

I stepped back another pace, trying to find my brother. Although my night vision was very much improved since the Change, the light of the candles made all the shadows waver, dance. I couldn't focus. If Tucker had been with me instead of Rhys, I could've easily spotted his red hair, but Rhys' dark head blended in too easily with the crowd. Plus he was several inches shorter than Tucker.

"He died of a broken heart, Sam did." The old man kept babbling at me, even though I put up my strongest "do not want" body language. "Just like the others. Old, not wanted, then they came and offered peace."

"I'm sorry to hear that," I mumbled, and turned on a heel. "Rhys," I called out as I spotted my brother.

"Over here, Keira." He waved an arm.

"Keira?" The old man muttered. "I know that name."

Yeah, you're probably a big Keira Knightley fan, you dolt, I thought, letting my frustration at the fruitlessness of the night turn into inner crankiness. But I said, "Keep safe," to the old coot as I went to join Rhys.

"The shining . . ." The old man's voice got lost in the crowd as I hurried away as quickly as I could.

"What was—" Rhys swung down from the bench he'd been standing on and approached me.

"Nothing," I said before he could finish asking the question. "Just some poor old guy with delusions of seeing lights that aren't really there. I think he had a few too many at his friend's wake." I totally didn't mention the royalty comment. I didn't want the ramblings of some drunk tramp getting in the way of finding Daffyd.

"Ah." Rhys nodded. "I asked several of the people around here if they'd seen anyone who looked like Daffyd."

"Any luck?"

"Like you, nothing," he said. He looked around at the gathering. "There's a lot of people here, but nothing that says Sidhe."

"They didn't see anyone?"

"Opposite," Rhys explained. "They saw too many."

"Sorry? I don't get you."

"The folk music festival," he said. "A lot of the musicians are here already, wandering around. Bunch of them look like something out of the Renaissance or their interpretation of it. You know the sort, leather, lace-up boots, flowing pirate shirts . . ."

"You mean something like a cross between a great fantasy and a bad romance novel cover?" I smirked at the thought. Granted, my Sidhe relatives and other fey I'd seen could get away with that look. Something about their unearthly beauty. For that matter, some human types could, too. I'd once joined up with a college group that was into the Society for Creative Anachronism, just for a lark . . . okay, and for a chance at a really hot guy who played bagpipes. He looked fantastic in a kilt—the traditional kit, including going without the things one traditionally went without underneath. Several of the men in the local group definitely did justice to various types of historical garb . . . others, not so much. But it was for fun and we all played the game.

"Yeah, just about," Rhys said, agreeing with my cover comment. "One of the folks I spoke with was a social worker. She's been working this area, here, around West Hastings, those empty storefronts. Mostly making sure that the people were okay, had access to food, shelter, the lot. She said she knew the dead man."

"Was it foul play?"

Rhys shook his head. "Nope, not even going to have a coroner's inquest. They figured it was just old age, malnutrition and all the usual things that happen to the discarded and forgotten. Sam was a fairly popular guy. He sang."

"Thus the tribute," I said, nodding toward the crowd that we were quickly leaving behind as we walked.

"Thus the tribute," Rhys agreed. He kicked a piece of trash with his foot, then bent over to pick it up and place it in a nearby bin. Rhys had become the quintessential Canadian. Unless they were totally into ecology, most of my American male acquaintances would probably have kicked the wadded-up paper for a while and then either left it on the ground or finally picked it up after being nagged by a girlfriend or wife.

Although Rhys and his twin Ianto spent a great many years in Texas, many more years had been spent in Canada. Gigi had bought the land up north some decades ago, when Vancouver was a only a glimmer of a city, its modest beginnings far from the third-largest metropolis in Canada it had become. I didn't know details, but no doubt my family had picked up the land for a song, acres and acres of prime wilderness, because in those days, who on earth would be interested in living in western Canada? Now, the population continued to grow, just like everywhere else. The climate was fabulous, enough weather to keep it from becoming boring, and close enough to the city to make it attractive to new settlers. Luckily, since we'd gotten in early, we had plenty of land to roam in. Gigi had remained in Texas, though, happy to stay in one place for years. But after the influx of too many tourists and outsiders into the Hill Country began a few years back, she'd decided to pick up stakes and move. I remembered a remark she'd made while in the midst of packing up to move, not long after I'd returned home from England.

"It's not my first choice," she'd said. "I bought the land because your brothers and father liked it so much. But it will do, it's isolated enough. No people." And likely to not be any, as we'd basically bought everything from the coast to the mountains. Besides, winters were severe enough, sometimes, to put off new land buyers. My brothers preferred the cooler weather and the tall trees and mountains. Not something one finds much in the Texas Hill Country, despite its great beauty. Hills do not equal mountains . . . and there's no skiing of the snow sort in the Lone Star State, a sport both twins enjoyed equally.

We walked in silence for a while, each of us wrapped in our own thoughts. Now that we were away from the park, the streets held the hush of the late-early hour.

"Did you see something shimmer not long before I found you, a flash of light perhaps?" I ventured to ask as we turned down a street and headed back toward the steam clock to meet up with Tucker and Niko. We'd agreed on the meet-up place earlier, figuring that by splitting up, we'd cover more ground. Niko and Tucker had taken the other side of Gastown and further toward the wharf and hotels. Rhys and I went down West Hastings, across to the more touristy areas. Until we'd seen the group assembled for the vigil, most of the streets had been just as deserted as the one we were now on. Despite the often late-night crowd in this area, most folks were long since in their beds, whether in a hotel or at home. We'd been searching for going on two hours now, plus our short interlude at the park.

"A shimmer, where?" Rhys asked.

"Off to the side, at the edge of the park," I said. "About fifteen, twenty minutes ago, when I was talking to the old man . . . or rather, when he was talking to me. I caught it at the corner of my vision . . . just outside my sensory range."

"Not a thing," Rhys said. "Do you think it's anything to worry about?"

"Not sure," I said, the uncertainty welling up. "It might've been candle flames catching a breeze or something. For a second, I thought—"

Rhys stopped and took a good look at me. "Could it have been Daffyd behind a glamour?"

"I don't think so, just a shimmer of light," I said. "The old man said he saw it, too, but he was in the middle of rambling about, I don't know, aliens or something. Probably watched too many *X-Files* or *Stargate* episodes being filmed."

Rhys laughed and continued walking. "Aliens? That's great. First we lose one of the Shining Ones and then someone sees aliens."

I stopped dead in my tracks, in the middle of the crosswalk. A man on a bicycle swerved to avoid me. I stared at him in surprise, as I hadn't seen him despite his reflective gear. "Sorry," I said.

"Sorry, miss," he called as he pedaled past me. I had to chuckle at that: Canada, where they apologize even if you were the one at fault.

"Shining . . ." I turned to my brother, who gestured me back onto the curb before I got run over by another cyclist. I complied, still thinking. "The old man said something about shining," I said. "I didn't think that . . ."

"Could he have seen Daffyd?" Rhys said in alarm. "Damn it."

"Fuck, damn it to all the hells and back," I said. "We've got to go back and find him."

How stupid was I? The guy had practically handed me my missing cousin on a platter and I'd done the dumb-people trick of ignoring the homeless guy's ramblings. "Hurry, Rhys, before we lose him in the . . ."

We reached the top of the hill. The small crowd of mourners had now swelled to three times its original size. There was no way I could possibly pick one man out of the crowd, despite his red toque.

CHAPTER THIRTEEN

"OLD GUY, RED TOQUE." I finished describing the man to Tucker and Niko, who'd rejoined me. Liz came up in time to hear the last.

"He knows something?" she asked.

"Maybe," I said and explained what the man had told me. "I think we need to find him."

"Okay, we'll go over to the right," Tucker said, "and split up the crowd. Rhys, why don't you and Keira take the other side?"

"I'll go down the middle," Liz said. "Meet back up at the top of the hill in twenty?"

We split up and began to move down into the gathering—which was starting to resemble a really weird outdoor concert, that same anticipatory energy, but with a hush on the crowd like spectators at a pro golf tournament. The makeup of the crowd was getting more and more mixed as homeless person after homeless person continued to gather: women, men, teens, all wandering through in various states of layered attire, speaking to each other in low voices, acknowledging one another with a nod or a shy smile. Rhys slid around me, movement swift and graceful, disappearing down the side of the hill to the back of the crowd. I kept to my side, looking at people's heads, peering into the darkness hoping to catch a glimpse of the red hat.

If I'd realized earlier, I could have tried using a Talent

that I probably now possessed: imprinting. I hadn't thought about it before, mostly because it never occurred to me that I could try. I'd seen it done several times, one of my cousins in Montreal showing off to a new conquest. He could imprint anything or anyone onto his senses—sort of an instant digital all-senses image, creating perfect recall and the ability to then track that object or person within a certain radius. A quick flash of open senses and a memory key and boom, there you were. The red toque alone might have done it. Had I imprinted the old man, this search would have taken only a few minutes. Hindsight being just that, I continued my search the old-fashioned way.

A shimmery flash caught the edge of my vision and I turned my head, only to see a small, elderly woman determined to walk to the center of the crowd, her hands gripping the rubber on her aluminum walker. Nothing but a reflection from the metal. Another shimmer to the other side. Once again, when I turned to face it, there was nothing. I rubbed my eyes. Maybe I was tired. I tried to keep walking with the people. It wasn't so much a dense crowd, but a scattered one. Still dark in pockets, as the streetlights, though strong, couldn't illuminate the entire place. I scanned the heads of the people, hoping that a flash of red would appear. Another shimmer, far in front of me. I squinted but only saw a man lighting a candle.

Maybe if I extended my senses a little . . .

I focused, taking a few deep breaths to concentrate. I had to do this carefully and not lose control. Other than when I touched Niko earlier, I'd not tried this since my Change. The faint shimmer teased me again. I ignored it.

Around me, the hum of the voices and conversation

began to fade. My skin tingled, the slight breeze sliding across my hands, my face. I felt sad suddenly, a sense of loss and resignation to fate dancing past my ken. As I tried to extend more, a tear fell down my cheek. I blinked it away, trying to shield.

Some people were singing farewell songs, others quietly crying, others somberly reading passages from some worn book of prayers or just a poetry book. Most gathered in small subgroups, nearly everyone with a candle, flashlight or a Zippo held in front of them. I half expected people to start chanting or singing "Kumbaya." There didn't seem to be rhyme nor reason to the madness—no organized performances, no words all sung or spoken at the same time—each person was marching to his or her own drummer. Oddly enough, it worked. No one person outspoke or sang above another; you could move from small group to small group and catch fragments of lamenting song, snatches of poetry, appropriate Bible verses.

I could even swear I heard someone quoting advert jingles. I wanted to stop the confusion, silence everything and concentrate on picking up either Red Toque's location or any sense of Daffyd. But there was too much sound and feeling. My sensory skills felt like the powerful engine in an Italian sports car but, right now, my body was no more than a Japanese hybrid. I could unleash the energy, but it would be too easy to get lost in what now seemed to me a cacophony, like a brilliant symphony recording that's played at an overloud, overcompensated level; it becomes nothing but discordant noise, all melody and music overcome by overload—static, if you will.

I needed to focus.

Sound morphed into white noise, into music again . . . no, it was more singing . . . right? For a moment, I could have sworn it sounded like the music from—I gagged at a stray smell that assaulted my nose, not all that close by, but from someone no further away than a few meters. Forcing myself to ignore the odors, the heavy feel of the sorrow weaving through, I caught a hint of fresh green silver light shimmer—

A persistent sound broke my concentration. I fumbled in my pocket for my phone. Without glancing at the display, I flipped it open.

"Found him," Tucker said, a note of triumph in his voice. "We're going to meet you at the top of the hill, by the war memorial thing. Liz went to check something out over on the other side of the street."

"The Victory Square Cenotaph," I said, correcting him and sighing in relief, I went to join them.

"Poor Sam," the old man sobbed. "Known him for years, y'know. He was my friend."

"Les here says that he's known Sam since they were nearly kids. When they were kicked out of their respective family houses," Tucker explained.

"You've been on the streets that long?" Rhys said in astonishment. Homelessness wasn't a condition familiar to Kellys. No matter our status, our place in the extremely extended family, anywhere a group of Kellys lived, they would house, feed and care for us.

Les, the bobble on his toque flopping back and forth as he spoke, nodded rapidly. "Been around for a long time," he said. "Poor Sam and me. Tough times, sweet times. They say he went in his sleep though. Dreaming again, I s'pose. The beautiful dream." The man sighed, a dramatic gesture born of storytelling. A bemused look on his face spoke of his becoming lost in thought.

I stifled my irritation at his ramblings and fought my initial urge to say something to hurry him along. I had to treat him with kindness, get him to tell us what he remembered. I put a hand out, touching his arm in a gesture of friendliness, reinforcing my shields as I did so, as a precaution. "I'm sorry about your friend, Les," I said. "Could you perhaps tell us if you've seen my cousin? The one we're looking for?"

The man quickly doffed his cap and twisted in his hands as he gave me a bow. "M'lady, I apologize. I'm an old man, easily distracted. Please forgive me."

"No worries, Les," I hastily reassured him. "We understand."

"The shining one . . ." he began, but stopped at Niko's audible gasp. Visibly paler than normal, he gripped Tucker's arm, his mouth set, lips tight.

Les waited a moment, then when none of us said anything, he continued. "He was tall, so beautiful, all dressed in black. He shone in the night. I thought he'd come because of Sam's dreams. He dreamed of angels, a lot, Sam did," Les said. "Nearly every night recently. I thought at first the man was someone Sam knew, and was here to pay tribute. He was like a dark angel—all light and beauty, but with black clothing."

"Daffyd," I said to my brothers. "Has to be. Where did you see him?"

"Is the angel part of your entourage, then?" Les asked.

"Entourage?"

Les nodded with enthusiasm. "You are obviously a queen, m'lady. You must have your entourage. You have the strong one, the beast here." He pointed to Tucker.

"And the nightwalker and the smaller beast." Les scrunched up his face. "I told you. Royalty, I said, and I was right."

I gripped Rhys' arm and stood dumbfounded. How could this human man know us? A queen I wasn't, but, thanks to my twisted genealogy, I was heir to the equivalent of a Clan throne and, although I hated the connection, of royal Sidhe blood. My mother's cousin was queen of the Seelie Court; my mother was her begrudged heir presumptive who ruled a lesser court in her own right and I was my mother's only child. And he knew to name Tucker and Rhys as beast and Niko as nightwalker. How on earth?

"I see things," Les said, his face once again bland, the soft smile returning.

"I suppose you do at that," Tucker said, his own voice gentle as he put his hand on the old man's shoulder. "Perhaps you can tell us where you saw the dark angel?" He led Les to the nearby bus bench. The man sat down and frowned as he picked at a loose thread on his neck cloth, which he'd removed and was now holding in his hands.

"I don't remember," he said in a quiet voice. "I tried and tried, but I don't—" Les closed his eyes and covered his face with his hands, the neck cloth fluttering between his fingers like a warning banner. "They took Sam's soul," he said, words muffled behind the cloth. "If I tell, they'll take me." He looked up in a sudden move and stared directly into my eyes. "Not that I don't want to go with angels, m'lady," he said. "I'm down with that, I am. But not yet." His serious countenance suddenly broke into a huge grin. "He went with angels," he crowed. "Sam, who slept with all the women in the world who would have him—and there were loads of those in the old days. Angels."

I bit my lip, trying to hold back the exasperated words. Damnation, first the guy was fairly coherent, now he'd declined into some sort of semi-confused state. Angels, indeed.

I looked over at Tucker, Niko and Rhys. Each of them had the same expression on his face—probably a mirror of my own confusion and full of "what do we do next?" questions. I didn't have experience talking with someone in this state. Rhys had talked to a social worker earlier, and we could probably track her down, but I didn't want to bring any humans into this mix. How to explain that I was trying to find someone who was not only missing, but vanished into thin air, and oh, by the way, not legally in the country because he was technically invisible to the customs agent when we landed in the plane? Oh yeah, that would go over like a thousand lead balloons.

"Look, guys," I said, trying to keep my voice down. "Why don't I take one of you and keep searching and the other two can stay here with Les. Maybe he will sober up some. We'll do another hour and then, if we don't find Daffyd, call it off for the night. We need to make it back to the condo by dawn."

Tucker nodded. "Yeah, sounds like a plan. Niko, go with Keira, and Rhys and I will stay here. Be back here in an hour. Maybe we'll get lucky, I mean, how hard can it be to find a shiny white blond guy in Johnny Cash colors?"

"True, but we've—"

Les's grumbly mutter interrupted me. "He wasn't blond," he said in disgust. "Did you people not listen to what I said?" He stood and held out his hands to me, as if in supplication. "Oh, I am so very sorry, m'lady," he apologized. "I didn't mean you."

"Accepted," I said. "But what did you mean, not blond?"

"The shining man," Les answered. "He had dark hair."

CHAPTER FOURTEEN

"DARK?" I SAID. "Are you sure?"

Les gave me a look of disgust, then dropped his eyes and pulled off his toque, clenching his hands around the red material. "My apologies, but yes. He was dark-haired, dressed all in black." A dreamy smile appeared on Les' face again. "So very beautiful. A dark angel. He took Sam's soul, he did . . . inside the dream."

I threw my hands up in exasperation and walked away toward the street, enough so that Les couldn't hear me. Tucker, who probably knew me well enough to see the signs of a full-fledged Keira Kelly frustration rant coming, followed me. I stopped by a boarded-up store window with a poster advertising some sort of video game glued to the pressboard. A flyer for the folk music festival hung next to it.

"Damn it, Tucker, he's still rambling." I said. "He didn't see Daffyd. He could be talking about some alcohol-fueled dream."

"You're probably right, Keira," Tucker agreed. "Let's wrap up and go on back to the condo. It's too close to dawn to dawdle much longer."

I looked at the horizon. The sky had started to lighten perceptibly. "We'd best get back, then. Round up the troops, would you? I'm afraid if I have to listen to old Les there anymore, I might totally lose it."

Tucker waved the others over. Rhys said something

to Les that I couldn't hear. Les gave him a nod, then said something in return. He turned to leave, then stopped, faced me and gave me a deep bow, hand over his heart. I nodded back at him and he turned and left.

"Why is he calling you m'lady?" Liz asked as we began the trek back to the condo.

"Beats me," I said. "He started that earlier. Then said something about me being a queen."

Niko's eyes narrowed. "He also knew of our natures, Keira," he said. "Still think he is nothing more than a dream-ridden old man?"

"Perhaps he is one who is touched with Sight," Rhys said. "It happens."

"It does?" Niko sounded surprised. "How so? I had thought humans and your Clan did not intermix—could not."

I stepped around a large cement plant pot set outside a store. We'd taken the most direct route back, down Water Street, the heart of the tourist-focused area. "We can't," I confirmed.

"But he could have fey blood in his background," Rhys explained. "I've known people in the past who were mixed race."

Niko looked thoughtful as he walked beside Tucker, evidently digesting this scrap of news. Our Clan was biologically incompatible with humans but, as Rhys said, several friends of Clan were part fey, part human. "I was not aware the Sidhe could interbreed with humans," he said.

"They can't," Tucker said, his voice patient. "It's complicated as hell, but high court Sidhe are as unable to breed with humans as we are. It's the lesser fey who can." At Niko's continued puzzled look, he continued.

"Brownies, selkies, phoukas and the like. They have always been closer to human evolution."

"Hmm." Niko's brow furrowed. "This is rather complex. I had thought . . ."

"Thought, *cariad*?" Tucker asked.

Niko shook his head, red hair gleaming in the light of a nearby shop window. We were nearly to our building. About time, too, as I noticed that the sky was definitely lighter.

"Nothing, really," Niko said. "Just something Adam once said."

"Oh, bloody everlasting hell," I exclaimed and dug my phone out. "Adam."

Four pairs of eyes stared at me as I stopped walking and began pressing numbers. "I forgot to call him," I said. "In all the hubbub of Daffyd disappearing."

The phone rang several times and went to voice mail. "Damn it, Adam, I'm sorry," I said into the speaker. "Daffyd's gone and pulled a Claude Rains on us and I totally lost track of time. If you're still up or when you get up, please call?" I ended the connection and slipped the phone back into my pocket.

"Claude Rains?" Tucker questioned.

"It seemed apt."

"So what's the plan?" Liz asked. "We going to keep on looking?" She waved a hand, indicating that she meant those of us not of the vampire persuasion.

"I think we need to regroup," I said. "Let's get some sleep and meet again in the early afternoon and see if we can figure something out. If we're lucky, the weather up north will have cleared and we can consult with Gigi."

"Or Dad," Rhys reminded me. "If he's done in Seattle,

he and Isabel can be here pretty quickly. It's only about a three hour drive."

"If the wait at the bridge isn't horribly long," Liz said.

"True."

"Would be great if we had more eyes to search," I said as we reached the front door of the building. "Liz, you going to stay over or head home?"

She eyed Rhys, who gave her a broad grin and a slight nod. "I think I'll stay," she said with a smile.

I placed my palm on the access plate. The doors swung open.

RHYS, LIZ and I all slept for hours, until late afternoon, and woke up to a gray, overcast day. In the quiet of the afternoon before the others woke, I'd tried calling Bea again. All this running around with family looking for Daffyd was making me crazy—and Bea had always been a great grounding force in my life. Even now, with her so freaked out about seeing who I was underneath all this façade of humanity, I trusted that, eventually, we'd repair the relationship. I had to believe that. Anything else wasn't acceptable.

The phone rang four times and went to voice mail. I left a brief message, telling her of the delay and that I was still at the condo. Maybe, just maybe, she'd be willing to call when it was over a long distance—far enough away to have an uncomfortable conversation. I flipped the phone shut, shoved it in my jeans pocket and went out to the kitchen to start a pot of coffee.

"IT'S STILL craptastic weather up north," Liz announced over a steaming mug I'd poured for her. "I tried to call up there but no dice." She took a long sip. "I'm afraid I've got to run, too. I've gotten a call about a job out in the Fraser Valley. Some new TV show. They need a stunt pilot for at least a few days."

"You're leaving?"

"I don't know if there's anything else I can do, Keira," she said. "I'm happy to help, but to just sit around or go back out and do the same thing we've been doing all over again?" She shrugged. "I think I'd rather take this job. I'll have my phone. Call me if you need me."

Liz finished her coffee and Rhys said he'd walk her down to her car in the garage. (*Riight.* Like she'd get lost? At least my brothers were gentlemen . . . when they wanted to be.) I poured myself another mug and went to the window wall. Pulling back the blackout drapes revealed a multimillion (Canadian) dollar view for me to contemplate. Not that I felt too contemplative. My mind was spinning faster than a Texas tornado.

"Is there any way to provide a magical trace?" I asked Rhys when he returned. "Cast some sort of spell?"

"There's no dowsing rod for fey, Keira," Rhys said. "The best we can do is keep trying."

"Damn it. How the hell are we supposed to find Daffyd, then?"

"We can call Dad," Rhys said, "and see if he has any suggestions."

I pulled out my phone. "Perfect idea." I dialed Dad's number.

"Hey, honey, what's shaking?"

"Weather better, Dad?" I asked. "Phone sounds better."

"Yeah, cleared up a bit ago. 'Bout time, too. So what can I do for you? I don't imagine you called to ask about the weather."

"I wish it was that simple," I muttered.

"What was that?"

I shook my head. "Nothing, Dad. Where are you? We've got something of a situation here." I filled him in.

"Damn, Keira," he said, his voice amused. "You do manage to get yourself into some situations. We're still in Seattle, but we're heading to Van in a few hours. Hang tight; we'll come help look." My dad paused a moment. "Keira, did you ever think maybe your old man—Les?—actually did see another Sidhe?"

"Dad, that's ridiculous," I said. "It's not like this is the heart and soul of ye olde country. Why would any Sidhe be here—in Vancouver?"

"Daffyd is there."

"Point taken, Dad, but he came with us."

Dead silence on the other end of the phone. "Oh, duh, you mean someone else could've come here just like Daffyd."

"It's not outside the bounds of believability, sweetheart."

"No, but . . . why would another Sidhe be in Vancouver?"

"Keira, perhaps this other Sidhe came for the same reason Daffyd did."

"For me?" Evidently, however slow I was in first getting on this clue bus, once I got on, I got up to speed fast.

"Brilliant, sweetheart. You've got it," Dad said. "I'm sure Minerva's lost no time in announcing the fact that she has a new heir. I expect there to be an influx of visitors over the new few days."

"Visitors who are stuck here in Vancouver, like we are," I said. "Damnation, Dad, did she have to go throw open the doors before I even got there?"

My dad laughed. "Honey, since when did our leader ever do things the simple way?"

"True. Hey, Dad, that old guy who died . . . Les said he

went with the angel. Do you think the Sidhe, if there is one, is draining humans here?"

"Hmm. I don't know. It's a possibility. Sidhe rarely go for humans unless they're desperate. If they didn't realize the distance . . . which is very possible . . . some of the older ones are still unlikely to understand the great distances in the new world . . . they may not have come prepared. If this Sidhe is loose in the city, the metal, the modernity could be hurting him, draining reserves. Then again, your old man may have seen someone else. Can't rule out the possibility, though."

"Dad, you're the closest thing I have to an expert on that part of my bloodline," I said. "Do you know anything about them having the ability to vanish?"

"I don't know about the vanishing, although I did see something odd a few times when visiting your mother's relatives. Things Underhill in Faery aren't necessarily what they seem, and they weren't good at answering questions. Besides, I was actually only there for one thing."

Egads, was my dad going to share his lust for my not-lamented and, as far as I knew, still much-alive mother? Not something I really wanted to hear about.

"So you never saw anyone vanish?" I asked, trying to keep to the subject we'd been discussing.

"Not as such," he said. "But if memory serves, that's not a Talent I'd cross off the list."

"Okay, one more question, Dad. Do you know if there's any way we can do some sort of tracking spell?"

"A tracking spell . . ." His voice trailed off. "Perhaps. Do you have anything of his?"

"No." I shook my head automatically. "He had nothing but the clothes Niko lent him."

"That could work," Dad said. "Have you tried tracking

Niko's scent? The boys can help you out since you've not done a tracking spell before. It's fairly simple."

I slapped my own forehead. How could we have overlooked that? Daffyd may not have a traceable scent, but Niko's clothing did. "I can't believe we didn't think about that."

"You're tired, honey," Dad said. "Talk to your brothers and I bet the three of you can come up with a way to cast the tracking. You may be new at this, but the ability's within you . . . and the boys are great trackers as wolves."

"Thanks, Dad."

"Anytime, Keira. You all do what you need to. Isabel and I will give you a ring when we've crossed the bridge. I expect that'll be somewhere around eleven or so. We should be leaving Seattle right around sunset—say eightish."

"Why wait so long? Can't you all come now?"

"Wish I could, sweetheart," he said. "But I've got something on and it's difficult for us to leave any sooner. No worries, we'll be there before you know it. Hopefully, you'll have located that missing cousin of yours by then."

"Yeah, hopefully," I said.

"Take care, Keira. See you soon."

"Bye, Dad."

"THIS SHOULD work," Rhys mumbled around a strip of cloth he was ripping from a shirt. Tucker had fetched it for us after we'd awakened him from his blissful slumbers with his vampire boyfriend. It was the shirt Niko had worn on the trip and while we were roaming around Vancouver. We'd dug up a locator-type tracking spell that Tucker thought might work. It worked more like an enhancement, not a real tracker, per se. I was hoping that Rhys' and Tucker's natural tracking ability would help compensate.

"What the hell are you doing with my shirt?" Niko strode in the living room, yawning. "It's custom tailored . . . or, rather, was."

"We're using it to help locate Daffyd, *cariad*." Tucker rose and pecked Niko on the cheek. "Don't be angry. It's for a good cause."

"It's not your shirt that's been sacrificed for a cause," Niko grumbled. He walked over to the blackout curtain. "It doesn't feel like night." He raised the curtain on the standard Vancouver late afternoon—overcast and an unmitigated gray. Pulling open the overcurtains, he fastened them with the ties. "The sheers are enough," he said. "It's dark enough with the overcast. Are you all going out now?"

"Yes, I don't want to lose any more time," I said.

"Damn. I can't go with you unless you wait until later. When is sunset?"

"A couple of hours at least," I said. "It's pretty dark out, though. Sure you can't—"

"No, can't risk it. The weather's too unpredictable. I was just hoping . . ."

I looked at him staring at the pieces of cloth. "The magick," he said. "It's fascinating, though still a bit unsettling."

"Unsettling?" I stood up and handed my strips of cloth to Rhys.

"In my youth, magick was feared; the work of the devil."

I laughed. "No devils here. Just energies harnessed in a way not known to humans."

"Do you think it's a Sidhe—the dark man? Could

it be?" Niko's voice, though strong, still held a note of something not right.

I explained what Dad had said. "I hope I don't end up like Aurora," I said in an attempt to lighten the mood. "Though I don't plan on trying out any spinning wheels anytime soon, even if a dark faery curses me."

"Come again?"

"'Sleeping Beauty'?" I looked at Niko. "I don't suppose you read many children's tales in the last couple of centuries."

"Ah, yes," he said, "I do recognize the spinning wheel allusion, but don't recall the princess being named Aurora. I don't think we knew of a name."

"Figures," I muttered. "Don't name the women in a story."

Rhys laughed. "I doubt that our fearless leader plans to ignore or slight anyone, Keira," he said. "Much less take the piss from a bunch of Sidhe. Plus, I don't really think they can curse anyone."

"No," I said. "Leave that to our own family. Sidhe just steal children and take lives." And vanish into thin air, I didn't say aloud.

CHAPTER FIFTEEN

As we climbed the steep hill toward West Pender, the near quiet of the early evening was broken by a loud buzz that got clearer as we got closer to the park. A crowd was gathering, people coming from all directions making their way toward Victory Square, the same place we'd been the night before, only this time, instead of a vigil, we saw a gathering that looked more like it belonged here. Bands and small music festivals often congregated in the park, like wee Woodstocks, complete with drugs, sex and loads of rock'n'roll. Except a lot of these people looked more like the type who listened to bagpipes and bodhráns rather than amplified electric guitars and headbanging drummers. If I didn't know any better, it could even be a Clan gathering. The difference was that none of these folks had any more magick than could be found in a well-sung song. No Clan members here, other than three Kellys and a vampire.

The folk music festival had started.

We'd each taken a strip of the magic-infused cloth and tied it around a wrist. According to my brothers, the scent of the fabric, enhanced by the spell, should help us in tracking Daffyd. We'd set out toward the park, figuring that if old Les had seen one Sidhe here, there might well be another.

Tucker and Niko slowed, waiting for Rhys and me

to catch up. We'd waited until dusk after all, figuring Niko would be more help with us than hanging out at the condo.

"Listen," Tucker said sotto voce. "Something's going on."

I closed my eyes a moment to focus on the sounds. The general crowd buzz faded as I concentrated. Snippets of conversation began to come clear.

"Did you hear . . ."

". . . they found . . . at the hostel."

"Did anyone tell Rodney?"

"John's over there, maybe Rodney's with him. Wasn't he their friend?"

"Found him in one of the rooms . . ."

The sounds began to fade, an almost doppler-like effect morphing into the drip, drip, plink of a leaky faucet.

The tiny room was too dark; its only window covered by a threadbare Hudson Bay blanket—a dingy cream, striped in red, yellow and blue—held up by a ragged rope wound around a couple of large nails. A small graying mattress topped by yellow and green sheets and a ragged flat pillow held the body of a thin, older man. Bushy salt-and-pepper hair framed his ascetic face. A neatly trimmed beard completed the picture. His eyes were closed in death; the expression on his face serene, as if he'd finally found peace. There were no marks on the body. His torn, but clean clothes showed no signs of blood, or any evidence that he was dead by foul play. Yet something was off here. Something wasn't quite right. It's a good thing they called me in. I need to get back to the sergeant and figure this out. Only . . .

"Keira?"

I opened my eyes.

"You still with us, sis?" Rhys poked me in the side and cocked his head, a worried look on his face.

"I'm sorry, what?" I looked around. Most of the crowd had moved on down the street, and the four of us stood in the middle of the sidewalk about six meters from the corner.

"You were out of it for a few minutes, sis," Tucker said quietly. "You okay?"

"Yeah, I think—weird." I looked around and saw a couple of sidewalk benches about halfway up the block. "I think I need to sit down a minute."

I didn't say anything until I reached the bench and slumped onto it. What the hell had that been? It wasn't like the visions I'd had before, more like I'd been watching a really vivid TV show.

Tucker sat next to me and grabbed my hand. I let him do it, even though I was still a little freaked and wasn't sure how strong my shields were. He was pretty tightly shielded, so I let myself relax.

"I kind of saw something," I began.

"A vision?" Tucker asked, concern coloring his voice.

"Sort of." I explained what I'd seen and how it was different. "All I could think was that I needed to get back and report this. Weird thing is, I'm not touching anyone. Not smelling anything peculiar—those two things were what triggered visions before."

"Things could be different now," Niko said. He stepped closer and sat on my left side, leaning in so he could speak in a lower tone. "Do you think it's what those people were talking about?"

"Could be. Old dead guy in a grungy room. Could've been a hostel." I shrugged. "I don't know. Closest thing to roughing it I ever did was to stay at a Days Inn one time in midtown Manhattan."

"Really?" Niko sounded surprised.

"Don't forget, *cariad*," said Tucker, "Keira's young and rather spoiled. In all her traveling, I bet our dear matriarch, or perhaps even our dear papa, spared no expense."

I smacked my brother's arm. "Spoiled, my ass. You both know very well that the Kellys own a metric ton of houses all over the place. I stay in them on the cheap and don't stay in hotels. Besides, the idea of trying to stay in a hostel among a bunch of humans—you couldn't ever relax. Of course I stayed in nice places."

"Exactly." He grinned at me, and then looked up at Rhys. "Wouldn't you say she's spoiled?"

Rhys grinned back. "Leave me out of this one, brother. I pass no judgments on someone who'll soon be able to hex me into next week."

I stuck my tongue out at the both of them. "Take advantage all you want now, boys, while I still don't know how. I *will* learn, though."

"All kidding aside, Keira," Tucker said, "you're okay, right?"

At his words, I took a deep breath and did a quick check of myself. This was a technique that Aunt Jane had taught me years ago, but I'd grown out of the habit of using. I hadn't needed it until a couple of days ago. Tucker had reminded me of it when we'd come back from our first outing as wolves. It's kind of an internal awareness systems check—high level to be sure, but it was a quick way to see if anything felt off.

"I'm good," I replied. "Not woozy, dizzy or even faintly light-headed. I guess I tuned in to some local cop somehow."

"Hmm," Tucker looked me over once more. "I'd feel less worried if you'd tuned in to one of us. That would be a natural extension of Kelly Talent. This, I'm not so sure about."

"I'm fine, Tucker," I said. "Can we concentrate on what we're doing for now? We can ask Isabel about this when we see her." He didn't say anything, just kept looking at me.

"Do you think it was the friend Les was talking about? The guy you saw in your vision?" Rhys asked.

"Maybe," I said. "I have no idea. I got the feeling though, from what Les said, that he and his buddy were in some sort of shelter-like place, with a row of beds. This looked like a single room—really tiny, but individual."

"Hmm," Tucker mused as he studied me. He placed a broad hand on my forehead, like a parent checking a child for a fever. I tried to bat his hand away, but he wouldn't let me. No sense in trying to out-strength my brother, so I put up with it.

"What are you doing?"

"Shhh, let me . . ." Tucker closed his eyes, and began to hum something that sounded vaguely familiar. I began to relax, the quiet melody weaving its way into my consciousness, then soothing me, much like a meditation CD I'd once had. My breaths became deeper. My thoughts began to drift . . . music, sunshine, a tiny room holding the songs that mattered. The sound of so sharp, so clear a note that one could cut one's soul on it. A wind instrument, shiny silver flute holding the melody, slowly wending its way inside, touching that part of us that we'd thought dead, lost forever in the morass of guilt and shame that was our past. Tears forced themselves past my closed lids, carrying with them every moment of regret; washing away my plethora of sins—both real and imagined. I gasped at the perfect beauty and died.

With a start, I came back to myself and wrenched away

from Tucker's hold, standing and stepping away from the group.

"What in all the bloody hells was that?" I demanded.

My heart still pounded with an adrenaline response that I couldn't control. "I just died, Tucker . . . or rather, I was . . . I felt . . ." The rest of the words failed to come. I had no idea how to explain what I'd experienced. Unlike my visions before, unlike the one where I was the cop, this was living and breathing and feeling another person. Knowing his history, his sins, peccadilloes and a lifetime of ugly self-recrimination that colored his world. Becoming someone else for the space of—how long was that anyway?

Tucker stood and approached me, hands held out in a peaceful gesture. "Damn, Keira, I'm sorry. Isabel showed me how to do that before she left. It was supposed to be a way to relax you, to help you remember. I was only—"

"Yeah, yeah, I know," I said. "Only trying to help." I waved him off as he stepped closer. I wasn't sure I could deal with him touching me right now. A buzzing sound morphed into the electronic strains of "Don't Fear the Reaper." I shot a look at Rhys.

"I had to," he said, not even trying to feign innocence.

I rolled my eyes. Of course he'd reprogrammed my ringtone with the Blue Öyster Cult song. Typical. I pulled the phone out and saw it was Adam calling.

"Hey there," I answered. "Where—"

"Miss Keira." The voice on the other end was not Adam's. "This is Lance. Mr. Adam asked me to ring you and let you know he got your voice mail and that he will touch base with you soon." His formal tone was at odds with the Lance I knew in person.

"He did what?" I asked, stunned at Lance's words.

"He couldn't be bothered to call me himself?" A week or two ago, I would not have been fazed by this, since our relationship had become so strained. But all that had changed . . . hadn't it? True, we'd only had a couple of nights together to mend fences, but I'd thought we'd more than patched things up.

"My apologies, Miss Keira," Lance said. "I neglected to explain. Mr. Adam has had to leave on travel. He is out of pocket right now, but will contact you soon."

"Leave? Where?" I looked over at Niko, who, like Tucker and Rhys, was listening in to both ends of the conversation. All three men looked as stunned as I felt.

"I'm afraid I don't know. I wasn't told."

"When did he go?"

"A few hours ago," he said. "He did say to tell you that he'd speak with you soon."

"Yes, well." I didn't know what else to say. It was obvious Lance either knew nothing or had been instructed to pretend so. I voted for the former. Adam didn't seem the type to confide in a secretary/assistant—at least not in the case of a situation where he didn't tell Niko first. Niko was his right hand. Yet he'd let Niko come with us to Canada. Would he have done that if something was seriously wrong? Maybe something had come up suddenly?

"Did you need anything else, Miss Keira?" Lance asked.

"I guess not," I said.

"Thank you, then." Lance disconnected the call.

I shut the phone. "Niko?"

"I am as in the dark as you are," Niko said. "He said nothing to me."

"He doesn't do this type of thing on a whim, does he?"

"Travel?" He paused, as if thinking. "Unlikely. He

doesn't particularly enjoy traveling. Especially as it's difficult for us to do so with our restrictions. We have to charter a plane."

"Or own one," I said absently. "Adam doesn't own a plane?"

"Not locally," he said. "He's got several in the EU."

"Then I really don't get this," I said. "Why would he just up and leave, especially if you're not there to cover for him?"

Niko rubbed his eyebrow with a thumb. "I don't know and I'm afraid this doesn't bode well. Perhaps word of his recent . . . incapacitation . . . got out and he's had to go take care of things."

"Take care of—what things? With whom? I thought you all didn't have any sort of ruling body or council; that your tribes are all independent."

"They are, Keira. Adam rules our tribe, but it's pretty large." Niko hesitated a moment as he looked around us. "Perhaps we should talk about this in a less public space."

The streets weren't crowded by any means, but there was a fair amount of pedestrian traffic enjoying a temporary respite from the all-day rain.

"How about we go over there?" I pointed to an area set back from the main walk, with a couple of benches, set off to the side of an office building. A small path led there, but since it didn't look as if it connected to anywhere but the benches, no one was walking on it. The area was probably used by workers during lunch hour or something.

"So, talk to us, Niko," I said. "What do you mean by large? Weren't there only a few handfuls of vampires at the ranch?"

"The ranch is not the only location for our tribe, Keira.

We have other branches, in the UK, other places throughout the EU."

"Now you tell me?"

"It wasn't my place."

"Did you know?" I asked Tucker, who was staring at Niko.

"No," he said. "No one ever told me."

Niko put his hands up. "I am sorry. I—" He touched Tucker's arm. "Tucker, I am not used to having someone I can trust with our—"

"Secrets?" I wasn't angry. I totally understood Niko's position. As for Adam . . . if I knew the extent of the Kelly holdings, all the convoluted political machinations, allies, treaties and bonds, would I share them with Adam?

A sobering thought struck me. As the Kelly heir, I'd probably be expected to learn all this shite. Damn.

"Look, this is not the time or place for this talk," I said. "Adam and whatever he's doing is going to have to wait. We're on a mission here." I tugged Rhys' arm. "Shall we keep looking?"

Rhys nodded, his uncomfortable look changing to one of anticipation. "Niko and Tucker, why don't you guys go around to the east and south. We'll go west and north—see what we find. If you feel anything, sense anything, call. Meet back up here in about an hour?"

We all nodded. "Once more unto the breach," I said.

CHAPTER SIXTEEN

WE TRUDGED BACK to the condo building, having found nothing and no one that even vaguely felt Sidhe. A lot of lookalikes, with the music festival going full swing by ten P.M., but no one of magickal means other than ourselves. We'd called it a night around three A.M. At one point during our search, Dad had called and pleaded another delay. He and Isabel wouldn't be in Vancouver until at least morning.

"I'm beginning to think we're spinning our wheels," I said as I punched the penthouse button in the elevator. "Maybe we *should* give up. Daffyd's not only grown, but he's at least as old as you two." I motioned toward Tucker and Rhys. "If he chooses not to be found, then so be it."

"He's both grown and old enough," Tucker said. "I'm at a loss for what to do, also. Perhaps Keira is right. We should let it, and him, be."

"I'm for that," Rhys said. "We've done all we can for now . . . unless we want to call in the Horsemen."

"Yeah, right," I said. "And what would we say, exactly, to the Royal Canadian Mounted Police? Hey, we've lost a faery and—" I stepped out of the elevator and opened the door to the penthouse. "What the fuck are you doing here?"

Behind me, Rhys laughed. "I'm sure the Mounties wouldn't feel that was appropri—"

Adam Walker stood inside, standing at the edge of the living area, as if he belonged there.

I blinked my eyes and shook my head. Well then, that was one question answered. Adam could still shield from me. I hadn't felt his presence.

"Keira."

No, visions tended not to sound as if they were in the same room I was. Without looking at the others, I continued on into the apartment, pushing past Adam. My brothers and Niko followed behind me, each of them speechless.

I stopped when I reached the center of the living room. "Adam, I'm not sure I get this," I said, turning to face him. "Lance called—"

"Yes, I asked him to," he said. "I wanted to surprise you."

"Well, that worked." I threw up my hands. "But how are you—"

Niko spoke up. "Yes, how are you, indeed?"

"Here," I finished, glaring at Niko. "In Vancouver."

Rhys frowned. "How did you get in the building?"

"I can explain everything. Shall we sit?" Adam said, and walked on into the main living area. "I apologize for the sudden appearance, Keira, Nikolai, Tucker." He inclined his head toward Rhys. "I suppose you are another Kelly?"

"My brother Rhys," I said and sat on one of the couches. Adam sat next to me. Niko and Tucker settled on the couch opposite. Rhys chose to perch on the arm of the couch next to Niko. Odd that they should choose to flank Niko instead of me. Not that I minded; I could most definitely handle myself—whatever weird reasoning Adam might have for showing up unannounced.

Adam took my hand. I couldn't suppress the electric

thrill that ran through me at his touch, energy snapping into place, establishing a balance I hadn't realized I'd been missing. Immediately, I felt more at ease, less unsettled. Damn. Not only was I reacting as if we'd been apart for weeks instead of days, Liz had been so right about the energy bond, or whatever.

"I missed you, Keira," he said, his voice dropping to that melted dark chocolate tone I knew so well. "After you left, I had a change of heart. I hurried to finish some business, then chartered a plane."

"You couldn't have realized that before we left?" I pulled my hand away, not wanting his touch to distract me. Oh sarcasm, how I missed you.

Adam smiled at me, knowing I was hiding my joy and confusion in my usual snarktastic self. "I was stupid," he admitted. "I let my sense of responsibility override what I knew to be right." There was that word again: responsibility—something that caused normally balanced and sane people to do things that didn't make sense . . . like leave your girlfriend to face an uncertain future by herself, while you stayed behind to be "responsible." It was no wonder that I didn't particularly want to find out what new responsibilities were ahead of me.

"A change of heart." Niko's own voice was full of the same sarcasm that colored mine. Except I could tell his wasn't backed up by joy, but by suspicion. What did Niko know—or suspect—that I didn't?

Adam's face remained neutral as he regarded his second. "Yes," he said, voice as expressionless as his face. "I changed my mind."

"And the tribe?" Niko pressed.

"Everything is fine, Nikolai," Adam insisted. "You know I would not leave otherwise."

"Then I ask the same question as Keira," Niko said. "Why now? Why not two days ago?"

Adam said nothing, but continued to regard Niko with that "I am king" look—neutral, no challenge, a reminder that no matter what, he was the leader and his word was law.

The silence continued, Adam staring, Niko staring back. The rest of us remained quiet. I didn't want to get in the middle of a vampire fight—been there, done that. Not something I cared to do again. Seconds stretched into minutes. Behind me, the hum/tick of a clock was the only sound, other than our breaths.

"So, Adam . . . how exactly *did* you know where to find us?" Rhys finally broke the tension. He didn't repeat his earlier question.

Rhys had a point. I'd never told Adam the location of the condo. When I'd left voice mail, I'd only said we were stuck in Vancouver because of weather and would be at the Kelly condo. Neither the penthouse nor the building was listed under the Kelly name specifically, but under one of our holding companies. I didn't even know which one. Ciprian kept all that information and frankly, I'd never been all that interested in the details.

Adam blinked and smiled at Rhys. "Your father told me."

"Say what?" I turned in my seat to face him directly. "You talked to my dad? When? How do you even know him to talk to him?"

Adam relaxed back into the couch, a picture of confidence. "Your father remained in touch with me after Marty's death, Keira. He wanted me to keep an eye on you. He knew you were more affected than you were allowing to show."

I stood up and walked a few steps away, then back. "You knew my father well enough to stay in touch?"

After a moment, Adam answered. "When you left London," he began, "I petitioned your leader to help find you. By then, though, they'd all gone to Canada and were no longer in Texas."

I was dumbfounded. When Adam had shown up in Texas he had acted as if he thought I was human. Now he was telling me he not only knew I was Other, but that he was acquainted with my family.

He sat there, studying me in silence, then continued after I gestured, speechless, for him to continue. How this was playing out, I didn't know, but I needed to hear the rest.

"Minerva refused to tell me where you were, but I managed to communicate with your father. He had no qualms about telling me you had returned to Texas. That's how I initially found you in Rio Seco. Then Marty died and your father contacted me. We've spoken since then a few times. Last night, I rang him so I could get information as to your location here in Vancouver."

"You stayed with me because my *father* told you to keep an eye on me?" Could this really be true? Everything I'd thought for the past half a year was wrong? I thought Adam loved me, fought for me, risked his life for me. Now, here I was finding out that for some bizarre reason in some not-so-random twist of fate, Adam Walker and Huw Kelly had been BFF for years. And that my wonderful father, in all his absentminded glory, had encouraged Adam to become my boyfriend.

"That's not at all what I'm saying, Keira," Adam said, his voice taking the patient tone that I detested in adults. It was as if he were talking to a cranky child. I might be cranky, but I'm definitely no child. At this rate, it'd be a hell of a long time before the softer side of this Kelly returned.

"So what are you telling me, then? That Dad had nothing to do with *this*?" And by *this*, I meant our relationship *and* the fact that he'd followed me to Vancouver, changed his mind after giving me extremely valid reasons why he wouldn't accompany me. "What changed, Adam? First you tell me you can't come, then you show up several hours after we arrive with some lame-ass excuse."

He started to interrupt, but I held my hand up. "No way, buster, I'm getting my say in first." He closed his mouth and nodded, keeping his expression completely neutral. Damn it, I hated the fact that he and Niko could both do that so well. Must be the vampire in them.

"As much as I'd like to believe I'm that irresistible, I highly doubt that you up and chartered your own plane almost immediately after I left you so you could join us here on a whim. Something happened in that time that changed your mind. The only guess I have is your conversation with my father, a man I never even knew you knew. Hell, when I first figured you for a vampire . . . when we first got reacquainted in Rio Seco, you acted as if you had no idea I was not human, let alone anything about the Clan. When I was trying to explain about my family, you even pretended to not know about shapeshifters!" I shook my head. "Has all this been a game to you? I don't get this. Any of it." I looked at my brothers. "Why on earth did the both of you keep this from me? Tucker? Rhys?"

My brothers were still gaping at Adam and me. With a slow shake of his head, Tucker answered. "Keira, I know no more than you do. First time I'd even heard of Adam was when you told me about him in Rio Seco. You never even mentioned him during your London stay."

"I'm afraid we're all completely baffled, Adam," Niko said, a note of anger in his voice. "I've been your second for more than a century. We've shared everything . . . or so I thought."

I sank into the closest chair. I couldn't be on the couch with Adam. Not Niko, too. If anyone had known about this, I would've expected Niko to be the one. He was right. As Adam's second, he should know everything. That was kind of the point of being the second. Ready to step in should anything happen to Adam—as it almost did a few days ago.

"Is everyone done?" The wry tone didn't escape me. Mr. Neutral Vampire's emotions were bleeding through.

We all remained silent and let him speak.

"First, I did not share my relationship with your father, as he requested me to keep silent," Adam began. I started to say something, but, as I had, he put up his hand to stop my questions. "Please, allow me the same courtesy I allowed you, Keira. Let me finish. Some three or four years ago, when I first met you," he said, "I knew there was something about you. Something I wanted to know more about. In trying to discover more about you, I stumbled across your family. Well, stumbled being less exact than that, actually. I reconnected with your family."

"Reconnected?" I squeaked, the word escaping before I could stop. Tucker's mouth dropped open as he, too, fell into a nearby chair. Niko's frown turned into a scowl, lines on his forehead deepening as Adam explained.

"I'd met some of your family before," said Adam. "And I met your parents before you were born."

"Did you just say you knew my parents? As in *both* of

them? Oh, do not tell me this is some godawful disgusting thing like you knew me in the womb and imprinted or something gross like that," I blurted out. "By all the things that are holy and un-, you are seriously not going there, are you?"

"When you were—" Adam looked puzzled. "What—oh my, that's not—absolutely not," he said. "This isn't some badly written young adult stalker romance, Keira. I met your parents during a . . . let's call it a political meeting—before you were even conceived. And as to not knowing about shapeshifters—not one member of your family ever let on. I was absolutely honest with you about that."

I eyed him warily, unsure of what to believe. "Okay, I'll give you shapeshifters . . . we've been known to hide a lot about ourselves, but a political meeting? Sorry, I'm just trying to get over the whole idea that you knew—after London—that I wasn't human, that my family—"

"I'm sorry, Keira. I did deceive you." Adam nodded. "But I also did not realize you were going through the Change until that first time we touched. I had no idea you were coming into your family heritage. It . . . took me off guard. As for me knowing your family . . . I should have told you, I know. But there were implications you couldn't understand."

"Politics," Tucker said with a grimace. "I get it. You not only met Keira's parents, but Gigi, as well. Summit meeting, I take it? You represented the vampires?"

I stared at Adam, trying to decipher what he was going to say next. He let me look into his eyes for a brief second, then just as quickly looked away.

"Not specifically," he said after a moment. He raised his head and looked directly at Tucker first, then Niko, then me, then back to Tucker. "At the time, more than thirty-eight years ago, many of the leaders in the supernatural world were called together. Not for the first time, but this was the most recent of the times. And yes, by your Clan chief," he said as he caught my questioning look. "Minerva Kelly put out a call to all of us, whether vampire, wer, fey . . . anyone who could claim to be outside the so-called normal world. Niko was in Greece at the time, handling some of our own business. Since I was not attending as a representative of the vampires, per se, I did not involve him. A distant connection of ours, one of the London tribe, came to formally represent our people." He paused and looked at me before continuing. "Keira, I know that I should have told you this before—"

"I'm hearing those words a lot tonight," I said. "But I've yet to hear what this is and a reason."

"I apologize again," Adam said. "There were too many things at stake." He made a wry face at the inadvertent pun. "When your great-great-grandmother called the summit meeting, I went as a rather reluctant representative of my father's people: the Unseelie Court."

CHAPTER SEVENTEEN

I SPRANG UP from the couch, arms instinctively crossing, my mouth gaping open like a surprised fish. Tucker and Niko both began to sputter. Rhys, bless him, remained quiet, a thoughtful look on his face.

"No. I did not just hear that," I said and took a step back. "You absolutely can't be saying what I just heard."

"How, Adam—" Niko clasped Tucker's arm, his knuckles going even paler with the grip, voice shaking with anger. "Were you one of them, then? The ones who came in the night?"

Adam's brow furrowed as he regarded Niko. "I don't understand," he said.

Niko's breath caught as he tried to speak. "When I was a child," he said.

Tucker closed his hand over Niko's and gave it a squeeze. The expression on Tucker's face reminded me of the way he'd looked when a school bully had threatened me and Bea during elementary school. He'd been acting in loco parentis then, my father having gone to London on some errand of Gigi's. I'd been all of eight years old, still coming to terms with living Above, and often frightened of others. The bully girl had demanded our lunches, homemade tacos and desserts made by Bea's mom. Tucker had been at the school helping to organize some fall fair or something. One look from my very big brother and Little Miss Future Gangster never bothered us again. She may even have decided to become a nun. Tucker took the role of protector very seriously. And now, he was protecting Niko, too.

"Niko was in an orphanage as a small boy," I explained, my voice hard as steel. "He only recently remembered having seen Sidhe come in the night to steal children."

I was attempting to explain Niko's emotions, but I had no idea how to even begin processing this information myself. Adam, Unseelie Sidhe? My mother's people, the Seelie, might be unkind and uncaring, but the Unseelie had even less regard for humans—or unhumans. Not evil, but . . . a darker breed. What else did he hide from me and how did I not sense this before? How could I have been sleeping with—no, making love with—laying myself bare in so many ways to one of *them*? I'd suffered so much as a child in my mother's land, living among the Seelie in the Welsh hills, underground, starved for affection, noticed only when reviled. And Adam was Unseelie, a race that made my mother's people look sweet and benevolent. I strode over to the window, turning my back. I couldn't look at him right now.

"You were—Niko, I—"

Reflected in the glass, I saw Adam rise and cross over to Niko to kneel at his second's feet. He took one of Niko's hands in his. "I am so sorry," Adam whispered. "Nikolai, I am so . . ."

I turned as Adam raised a hand and cupped Niko's face. Niko stared, eyes stony, muscles tight as he held himself utterly, perfectly still, as only the dead can. I watched in silence, holding in my own anger and feeling of betrayal.

Tucker sat nearly as still as Niko, only a twitch of his jaw disclosing the tight rein holding in his emotions, a scowl on his face as he studied Adam. We both knew that Adam and Niko had been lovers in the past, together for many decades, even centuries. Theirs was a bond that extended beyond sex: a blood oath from vassal—from trusted advisor and second—to king. In many ways, Adam not telling Niko was more of a betrayal than him not telling me. I was only his lover. From what I understood of the vampire world, Niko was as much Adam's heir as I was Gigi's . . . closer than kin. Closer than blood, as this was voluntary.

"I never meant . . ." Adam dropped his eyes and whispered, "For all that you know of me, all that we've been to each other, I swear . . . on my own grave and on the blood oath between us, I never intended to hurt you. I wanted to save you."

Niko started at Adam's words. "You knew?" His own voice was barely above a whisper. "When you found me later on, dying in the streets. You knew who I was?"

Adam nodded. "I'd known for years. I'd seen you once or twice, but you were too young, unfinished. I recognized you, but I never remembered from where. Only that I'd seen you."

I pressed my lips firmly together, trying to keep my reaction from becoming verbal. Adam had as much as admitted to stalking Niko in Niko's boyhood, similar to the way he'd sort of stalked me. I didn't want to jump to any conclusions, but the facts were pretty damning. This man, this vampire/Sidhe seemed to have a habit of stalking those who would become his lovers. Did he then glamour us? Was this some twisted, sick fantasy of his? How could I not have sensed any of this? I gripped my own arms in an effort to remain still, to not walk right out of this apartment and onto the next bus to somewhere else. Out of the corner of my eye, I could see Rhys' hand drop onto Niko's shoulder as Niko tried to deal with Adam's revelation.

"You took my best friend, my only friend," Niko whispered, anger laced with so much emotion I could nearly feel it. "And you stalked me as a boy. How could this not be bad? How could you have done this?"

I could barely see Adam's face, but I could hear the emotion in his voice. "I, too, was but a boy, Nikolai," he said. "So young, so . . . forgive me, please. I only knew to follow my father. To do as he did—I was still young myself. I never knew you were one of those boys. It wasn't until later, until I saw you dying, that I knew I must save you."

Niko's eyes were wet, tears glimmering, on the verge of falling. "Yet you never told me," he said, still whispering.

"And I shall regret it forever, love," Adam said and with a squeeze to Niko's hand, leaned forward and kissed his second's forehead. A benediction, perhaps? A plea for forgiveness, most certainly. Niko, to his credit, did not flinch. He remained stoic, emotions barely leashed.

"You are my heir, Nicholas. No matter whose bed you share, nor whom you love, you will always be my second." Adam nodded to Tucker, who, after a moment, nodded back. "I made some very regrettable decisions as a youth, and later on, when made vampire, I realized the errors and worked to correct them." He turned his head to look at me at that last.

"So, vampire?" I finally let the question loose. "How? Wasn't being Sidhe enough?"

Adam gave one last caress to Niko's cheek, then rose and came to me. Involuntarily, I stepped back, arms still wound tight around myself.

Adam opened his hands, a nonverbal plea for understanding. "I was content being who I was," he said. "My father, however, wanted to expand our territory—"

Rhys interrupted. "Your father. You said you represented his people. Who is your father, Adam?"

Thank his shapeshifting soul, my brother could have been a good trial lawyer, asking the right questions, the ones my currently befuddled brain couldn't quite frame. My synapses weren't snapping.

"The Unseelie king. He knew, even so many centuries ago, that the world was changing. New religions replacing old, most people no longer acknowledged us outside of plays or poems. The magick of Above was dying, becoming lost."

"He sold you to the vampires," Tucker said, his voice laced with an underlying growl.

Adam shook his head. "Not sold, so much as bargained with," he said. "Like the summit I attended some decades ago, we'd all met before—several times. My first was when Elizabeth had just become queen. My father brought me as my people met with representatives of all the courts: Seelie, vampire, wer, the various fey groups, your own Clan. At the time, and after much discussion, it sounded like a good idea to marry into the vampires, to join our peoples. That meant becoming one first." He looked at me as he finished. "I had no idea what that meant."

"What was the point?" Rhys asked. "As far as I can remember back—and I do remember that time—nothing ever came of that so-called summit. Wasn't the idea to try and connect all our people under one rule or a council of rulers?"

"It failed," Tucker said. "No one wanted to make concessions."

"But by then, I'd already been made vampire," Adam said. "My father, angry at the outcome, then cast me out to live with the vampire tribe. I had to make my way amongst a clan that, for all intents and purposes, despised my own."

"You seem to have managed that fairly well," I said, a note of sarcasm finding its way back into my voice. "You kept all of this from me because . . . ?"

Adam regarded me with a steady gaze. "Because I knew how you felt about the Sidhe," he said. "Despite the fact that my own Court was in no way your mother's people, I felt I could not share this information with you. I did not want to lose you." He looked back toward Niko, whose own expression had cleared somewhat. "Or you.

"Keira." Adam knelt at my feet, as he'd done with Niko. "You two are the most important people in all my life. I was frightened. And until you came fully into your Talents, I did not know you would be the Kelly heir. Without the heirship, you would never need to know the . . . politics involved. Then there was no time . . ."

Everything I knew about the Sidhe warred with what I knew about Adam. I studied his face, trying to figure out which version of Adam I believed. Or was it his face at all? Perhaps it was merely a mask. He had been a consummate actor since the moment we'd met in London. His performance in Texas went beyond Academy Award level. Johnny Depp was an amateur compared to Adam. Why not? The Sidhe were lords of deception and he was their prince. And centuries of self-preserving vampiric thespianism had protected not only himself but his tribe. Fooling me so completely was probably one of the least challenging roles he'd ever played.

On the one hand, other than his humongous whopper about him not knowing my supernatural connections, he'd never outright lied to me in the time we'd been together. Obfuscated, misdirected, yes, but nothing of consequence . . . until now.

And—he was right. Had I known he was Sidhe-made-vampire, I'd have probably gone running.

Would I still? I didn't know. This was Adam Walker. I cared for him. I loved him. I needed to think.

"Tucker, Rhys," I said to my brothers, as a thought occurred to me. "You both were there, you said, at the summit. Did you meet Adam then?"

Rhys shook his head in denial, as did Tucker. "I never met him," Rhys said. "Neither Tucker nor I were ever allowed into any of the meetings. We were there as muscle—sort of."

I frowned. "But neither of you are Marked," I said. "Gigi always Marks her Protectors."

"Marked?" Niko asked, his voice calmer than I expected after all these revelations.

"Each leader selects his or own guards, Protectors with a capital P," Rhys explained. "They are then given a special tattoo, a Mark infused with magick, binding them to that Clan chief until he or she steps down."

Niko nodded. "Like a blood oath, then. As we do ours." His eyes narrowed as he stared at Adam, who remained silent.

"Similar," Tucker said. "The design is always something particular to the chief. Rhys and I weren't officially at that summit, nor any of the others," he explained. "Gigi always told us we'd be wasted as just muscle. We were there to simply keep an eye out." He looked over at Adam. "I never saw any of the higher-ups. Never saw Adam. Gigi kept us out of the talks."

Ah, my great-great-granny, always up to something.

"So, now, any more revelations?" I asked the room in general. "Or have we done enough of that for the night?"

"Perhaps we should all retire early," Adam said. "I'm

sure Niko and Tucker would like to speak alone, as I would with Keira."

"Do you know about Daffyd, then?" I asked, not sure if I wanted to be alone with Adam yet.

Adam looked around the room. "Wait, I just realized. He is not with you."

"Yeah, not so much." I told him what had happened. "We've just given up the search and come back here."

"Disappeared, you said?" Adam looked thoughtful. "Sounds like he was Called."

"Called?"

"Normally, we—Sidhe—cannot just disappear. However, if another, more powerful Sidhe Calls us, it's as if we vanish from where we are and appear in the presence of the one who did the Calling. There must be another Sidhe in Vancouver."

"Other than you?" Tucker asked drily. "Perhaps the dark angel dressed in black that old Les saw was you?"

Adam scowled. "Who is this Les? I came directly here from the airport," he said. "I was never in town proper."

"Which reminds me," I said. "How the hell *did* you get in the building? Tucker couldn't even trigger the doors with the upgraded wards."

"Ever since this building was warded, I have had access," Adam said.

"Excuse me?" Yet another thing I didn't know.

"Keira, I ap—no, I do not wish to spend the evening continuing to apologize." Adam looked at each of us in turn. "I was given access to the wards some years ago," he said. "Although I've never been here prior to tonight. Your father explained this when I spoke to him."

I shook my head. "You know what? I'm not even going to bother asking anything else," I said. "This is getting to be more than ridiculous." I filed the new information away. Next time I talked to my dad, there'd be an extremely serious conversation. What the hell else had my family been doing behind my back?

"I'd like to ask something about Daffyd's disappearance, though," said Rhys. "How could another Sidhe have known of Daffyd's presence? You were all in a taxicab and Keira said he wasn't exactly broadcasting his presence."

"But this other Sidhe could have been," Adam said. "The music Keira heard was probably Sidhe music, cast by the other Sidhe. It would be natural for Daffyd to have answered the Call—subconsciously perhaps, but still, it would have been a flag to the other one."

"And he Called Daffyd?"

Adam nodded. "He did. Probably to find out who Daffyd was—in territory that he'd claimed, probably temporarily. I would have done something similar—if I still could."

If he could? That was a curious way of putting it. "What do you mean?"

"When I became vampire," he said, "at first, it seemed I lost much of my Sidhe ability. My father felt it was evident that merging our two peoples meant the loss of who I was as Sidhe. That was why he threw me out."

I blinked in reaction, then grasped his hand. "Like me," I said. "They didn't want me because I never showed any signs of magick."

Adam's thumb ran across my knuckles. "We are more alike than you think, Keira Kelly," he said, his voice nearly as quiet as when he'd been speaking to Niko. "Why don't we all get some rest and regroup later?"

"Yes," I said. "Let's. Niko, Tucker, you okay?"

They both nodded in agreement.

Rhys stood and stretched. “It’s nearly dawn,” he said. “I’m for getting a good day’s sleep.”

“Leave a note for Dad,” Tucker said as he and Niko headed to their bedroom. “He and Isabel might show up while we’re asleep.”

“Will do,” Rhys said. “Get some rest, you four. I’m sure you have a lot to discuss privately, but make sure to sleep.”

I looked at Adam, who rose and extended a hand to me. A lot to discuss, indeed. I’d forgiven him—mostly. Perhaps I should let this go. Yet, there were so many things I wanted to talk about. He’d nailed it. There was more similar to our backgrounds than different. Both of us born to fey royalty. Both of us rejects from the Sidhe; him from the Unseelie Court, me from the Seelie. He was now a king in his own right and I was heir to another leader. How much more convoluted could our lives get?

CHAPTER EIGHTEEN

"I DO LOVE YOU, Keira," Adam whispered, his mouth inches from my ear. "I still love Nikolai, and am beginning to love your brother."

"I'm not jealous, Adam," I said, turning to face him. We'd gotten ready for bed in silence, the both of us seeming reluctant to bring up the subject of Adam's background again. "I know you love Niko. He's part of your life and always will be. I'm fine with that."

"You are?"

I stroked his face. "I come from a long-lived family, Adam. We have as many ways to express love as has ever existed. We're not tied into some couple-centric human tradition. I've told you this before. I've not changed my attitude."

"Even though you know my secret?"

I regarded his face. The room was dark; light from a few candles played over his skin, the pale gleam reminding me now not only of his vampire nature, but of his Sidhe heritage as well. The Unseelie were often dark of hair with light eyes, as I was—although the Seelie, in general, tended to be fair-haired. I'd inherited my father's dark hair, one more difference for young Keira in a court of blonds.

Family on my father's side, like the Celts and Vikings they lived among centuries ago, were fair-skinned, as were the Sidhe on my maternal branch and Adam's own family. Many Clan members came from other parts of the world, from Africa to New Zealand, but this branch of the Kellys hailed from the colder northern areas.

"It is the last of your secrets, Adam?"

He nodded. "It is."

"Then, yes, I'm satisfied," I said. I didn't say: For now. Part of me remained wary. I'd never been able to trust the Sidhe. I wanted to trust Adam—before now, I'd trusted him implicitly. We'd fought. We'd disagreed on fundamental beliefs, but at the core of who I'd thought he was, was honesty and trust. No longer certain of this, I had to take a leap of faith, however difficult this was for me. "What happened is in the past and now we all know." I ran a hand through my hair. "Do you want to find the other Sidhe?"

"I do," Adam said. "If this is someone from my father's court, I want to know. No matter how long I've been gone, I am still my father's son. He threw me out, but never officially disowned me."

"So you are still his heir?" This certainly put a different spin on things. "Is this why you represented your father at the more recent summit?"

Adam sighed. "My father's whim dictates my status in that court. He claimed he could not be asked to show up for another one of Minerva's meetings and sent me in his place, despite the fact that I haven't set foot in Faery in many decades. Then, to my surprise, he came with an entourage after all. Showing me my place, you see. Officially, I am still considered heir—in disgrace, but heir nonetheless."

"If your father should step down . . ."

"Yes. Somehow, I would have to figure a way to handle the succession. And since I am still heir, I need to find the

Sidhe who is here. I'm reasonably confident I know why he is in Vancouver and why he was sent."

"Sent?"

"To greet the Kelly heir," he said. "You."

"Oh, bloody hell," I said. "Really? We joked about this earlier, but you think that's why?"

"My love, this is an understood requirement. When a new heir is recognized, representatives of each group come to pay their respects. I'm sure your Gigi sent the word out."

"But wouldn't you have gotten the word?"

He chuckled. "It's highly unlikely that she sent me a formal invitation," he said. "Since you were with me and I'm the catalyst for your Change. Minerva would have assumed I knew to come."

"But you didn't come until now," I said, still miffed that we'd had the "you're not coming" argument to begin with, if he'd intended to come all along. More of his great acting.

"You are correct," he said. "I honestly wasn't sure how much to tell you, or how even to tell you. If I'd said anything before you left, I was afraid you'd not go—or go forever." He kissed my hand. "Forgive me?"

"I already have," I said and kissed his hand in return. "I'm trying to be adult about all of this. Now that I am one."

"You are that," he said. "And I deeply appreciate it."

"Thank you," I said. "Now, let's get some sleep so we can work out what to do next."

Adam's eyes glittered green in the dim light. "Are you sure you want to sleep right away? Could I not persuade you otherwise?"

I stared into his eyes and smiled in answer.

He reached for me and I let myself be persuaded.

Adam leaned forward. "You had two visions, that clearly?"

We were all sitting around in the main living room, mostly because even though the condo was large, this was the biggest room in the place. Adam and I perched on one couch, Niko and Tucker on the other, Rhys in a chair—same as earlier, but all of us were a lot more relaxed. After some much-needed time reconnecting, Adam and I had slept several hours and regrouped with the others mid-afternoon. Thanks to the blackout draperies, both Niko and Adam could be comfortable.

When we'd woken, Adam had excused himself and gone to speak with Niko. Tucker, Rhys and I made a quick trip to Tim Hortons and brought back coffee and pastries.

By the time we got back, Adam and Niko were in the living room, both smiling. I could tell by Niko's body language that he'd come to terms with Adam's revelations.

Adam had asked for all the details of our recent searches for Daffyd. I'd supplied them. Then he'd asked about the visions.

I shrugged as I answered his question. "If that's what they were. I could be channeling someone's fantasy world."

"I doubt that, Keira. You've had plenty of visions before." Adam reminded me of recent and not-so-recent events involving my visions.

Rhys leaned into me, looking deep into my eyes. "Oh yeah? How come you never said anything about that? This is going to be fun. We'll point you in the direction and you can have a vision about—"

I pushed him away and settled into the corner of the couch. "Yeah, fun. Like the time you and Ianto shifted into wolfhounds and made me take you to Victoria and walk around so you could have women fawn all over you?"

Tucker burst into laughter, startling Niko, who stared at Rhys. Adam kept the same amused smile on his face.

"My brothers, Niko, may have been around for centuries, but that doesn't mean they've grown up." I patted Rhys on the head. "Don't try that again, bro. I'm not as naive as I once was." He laughed and gave me a hug. I'd spent hours walking around Victoria with the two of them in Irish wolfhound form one afternoon. I'd been bored stiff. Eventually, they'd tired of the game and accompanied me back to the car. We'd barely made the last ferry across.

"Damn, girl, I've missed you. I haven't had much of a chance to say that in the past couple of days."

I relaxed into his hug. Not being around my brothers was the only reason I regretted not living at Kelly Central. I had Tucker, sure, but one brother couldn't substitute for all six of them, plus my dad, my aunts and the cousins I'd grown up around. As much as I sometimes hated the overbearing presence of Family with a capital F, there was something to be said for a built-in support group.

Rhys let me go with another squeeze. "You think this Sidhe is doing something hinky out in the streets of Vancouver, yeah?" He addressed Adam, but I answered.

"Maybe," I said. "Adam, those folks last night talked about someone found dead in a hostel. But if it was the guy I envisioned, it seemed like he died of natural causes. Seemed peaceful . . . although . . ."

"Although?" Adam asked.

"Last night, you talked about the music I heard in the

taxi," I said. "In my vision, the old man heard music. I blew it off, thinking it was some dying-induced dream—some human idea of angelic choirs or something. I've escorted way too many Kelly family members to believe in that, but now that you explained it, I bet it was Sidhe music."

"Could be," Adam said. "But there's no need for one of my father's Court to kill a human. You mentioned there has been news of two homeless men recently being found dead in the area. There's been a lot of outsiders—musicians and such—coming in for that music festival you encountered. Events like this sometimes attract petty criminals, thieves. Maybe someone got carried away and accidentally hurt them."

"That doesn't make sense," I protested. "Why would anyone try to rob a homeless person?"

"Who knows why humans do anything, Keira?" Rhys answered. "Maybe they had some coin and they were easy marks. In any case, take a look at this." He shoved a copy of today's *Vancouver Sun* at me. "Look, here's an article about the Vancouver Police Department investigating that man's death as a drugs case and calling in the RCMP."

"I'd like to think I know a little something about humans, Rhys," I retorted after skimming the article. "After all, I grew up with them."

"But not with criminals, little sister," Tucker said. "Our brother and Adam are probably right. Daffyd taking Adam's energy was one thing, but the idea that a Sidhe, even from the Unseelie Court"—he acknowledged Adam with a nod and a smile—"is murdering humans? Highly unlikely. Besides, we're not investigating the murders. Just looking for Daffyd and the other Sidhe."

"Maybe. I don't like it. This is a nice city. There shouldn't be this type of murder here."

"It's a *city*, Keira," Rhys said. "Bad things happen here just like anywhere else. There are shootings, theft, drugs—Vancouver's not some shiny utopia, no matter how much you love it. Plus, it's not our turf, so we can only sit back and let the Horsemen handle it."

"Why on earth would the PD bring in the Mounties?" That wasn't normal. "I'd have thought that the Vancouver police would handle this."

"No idea why they called the RCMP," Rhys said. "All I know is what I read in that article." He looked at me as if a thought suddenly occurred to him. "This isn't some silly excuse to delay the inevitable, is it?"

"To what?" I stared at my brother, who crossed his arms and stared right back. The other three echoed his stare.

"Delay seeing our matriarch," Rhys suggested. "With your Unseelie vampire prince in tow? Now that the weather's clearing, there's nothing to stop us from either driving up or calling for a plane."

"Ha funny ha, Rhys. I'm not avoiding anyone. The weather might be clearing up by the enclave, but I've not gotten any phone calls yet—not even from Dad or Isabel—so as far I know we're here for whatever the duration is."

I tried to remain indignant, but staring down both my brothers and Niko was an entirely futile undertaking. "Okay, okay, maybe I'm not exactly sorry no one's called, nor that Dad and Isabel haven't shown." Indignity turned to defiance. "I hadn't consciously thought of that, but yeah, I'll grant you that avoiding Gigi legitimately for a couple of days—especially considering what Adam's now told us—I'd like nothing better. It's just . . ." Damn it, could I be more lame? "I kind of have a feeling." Sheesh. Lame times a thousand. I really couldn't describe it well, it was sort of . . . *something* . . . I'd had visions, heard Sidhe music when no one else did. I *needed* to follow this through.

"A feeling?" Adam stood and approached me. "Are you having another vision, then?"

"No visions, not now," I said. "But I hate leaving this unfinished—Daffyd out there who knows where, another Sidhe responsible, a couple of dead homeless guys right in the area where we think Daffyd and this Sidhe might be . . ."

"Murder's not right." Niko put in his two cents from the couch, where he'd made himself at home. "But that doesn't mean there's anything other than human greed involved."

"You're correct there," I agreed, however reluctantly. I really hadn't seen or heard anything that led me to believe there was more to the murders than met the normal, nonsupernatural eye or ear here. Nothing paranormal or outside the realm of human actions. Maybe Rhys was right and my subconscious was trying to come up with another excuse not to go the enclave right away. I wanted at least a full day or two with Adam to process everything before I faced my great-great-granny.

"Rhys, we should really try to see if we can find out about Gideon's status and fill folks in on Daffyd and all," Tucker said, shooting a quick look at me. Damn it, now *he* was being right, too. Despite Isabel's assurances, we really needed an update about Gideon. Even though no one had called us, the phones could possibly be working.

"I'm sorry, I—"

"Never mind, Keira," Tucker said gently. "I know you

really want to put this out of your mind and trust Isabel's assessment of the situation. I'm not blaming you for not asking. Just wanting to know, that's all."

"Oh, damn. I meant to tell you. It's okay," Rhys answered with a sheepish look. "I talked to Ianto. Dad and Isabel arrived and told him to relay the message and that it's fine to stay. They're handling Gideon."

"They, huh, what?" I couldn't have heard that right. Dad and Isabel were at the enclave? "What happened to Dad and Isabel driving here from Seattle? To someone calling us when it was okay to fly there? I don't get it, Rhys—why hasn't anyone called to tell us we could come on up?"

"Ianto called before you guys were awake," Rhys said. "Sorry. I should have totally gotten you up so you could talk to him or Dad. I didn't get a chance to talk to Isabel at all but I could hear Dad in the background mumbling something about 'the boy' and having had to change plans. When I asked about it, Ianto just laughed and said Dad had been pacing around the place for a couple of hours and not talking. Isabel went directly to Gigi and the two of them were still sequestered."

"Now what?" I asked.

"No idea, sis, but my twin relayed Gigi's message."

"Which was . . ." I prompted my brother.

"To stay put."

"You're having me on, right?"

"Toss me one of those glasses, eh, brother?" Rhys waved a hand in the direction of the highball glasses adorning the side table next to Tucker. My other brother complied and Rhys poured himself a couple of fingers from a decanter. I could scent the single malt whisky's distinctive aroma even from across the room.

"Lagavulin?" I asked.

"Yeah, sixteen-year-old," Rhys replied. "Want one?"

"Damn right," I said, and grabbed a glass for myself. "Anyone else?"

Nods from everyone.

"Well then, whisky all around, brother." I definitely needed strong spirits with this news. What in the world was my dear granny playing at? First she tells Isabel to come get me right away because Gideon is dying. My father and aunt were headed here, but instead, drove directly out to the enclave without even calling us. Now, I'd basically been told, oh, hey, no rush, go ahead and stay at the condo. This did not compute.

I settled back in the wide leather couch, sipping my whisky. We were all quiet, no one speaking for several minutes. I studied Rhys, who was still watching me over his own glass. He was definitely amused. His mouth twitched as he raised his glass. "*Sláinte*, dear sister and heir apparent."

"Fuck you very much, dear brother," I teased back. "I'll give you good health, but can the heir apparent shite, okay?"

"Not enjoying it, then?" Rhys grinned.

"It's been all of a few days, Rhys. Not much to enjoy . . . except . . ." I smiled as I remembered Tucker's and my sojourn as wolves the other afternoon.

"I taught her wolf, brother," Tucker said. "She enjoyed it."

"Ah, and well you should have, sweetheart," Rhys said. "Wolf is my favorite shape."

I raised my own glass. "Then to the wolves. Brothers, Niko, Adam."

The men raised their own glasses to me. "To the wolves." We all sipped, enjoying the peaty smoke flavor of the best whisky in existence.

"So, seriously, Rhys," I said, putting down my glass. "Gigi's okay with us staying here?"

"Absolutely," he said. "Seeing as how she'll be here soon."

I knocked over the cut-crystal glass, spilling what was left of my drink on the table.

Oh. Bloody. Hell.

CHAPTER NINETEEN

"YOU DID *NOT* say that." I bent down to mop up the spill. "You are totally kidding me, right?"

"'Fraid not, Keira," he answered. "Look, it's going to be fine. She's meeting you here instead of the enclave, yeah?" He took another sip of whisky, then refilled my now empty glass. "Saves you a trip and you can enjoy the luxuries of Vancouver longer—and we can do another reccy for the Sidhe."

Frowning, I bent my head to my glass and inhaled the aroma of the Lagavulin as I tried to marshal my thoughts. Was this one of Gigi's power trips? But no, the mountain was indeed coming to me, so what was her game? Our matriarch was forever playing them. I couldn't recall anything she'd ever done that was free of her unique flavor of gamesmanship. But this time her moves had left me beyond confused. It was as if she was kicking over the chessboard and resetting the pieces. About the time the game started making sense, she'd kick it over again. "I don't know, Rhys. Why would she come here? Did you tell her about Daffyd?"

"I didn't," Rhys said. "Wasn't sure if that was a good idea or not. All I said was that we were spending time here and were looking forward to seeing her. I could've told Ianto the truth, but I didn't want him to get in the middle of an explanation he couldn't handle."

"She may still know," Tucker reminded me gently. "She

is our matriarch, our kin—and as the Clan chief, she's got the same Talents you inherited . . . with several centuries of practice."

He was right. I should have known. Gigi wasn't omniscient, but she'd known I was Changing before I did and had sent Tucker to me. Why on earth couldn't she know what was going on here? I sighed a deep and utterly exhausted sigh. "I need to process this a while," I said, looking at the three men. "I think I need some air." I got up and headed for the door, intent on taking a long walk before dark. I wanted to think.

"I'll come with you," Rhys said. He tossed Adam a look I couldn't decipher. "We won't be long."

NEITHER RHYS nor I spoke until we got outside. It was sometime in the late afternoon, but I had no idea of the actual time. The city buzzed with its usual quiet Vancouver version of a workday heading toward rush hour. Downtown tended to lose momentum early during the weekdays, workers bicycling, busing or driving home politely winding their way through the streets. We ambled in the direction of Gastown, my brother matching his longer strides to mine. I really did want to go back over to where we'd seen all the people earlier, to poke around, take my mind off things. I said as much to Rhys, who, to my surprise, agreed.

"Maybe we can stop by the music festival. According to the *Sun*, there's nothing formal going on today or tonight, just folks gathering as they arrive in Vancouver. Impromptu jam sessions and such. Like home." The corners of Rhys' mouth turned up in a fond smile.

"Like the home I was glad I left," I said.

"I meant our home, you dolt." Rhys cuffed my head in a brotherly gesture of amusement. "Not Wales."

As we got closer to the park, we began to see more pedestrians than usual—musicians, their families, perhaps, or companions. Many of them carrying some sort of instrument case, most of them dressed outside what the average North American would wear unless they were appearing in a play or going to a Renaissance fair, and I wasn't sure you counted as average if you did either of those. I'd wondered why the festival was being held at Victory Square instead of the much larger Stanley Park, but a quick perusal of the *Sun* earlier explained it. Some movie company was using the larger location for a shoot. Plus, according to the write-up in the paper, this festival normally only attracted a small crowd. As I watched the increasing numbers of creatively dressed pedestrians, I wondered what the reporter considered small.

"We saw a lot of these people earlier," I said to Rhys. "A bit weird, really, it's like a gathering of the Sidhe, except . . ."

"What?" Rhys asked and moved closer to me. We kept walking, but slowed our pace to more of a leisurely stroll.

"Except they all feel human—not that I've tried to sense them." I tried to explain. "Things are more intense since . . . I've had to reinforce my shielding. More so since I got here."

"You've not really been around many people since you Changed," Rhys said. "At least many people where you could let go."

"Not bloody likely to have been," I said, feeling my temper rise for no real reason. "I Changed all of four days ago, Rhys, it's not like I've been on some cozy tourist excursion."

He put up his hands in a conciliatory gesture. "Okay,

okay, Keira, no sense raising your hackles. I was—"

"I know, I know, damn it." I ducked my head, embarrassed that I'd almost bitten off his head—metaphorically. "Sorry. It's been difficult, what with Daffyd having gone AWOL and now Adam being here. Not what I expected, really."

He threw an arm around me. "I'm sure it has, little sister. Now, what say we go find ourselves some music and let some of this energy loose?"

"Excellent idea," I agreed. We increased our pace and headed in the direction of Victory Square. Rhys, like Tucker, was one of my favorite brothers. I'd seen so little of him over the past few years. He and his twin, Ianto, spent a great deal of time at our British Columbia enclave and in Vancouver, even when the bulk of the Kellys had been in Texas. They loved the weather here as did their current more-or-less spouse, Adela. Several of their sons and daughters (by much earlier alliances) lived in the Fraser Valley. Rhys and Ianto often split their time at the condo, at the enclave and with Adela. She wasn't a Kelly cousin by birth, but had come from a distant Clan branch in Spain some century or so ago. She'd hooked up with my brothers around seventy years back, and they'd been a happy sometimes trio ever since.

We walked by a souvenir shop, its doors open, a silly fake moose dressed in red Mountie serge posed in the window, the store full of shoppers. "Hey, is Gareth still up in Inuvik?" I asked, the moose reminding me of Rhys' youngest, who'd Changed twenty some years ago. A weather watcher, he lived near Inuvik, in the Northwest Territories, an Inspector with the RCMP detachment there. I never learned how he'd managed to fool modern medical technology and go through Depot to become a

Mountie. I'd asked Rhys that once. He'd just said that Gigi had arranged everything. At twelve, I'd been too young and too frightened of her to ask any more questions. In my head, Gigi had somehow bought out the RCMP and was controlling them, too. Hell, for all I knew, that was true fact.

"He transferred to North Van a while back," Rhys said. "Haven't talked to him in ages, though. He's always busy."

"You ever find out how he passed all the physical exams and such—for the RCMP?"

"Still no clue, sis," Rhys replied. "I think some things are better left as mysteries."

"You don't think she's bribed the RCMP at the very top levels?" I wondered in hushed tones, the awe I'd felt as a child creeping back in.

Rhys let out a belly laugh. "My brilliantly wonderful little sister," he said as he pulled me into a crushing hug. "I really don't think that's possible, but I'm sure if anyone could do it, Gigi could."

I was enjoying my brother's company. My new Talents were still so raw, so unrefined, I could feel them lurking just below my skin. With the few non-family members I'd been around since my Change, I'd kept myself under tight control, shielding as if I was a nuclear bunker and my shield was the only thing between me and a worldwide holocaust. I was still too new at this to feel entirely comfortable around anyone but family. Adam and Niko had crossed the line into family by dint of having been there when I Changed. Daffyd was family by blood, though our kinship was strained. Still, his energies didn't disrupt mine. Unlike . . .

"What was that?" I started at a brush of something . . .

energy? A wisp of thought, of feeling slid past me. Other. A shimmer and then nothing.

"What was what?" Rhys immediately stood in front of me, scanning the area for potential trouble. "What did you see?" We weren't at Victory Square yet, but a few blocks away. Nothing but storefronts and a rather run-down hostel across the street. There were a few men standing in front of the place as if on guard, but I could tell they were human. Whatever I'd felt had brushed by me, gone past in the direction we'd just come from.

"Feel," I said. "Other, something different. A not-human. Headed back that way." I cocked my head to indicate direction. I wanted to keep a low profile.

"Shields up, sis," Rhys said. "Let me scan."

I nodded and held still, letting him do this thing. Wolf, or hound, he might be, but Rhys always had a touch of sensitivity, a trait that had allowed him and his twin to get away with their crazy antics more times than not.

Rhys dropped out of sentinel mode and turned to me with a frown. "Are you sure you felt something? I'm getting nothing but human."

I shook my head. "Not sure. It was too quick, like a breath of air passing me." I looked around, seeing nothing more than the three men in front of the building, a small group of folksy hippie types and some locals, probably residents of the hostel, huddled in a group, heads bent, several of them in what looked like intense discussion. It occurred to me that this wasn't standard behavior. "Hey, Rhys, look—what do you think is going on over there?"

Before my brother could answer, a man stepped up next to me, his attention focused on the gathered group. He was tall, thin, narrow-shouldered; a shock of dark hair topped his black-on-black attire; slung on his back was a battered leather guitar case. Next to him, a broader man stood quietly, a frown marring his face. Thinning brown hair fell back from his forehead. He was dressed in jeans and a hoodie and carried a bodhrán. The first man sighed and ran a hand through his messy hair.

"Excuse me, sir," I began and stepped closer to them. "Could I ask if you know what's going on?"

The first man looked at me, his frown deepening as he obviously tried to figure out if I was some sort of cop or reporter. Seemingly satisfied, he answered me. "Someone else dead," he said. "This time at the hostel, in one of the rooms. Wasn't from Van." He looked at his companion. "Rodney and me, we tend to stay at the hostel for the festival."

Rodney spoke up, his own voice carrying a note of weariness. "This is the third one," he said. "Two over the past few days. John and I don't feel so safe anymore." I guessed John was the name of the first man we spoke with.

"Dead how?" Rhys asked. "Murder?"

"That's just it," John said. "Police don't know much right now. Not really sure they care 'bout us. They haven't even come to tape off this place yet." His disgust was evident in his tone. "Nothing but a bunch of street folk, us. No autopsies back on the other guys. No signs of anything weird. Just, you know . . ."

"Dead," Rodney butted in. "Nobody knows anything. Could be us there . . . dead."

I guessed that the two of them couldn't afford safer lodging, studying their clean, but shabby clothing. Transients, drifters, musicians the world over.

"Drugs?" I ventured a guess.

"Maybe with this guy," John said. "Didn't know him. Saw him earlier, though, over at the park. We jammed a bit."

Rodney's head shook in vehemence. "Not in Sidney's case."

"Sidney?" I asked.

Before either Rodney or John answered, Rhys nudged me. "I'm going to take a look around."

"Yeah, I'll stay here," I said.

"Right then." He skirted the small group of people huddled at the corner lamppost, and crossed the street. I turned back to Rodney and John, who seemed to be conducting a wordless conversation, all eyebrows and forehead furrows. Rodney's mouth suddenly dipped on one side, slanting disapproval. John tucked his hands in his jeans' pockets, shoulders hunched.

"Didn't know the first guy," John said. "Some older guy, regular during spring and summer, they said. This new dead guy was a visitor, too. But Sidney, though—"

"Sidney," I cut in to clarify, "Sidney was . . . ?"

"Yeah, right. We go way back. I've known him—"

"Knew," interrupted Rodney softly.

"Knew," John repeated, tossing a worried glance at his friend. "Sidney was a good guy. Clean. Sober. He had one of those twenty-year chips."

"Twenty-year chips?" I didn't know what he was talking about.

"AA. He always kept it in his right pocket. His lucky charm. Used to say it reminded him of where he'd been." John shuffled his feet and looked down at the ground. "He wasn't a bad guy, miss." John raised his head and looked directly at me, the first time since we'd begun to talk. His eyes were a lovely clear hazel green, no sign of drugs or alcohol abuse in him. In fact, neither of them smelled or felt as if they were users. "He played the clarinet," explained John. "In his heyday, he was in an orchestra. Back when dance clubs meant suits and fancy dresses. Fell to the drink in the late seventies, Sidney told me. Disco drove him to drink."

I held my burst of laughter inside as I realized that John was dead serious. He smiled at me, a sheepish look on his face.

"Oh, I know what it sounds like. Dumb thing to say, but for Sidney, it was the honest truth. He drank himself out of a family, home and nearly out of his music. Rodney 'n me found him a couple of years ago over near Simon Fraser, playing for coins and damn well determined to stay sober. Three of us sort of made an informal trio. We'd meet up here for the music, then go our separate ways until the next time. Sidney worked part-time up at the Tim Hortons and at a couple of the hotels when they needed labor. He made enough to live in a small place."

"So why was he in the hostel?" I found myself getting more and more curious. Not that any of this had anything to do with me, but it was certainly keeping me from dwelling on my own situation. Besides, I liked these guys. Many of my own family were musicians, and despite my banter with Rhys earlier, music did have a more positive association than the Sidhe. I'd enjoyed clubbing in London and going to as many folk music festivals as I could find during my time in England. There was very little music I didn't enjoy.

"Old times' sake," Rodney replied. "He liked staying here during the festivals instead of traveling back and forth from Burnaby."

"So what do you think killed him?" The question burst out of me before I could temper it. "Sorry, I mean . . ."

"No worries, miss," John said. "I know you're just interested. Not creepy ghoulish like them over there." He nodded his head, indicating four obnoxious tourists at the corner. They'd pushed past the small group of the homeless and were trying to crowd even closer to where the men barred the door of the hostel, self-policing, it seemed, until the officials could arrive. One of the women was yelling at the other one to get a picture already.

I sighed. "Tourists."

"Yeah, they're a lot of trouble, even though they give good coin." John laughed, showing even white teeth. His eyes crinkled in amusement as he took a proper good look at me. "You're not from around here, but you're not a tourist."

I studied him back, wondering where that insight had come from. "Nope, I don't live here now, but my family owns a place here. They've got some land up country a ways. Been there a while."

"I figured something like that," he said. "I'll answer your question."

"About Sidney?"

"Yup. Not drugs. Not drink. Maybe just old age." Rodney guffawed at this.

"You don't think so?" I asked.

"If it's just old age," he replied, "then why all the fuss?" He waved a hand toward the crowd. "It's only another old, dead homeless guy, nothing for real people to worry about. Why call in the Horsemen?"

"They've called in the Mounties?" I asked to see what they knew. So far, nothing I'd heard led me to believe the auspices of the RCMP would be needed. That said, I had to admit to myself that I didn't have much of an idea of what *would* constitute a case needing said force. The RCMP often had jurisdiction when there was no local police, but that wasn't the case here. Vancouver had a police force. It seemed odd to me. Perhaps the police knew a hell of lot more than was being said publicly.

Rodney scowled. "That's what I heard. Sidney would've liked it, though—bringing in the Horsemen for him."

"Maybe they do suspect a drugs case," I said. "Otherwise, why bring in the RCMP?"

"That, dear cousin, is exactly why I'm here."

I whirled to see Gareth Evans Kelly behind me in his everyday uniform, a twinkle in his deep blue eyes—a color very close to the blue of his tie.

CHAPTER TWENTY

"WHAT THE—"

"Gareth!" Rhys, who'd just walked up beside me, ignored my splutters and swept the man up in a hug. "It's been how long?"

"Much too, Rhys," Gareth answered with a smile. "Why are you two here? I mean, last time I saw you, Keira, you were in London, partying up a storm. What was that—eight, nine years ago?"

"Long story, neph—um, cousin," I stumbled on the words, remembering the two human men beside us. It wouldn't do to call Gareth nephew, though that's what he was, despite the fact that he was at least three decades older than me and looked it with his silvering hair (courtesy of discreet dye jobs in order to look more mature). He was, after all, my brother's son. "So you're here about this?" I waved over at the crowd.

"I am," he replied. "Was all nice and snug in bed yesterday when I got the call that there'd been another death in the same place. I hightailed it here. Been talking to people since about four or so, haven't even settled in somewhere to stay." He sighed in exasperation. "Great folks the local PD, but sometimes, when it's these guys"—he motioned toward the obvious residents of the hostel—"the communication isn't exactly the best. Folks tend to respect this uniform, even though it's not the serge. Was hoping I'd get more out of people, though. No one seems to have seen anything."

"So why did the Vancouver PD bring you all in, then?" I asked. At least now, I could get an answer from the Horseman's mouth.

Gareth looked pointedly at me. Oh, yeah, civilians next to us.

"Why don't I catch up to you later? I need to do some more work. You at the condo?"

"Yes," Rhys said. "Do you need a place to crash or you going back to your place in North Van?"

"I'd love to not have to drive back and forth during the investigation. It's not horribly far, but plenty painful in rush hour, especially with all the damned construction on the bridges. I'll go on over to the condo when I'm done here."

I turned to the musicians. "John, Rodney. Thank you for putting up with me and my questions." The two men nodded.

"Our pleasure, miss," John tipped an imaginary hat, his eyes twinkling. "I believe we'll be going now." They turned in unison and walked away.

"THEN WHAT do you think we should do, Keira?"

Tucker and I stood at the windows, taking in the spectacular view from the penthouse. The city's lights began to blink on as the evening skies darkened. Rhys had disappeared, probably to his bedroom. I didn't blame him. Our innocuous chat was starting to become a Kelly confrontation and that wasn't ever comfortable for the spectators, even if they themselves were Kellys. Rhys knew better than to stick around. Tucker and I rarely butted heads, but when we did . . .

"The more I think on this, the more I hate the fact that

Daffyd and some unknown Sidhe are wandering around Vancouver. We need to keep searching."

"For pity's sake, Keira, don't get your knickers in a twist. And be quiet, you'll wake Adam and Niko. They went back for a nap." Tucker was near growling at this point, more than frustrated, he was pissed off at me. "Daffyd may be just this side of naive, but he's an adult—in fact, he's centuries old—more than capable of making his own damned decisions and doing whatever the hell he damn well pleases. If he wants to vanish and wander the city, he can. We're not his jailers, or his babysitters. He asked neither for Sanctuary nor companionship. You've got to cut him some slack, sis."

"I do have some responsibility here, Tucker."

"Right. If he's gotten himself into trouble, then we'll go get him out. It's our way."

"We have to find him first. Plus," I added, "that's not the only thing I'm worried about. He's a Sidhe, dear brother, and lives off the energy of humans. Setting him loose in a city of nearly six hundred thousand people? It's like releasing a hungry lion in a herd of staked deer. Do you want to be responsible for that? Some unknown person's death, because we couldn't keep an eye on one Sidhe?"

"Oh, for . . ." Tucker took a deep breath before he continued. "Keira, Daffyd—your family on that side—are Seelie Court. Draining humans is *not* what they do."

"Then how about what happened in Texas, with what he did to the men Pete Garza would bring him? What he did to Adam?" I had more or less accepted, under the circumstances, Daffyd's actions, but it wasn't as if I could condone him doing the same thing here. And evidence was mounting that someone was up to no good—whether Daffyd or the mystery Sidhe.

Tucker's tone gentled. "You really don't get it, do you?" He seemed genuinely puzzled. "C'mon, let's go sit down. I think I've got a lot of explaining to do."

"Explaining?" Was every person in my family keeping secrets? I let my brother lead me over to the kitchen table. He went to the cupboard and pulled out a bag of chips and a fresh jar of salsa, then grabbed a couple of beers out of the fridge. I smiled despite myself. Even in Canada, Kelly boys could always find Texas-style food.

"What are you trying to tell me, Tucker?" I asked as I watched him scoop up some salsa and begin to chow down. "That what Daffyd and his companions did in Texas was different? That accepting humans who were given as payment—appeasement—from someone who held their lives as less valuable than a cockroach doesn't count?" I pulled my knees up to my chest and hugged them, full of confusion, anger and the need to go back out to talk to Gareth, to somehow make sense of the emotions warring inside of me. I'd promised Tucker I'd hear him out, though, so I needed to get a grip.

"I don't know what Daffyd said to you, or how he explained the lives he took recently, Keira, but his being in Texas—"

"Was because of me," I interrupted.

"Damn it, let me finish," Tucker said. "You're making this more difficult than it has to be."

I bit my lip against the automatic sarcasm threatening to leap out of my mouth.

"Sidhe have to absorb energy to live. In their homeland, where you were born and used to live, they get much of it from the earth around them. It is Home, it sustains them. When they are taken from there for any length of time, they begin to fade." My brother shook his head, instinctively knowing that I was about to interrupt again. "Let me finish," he repeated firmly.

I nodded and tried to pay attention. He washed a chip down with a swig of beer, then continued.

"I don't condone what happened, but from what I know about your cousin, what I've seen of him so far, he only did what he did to survive. You were a *geas*, your well-being his imperative. I know you don't like that, but it's a fact. No one blames you or holds you responsible. It is what it is."

I waited a moment to see if Tucker would continue. Before I spoke, I took a deep, calming breath. I didn't want to start a shouting match. Tucker knew how much I felt the responsibility. "I know that what happened to Adam was a result of Daffyd reaching out blindly to a source of energy that sustained him. He'd had no idea. I've forgiven him for that."

"But . . ." Tucker motioned for me to continue.

I bit my lip again, trying to choose my words carefully. "But . . . I lived among them, Tucker. I was a child, yes, but I remember the cruelty, the abandonment. They treated me—" My voice broke. I hated thinking about then, about . . .

Tucker reached over and put his arm around my shoulders. "That was a long time ago, sis, and you're with us now."

I nodded, fighting back tears, the old emotions welling up in me, past the walls I'd erected in front of them. "Damn it, Tucker. I hate this."

"What?"

"Feeling like this. All this disruption—and Adam being Sidhe? I forgave him for not telling me. I get it, I do, intellectually, but—"

"Yeah, I know. I feel the same way about his revelation.

Niko's still barely holding it together. They talked, but . . ." Tucker shook his head. "Honestly, Keira, if it hadn't been for your relationship with Adam, he'd probably be a former vampire at this point."

I could tell he was about as far from kidding as possible. "Yeah, I know," I said. "Don't think I don't appreciate it. I'm not so sure of how this is all going to work out, either. I'm none too excited about Gigi coming into the mix in a couple of days."

"Agreed," Tucker said. "She doesn't bother me so much as she does you, but damn." He patted my arm and shot me a smile. "Don't worry, sis, I'm here. Niko's got your back, too. So does Rhys."

"Thanks, bro. Gratefully appreciated." I smiled back at him. "Sorry I'm so . . . bugfuck emotional, I guess."

"No worries, Keira. It's all pretty normal. You're likely to be an iota more . . ." He paused. I looked up at his face. He, too, was struggling for words. "More volatile?"

"Oh, great, exactly what I need," I said. "So Changing brings mood swings? How bloody wonderful."

Tucker shook his head. "Not so much Change itself, but your particular one. Your body's going through all sorts of adjustment now. It's not only for political reasons that heirs are brought back to the family fold, Keira. It's a hell of a lot easier on you to be around family, to be with people who know you and can help you through the next few months or so."

"Months?" I pushed away from him, nearly shrieking the word.

"Whoa, hold on there," he said. "I'm just speculating on the time frame."

I narrowed my eyes at him. "It damn well better not be months," I threatened. "And you've changed the subject.

So why shouldn't I be worried about Daffyd loose in Vancouver again?"

"Because, little sister, there is a lot of native energy in a city," Tucker answered. "A—Daffyd recently topped up, so to speak, so he's not likely to need to replenish his resources anytime soon. And B—a city is full of energy—from the people, from the vehicles, the electrical grid. All sorts of ways that Daffyd can top off the tank if need be, without resorting to people."

"He can do that?"

"Seelie Court," Tucker said. "Although . . . the Unseelies do that as well, they just, once in a great while, prefer humans."

"I thought Unseelie Sidhe were no more evil than Seelie, just had a looser moral code," I said.

"Exactly," Tucker agreed. "If presented with loose city-type energy versus a fresh, sacrificial human, Daffyd—any Seelie, for that matter—would usually choose the former. Unseelie? It's a toss-up."

This certainly put a different take on a lot of things I'd thought over the years. I'd known about the other side of the coin, the Unseelie Court, because there was nothing the Sidhe liked more than to talk politics and intrigue. But I'd been a child and the only thing I'd gleaned was that the Unseelie were other, kind of like me. So at first, I'd sort of identified with them. It wasn't until much later in a human school, when we'd done a semester on legends and myths, that I'd discovered that the Unseelie Court was seen to be Dark. Of course, this was Western society's human interpretation, where Dark meant not Christian, not Jewish, but Other. I had a feeling that the poets of earlier centuries imbued the Seelie Court with angelic qualities and assumed that they were Good with a capital G, with all the weight of Biblical definitions behind it. I knew better. I'd asked my Aunt Jane, who filled me in on reality. Good and evil meant nothing to Faery. Their mores and ethics resembled Western humanity's versions about as much as I resembled a stoat. We both had four appendages, two eyes, two ears and a mouth. After that, not much in common. Of course, the same could be said about the Kelly Clan and our sister Clans around the world. Our very natures precluded us from following the same code and standards as our distant human cousins. We were, however, closer to humans than the Sidhe were. After all, we lived among them. The Sidhe, both Courts, had chosen to remain separate. The taint of the Unseelie Sidhe, though, had lingered, and my aunt had told me how they weren't to be trusted, even less so than my mother's family.

"Keira? You okay in there?" Tucker knocked lightly on the side of my head, an old joke. I'd often gone "into my head" as a young teen, losing myself for hours thinking and dreaming.

"I'm good," I said. "Sorry. Just had to work this out. I'll take your word on it for now about Daffyd, but you've got to promise me something."

"If I can," he said.

"If we find him, would you keep an eye on him? Please, for me. I'm still not all that comfortable around him."

Tucker nodded. "Rightly so," he said. "He's not exactly a serial killer, but neither is he harmless. I mean, look at me." He spread his arms. "On the outside, I'm just a guy. On the inside . . ." He gave me a feral grin, only a faint echo of the Berserker I knew lurked beneath; the predator wolf shape he adored.

"True that." I smiled at my brother, a sense of relief taking over the uneasiness. "I don't think anything . . .

untoward is going to happen, but still, I'd like to make sure we keep tabs on him." Assuming we found him. If we didn't, what then? I had no freaking clue.

"You all done yelling in here?" Rhys poked his head out from around the corner.

I gave him an abashed smile. "Coast is clear. No more yelling."

"Great," he said as he plopped down on the chair next to Tucker and grabbed the beer I hadn't even begun to drink. "So, what's the game plan?" he asked and took a deep gulp of the brew.

"Game plan?"

"Yeah, bro, what game?" Tucker asked.

"Well, it's not likely that my son the Mountie gets called in to investigate suspicious deaths of the city's homeless population," Rhys said wryly. "Gareth usually handles much wider-ranging cases. Reality being what it is, it's rare for homeless victims to get this kind of attention. So, what's really going on? I mean, you did want something to distract you, Keira. Here's a prime opportunity. Family's involved now." My brother grinned like a loon. I grinned back.

This certainly was an opportunity for distraction. Now that Gareth was investigating, we could do some semi-legitimate poking about of our own while we waited for Gigi to make her royal appearance. I recognized this was nothing more than said distraction and that Rhys was reaching out to me in his own way. Because honestly? What good would it do us to "help" the RCMP? To be perfectly fair, if it weren't for the fact I was here in Vancouver and desperate to think about something other than my upcoming meeting with Gigi, I'd have been quite content to spend the next couple of days spending time with Adam, shopping, reading and doing a little sightseeing. Now that Tucker had convinced me my concerns about the possibility of a murderous Sidhe were misplaced and reminded me that Daffyd could, and probably was, taking care of himself, the reports of the murders would have been nothing more than something I heard about in a newscast . . . if even then. I wasn't the newscast-watching type.

Tucker shook his head and *tsked* at us.

"What?" I said, every inch of me trying to radiate indignity.

"Look at the two of you," he laughed. "It's like someone's given you this fascinating puzzle to solve, a new toy to play with."

I stuck my tongue out at him. "Yeah, and like you're not as interested as we are. Your inner child is squealing, 'ooh, shiny.' "

Tucker threw his head back and laughed. "So right, dear sister, so right."

Niko appeared then, confusion written on his face. Poor guy wasn't used to all these Kellys, yelling at each other one minute, and laughing like idiots the next.

"What is she right about?" Niko asked with a yawn.

"Looks like we're going to help Gareth solve some murders, *cariad*."

INTERLUDE

Death

"DEAD, DEAD?" The tall woman hunching over her cigarette asks the man in the wheelchair. Her eyes dart back and forth, watching, observing, lighting on nothing, no one specific. She's a denizen of the streets, like the rest of them, more comfortable when she's not in the middle of such commotion.

It's gone full dark now, but the brightness of the streetlights chase most of the shadows away from the sidewalks and main walkways. The Muni really likes to keep this section well-lit for all them tourists. Got so a girl couldn't find a good dark spot to hide in no more.

Her companion nods at her question, his wild gray-brown hair obscuring his face. He brushes back the hair and takes a long drag of his own cigarette, the cracked leather of his fingerless gloves reflecting his social status as much as the company he keeps. The foot of one leg is clad in a beat-up sneaker; his other leg ends at the knee, the trouser leg pinned neatly under the stump.

The man's raspy cough turns into a hacking fit. The woman bends over him, a surprisingly clean handkerchief at the ready. He grabs it from her and wipes his mouth. "Thanks, Marla."

"It's getting better," she says as she tucks the man's blanket more securely around him. "You've got to stay out

of the wind, Ernie. Make sure you keep on getting better, yeah?"

"I know, I know," he says in a mutter and waves away her ministering hands. "Got some meds from the walk-in clinic," he wheezes around another puff of smoke. "I'm handling it."

"So you were saying . . ." The woman presses him to finish what he'd started to say.

He peers up at her, dark eyes glittering through the wild fringe of hair. "Over there." He motions with his cigarette toward the building cordoned off with crime-scene tape. "One guy. Didn't know him. Saw him, though. Last night and night before. Looked like a hippie."

"Don't we all." It isn't a question. Marla laughs the croak of a longtime smoker. "I mean look at us." She twirls, arms outstretched, fingers elegantly pointed as if she were dancing. Layers of draped shawls, sweaters and at least two skirts on top of a pair of skinny men's trousers float around her, a poor woman's version of Joseph's coat.

Ernie's laugh turns into a cough. He quickly covers his mouth with a hand, some semblance of polite company behavior still remaining. He looks at the crowd gathered around the perimeter of the police-strung crime-scene tape.

Most of them look like they belong there, people like Ernie and Marla—residents of West Hastings, where they all hang out, the disenfranchised, the homeless, the ones who have no place other than a hostel or an empty storefront or even a doorway to huddle in. In Vancouver, they are mostly clean, mostly polite, but still, their eyes are hollow, emotions long since wrung out, leaving nothing but empty shells. Two men in the distinctive blue-gray of the police walk among the crowd, talking too quietly to be heard, taking notes. Another, in RCMP gray-and-blue, stood watching.

"He weren't none of our kind," the man says to Marla. "Nothing like us . . . only like who we might dream of becoming . . ."

CHAPTER TWENTY-ONE

I STAYED IN THE alcove of a nearby office building with Rhys, eavesdropping on the man in the wheelchair and his colorful female companion.

We'd all agreed that five of us out in the city playing street detective might be overkill. Even though we expected Gareth to eventually show up at the condo, Rhys and I decided to try to track him down and find out what he'd learned. Adam wanted to see if he could get in touch with any of his father's people. I still had a great deal to discuss with him, but our first order of business was to find out what was going on right here in this city.

After a quick coffee at Sciué Caffé, Rhys and I walked back over toward the hostel, only to see more of a crowd than before. We couldn't even see the doorway beyond the throng. I wondered why they were still there—it had been at least a couple of hours since we'd first seen Gareth. I'd have figured the police would have dispersed the crowd by now.

I'd wanted to eavesdrop so, between the two of us, we'd remembered a small glamour charm, an Unseeing, that helped hide us. Didn't make us invisible or anything, but as long as we stayed in the shadows, people would be less likely to notice we were there. We'd been eavesdropping on the man and woman for a while.

"Nah, not like us so much as like one of them music freaks from the sixties. All long hair, leather vest thing.

I don't dream of anything of the sort." Marla dragged on her cigarette and twirled her long scarf in her other hand. "There's a festival on this week, yeah? They be coming in and all that. Music folk. All la-di-da and fiddle-dee-dee and music from the old times like my gran sang."

"Yeah, could be," the man agreed. " 'Cept . . ." He shrugged. "Nah, never mind. Silly, really."

"Ernie . . ." Marla pleaded. "You know something? Tell me." She squatted down next to Ernie, hanging on to the arm of the wheelchair. "C'mon."

"Was kind of different. You know. Music man, maybe, but old eyes, yeah? Saw him up by Tim Hortons. He held the door for me as I come down the street. Early, not quite sunrise. Felt odd."

"Felt?" I whispered to Rhys. Even though there was no way Ernie and Marla could've heard me under the glamour. Rhys poked me, signaling me to be quiet.

"Felt?" Marla echoed my own question.

"Yah, got a small shock from him when I shook his hand. Thought it were the metal on the door, but I weren't touching it."

Marla stood and put her hands on her skinny hips, elbows akimbo. "You sure about that, Ernie? No person shocks with a touch like that in a wet climate."

She was right. It had been misty and raining this morning and would be so for days. Not that I pined for the relentless sun of Texas, but the only other times I'd visited the city had been in early fall, the few weeks of the year that the sun beat out the rain. I wasn't used to the constant overcast. Weather like this didn't lend itself to static electricity shocks . . . not even from the metal of a door pull, and much less from a person's skin.

"Sidhe?" I looked at Rhys, who shook his head.

"Spark guy? Could be."

We'd been trying to approach the crime scene under our glamour, but there were too many people around and too few safe shadows. We were both fairly good at this, and no doubt my own ability had increased exponentially with the Change, but I hadn't cast an Unseeing in years. It was difficult enough at the best of times, and much harder when surrounded by all these people.

Our glamour wasn't strong enough to step out in the crowd who, by now, completely surrounded the cordoned off area. Most of the people seemed to be locals, the usual vagrants and homeless who made these blocks of West Hastings their turf. A few scattered tourists approached in caution, curiosity getting the better of their common sense. Although there really wasn't anything much to worry about. Pickpockets, yeah, but more than that was unlikely. A couple of Vancouver PD's best stood outside the tape, asking the crowd to keep back. I couldn't see Gareth anywhere.

"We could always go play tourist and ask," I ventured.

"True," Rhys agreed. "Maybe we can get close enough to tell what's in there."

What, not who.

I walked around Ernie in the wheelchair and Marla of the twirling scarf, who were now counting spare change and muttering something about getting a coffee and something to eat.

My brother took my arm as we crossed the street to join the crowd. I stepped onto the sidewalk and around a small pale man who was trying to video the goings-on while his wife and children stood beside him, all of them whispering in embarrassment for him to stop. Rhys and

I exchanged an amused look and stepped onto the curb. I stopped suddenly and Rhys stopped with me.

"What on earth—?" He whispered the words so low that I had to strain to hear them. I knew why, though. The feeling was unmistakable. Mere yards away, inside the empty space that had once, according to signage, been Mosel's Mercantile—the storefront just a few doors down from the hostel—the raw *scentfeelglow* of power throbbed. The abandoned store's windows, through dirty, weren't boarded over like so many other closed shops. The pulse of raw energy I could see through the filthy glass was so intense I could barely make out the police and forensics technicians bustling around inside. Bright lamps of some sort illuminated the scene, but the figures paled to ghosts obscured by energy that seemed ready to burst out of its confines.

My knees buckled and Rhys caught me before I fell to the ground. Power arced through me, singing its energy, a burst of light so strong my vision whited out. I fought to catch a breath as the power lanced every muscle, stifled my autonomic system. The touch of my brother's hands reverberated through me, two points of pressure magnified. I wrenched myself away and dropped to my hands and knees panting as everything slowly came back to normal.

The heightened buzz of conversation pierced my awareness. "What happened . . . is she all right . . . call 999 . . ."

"Miss, are you well?" "Keira, you okay?"

The deep voice of one of the police officers battled the sound of my brother's concern. I waved them both off and struggled to my feet, grasping for Rhys' arm to steady myself. "I'm fine, I'm okay," I said. "Thank you, officer, I felt dizzy and stumbled."

"There's a walk-in clinic close by," the police officer said. "Perhaps you should—"

"Thank you, Dean." Another voice cut in. Gareth pushed through the now closer crowd. "I'll take care of this. She happens to be a relative. Can you and Samuels see if you can handle . . . ?" He motioned to the people surrounding us.

"Right away, sir," answered Dean. "Samuels, your assistance, if you please." A second police officer joined the first and they both began asking the crowd to please disperse. They were so damned polite. When I'd first visited Canada as an adult, I'd been determined that the myth of the polite Canadian was just that. Funny thing is, I kept being proven wrong. Even here, in a tense situation, polite cop attitude rather than rude cop every time.

"Keira, why don't we go sit down?" Gareth came closer and reached to help support me. "May I?" he asked before he took my arm. I nodded and began to laugh, a ragged sound that even to my own ears sounded off.

Rhys and Gareth helped me to a nearby bench. I loved the fact that throughout the city, one could come across benches on the sidewalk, meant for nothing else but sitting and relaxing.

"You sit tight, Keira," Rhys said. "I'll walk over to the Tim's and get you a coffee. Gareth?"

"Yeah, that'd be good," he said. "Thanks . . . Dad." Gareth grinned at Rhys, who rolled his eyes and trotted away.

"You okay, then?"

"I'm all right, really," I protested. "That was . . . unexpected."

"You can say that again," Gareth agreed. "That power

signature wasn't there a few hours ago when I was investigating the hostel deaths."

I took a deep breath of the clean air. I always loved how the air in this city had no real urban scent—buses ran on compressed natural gas or electricity, so there were no diesel fumes to taint the air. City workers kept the place tidier than one could expect from a city this size.

"When were you last at the scene, Gareth?" I asked. "Or have you been here since we saw you?"

"I left not long after you did for about an hour or so," he said. "Went back to the police station to pick up some paperwork. I intended to stop at the condo and perhaps catch some rest, but then I got word that another body had been found."

"What, wait—*another* one?" I grabbed his arm. "You mean this isn't the same one from before?"

"No, and the weird thing is, they looked a lot alike."

"I'm sorry, what?"

"First guy was human, definitely," he said, keeping his voice low so neither passersby nor fellow law enforcement officers would hear if they wandered too close.

"Those two men from earlier, Rodney and John, they'd seen him before. You talked to them, right?"

"I did, but the dead man in the hostel wasn't the man they'd seen before, though I could see the resemblance. Both were tall and blond and dressed in similar clothing, but the hostel guy was just a musician passing through. He and a couple of his friends got into a drinking game and well, let's just say their judgment was less than stellar. I turned that case back over to Vancouver PD. It's no longer considered a suspicious death, but we're going ahead with the coroner's inquiry just in case." He ran a hand through his close-cropped salt-and-pepper hair. To the un-Clan eye, my nephew looked nothing like his fathers (neither Rhys nor Ianto was sure who was the biological sire, but since they were identical twins, the genes were the same); his brown hair, high cheekbones and deep brown eyes definitely came from his mother. The twinkle in his eye and sense of humor: all paternal.

"Then this victim—?"

"A dead Sidhe, I think," he said. "The power's definitely Sidhe-flavored. Dark but with a golden tinge."

"You see power as colors?"

"Yeah."

"I thought you did weather," I said.

"I do. Weather sense is tied to energies in the atmosphere. I see energies as bands of color."

"Fascinating."

"I guess you'll be doing much the same soon, eh, auntie?" He grinned at me. "Soon as you learn, that is."

"True." I scrubbed my face with my hands. "Where the hell is my brother with those coffees?"

"Tim Hortons is pretty busy this time of day," Gareth replied. "People grabbing a last-minute coffee on their way somewhere."

I looked around, realizing that as we'd been speaking, the weather had cleared a smidgen—the ubiquitous mist giving way to overcast skies with no precipitation—and the number of ambulatory bodies passing us had increased. Downtown was reawakening, as the nighttime crowd replaced the office workers. And in the midst of all this dull normality, someone was killing with magickal power.

CHAPTER TWENTY-TWO

"I THINK KEIRA should go in there with you," argued Rhys. He'd returned with two extra-large coffees, loaded with cream and sugar, and a box of Timbits. Gareth was getting ready to go back to the crime scene, now nearly blessedly free of spectators as the two police officers had taken their directive from the RCMP inspector to heart. They'd stationed a third man to patrol the perimeter of the taped-off crime scene and ask pedestrians—politely, of course—to please cross to the other side of the street.

Buses filled with evening commuters punctuated the traffic. A few cyclists sped by on the bike path as we crossed the street, heading back to the no longer empty storefront. I paused a moment before stepping off the sidewalk.

"You going to be okay?" Rhys asked, hovering protectively to my right.

I nodded. "Extra shielding, no glamour to interfere, I'll be fine." I hoped. I could still feel the energy buildup, even this far away—less debilitating, but insistent. I was beginning to wish I'd chucked my nerves and contrariness and gone straight on to the enclave like a good Kelly heir.

Gareth took the lead and motioned us under the crime-scene tape. "They're with me, Bob," he said to the police officer at the perimeter. The man nodded and let us pass without comment.

The other two officers were inside the entryway, overseeing what looked to be a forensics team. "They almost done, Samuels?" Gareth asked.

Samuels, the taller of the two, nodded and gestured to a small woman in a white coverall packing up some gear. "Dr. Woo just finished, Inspector."

"Maggie, good to see you again." Gareth greeted her with a smile and a warm handshake.

"Been a while, Gareth. Thought you were in Ontario."

"I was, yeah," he replied. "Came back to North Van a couple of weeks ago. Got called here for this."

The coroner studied him, a perplexed look on her face. "For some homeless guys? The Horsemen investigating that? Autopsies aren't even done yet on the first couple of them. Why'd you get called in already?"

"I know it sounds odd," Gareth answered, "but the PD asked for help; too many dead in too short a time. This can't all be due to malnutrition, old age or too much alcohol."

"This one sure isn't," she said. "Blunt-force trauma, some stab wounds. Not so sure of time of death, body temp's all wonky." She looked at Rhys and me. "Who's the company?"

"Dr. Margaret Woo, coroner, meet Rhys and Keira Kelly."

Dr. Woo's eyebrows raised in surprise. "You brought your relatives to a crime scene?"

"Rhys is an investigator in his own right, Mags," Gareth said.

I nearly giggled aloud at this extremely unlikely lie. My brother was only an "investigator" by dint of his ability to shapeshift into some sort of canine or lupine form, which upped his sense of smell, which, I was pretty sure, was one of the reasons Gareth had brought us to the scene. Gareth's talent didn't lend itself to investigating crimes. I sincerely doubted that the Coroner's Office would agree that his ability qualified him as an investigator of any type.

"Whatever," she said. "It's your crime scene now. There are some . . . unusual aspects to this one. But I'll let you take a look yourself. I'll text you when my initial report is ready. Or call me if you want to discuss anything. Otherwise, check back in later. My guys will wait outside. Let them know when they can take the body."

Unusual aspects?

"Of course." Gareth nodded at her. "Take care, Maggie; no offense, but let's hope I don't need to see much more of you while I'm here."

"Oh, I think we'll be chatting again quite soon." A slightly bemused look flitted across her face before being replaced with a professional smile. "Rhys, Keira, a pleasure." Dr. Woo nodded to each of us and hefted her kit on her shoulder.

"Likewise," I murmured back. Gareth said nothing. Was he taken aback by her reference to unusual aspects, too?

The petite doctor exited the building, leaving the dead body to we three Kellys.

THE DEAD man—Sidhe, whatever—lay on the floor, atop some sort of bedroll. A long rectangular wooden case with rounded ends lay next to him, broken and empty; the empty space inside looked as if it had once carried a flute. The man was tall, perhaps even as tall as Tucker, and slender in the way Sidhe often are. Long blond hair was now dyed red-brown with crusting blood. A small, festively beribboned braid lay across his face; the rest of his hair was loose and spread out across the floor. Skin so pale beneath the bloodstains, it was almost translucent. He was clad in a leather vest over a green flowing shirt, soft leather breeches tucked into knee-high brown leather boots. The shirt was torn in several places—the knife wounds, I supposed. Every piece of clothing was soaked in blood. A snake-shaped pendant of green jade hung from a leather thong hung around his neck. A silver band on his right ring finger was the only other piece of jewelry.

I could barely look at the ruin of what was once his face. It was no longer recognizable, but one hazel-brown eye peeked out, still open in death.

"He has no papers, no passport, no ID." Gareth spoke quietly.

"Looks like someone tried to rob him," I heard myself saying in a flat tone. I seemed to have gone into some sort of analytical mode, shields tight and hardened against the power I still felt thrumming against my skin. It hadn't decreased any in the time we'd been standing there.

"Yes, that's what young Dean said earlier," Gareth said in a low voice. "He texted me some details before the crime scene investigators got here. He was first on the scene."

"If it was robbery, then why leave a silver ring and what might be a valuable pendant?" asked Rhys.

"Good question, Dad. Dean wondered the same thing."

"There's a lot of blood," I said. "Rhys?"

My brother crossed the room and squatted down close to the body. His sense of smell would be less precise in human form, but would still be better than mine . . .

Wait, I kept forgetting my new abilities. Maybe I could tell, too. I approached my brother, intending to help him. Before I got even one step closer, an arm blocked my way.

"Do not even go there," Gareth said.

"What? I was going to—"

"Help Rhys out?" He smiled briefly. "I could tell exactly what you were going to do. You remembered you have the Talent now and were going to see what you sensed, right?"

I narrowed my eyes at him and frowned. "How did you—"

"I'm a cop, aunt," he said. "I saw the look on your face."

"But why did you stop me?"

"Because, Keira," Rhys replied as he rejoined us. "Not an hour ago, you were brought to your knees by whatever power surrounds this body. Do you really think it would be a good idea to concentrate on anything other than keeping your shields in place?"

"Okay, one point to the twin," I said. "Did you find anything?"

"Most of the blood isn't his," Rhys said.

"It's not?" Both Gareth and I spoke at once.

"It's primarily human. The stab wounds, the blow to the head—looks like they were postmortem. Very little blood from those locations."

"That changes everything," Gareth said.

"How so?" I asked.

"If those wounds were postmortem, and the blood isn't his, Keira, then why on earth is a Sidhe bard dead?"

"Bard?"

"The ring, the snake, I recognize them."

"You do?" Rhys stood and rejoined us. "Gareth, do you know this man?"

"Sidhe," I insisted and looked at Gareth. "How do you know him?"

"About forty years ago, this very bard was at our home. Don't you remember, Rhys?"

Rhys studied the man's battered face again, a look of concentration on his own. A slow shake of his head, then: "I'm not at all sure that I do."

Gareth replied, "He came with the envoys one year. Gigi had come to Canada for the summer that year because of a heat wave in Texas. It was before you were born, Keira. I think that may have been when Gigi was buying more land, I can't remember exactly, I was young—and honestly, I was busy chasing Megan."

"And catching her." Rhys poked Gareth in the side.

"Giving me a good excuse for not being able to remember every detail, but you should. Weren't you there?"

Rhys thought a moment. "I honestly don't remember him," he said. "You sure it was me that saw him?"

"I guess it could've been Ianto," Gareth said. "The bard sang for us a couple of times after the day's meetings."

"Probably Ianto, then," said Rhys. "Tucker and I were pretty much relegated to being Gigi's errand boys during that Summit—including during the entertainment. I don't think I saw any of the bards."

"Hello? Little sister here," I interrupted. "Are you all telling me this Sidhe was someone involved with Gigi?"

"I don't know if I'd use the word involved exactly," Gareth said. "But yeah, I'm pretty damned sure this guy was in the entourage."

"Whose entourage?"

"The Unseelie Court's."

I stepped back, stumbling over some trash. Rhys caught my arm. Pressure began to seep through my shields, the power pushing past my defenses as I tried to catch my breath. That couldn't be. I started to pant, fight against the pervasive thrum, to gather my wild thoughts, to push back the memories that threatened to escape. I couldn't catch a breath, was suffocating, air, I needed—

The darkness of the caves surrounds me, the light of my small candle a pitiful measure against it. I make my way down the corridor, to my rooms, needing to hide. They'd been talking of me again, using words I didn't understand. Sending representatives, my mother had said.

"Entourage," Geraint said. "We did that before. So did our Unseelie brethren. Look where that got us. A sickly child with no magicks. The other one, Drystan's son, what do you know of him?"

My mother whispered words I could barely hear. "He is strong."

Geraint had snorted at her whispers. "So we are the losers in this arrangement, then." My mother had mewled at this.

"You cannot know, Geraint. It is still early. She is young."

"She is useless."

"Keira, what is it?" Rhys put his arm around my waist. I came back to myself, to the present, with a gasp.

"Let's get her out of here," Gareth said. "We've seen enough."

My entire body was shaking by the time they led me outside and into the fresh air. Gareth said something I didn't catch to the police officers as we passed by. The men led me back to the bench where I'd sat before. Luckily, no one was sitting there. I sank down onto the seat, grateful for the support. Rhys sat next to me, keeping his arm around me.

"Was it the power?" Rhys asked, keeping his voice low and steady.

"No, not . . ." I leaned into him and buried my face in his shoulder. I didn't want to remember, but the combination of the dead Sidhe's power plus hearing that word, entourage, had triggered a memory I'd suppressed for decades.

"Vision?" Gareth prodded.

"No. Memory," I answered, my voice muffled as I kept my face where it was. Rhys was slighter and shorter than Tucker, but his shoulders were plenty broad for me to use as an anchor. He tightened the hug and let me stay there for a few minutes. Neither man spoke as they let me compose myself.

"It hurt," I said finally, raising my head and looking at them both. Gareth squatted next to the bench, a worried frown echoing that of Rhys.

"The power hurt you?" Gareth stood and sat next to me, his hand on my arm.

"No. It—when you spoke about the entourage, the Unseelie Court, I remembered something I'd overheard as a child." I forced another deep breath. My heart raced every time my thoughts went back there. If I'd been human, I'd be in dire need of therapy. I'd never dealt with the emotions caused by my first seven years. Never wanted to. The events of these past several days kept dredging them up, though, calling up memories I'd kept buried successfully for most of my life.

"My mother and Geraint talking about an entourage, about Drystan's son, about how . . ." Useless. Say it, Keira, how absolutely less than useless your own mother thought you.

"Drystan's son?" Rhys stiffened and pulled away from me. "Are you sure that's what you heard, Keira?"

"Yeah, why?" I looked at my brother, puzzled by his reaction. Granted, I'd been practically bawling on him a moment ago, but I was sure that wasn't why he was acting this way.

"Drystan is Gideon's father's name."

CHAPTER TWENTY-THREE

"IT TOTALLY IS NOT," I said hotly. "His father is named Tris—oh, bloody hells." His name was Tristan. Drystan was—duh—the Welsh version of the same name. In Latin it was Drustanus. Name of a character in Arthurian legend who was a trickster, possible shapeshifter, and oh, my freaking insane world had done a leap into ridiculousness.

"Are you telling me that Gideon, my Gideon, the man I once—he's half Sidhe? Like me?" Was everyone I knew Sidhe? Okay, not everyone—only the only two men I'd ever been in love with. Like that wasn't more than enough.

"I can't tell you that, sis, but I do know that someone named Drystan used to come visit Gigi and at some point, I learned that he was Gideon's father. I never actually met him; neither did any of our brothers, as I recalled. Wasn't all that curious, to tell the truth. I really was never interested in Gigi's political machinations, but this—" Rhys motioned toward the building across the street, where the coroner's van was pulling away. "This leads me to believe that something is going on and Gigi needs to know about it. What's the likelihood that this unnamed Sidhe shows up in Vancouver the exact same time that the new Clan heir arrives? At first, I was ready to blow off the whole mystery Sidhe business as a fluke, but this . . . now?"

Clan heir. He meant me. Oh, crap. The clue bat smacked me upside the head. This wasn't necessarily a weird Gigi thing, it could very well be a weird *me* thing. That Sidhe, the Unseelie bard, could have been here to find me. Why, I had no idea, but it couldn't be for a good reason. The Seelie and Unseelie Courts had long since been, if not enemies exactly, then at least rivals. Battles fought for dominance filled legendary stories and songs. Not all of them were only stories. In fact, most of them were based on reality, only it was a reality known to few humans these days. I had to admit that in spite of my own gene pool, I'd been woefully ignorant of any of this until we'd studied Malory and Marlowe in high school. Bea was the one who had been excited about the stories and she did an extra credit paper. Helping her research, I'd run across names I vaguely recognized; Sidhe who still lived Underhill. But I didn't mention it to Bea. She had enough to accept about my father's family who lived right there in Hill Country. I wasn't about to tell her I was a faery. Even researching the paper had become another set of memories to repress. Way to rock, Keira. Motivated suppression of childhood trauma was one thing. Disassociating something as mild as Bea's high school paper? I was beginning to think I was definitely a better candidate for the loony bin than the heir to a lot of Clan responsibility.

"I think we need to call Gigi and get her down here sooner than later," Rhys said. "Or we should hightail it out of here and go on up to the enclave. Can you get Liz back?"

"I have no idea," I said. "But you're right; much as I don't want to involve Gigi, I think we have to."

"Sensible girl." Rhys patted my head.

"Not sensible, just hella freaked out," I replied. "There

is so much about this whole thing that I don't like. If this Sidhe came to find me, what was he doing here?" I waved my hand around, indicating the neighborhood. "Not likely to find me among the city's homeless population. It's not like we're completely unfindable. I know a holding company is listed as our building's owner, but I'm pretty sure that you can call directory assistance and get the phone number for the penthouse. We may be hidden, but we're not *hiding*."

"He's a bard, aunt," Gareth pointed out. "There's a music festival. If he were lost, or even just happened by, it would be difficult for him to ignore the music. Or he might even have added it to his intended agenda. Music is what he is—was—and what he *did*."

"Okay, makes sense," I conceded. "That said, why's he dead? It's not exactly easy to kill one of them."

"That, my dear sister," Rhys said, "is precisely the point."

"And that's my job." Gareth stood up. "I need to go do it. Rhys, why don't you take Keira back to the condo and I'll come there when I've checked in at the police station. I want to read the witness reports, check with Dr. Woo and see what's what."

"We should help you," I protested.

"You can't," he said bluntly. "It's one thing to have you at the scene as investigators, but another thing entirely to have you at the police station. You'd need actual ID for that and frankly, although I'm sure we could get it, we could not get it immediately. Even if we could, I don't think it's wise. You've been through a lot, Keira, and you need to rest. You've not slept, am I right?"

"I have," I protested.

"But you got hit with some weird power whammy,"

Gareth said. "You look tired—exhausted. Go back to the condo and get some rest. Tell the rest of your group what's been going on. I'll be there as soon as I can."

"Gareth, there's one more thing," Rhys said. "Daffyd, Seelie Sidhe cousin on Keira's side. He's gone missing . . . sort of."

"Sort of how?"

Rhys quickly explained.

"Damn it, Rhys," Gareth said. "I'm not fond of coincidence and the fact that a member of the Seelie Court is here in town at the same time one from the Unseelie is found murdered—well, it bears looking into. I'll be asking him a few questions myself."

"Once we find him," I said. "He's been gone a while."

"I don't like this," said Gareth. "Two High Court Sidhe in Vancouver at the same time. Both on opposite sides, rivals. Both wandering the city alone."

"Keira, do you think Daffyd could have something to do with the death of this other Sidhe?" Rhys asked.

I thought about Rhys' question a moment. Could he? I had only known of him for a few days. He'd been watching me for decades.

"It's possible," I said. "He seems a quiet, gentle type, but he did kill someone—a human man. On my behalf."

Gareth's eyebrows raised. "Here?"

"No, at the Wild Moon, in Texas," I said. "Long story short, the man was trying to kill my best friend. Daffyd took him so neither I nor Tucker had to." Daffyd had killed other humans, too, in order to survive. No reason to bring that up to Gareth right now.

"Ah. Interesting." Gareth checked his watch. "It's getting late," he said. "Nearly ten. I think I'll come back to the condo with you instead of going to the station. I'll have

Officer Dean fax me the statements and coroner's report there. I'd like to talk to your vampire—the Unseelie Sidhe one, see if he can shed any light on this."

"THEY'RE NOT here?" Rhys's voice was getting louder. "Tucker, what the—" We'd arrived at the condo to find Adam and Niko gone. "Did you not think to keep them here?"

"I told you both this before about Daffyd, and I will say it again." Tucker spoke calmly. "I am not their keeper. Adam and Niko are both adult beings fully capable of taking care of themselves—like Daffyd. If they want to wander about the city, why on earth should I care to stop them?"

"That's not the problem," I butted in. "There's a new situation." I quickly explained.

Tucker let out a breath with a whoosh. "Damn it, you three, why in all the hells didn't you call me? They only left about half an hour ago. If you'd used your brains—and your cells—I'd have kept them here."

Fuck. He was right. We'd all failed. "Damn it, I'm sorry," I said. "I didn't think. How stupid can three people be . . . including a member of the Royal Canadian Mounted Police."

"Now, Keira, that's unfair," Tucker said. "Gareth had no way of knowing. Nor did you all," he admitted. "Sorry back at you. I overreacted."

"Did they say where they were going?"

Tucker shook his head. "No idea. They said they wanted to wander about some and that they'd be back." He gave me a solemn look. "Keira, no doubt they wanted time alone—to talk. After everything Adam told us, and Niko's past, there's a lot there to work out. I'd have done the same in Niko's place."

My brother, as per usual, was more than right. "Yeah, I suppose," I agreed. "I just wish that they were here, in light of what we've found."

"Speaking of calling—we can always call Adam on *his* cell phone and see where they are. Tell them what's going on. I'd like them both in on this, too." Tucker, at least, was thinking now.

"Why don't we all calm down and have something to eat," Gareth said, playing the voice of reason. "I don't know about you all, but I'm starving. Is there any food in this place?"

"Tons," said Rhys. "I had groceries delivered earlier. Help yourself. I'm going to go shower. Would someone brew up some coffee?"

"I'll do that," said Tucker. "Keira, you look wiped. Why don't you go rest for a while? Gareth can call his headquarters while I put together some food and then we'll eat and figure out what to do next. There's no sense going off half-crazy trying to find Daffyd again—or even asking Niko and Adam to—we haven't exactly gotten anywhere with that."

"I could always call Daffyd in as a person of interest," Gareth said. "Get the PD to help look for him."

"Yeah, and what are they going to do when they find him . . . if they find him?" Tucker replied. "He's a full Sidhe, nephew. Glamour, power, everything. I'd rather not be responsible for him harming police officers. I think it's best he's left to us."

"You've a point, uncle," Gareth said. "Apologies; I do tend to think as cop more than Clan sometimes."

Tucker ruffled Gareth's hair. "I'm sure you're an excellent cop, nephew. Let's use some of those skills to help us figure out how to find him." Tucker turned to me. "Go on, Keira, you're exhausted."

Sleep. I could do that. I nodded at my brother and wandered off down the hall.

Dreams assaulted me the moment I lay down. I didn't even remember my head hitting the pillow before I was off in a nightmare.

INTERLUDE

Dreaming

HE ARGUES WITH the others, my name said over and over again. I cower in my hiding place, making sure to keep out of sight. If they can't see me, they can't hurt me.

"She is ours, Geraint—Father," he says. "You cannot—"

"I can, and I will," Geraint argues. "She has no magick, Daffyd. She cannot be heir."

A shimmer of light and then I am watching Daffyd somewhere different: modern, glass reflecting him dressed in black, people of all ages and races walking behind and around him. He stares at the glass, into the store window, row upon row of flat-screen LCD displays showing some sports event. He turns away and walks down the street, hands to his side, held out a little as if gathering the very air and feeling. A steep walk up a hill, then he sees them. A couple with a guitar and a bodhrán, two men arguing while walking, but talking about music.

He follows them to the large concrete pillar, some sort of memorial. They pass it and join the others in the crowd. Daffyd touches the pillar, stops, then walks further into the park and sits on the grass to listen. A song begins; string, drum and voice joining to rise above the crowd's murmur. He stands, called by the music.

He concentrates, eyes closed, the music weaving inside him, sound of a flute joining the guitar and drum. He sees, oh Mother of All Holies, he sees.

He is taking the song and choking the life from it, killing the music. The dead Sidhe's eyes stare back at me, hazel, sad, regretful. I'd come to see you, *he says in my head.* Come to find the heir. *Daffyd's grin behind him turns into a rictus, his face into a skull, eyes left gleaming in the bare bone, searing my thoughts, burning my brain. I fight the pull, fight the pressure, can't breathe, can't see, can't—*

CHAPTER TWENTY-FOUR

"KEIRA, WAKE UP." My brother's voice was too loud in my ears. I shoved my hands over them to block the noise.

"Tucker, it hurts," I mumbled. "Stop."

His voice dropped to a whisper. "You were screaming, sis." He placed a cool hand on my brow. "You're overwarm, a bit feverish. I'm going to get you something to drink. Stay here."

He disappeared and I closed my eyes and turned on my side, clutching a pillow to my chest. A few minutes later, Tucker came back in.

"Here," he said. "Drink this."

I struggled to sit up, lethargy still keeping hold of all my limbs. "What is it?"

"Tea."

I inhaled the smoky aroma. Mmm, Lapsang souchong, my favorite. "Thanks, bro," I whispered. "What time is it?"

"Not quite one," he said. "You've not been asleep long."

Seemed like forever. "I had a nightmare." I sipped the tea, both my hands wrapping around the big mug.

"Not a vision?"

I shook my head. "No, don't think so. Too jumbled, memories wrapped around dreams, nothing I could definitely pinpoint as visions. Have Adam and Niko come back?"

"Not yet. I got Adam's voice mail. Gareth had to go back out. Cop biz."

"Damn."

"Indeed." Tucker perched on the edge of the bed, concern written all over him. "Keira, do you think Daffyd did it?"

I took a deep sigh and set my mug down on the nightstand. "I don't know. Is he capable? Yes, of course, we both know that. But did he either run across the bard and kill him or deliberately seek him out? No clue. For all I know, he came with us to do precisely that."

"Seek the bard out." It wasn't a question.

"Yeah. I think that was part of my nightmare. After what Gareth said, about the Courts having come years ago to visit Gigi here at the enclave. What if Daffyd was tangled up in that? After all, what I know about him and why he was in Texas was what he told me. How can we be sure he was telling us the truth?"

"Or all the truth," Tucker reminded me. "They are good at lying, shading the truth or only telling part of it."

I snorted. "Probably why our dear great-great-granny consorts with them," I said. "She's pretty damned good at that herself."

"That she is, sis. That she is."

I picked up the mug again and warmed my hands. "So, brother," I began, then took a sip of the still-hot tea. "What do you remember of those days? Were you there when the Courts came?"

Tucker regarded me solemnly. "I was, Keira. Though, to be honest, you know none of us brothers have ever been involved in the political side of things. Both Courts came, separately: first the Seelie—your mother as the envoy for her aunt. Don't know why she came rather than her cousin, the heir apparent. Others came, too, of course. They stayed for several weeks. Sometimes closeted with Gigi and her advisors, sometimes wandering around the enclave. I mostly remember fancy dinners and elaborate entertainment neither Rhys nor I got to see. Their bards, our bards."

"That's where Dad met her, then."

He nodded. "Yes, he was assigned to escort her at dinner most nights, to partner with her in dancing. I guess one thing led to another."

"Therefore, me," I said with a wry grimace.

"It's not like that was a bad thing." Tucker smiled and patted my knee. "I kind of like you."

"I kind of like you, too, brother." I smiled back. "So, the Unseelie Court . . ."

"Yeah, they came later. A few weeks, I think. Drystan, their king, came with a much bigger entourage. Gigi was enchanted. She squired Drystan all over the place, even took him down to Vancouver once or twice."

"I don't get this, Tucker," I said. "How the hell did we not know that Gideon was part Sidhe? Surely, you'd met his father?"

"That's just it, Keira," he said. "I never did. After that summer, we went back to Texas and stayed there for years. Gideon's mother went to London. A few years later, we heard about her son. Frankly, the only reason I remember the announcement is because I was having dinner with Gigi and Dad the day it got delivered. Gigi said something to Dad about him getting on the ball. Dad was pretty uncomfortable about the whole thing. I asked him about it later and he said it was some ridiculous notion of Gigi's and not to worry. So, I didn't. About a month or so later, we heard Branwen was pregnant."

"It certainly explains a few things," I muttered into my tea.

"Such as?"

"Gideon's fascination with the dark," I said bluntly. "Unseelie aren't as squicked by that sort of thing."

"Do you think he knows?"

"What?" I asked.

"That he's half Sidhe," Tucker replied. "Remember, Gideon was raised by his mother. None of us ever met his father . . . or at least, that we knew of."

"Huh." I sat up straighter. "You know, you're right. He told me his father's name was Tristan, but I never met him. I know when I asked what happened to him, all Gideon ever said was that his mom told him that his father had been a mistake."

"We're calling Gigi. Now."

"It's after one A.M., Tucker."

"Like I said: now."

"I WANT you here at the enclave." Gigi's steely tones rang loud and clear through the speakerphone. Instead of using my cell phone, Rhys, Tucker and I had decided to use the landline. Adam and Niko had returned and were waiting to hear the outcome of the call. They'd gone hunting Daffyd and the other Sidhe. Adam had hoped that his affinity to his Clan would help, but he'd found no sign.

Rhys and I stood next to a beautiful Euro-style desk, its clean, elegant lines broken only by the single multiline speakerphone sitting in the center. Tucker sat next to us in a very expensive ergonomic chair. The room had been outfitted as an office with the best furniture money could buy. From the looks of it, no one ever used it.

"But Gi—"

"Keira, there's danger there and I can't have you exposed. Not now."

"Daffyd's still missing," I said bluntly. "You want we should leave him behind? And what about the dead Sidhe?"

"Neither the living nor dead Sidhe are my concern," she replied, even more bluntly. "You and your siblings are. I want you out of the danger zone and here with me."

"And our guests?" Rhys asked.

I shot him a look and mouthed "Guests?"—amused that my brother, honest and open as the years were long, still used polite and noncommittal terminology when speaking to our leader. Probably more politic that way.

"The pilot will be at the airport ready to take off at eight P.M. tonight," Gigi said. "Since you are bringing along your . . . guests, you can't depart until dark anyway." I could almost hear the shit-eating grin on her face as she contemplated meeting our significant others. Bloody hell, I was bringing my boyfriend home to meet my family.

"Until then, I want you to stay in the condo, Keira. Do you understand?"

Gigi was also grounding me. Holy teenagehood, Batman. "Yes, Gigi, I understand."

"You need some rest anyway. Rhys?"

"Yes, Gigi?"

"Rhys, on second thought, I want you to stay in town, work with your son. Someone from the family needs to be on-site. I'll see who else I can send down. Tucker?" Gigi didn't give him time to reply. "You will accompany Keira as previously planned. I want Keira safely here."

Where she can keep an eye on me, I wagered. That said, I was kind of okay with it. Still uneasy—Gigi always made me feel as if I was on notice—but I understood, more or less.

"We'll meet Liz at eight, then," I said.

"No, you won't." Gigi's delicate laugh echoed in the room. "I'm sending my personal plane."

Oh, yeah, that again. All right, then, whatever.

"I'm looking forward to seeing you, child," Gigi continued, her amusement evident. "And your brother."

"See you tonight." Before I could touch the button to hang up, Gigi had already done so on her end. Tucker stood up and walked out of the room without saying a word. After all, what was there to say?

"Well, that was interesting." I leaned back against the desk and crossed my arms. "So she wants you to stay here, Rhys? Give you a chance to escape the madness of whatever she's got up her sleeve with me?"

"She's not that bad, Keira," Rhys insisted. "You've been gone from the family more than you've been with us. You spent how many years in London? Eight? Then you get back and still stay apart."

"You were the ones who left Texas, Rhys, remember?"

"You were the one who decided to nurse your wounds alone." Rhys sounded hurt. "Did you ever stop to think that we hurt along with you, little sister? That we didn't want to see you alone, emotional and angry at all of us?"

"I wasn't angry with you, Rhys, or with Ianto, Tucker, or any of my brothers. I wasn't even mad at Dad. I laid the entire thing on Gigi. I didn't really understand why she felt she had to move to the Canadian enclave right then. Okay, I was being totally self-centered and completely selfish at that point, but I felt staying in Texas a few more years—hell, a few months—wouldn't have been a problem. That's all I wanted. My family to be my refuge for a while. I'd have been over it by Solstice and then we could have all come here. Instead, Gigi stuck to her guns. I got my stubborn pride up and decided to stay. So she punished me with Marty duty—and you see how well that turned out."

"I know, Keira," Rhys said. "You were angry, she made you angrier. You are both so much alike."

"We are so *not*!" I stomped away from my brother and went into the kitchen. Tucker was in there, making a sandwich. I didn't even pause to look at Adam and Niko, who were sitting on a couch, heads together and talking about something.

"Here, sit down and eat this," Tucker said.

I sat down at the kitchen island on a tall stool.

"And yeah, you are." Tucker sat a plate with a sandwich on it before me.

"Am not," I mumbled around a bite of roast beef on rye. I realized I hadn't eaten since—egads, how long had it been? "So are we going to the enclave and leaving this mess here to Rhys and Gareth?" I took another bite.

"We need to, Keira," Tucker said gently. He put a cold bottle of ale next to my plate. "I'm worried that your new Talents will start manifesting without control. From what Rhys said, you came too damned close to collapsing in that storefront. It's nothing like the visions and occasional bouts of Talent that showed up while you were Changing. If anything happened now—say a run-in with a rogue Sidhe—you could be seriously hurt." He took a swig of his own bottle.

Mouth full of ale and sandwich, I shrugged in reply.

"You really do need to be among family. Plus, we can talk to Gigi about Gideon, find out about this half Sidhe business and what's really going on. If we need to come back to Vancouver, we can do so."

I swallowed and sighed in defeat. "So we go. At some point, I'm going to have to figure out how to ask Gigi for a reprieve."

"From what?"

"Heir duties. I'm perfectly willing to get some training on my Talents, but I want to go home, back to the ranch, with Adam." I snuck a peek out at the living room, but Adam and Niko were still deep in conversation, not paying attention to either of us.

"I just found him, Tucker, and nearly just lost him. I'll be damned if I let this heirship pull me away now. Gigi's not abdicating her position anytime soon. She can send me reading material or something. Hell, she can send someone to stay at the ranch and help me learn whatever it is I need to learn. I want some years with Adam. I'm sure we can work something out." Like perhaps Adam buying adjacent land near our enclave. He would enjoy British Columbia.

"Not a bad idea, sis, but I wouldn't hit her with that right away. Let's figure all of this out first, then I'll help you convince her."

"You will?"

"Absolutely. You're happy with Adam," he said. "It's been a long time since you've been happy."

"Did you tell Niko and Adam about Gideon, about what we've found out?"

"A brief overview. We can supply details on the plane. Right now, I really want you to get some rest with no nightmares and then, tonight, I want to get you out of here and safe."

"You're a good brother, you know that?"

"I make a good sandwich, too," he said, noting my near-empty plate.

"Excellent taste in ale, too." I took another drink. "And, Tucker? Thanks for backing me up about Adam."

He smiled. "Don't forget, sis, I'm happy with Niko and I have every intention of continuing. This isn't all about you."

"You being with Niko isn't exactly predicated on my being in the same place, Tucker."

"Actually . . ." Tucker went to the fridge.

"What?"

He came back to the island with two more cold bottles. "I haven't really said anything up to now, but you know that Gigi sent me to keep an eye on you."

"Yeah, because I was Changing, and she knew it."

"Well, that and . . ." He stopped a moment as if to figure out how to say whatever it was he was trying to say. "It was kind of more than that."

"How so?"

"I've been assigned to you." He opened his ale.

I took a bite of my sandwich and chewed it before I could say something I would regret. I put the rest of it down on the counter, finished off my ale and took a deep breath once I'd swallowed.

"Assigned. As in . . . bodyguard. For the heir." This was all falling into place. Gigi had known—or suspected—my eventual Change results. To that end, she'd formally assigned Tucker to be my body man. The person who would be by my side constantly, my companion, my guard, my advisor—my official Protector.

It wasn't as if I didn't have a say in it; from what I recalled of how this worked, I could request a new companion at any time. I looked at my brother. "I'm not going to request a replacement," I said. "You could have said something, though."

"I didn't know, honestly," he said. "At first, she told me that she was worried about you and for me to come watch over you. Then, the other day, after—"

"After I Changed."

He nodded. "She called me and told me the assignment was permanent. I would have said something, but we were having too much fun being wolves. I wanted you to spend a few days enjoying yourself."

"Thanks," I said and took his hands. "I accept your service, brother."

With a solemn look, Tucker squeezed my hands and bowed his head quickly. "I shall serve you well, my liege."

A burst of energy slid between us, wrapping our hands and shimmering about our wrists before vanishing.

Well, fuck. I'd just bonded my brother into service.

"Better open that bottle for me, bro."

CHAPTER TWENTY-FIVE

EXHAUSTION TURNED TO pleasure as I sank deeper in the giant Jacuzzi bath. Thank the powers that be that the person or persons who helped our dear matriarch build this penthouse believed in pure sybaritic gratification. The bathroom itself was larger than most standard master bedrooms, with two standalone showers, each large enough for sharing. The deep tub could hold up to four comfortably, six if you were very friendly. The entire decor mirrored that of the penthouse—luxuriant, elegant but deceptively simple. Clean lines and accents against rich woods complemented the silver steel of the fixtures.

Stored on the shelves of a hidden closet, I'd found a near endless supply of Lush bath products, lotions and other wonderful goodies. I'd unwrapped a lavender-scented bubble bar and prepared for a long, hot soak. Downtime. Something I hadn't realized I'd been craving. I needed to recharge something fierce. All this craziness: not conducive to relaxation. But a good built-in music system tuned to some Sarah McLachlan, a bubble bath, some candles and some quiet time: just what the new heir ordered . . . for herself.

"Keira Kelly."

Adam's voice, slightly louder than the quiet background music, didn't even startle me. I'd almost expected it—expected him. When I'd finished my sandwich, I'd walked past him and Niko, saying nothing, no intention of interrupting the conversation they were still having. I'd only smiled and touched his shoulder lightly and continued on to the suite we shared.

I opened my eyes and turned my head. I'd lit several vanilla-scented candles and turned out the overhead light when I entered the tub, preferring subtle luminescence over harsher artificial light.

Adam stood in the doorway between the bedroom and the bath, the light from behind creating a soft halo-like glow on his bare skin—yeah, all of it. He was nude, dark hair flowing loose down his back, hands open as if in surrender.

I studied his strength, the muscles smooth under the pale surface, lines flowing in pure elegance from limb to limb. He stepped forward, moving with the grace I'd once thought came from his vampire nature but now recognized as that combined with the sheer poetry of the Sidhe. Despite their treatment of me, I was always able to recognize their beauty, no matter how cruel. Adam, however, was never cruel—not to me.

"Will you have me join you, then?" The timbre of his voice remained steady, neutral, questioning. I knew what he was asking, what his body language said. Not just a question of physicality: could he join me in the bath, but a grander, more important query—would I have him, could he join with me as partner, lover, friend, even family. He'd bared himself before he entered—another symbol. An offering, perhaps—here he was, Adam Walker, nightwalker, vampire king, heir to the Unseelie Court, and my lover of less than a year. But so much more than that. This was a man, not human, but still a person who'd touched me in ways I'd not thought possible, bonding to me in blood, in mind, in spirit . . . so open to me that I'd thought I knew everything about him—why he'd stopped drinking human blood, how he'd survived in a concentration camp, the guilt, the sorrow, the deep sense of responsibility that laced his every action. Yet, he'd still had secrets. Now, though, he stood before me in all his naked glory, green eyes glittering in the candlelight, his very self offered.

Would I accept? Could I make this commitment? I was just shy of thirty-eight, a baby compared to every other soul in this penthouse. I had no clue as to Adam's real age, first Sidhe then vampire for more than four and a half centuries. Niko, closer to me in age but still 450 years from his human birth. My brothers, both older than Niko, and here I was, about to make a decision that might affect my life for centuries to come. Yeah, my family chose all sorts of familial and sexual companionships, but none of them were heirs. None besides me . . . and if I'd learned anything from reading historical novels and real history—the joining of two heirs: never that simple.

But hell, when was my life ever simple?

I extended my hand.

As he slid into the tub, his voice, its resonance now even deeper, richer, sent a shiver of pleasure up my spine. He whispered words so soft that even my preternatural hearing couldn't make them out. It didn't matter. I knew his intent, his meaning. He brushed his lips against mine, a touch delicate as a ghostly breeze, a promise of more. Fingertips grazed my side, touching nothing more than skin, yet sending a tingling along their path, energy that spread across my body, setting me afire. I shifted against him, the scent of the lavender oils in the water intensifying as energy built between us. I met the force of his gaze as he held my face in his hands, thumbs brushing along my cheekbones. Green eyes darkened to olive as his thumb swept across my lips. I licked and nipped its tip, my mouth dry, wanting his lips on mine. His tongue licking along my jawline, he slid atop me, hands sliding to my shoulders, down my arms to my waist.

His mouth pressed the curve of my neck, below my ear, breath hot against my skin, teasing with teeth, not yet a bite. I slid my hands up his back, cupped the nape of his neck and clasped his mouth to my neck, giving permission.

He'd offered himself, I was offering myself. I'd done this before, but it wasn't until I'd Changed, until he'd nearly bled me dry, that we'd shared blood voluntarily. Whatever demons he'd conquered coming out of that coma no longer shadowed his lovemaking.

One of his hands dropped between us, teasing, rubbing between my legs. My hips bucked against his hand, his hardness sliding against my thigh. Our hearts both pounded in time, the synchronous beat increasing as he finally raised his mouth to mine and took it, claiming it, not in possession but in acknowledgment. I was his, he was mine.

I growled as we both deepened the kiss, my need growing, energy rising—needing release, needing connection. With a strength I hadn't realized I had, I flipped him, water surging as I straddled his thighs and took control, sinking onto him, my physical body welcoming his, even as our energies merged. We gasped together, the power ripping through us as Adam raised his head to my neck and bit down hard. As I felt my orgasm tear through me, I grabbed his wrist, scratched deep enough to bring the blood and I, too, drank.

I SNUGGLED against him under the comforter, both of us relaxed, but still thrumming with the energy we'd shared, too wired to drop off to sleep.

"It's already dawn," I said in a whisper, not wanting to break the quiet afterglow.

"You can tell?" Adam murmured, his lips next to my ear as he drew me even closer.

I nodded, knowing that even in the pitch black of the heavily draped bedroom, he would feel the movement and perhaps even see a little. "The more I'm around you, the more I can sense it."

I felt his lips curve into a smile. "Indeed."

"Indeed," I echoed. "I guess maybe this is a good thing, huh?" I wasn't talking about my sensing the sun.

"That it is," Adam replied, understanding exactly what I'd meant. He brushed a kiss against my neck, the wound long since closed thanks to special Kelly mojo. I'd always been quick to heal from cuts and scrapes, but now, it was so very fast. "Thank you."

"For what?" I murmured. Surely he wasn't thanking me for the sex.

"For trusting me."

"Ah." Yeah, well, that. "You offered yourself," I said quietly. "No secrets, no more hiding."

"You understood, then."

I turned to face him, needing to see what I could of his face. I didn't want him talking to the back of my head. "I understood perfectly," I said. "I'll be honest. It wasn't an easy decision."

He nodded. "Nor was it for me."

"Being a leader can be craptastic, can't it?"

He smiled and cupped my chin, thumb brushing my cheek. "At the worst of times, yes, it can be utter shite," he said. "But there are . . . compensations."

"Like me." I smiled back at him and turned my face to kiss his palm. "And you with me."

"Yes."

I closed my eyes and took a deep breath. "I don't want to become Gigi," I said in a whisper. "I'm scared as all get-out that this power, these Talents, mean I'll eventually turn into her."

To his eternal credit, Adam neither laughed nor dismissed my fear. "You are not Minerva," he said in all seriousness. "You may be heir, may have become the future ruler, but you are yourself, Keira Kelly. You have loving brothers, a loving friend, a support network of people you can trust to help you, to teach you."

"I have you, too," I said. "But as far as a friend . . ." I buried my head in his shoulder. "I tried calling Bea again, Adam. She never picked up, never called me back. She's the only real tie I have to the part of me that was raised as a human—the part that balances all that Kelly ego, the Kelly hubris."

Adam stroked my hair, soothing me. "Although she is not your only balance, love, I have no fears that Bea will eventually work out her confusion and once again be a part of your life. Rest assured, your humanity, your compassion, is part of you—look at Tucker, at Rhys. They are no more egoistic than anyone. Perhaps more self-assured, but that comes with time, with learning, with experience. I promise you will not be alone in this. We shall all be here for you . . . even Bea."

I settled into a comfortable position, his words

reassuring as no one else's could be. After all, he was ruler of one world and heir to another; he had to know something about all of this.

"I guess it's my turn to thank you," I said.

"For what?"

"For giving me hope."

"That, my love, is the one thing that we can all give each other."

I kissed him lightly and closed my eyes, ready now to sleep. Things would work out.

"YOU CALLED a limo?" I zipped my phone into my backpack pocket, making sure that I'd put the charger and cord in with it. "Why, Rhys? We've got half a fleet of cars below."

"Because, dear sister, I really think someone should stay here, in case your wandering cousin shows up. You all could take a car, but leaving it parked in a lot for however many days is stupid. Thus, the limo."

I rolled my eyes at my brother and picked up a bottle of water. "Well, then, whatever. Shall we go downstairs and wait there?"

"Let's go," Tucker agreed. "I imagine the driver will be here shortly. We've got an account with that company. They tend to be fairly punctual."

"Figures," I muttered, even as I was hugging Rhys good-bye.

"Guess you'll need to get used to some of this froufrou stuff as heir." Rhys tugged my hair, which I'd left loose.

I batted his hands away. "Not if I can help it. I'd rather not play the rich and shameless game."

Rhys gave me another hug. "Just teasing, little sister. I

know you better than that. Besides, you know we won't let you get bigger than your britches."

At this, Adam gave me a small smile and a nod, as if to illustrate the point he'd made in bed. I smiled back at him.

I gave my brother another hug. "Take care of yourself, twin," I said.

"Back atcha, sis," he replied. "Call me when you get there, okay?"

"Will do."

I bent to pick up my backpack. "Let's to it, then."

Tucker and Niko led the way out of the penthouse. Adam and I followed. As we entered the elevator, I clasped Adam's hand and smiled at him. Whatever awaited us at the enclave, I felt nearly ready to handle it.

CHAPTER TWENTY-SIX

"SO THIS IS your vampire?" My cousin Raine scrutinized Niko, who stood next to me, obviously appreciating what she saw. Adam was still in the airport's private aircraft terminal, having received a phone call as we'd arrived. Tucker had stopped in the small café to buy coffees for us all.

"He's quite the pretty one, isn't he?" she continued, licking her lips as she studied Niko.

Déjà vu, much? Was every female pilot on my double-great-granny's payroll going to eyefuck the vampires? True, they were amazing to look at, but damn, it wasn't as if the Kellys weren't. We had plenty of gorgeous men and women in our family. Hell, at least Liz had leered with a grin. Raine was a complete opposite in demeanor from the cheery Liz. In fact, Raine Kelly was a snake. A seductive snake, but a snake. I'd never figured out how old she was, but I'd known her all my life. She'd drifted in and out of Texas, of London, always on the move. Raine had always said that after the first couple of centuries, who cares about age or where one lives?

The two of us looked a lot alike at first gander, both tall women, and—viewed from a short distance—we were similar enough to be twins. Not identical, mind, unless you allowed that at least one twin dyed her hair. Up close and side-by-side, Raine was a hell of a lot more exotic version of me. Her hair was the deep auburn of autumn leaves and fall sunsets. Her eyes, a changeable light amber; in some lights yellow, a hint of Asia in their shape. Raine's skin had always been a shade darker than my own Sidhe-pale, but with a sheen about it, reminiscent of a snake's scales. My cousin was a lamia, supernaturally seductive, and with the ability to speak to her reptilian pets.

Niko frowned and began to speak.

"Raine!" Tucker's voiced boomed from behind us. He pushed two cups of coffee into my hands and grabbed Raine into a bear hug. A low growl sounded next to me as Raine directed the hug into a deep snog, her hands sliding down to caress Tucker's ass. The subharmonics of the growl intensified as Raine's hands gave Tucker a squeeze. I didn't look over at Niko, figuring his fangs were probably out at this point.

I took a sip of my coffee, enjoying the spectacle just a wee bit. Raine had always had some rather interesting interpretations of personal space. Mostly because of her nature, but some of it was due to the sheer love of stirring shit up. She and Tucker had been together once or twice, simply for the hell of it. The last time had been years ago, when I was in my teens and she'd totally intimidated me while, at the same time, I'd been fascinated by her.

Tucker smacked Raine on the ass, stepped back and turned to Niko, hauling him in for an even deeper kiss. "You are mine, little vampire." Niko stepped back and looked at Tucker, eyes full of possession, cupping Tucker's face with his hands.

"And you are mine, wolf."

Raine laughed, a deep, throaty laugh that spoke to her love of chaos. She was like that—enjoyed messing with people. I hated that part of her. When I was in my early twenties—by then, she was less intimidating to me, but still as fascinating—I'd spent some time around her and her snakes. She taught me to like them. Tried to teach me their language, but I'd not managed to master a single meaningful hiss. I smiled, though, remembering some fun times we'd had.

"They are gorgeous, aren't they, cousin?" Raine smirked at the two men, then stepped over to me, and, before I could stop her, hauled me into a deep embrace and kiss. Surprised, I let myself sink into the kiss, sparks igniting between us. We'd never been lovers, mostly because I'd been with Gideon during the time I knew her and I tended to be a one-at-a-time person. I also was into the opposite sex more than my own, but—damn, she was good at this . . . a moment, then a gasp from Raine. She let me go, did a double take and dropped to her knees, offering the back of her neck.

Without thinking, I reached out and touched her nape with the tips of my first two fingers, stroking the skin. I snatched my hand back with a jerk. What did I just do? I'd as good as accepted my cousin as my sworn vassal.

"I'm sorry. Raine, please, get up," I urged her. "I didn't—"

"You are my liege, cousin." Raine's formal words chilled me.

I took another step back, shaking. "No, absolutely—" I hauled Raine up. "Don't fuck with me, Raine."

My cousin cocked her head, narrowed amber eyes studying me, then with a smirk and a smile, she tossed her hair back over her shoulder. "Well, I could take you up on the fucking part, but I think you're spoken for, wee cuz."

"That she is." Adam's voice came from behind me as he wrapped an arm around my waist. "You are her cousin?"

Raine's expression went from lusty to lewd in less than two seconds. "This one's yours?"

"I am," Adam answered. "And she is mine." He smiled, but behind the smile was a very clear warning.

Raine gave a slight bow. "My apologies, Sir Vampire," she said, then raised her head and smiled again. "You are very lucky, cousin . . . and like it or not, you are what you are."

She was suddenly right next to me, body scant inches from mine. Her nostrils flared, eyes gleamed. A hand came up between us, a long finger tracing down my cheek, across my chin and down the center of my neck. I shivered and grabbed her wrist as Adam's arm tightened around my waist. He held still, letting me handle it.

"Enough, Raine."

She laughed, leaned in to give me a quick peck and stepped away. "This visit is going to be a right treat. Our darling double-great-granny didn't . . ." She laughed again. "Yeah, a treat. Come along then, children," she said, motioning to the plane. "I think we'd best get moving."

"She didn't tell you?" I followed Raine onto the plane. This one was marked "Kelly 1" on the side. It was larger and better appointed than the one we'd arrived in. My granny's private plane. The Kelly version of Air Force One. Go figure.

"She was totally mum," Raine said. "All she told me was to get my ass to Vancouver airport and to pick up Keira, Tucker and the vampires."

Niko grumbled behind me. "The vampires, the vampires. Why does your family insist on not calling us by name?"

"Because, *cariad*," Tucker explained, "I didn't tell them your name."

"Whyever not?" Niko settled into a plush leather seat.

Tucker plopped down beside him. Adam settled into one across the aisle and I sat next to him.

Raine leaned close to Niko. "Because, little vampire," she breathed, "knowing your name gives us power."

Niko pushed her away. "The name I go by is not my true name, witch."

"Lamia," Raine snapped. "At least get your species right."

"Lamia, is it?"

"It is."

"And you fly planes for the family?"

"I like traveling," Raine said with nonchalance. "I get bored." She reached with her right hand and touched Tucker's arm. "I do miss this sometimes, though."

Niko batted her arm away. "Do not."

Tucker intervened. "Raine, don't. He doesn't understand."

"Understand what?" Niko asked, a hint of anger in his tone. "That she likes to paw you?"

"It's not that," Tucker said. "She's a lamia. There's a certain need to be around snakes, to curl up together in the sun and . . . to touch."

"You're not a snake."

"No, but I am family. We often need to be physically among our kind. There's an underlying energy that connects us. Some more than others." Tucker glanced over at me. "I wouldn't be surprised if you start seeing some of this need yourself, Keira."

"What do you mean?"

"Those with more advanced or the more physical Talents—even before they Change—need to recharge with other Clan. You're still too young to have had much need of this, I reckon. Plus, when you were younger, I think some of this was masked because of your Sidhe heritage. You've never really been all that touchy-feely."

"Unlike you and my other brothers," I said, remembering how much the boys would often throw themselves down into big piles, sleeping together after a hunt.

"I hadn't thought about this until now, but it might be something that manifests now that you're—"

"The heir." I finished his sentence for him. "Bloody hells. Is there anything else I don't know that I should?"

"Beats me, cousin." Raine smirked. "But I do know that we need to get up in the air, so buckle up, kids."

Raine went forward to the cockpit. As the engines were already running, I expected her to start taxiing almost immediately. We didn't move. Raine's voice, puzzled and angry, came over the speakers. "Sorry, but we aren't being allowed to take off . . . by order of the Royal Canadian Mounted—"

Before Raine could finish we were surprised to hear the thud of the rolling stairs as they were put back in place by the ground crew. The thud was quickly followed by a pounding on the plane's door.

"Open up, it's Gareth."

Raine growled but strode over to the door and worked the complicated controls. It swung open slowly, breaking the airtight seal.

Gareth pushed past her. "Don't go."

"What?" Raine's eyes flashed red as her growl grew louder. Fangs began to emerge from her gums. "No one, but no one . . ." she said as she approached Gareth and took his lapel in her hand. "No one fucks with my plane."

"Damn it, there's no time for this," Gareth blurted out. He didn't look afraid. "Stop it, Raine."

She pushed him back, head whipping from side to side,

the growl now turning subsonic, rattling the windows of the plane. The air thickened as the tension grew. With a shimmer, her body began to transform, scales slipping onto her skin, nose flattening, broadening, eyes changing shape, pupils narrowing to slits.

"Stop." Without thinking, I flipped open the seat belt buckle and stepped toward them, one hand raised in warning. "Now, Raine." Subharmonics in my voice that I'd never heard before echoed in the cabin and wrapped around the tension, pulling it away.

Raine shuddered and hissed, but nodded in my direction, without a word. She slid back and shifted, the scales that had begun to appear on her skin absorbed into its usual sheen.

"My liege," Raine said, her voice still rough. She turned, went through the cockpit door and shut it behind her.

"Keira, what was . . . ?" Niko's voice shook. Great, I'd not only freaked myself out, but the vampire, too.

Adam sat still, watching me, a thoughtful expression on his face.

Tucker unbuckled his seat belt and came toward me. "Sis, you okay?"

"Yeah, I guess," I said. "What the hell was that in my voice?"

"Command voice," he said.

"Well, crap." I went back to my seat and plopped down. Adam placed a hand on my arm. "I never expected that." I looked at Gareth. "Or you. Gareth, what's going on? Why didn't you call?"

"Couldn't take the chance I'd miss you. Calling Air Traffic Control was the surest way to keep you all here until I could talk to you." Gareth sat down across from me. "It's the dead Sidhe. I went over to the morgue to see what else I could find out. Look what I found." He pulled out his cell phone and browsed to a photo and handed it to me. Niko and Tucker rose and crossed to stand behind our seats, trying to get a look. It was impossible for all four of us to see the small screen at the same time.

"Is that—?" I looked at Gareth, who nodded. I passed the phone back to Tucker. "That Sidhe had our Clan symbol tattooed on his arm?"

"It is the symbol," Tucker conceded.

"Has everybody taken stupid pills? This is impossible," I said. "Even if Gideon is part Sidhe, they are not kin like we are. This Sidhe had to have copied the symbol. He couldn't have—"

"It's the symbol, Keira," Gareth said flatly. "This isn't a copycat tattoo."

"You're sure?"

"Absolutely. It resonates."

"How?"

"Only a true Kelly can bestow the symbol."

"But I thought that only a Kelly can receive it. Tucker?"

"That was my understanding, Keira. Gareth, do you have any ideas how this happened?"

My phone buzzed. I grabbed it and read the display, answering as soon as I saw who was calling.

"Rhys, what's up?"

"Have you all left yet?"

"No, Gareth came by before we took off. What is it?"

"You guys need to come back to the condo. Daffyd's returned. He's found something."

The four men in the plane looked at me as they listened to Rhys speak. "Found something? Where the hell has he been?" I asked.

"He said he needs to talk to you, Keira. He won't say anything to me."

How had Daffyd found the condo? We'd not gone there before he vanished.

"Put him on the phone, Rhys."

"No, he insists on speaking to you in person, Keira."

"We'd best go back and talk to him," Adam said.

"Yeah, I guess we won't get answers by sitting here." I turned my attention back to the phone. "Okay, we'll come back," I said to Rhys. "Let me fill you in on what Gareth found."

I told Rhys about the tattoo.

"That's not possible," Rhys said.

"That's what I've been trying to tell them."

"Who?"

"Everyone in the plane."

"Explain this to me, Keira," Adam said, interrupting.

"Hold on, Rhys . . . Remember I spoke of the Mark earlier? This is one—a ritual Mark," I said. "Given only to Kelly blood, to Protectors, those chosen as bodyguards. After a complex ritual of bonding—usually to your liege/ruler, you're given the Mark. It's imbued with your liege's magick. Every ruler has a specific Mark. Gigi's is a wolf's head."

Rhys broke in sarcastically. "So maybe he saw one and got it done. It's not like Vancouver has a lack of tattoo parlors. And wolves are pretty prevalent as images."

"I know, Rhys, but this one is different," I said. "It's not quite Gigi's standard wolf's head symbol. It's more stylized, with fangs, red eyes, still in a circle like the moon. Yet Gareth says it's a true Mark. It resonates. I have to believe him."

Gareth spoke up. "I'm not normally good at detecting

magickal signatures, Rhys—" I pressed the speakerphone button. Supernatural hearing was adequate, but the plain old natural phone needed help to pick up his voice. "But that's the point of the Mark. Its magick was meant to be recognized by all Kellys, no matter their own particular abilities."

"Well, it's not mine," I said. Tucker started to speak, but I stopped him. "I know I have to choose a design, but think on it. What's the likelihood I'd pick something that looks a hell of a lot like a graphic novel logo?" I turned to Gareth. "Can we go see it?"

"The body?"

"Yes. I'm not saying I can focus enough to figure anything out, but I think if we all go, maybe one of us can pin down something."

"Better come here first," Rhys said. "Daffyd's practically bursting at the seams."

CHAPTER TWENTY-SEVEN

"LET ME SPEAK," I said, pushing my way in front of Tucker, who'd instinctively moved in front of me. Out of the corner of my eye, I saw Niko doing the same for Adam. I had to be amused at our Protectors, doing their thing. Gareth had gone back to the police station, hoping to get more information out of the officers who had interviewed the spectators.

Daffyd, on seeing us, stood and approached, then stopped in mid-step, hands palm up in front of him, eyes wide. "No, you are not—" He took a step back, looked around and then again at us. "Why did you bring him here?" He pointed at Adam.

"You recognize him, then?" I asked and walked across the entryway to confront Daffyd, who raised his arms in a defensive gesture.

"He is of the other Court," he said. "Why involve them? He was not the one who Called me."

"Called?" Tucker said as he, too, crossed into the living room, remaining at my side. Niko and Adam remained standing in the foyer, both with a wary look in their eye. I glanced over at Rhys, who sat in one of the chairs, simply watching this play out.

"I disappeared from the taxicab," Daffyd said.

I managed to stifle my urge to say, "Oh, really, hadn't noticed," but Daffyd caught my expression anyway. "Obvious, yes, cousin," he said, "but I wanted to explain that I was Called. The music—" He looked at each of us in turn. "I could not avoid answering the Call."

"So where were you?" I motioned to the living area and sat. Daffyd copied my move, sitting across from me. Tucker stood next to me, every inch the guard. Adam and Niko joined us, sitting away from Daffyd. Despite the distance of several feet, Daffyd stiffened and moved slightly in his chair as if to keep as far from Adam as possible. "We looked for you, Daffyd. Several times for many hours."

"I saw the gathering, the vigil of sorts," he said. "I found myself in the center of a group of humans with candles. Heard them speaking about the music festival and of the tribute to their comrade. I felt the Other there, but could not see him."

"You know it was a him?" Niko asked.

Daffyd nodded, but didn't look at Niko. "His energy signature was all over that hill, over those people. I followed, casting a glamour so I could hide. The signature ended, just where the memorial marker stands—at the top of the Hill."

I heard the emphasis on hill and as he spoke, I immediately saw where he was going. "Oh, my bloody stars—they're Underhill, aren't they? No wonder we couldn't find them."

"Them?" Adam's voice chilled me, his icy tone nothing I'd ever heard, not even when he'd fought hand to hand with Niko last October. "There is more than one?"

"There has to be," I said. "One is dead, at least one Other, dressed in black, dark-haired. The dead Sidhe was blond. If there were two . . ."

"There are bound to be more," Adam finished, then addressed Daffyd. "You, then, what know you of this?

These deaths, these rogue Sidhe invading? Where were you hiding all this time?"

"I do not answer to the Unseelie Court." Daffyd stood and drew himself up to full height. Impressive, unless you were a Kelly and used to a brother fully six foot four and a Viking Berserker to boot.

Adam stood, pushing past a protesting Niko and stopping a scant foot from Daffyd. "I am no longer of that Court," he said, "but king in my own right." In the absolute silence following his statement, I heard a hiss from Daffyd at the same time that I felt Adam's power. He'd let loose his own personal wards, his shields now open. Energy surrounded him, dark light shimmering along his skin, his hair, his eyes flashing green-gold.

"Nightwalker," Daffyd whispered as he put a hand up to shield his face. "You are the one called Walker in name, are you not?"

"I am he." Adam's voice rang with subharmonics similar to my own when I'd commanded Raine. "I had forgiven you, Daffyd ap Geraint, but now, I must rethink that decision. You have caused a great many problems for those who are mine. Know, now, it is time for answers and for resolution. What do you know of the Sidhe who is dead and of the other?"

"I beg your forgiveness once more, Nightwalker." Daffyd bowed his head, hand over his heart. "My connection with you was never deliberate. I would never have—"

"Yes, yes," I said with a hurry-up motion. "Enough of this posturing, you two. Adam, stop already with the king stuff. Daffyd, get to the bloody point. Did you know that Sidhe or how he died?"

A corner of Adam's mouth curved up in amusement.

"Very well, Keira," he said and with a slight bow in my direction, sat down again. Niko, who seemed less than pleased, shook his head and remained standing next to Adam, hands clasped in front of him, the very picture of a bodyguard.

"The dead Sidhe was a bard," Daffyd began. "I see you know this already. I spoke to some of the people who live on the streets, looking for him. Trying to find a way Underhill. I could not glean enough information to even begin to guess the ritual. Nothing I tried worked. I left several messages for him, notes enchanted to look like random detritus." He looked sheepish. "Your city workers here are much too efficient. All trash disappeared within hours."

Oh, great, so if we'd had been in any normal rubbishy city, we might have found him.

"Do you have any idea why a bard from the Unseelie Court would have a Kelly Mark on his arm?" Tucker asked. "Why he would have been here in the first place?"

"Mark?" Daffyd asked, clearly puzzled. "I know of no mark. Perhaps the nightwalker can explain, as I have little dealing with their Court. To my knowledge, bards, as in our Court, have their bardic cloaks, perhaps an amulet or ring or both, depending on to whom they've sworn allegiance."

"We do—did—not mark our bards," Adam responded. The telltale slip made me wonder if all this exposure to Sidhe made him want to reclaim his place among his father's court. King of the vampires was one thing, but to be heir to the Unseelie Court as well? That kind of power could tempt even the strictest of ascetics . . . Adam was no more an ascetic than I was. And he was more accustomed to—and enjoyed—wielding power far more than I.

"We believe he was here because of Keira," Tucker said. "To welcome the new heir. Do you think that's possible?"

"Would the Unseelie Court know of her?" Daffyd asked. "I know your ruler had dealings with them, as she did with us, but I do not know in what regard she held them or holds them now."

"We have more connections than I previously thought. I am not the sole half Sidhe among the Clan. My distant cousin, Gideon, is also half Sidhe," I said. "His father is of the Unseelie Court—Drystan ap something-or-another."

Suddenly, Adam was crouching next to my chair in one of those blink-of-an-eye vampire moves that he'd rarely displayed around me. "His father is Drystan ap Tallwch? Are you sure?"

"No, I'm not sure," I said. "I only know the Drystan part. He's a king—"

"Not *a* king. High King," Adam put in. "My father."

I stared, my mouth open in shock.

"*You* are the missing son of the Unseelie king?" Daffyd's words were barely more than a whisper. "How then . . . ?"

Adam whipped his head around and glared at Daffyd. "This is no concern of yours. I suggest you remain silent."

I found my voice and surprisingly, it still worked. "Adam, what the ever-loving hell?"

"Wait a minute, you're Gideon's *brother*?" Rhys, the only one of us not too shocked to say the words, spoke. "Keira, that's—"

"Fucking ridiculous," I said, standing and walking toward the wall of windows. In the distance, past the lights on the water, past the lights on the road, a trail of lights from a ski run wound down the mountain. As I watched, one of the lights flickered and went out. I took a deep breath and turned around. Adam was now standing, Niko at his side again, his own expression a battle between bodyguard neutral and utter disbelief.

"There is no fucking way you are my former lover's brother," I stated flatly. "That would be too damned much."

"If, indeed, as you believe, your Gideon was fathered by Drystan, then yes, he is at the very least, my half brother," Adam said with an infuriating calm. "I must assume that his mother was of your people."

"How can you not be upset at this?" I asked, throwing up my hands. "I mean, this is something for an episode of Jerry Springer."

"Or a Lifetime TV movie." Rhys grinned. "C'mon, what's one more utterly insane thing to learn?" he said. "It's not as if we haven't had our fair share of revelations lately."

I turned to look at Niko. "And what about you? Are you the secret love child of royalty, too?"

Niko answered in an amused tone. "I never knew my parents. The nobleman who bought me always called my mother a whore and my father the whore's favorite pet. I doubt you need to worry about any more undisclosed royalty with me."

"This Gideon," Daffyd said, bringing the subject back to my former lover. "You are sure he is of your Clan?"

What the hell kind of question was that? "Yes, of course," I said, letting my impatience show. "Evidently that's never been in question."

Daffyd's face paled as he buried his face in his hands. "He impregnated a Clan woman . . ." he muttered, the words nearly incomprehensible.

"Yes, so?" I asked. "It's not like that hasn't happened—"

"Before?" Daffyd said, looking up at me. "Is he the elder?"

"Elder of whom?" Tucker asked, his frown growing deeper.

"Between him and Keira," Daffyd answered. "Which is the elder child?"

"He is," I said. "By some months."

"If this cousin of yours is indeed Drystan's get, if the nightwalker's father took a Clan woman and impregnated her, this could mean . . ." Daffyd shook his head as he studied me.

"What?" Three Kelly voices asked in near unison.

"A second heir."

"To the Court?" Adam waved his hand in a dismissive gesture. "Despite your Court believing I was missing, my father never disowned me as heir. There cannot be another."

"No, heir to the Kelly Clan," Daffyd explained. "Gideon could also be—"

"Excuse me? Again with the impossible," I said. "I don't know if you know the whole way this works, but there's only one in a handful of generations. I'm it, so QED—there are no others."

"So you don't know." Daffyd watched me as he spoke. "None of you know."

"Daffyd, this is getting beyond tedious," Tucker growled. "Either spit it out or I'll—"

"Please, calm yourselves," Daffyd said. "I will explain. About seventy-five years ago, your Clan chief, along with many other leaders, once again attempted to unite us—the fey, the Sidhe, the wers, vampires, all preternatural creatures and people of magick means. A summit of sorts."

"Yes, yes," I said, "She'd done that before. Back in the first Elizabeth's time, right? We were discussing it earlier while you were . . . missing." Discussing? Learning about the summits was a mere twig on a freaking tree of impossible knowledge that had taken root in my poor brain in the last few days.

"Yes, and it did not work then. None were willing to concede. But this time was different. She and all our leaders were concerned about modern technology and the intrusion of governments. Identification was being required in more and more places. They began to discuss how to keep hiding—or whether or not we should."

"Bottom line?" Rhys demanded.

"As they will, they spent decades arguing. Then, some four decades ago, they all came to agreement. I do not know the final result, but I do know that is when your mother, Keira, followed our queen's command and became your father's consort."

"Your queen?" Niko asked.

"Command?" My outburst came on top of Niko's question.

"Queen of the Seelie Sidhe, Maeve, and mother of the current queen, Angharad," Adam replied to Niko. "Keira's mother, Branwen, is Maeve's niece, her sister's child and underqueen of a lesser court."

"You did not know this?" Niko spoke to me.

"Not exactly," I said, still watching Daffyd. "It wasn't until recently that I knew about the royalty part. I knew my mother was Sidhe, but that's it." I stared pointedly at Daffyd, who had still not answered me. "My mother was commanded? Or was it my father?"

"Both." Daffyd's tone remained dry. "If everything my own sire told me was true—and I have no reason to believe it a lie—your leader and our own High Queen made an agreement."

"And my father did the same." Adam's eyes narrowed, a thoughtful look on his face. "I'd thought that—" He shook his head. "No, perhaps I underestimated Minerva."

"So Gideon?" Rhys mused. "His coma—perhaps he's—"

"Changing?" I breathed. "Well, by all the things holy and un . . ."

"If Drystan fathered your cousin, he may take precedence," Daffyd said. "I do not know your rules of succession, but Drystan is of higher rank, a ruling sovereign, and that may be a factor. Or, if absolute primogeniture of descendants applies, your cousin would inherit, as he is older than you. All contingent, of course, on him coming into all the powers that constitute heirship."

Those roots in my brain were getting gnarly.

"Drystan is of another Court," Adam said. "Did they then agree?"

Daffyd nodded. "Yes, the treaty was signed. All rulers were to be included."

"Keira, does this mean you aren't going to have to succeed Gigi?" Rhys asked.

I stared at Adam, whose expression remained as neutral as I'd ever seen it. Did he want this to be true? Could Gideon be his half brother and a Kelly heir? Bloody freaking hell, what had my great-great-granny spawned all those years ago?

CHAPTER TWENTY-EIGHT

"I HAVE NO IDEA," I said. "I think that we'd better call our dear leader and get some answers—as in now . . . right now."

Rhys got up and headed to the phone.

"Wait, Rhys." Tucker stopped him with a gesture. "Are we sure we just shouldn't go on up to the enclave—all of us? I'd feel more comfortable getting you out of Dodge right now, Keira. We've still got a rogue Sidhe running around out there possibly responsible for at least one murder."

"Not to mention the dead Sidhe's Mark," Niko reminded him. "There are still many loose ends. I agree with Tucker. As Adam's second and Protector"—he nodded to Tucker with a small smile, using the word as we Kellys did—"I advise we all leave the city. Your Gareth is on the case and can keep us informed."

"I'll call Raine," Tucker said. "She was going to hang out in case we needed her."

"Hold your horses, bro," I said. "I'm not all that sure I want to turn tail and leave yet. We've got two vampires, a high-ranking Sidhe and two shapeshifters, one of whom is a former Berserker. I'm thinking we can handle one lone Unseelie Sidhe who may or may not have anything at all to do with any of us."

"I'm an advocate of your safety," Adam said. "Our combined abilities and powers notwithstanding, it's not a matter so much of strength or who has the upper hand, but of politics."

"Okay, now you've lost me," I said. "Politics?"

"If this Sidhe is someone sent by my father," Adam said, "the fact of which I'm now fairly certain, we could very well cross some treaty line, or perhaps unknowingly spark a conflict. I am of the opinion that we go north. Minerva can help sort this out."

"No." I stood my ground. "I'm not simply turning tail and running away. Not this time."

"Then what would you suggest?" Adam regarded me solemnly.

"I'm concerned about the Sidhe we haven't yet found," I said. "If he—or they, however many there are—are indeed Underhill. And if there's a way into Faery at Victory Square, then I suggest we go there. We"—I indicated the group—"can deal with anything thrown at us."

"She does have a point," Rhys said to the room in general. "I'm game. Bro?"

Tucker gave me a look that was a cross between surprise and kudos. He nodded at Niko, who did the same. "If that's what you want, Keira, then let's be on with it."

Adam, still surly, muttered, "I'll go with you, however—" He motioned toward Daffyd, who sat in silence, lips tight as if to hold words back. "I do not think it is a good idea for him to be out there with us."

"I'll stay with him," Rhys said. "And I'll call Gareth to meet you all."

"He's a Mountie, brother, maybe it's not a great idea to have him mixed up in this. I don't want to have him need to—"

"Call him," Tucker said. "In case we do need the presence of the law."

"CAN'T MAKE it," Gareth said. "I'm in the middle of wrapping up this case. At the morgue." He paused, perhaps making sure he was not being overheard, then continued. "Since the victim is not . . . ah . . . Canadian, there are also certain matters I will personally need to deal with."

"I understand." I bet there would be matters. What would an autopsy of a Sidhe reveal? Probably a lot more than pointy ears. And how exactly would that be officially accounted for? I suddenly wondered if Gareth's career as a Mountie was purely, as the RCMP motto put it, about *Maintiens le droit*. Upholding the law was a noble calling and keeping the lid on knowledge of the supernatural was probably in the public's best interest . . . but said lid was also definitely in the Kelly Clan's best interests. Perhaps my childhood imaginings about Gigi's influence weren't so farfetched.

"Besides," Gareth added, "you four are better suited anyway."

"I'm good with that." I nodded to Tucker, Niko and Adam, all of whom were listening in. The three of them agreed. "If you change your mind, we're heading to the Victory Square Cenotaph to see if there really is access to Faery there."

"Faery?" Gareth asked. "I thought you were checking here, under the Victory Square hill—'under-the-hill,' right?"

"Oh, sorry, Underhill is sort of a generic word for the Sidhe world—Faery," I explained. "If there is access here, we can pretty much come out anywhere in Faery . . . or a specific place if someone's done a particular location-bonding ritual. We'll have to wait and see."

Gareth muttered something I couldn't understand.

"What was that?" I asked.

"Nothing, never mind," he said. "Be careful, damn it. And tell my dear papa that he'd better damned well keep a sharp eye on that Sidhe. We still don't know if he's responsible for any of these deaths."

Rhys, who was across the room talking to Daffyd, looked up slightly and nodded, a gesture Daffyd obviously missed. Evidently, my Sidhe cousin's hearing wasn't as good as my brother's . . . or he was concealing that he'd overheard.

"We'll take care, Gareth. If you learn of anything else, make sure to call Rhys. I'm taking the cell, but I have no idea if—"

Gareth's laugh interrupted me. "You think you might not get good reception in Faery?"

"Well, hell, I have no idea," I said. "Last time I was there, cell phones didn't exist. So how would I know?"

"Only you, dear aunt, only you would think to be concerned if your cell phone service area included the Sidhe realm. Talk to you all when you return." He disconnected the call.

"Shall we, then?" I motioned to the door and the three men followed me out.

"SORRY TO bother you again," I said to John, the guitarist. I'd seen him as we arrived at the park—the walk there was now almost as familiar as a stroll around the ranch—strumming on his guitar, lost in whatever melody had taken him. His partner, Rodney, sat next to him, hands sliding over the drum skin, as if remembering how he'd been keeping rhythm a few hours ago. The festival had ended earlier in the evening but, as always, several stragglers remained behind. A couple of boys ran through what was left of the crowd, checking in trash bins, looking on the ground, perhaps hoping to find dropped money or something of value they could then sell. "Did you happen to see another bardish-looking guy at the festival?" I described the dark-haired man as best I could without actually having seen him.

John rubbed his chin, tilted his head and nodded. "Yeah, pretty sure we saw him. Remember, Rodney? Up over by the Cenotaph. He didn't play, though, so I didn't pay much attention. He was there for a bit, then wasn't."

"When was he there?"

"Not really sure of the time. Guess it was not long after sunset?"

Rodney nodded, still concentrating on his bodhrán. "Yeah, about then," he said. "Never did see the other guy again, though. The one with the flute."

"Too bad," John said. "Guy played beautifully. As if . . ." He looked off into the distance, eyes unfocused. "Gorgeous music."

"Thank you kindly." Tucker tugged at my arm. "Probably should go on now, sis," he said quietly. John nodded and returned to plucking guitar strings.

I gave the guys a "what next?" expression as we walked toward the Cenotaph.

"In my opinion, there's still too many people around to try figuring out how to find the door to Faery," I said, trying to keep my voice low. "Canadians might be polite and let other people be, but if someone started messing around a war memorial in the middle of the night, I'd lay bets that someone would call the police. Damn it, I should have thought of that when I talked to Gareth."

"I think we'll be fine, sis. We can sit there for a while and wait until the rest of these folks— Hey, you there!"

Tucker sprang forward and grabbed the arm of a boy, one of the ones I'd seen rummaging around in the bins.

"What . . . what'd I do?" the boy protested, struggling to pull away from my brother.

"Where did you get that?" Tucker growled. "That flute?"

A shiny silver flute peeked out of the boy's jacket pocket. From my vantage point, I couldn't see much more than the end, but on that end, I saw at least one or two curlicued symbols—Faery writing.

"I—"

"Don't say nuthin', Daniel." The other boy, who'd been further away, came running up, yelling angrily. "We got given that. So leave us alone, 'fore we call the law."

"I'm with the law," I said in a serious tone. "We're investigating a death. Where did you get that flute?"

"Some guy," said the second boy. "We helped him out. Said his name was Gilliam or something—"

"*Gwil*im, Jack," Daniel supplied.

Jack shot Daniel a "shut up" look. "He gave the flute to us for helping."

"Gave?" Tucker's tone was more growl than words.

Daniel nodded, then on hearing another growl from Niko, who'd come up to flank them, started shaking. He held out the flute. "Here, you take it—please, don't tell the cops."

I considered both boys, too young to be mixed up in this. Too young to be on the streets, for that matter.

"What do you think, Tucker?" I asked. "Shall we believe them?"

Tucker, taking my lead, played bad cop. "I'm not so sure they weren't the ones who—"

"We didn't, we didn't, we swear . . ." Daniel blubbered

the words in between tears. "He was already dead," he said. "Honest."

"How did you know he was there?" Adam joined us. "Did you see what happened? How he died?"

Jack, arms wrapped around himself, all semblance of bravado gone, answered. "Yes," he whispered. "Danny and I were there. Trying to get some sleep in the back of the store. Old man Mosel still had a key to the place. He used to let us crash there. Woke up when I heard some noise. Thought it was someone else coming in to crash, but then saw the musician guy fighting with another guy who looked a lot like him, except he had dark hair. We stayed really quiet. The dark guy did something with his hand and the musician guy went down. The other guy picked up a knife and stabbed him, then used a big walking stick or something to bash his head in."

"We didn't want to be next," Daniel said.

Both boys were now shaking.

"Did you see where the dark man went?" Adam asked.

Jack shook his head. "Back out to the street," he said. "I didn't follow."

Daniel nodded. "I did," he said.

"Dumbshit, takin' a chance like that." Jack hit Daniel's arm.

"Ow!" Daniel rubbed where Jack hit him and poked the other boy in the side.

Jack flinched. "That hurt, damn it." He hunched over, as if protecting his side.

Tucker narrowed his eyes. "You injured?"

The boy began to shake his head, but changed it quickly to a nod. "S'nothin'. Cut myself."

"Bled all over the dead guy," Daniel said, in a tone between proud and embarrassed.

"So you followed the dark man," I prodded, hoping to get some more information.

"Yeah, miss. I wanted to make sure he was gone." Daniel looked around at the few festival stragglers. "He went fast, really fast, almost missed him, but I could've sworn he came right here," he said, pointing to the Cenotaph. "To the memorial thing. Then, I guess I lost him, because he wasn't there anymore."

The four of us realized what had happened at the same instant. The Sidhe had to have gone Underhill.

"Thanks for the info, boys. We won't tell the authorities," Tucker promised. "Here." Tucker pulled out a few bills and passed them to Jack. "Go and get yourselves some food and a place to crash tonight."

Jack snatched the money out of Tucker's hand and the boys hurried down the street, neither of them looking back.

"We're definitely going to have to figure out a way to get down there," I said, running my hands over the stone of the monument. "Daffyd said he didn't know the ritual. I'm totally at a loss here. When I lived Below, I never came Above, so never needed to know how to get back."

"I think I know how," Adam said, a grimace crossing his face. "I'm not sure—"

"Adam, don't," Niko said, putting a hand on Adam's shoulder.

Tucker frowned. "Why not? If he knows how to—"

Niko faced Tucker, eyes blazing. "If there is indeed an entrance here, to Faery, to the Unseelie Court . . ." He let his words trail off, but we all knew exactly what he meant. Adam was still persona non grata in his father's Court, despite the fact that he was still the official heir. Doors to Faery didn't work like human doors and had nothing to do with human geography. A door to Underhill here in Vancouver could lead to anywhere in Faery; it might be a direct gateway to the heart of the Unseelie Court—and Adam's father.

"I'll take my chances." Adam put his hand over Niko's.

I put my hand over theirs. "You are not going in there without me."

CHAPTER TWENTY-NINE

"Now?" We'd been sitting on a bench near the Cenotaph for what seemed to be hours, but was probably only less than a quarter of one. Impatience, thy name is Keira Kelly.

Adam stood and looked around the park. Victory Square was fairly well illuminated by streetlights around it and tall lamps along the curving concrete paths. Only John and Rodney remained at the bottom of the hill, both men seemingly absorbed in whatever music they were making at the moment. No one was passing. No one was watching.

"Now. Follow me." He began to walk, measured steps, a cadence we could easily follow.

In line like ducks or a grown-up version of a school trip, we trooped behind Adam, widdershins around the Cenotaph, careful to keep silent. Adam muttered below his breath, words I could barely hear, but almost understood. Words in a language I'd heard until age seven. A language I no longer wanted to know, but which still lurked beneath my memory.

One circuit, then another, a third and finally, I felt it. Power. Energy growing, shimmering sounds, light fading in, out and back again, turning the usual comforting glow of the nighttime street lamps into something unearthly.

The sounds and scents begin to blend, memories from childhood flash through my mind. My mother, striding through candlelit hallways, shining dagger at her belt, silver, not base metal. She drags me by one hand, impatient. I'm only five or so. Flash of light and another memory, a song, a bard in the front singing about a lady fair and a horse . . . or perhaps the lady was the horse?

I reached out, hand searching for some purchase, some way of grounding . . .

A silent pop, pressure of air changing as we stop, a rectangular nothingness—a doorway—now hung in thin air to the right of the Cenotaph. The air seemed charged, particles of light and sound swirling around us and the door. I sent a silent plea to whatever powers that be that we were invisible to passersby.

Adam, with a solemn gesture, motioned to the door. "Shall we?"

"We shall," Tucker said, grim determination on his face. Niko, behind him, bit his lip, but moved forward. I nodded at him as he passed. He nodded back and disappeared through the door. I followed; Adam came behind me. As Adam's head cleared the opening, it closed with the same pop of air pressure that had signaled its appearance.

I blinked in the sudden darkness. A moment, then a darkling light began to glow, the very walls, smooth stone, emanating enough luminescence for us to see by. I'd not lay odds for any human being able to see here, but I was doing fine. "Can you all see?" I asked in a hushed whisper.

"Yes," three voices answered, nearly in tandem, nearly as quiet as mine.

"Welcome to Faery," I said a little more loudly. "Enter at your own—"

"Keira," Adam warned.

"Just trying to keep a sense of humor. I could've said 'Abandon hope, all ye who enter.'" I gave up on the wittiness and moved down the hallway a short way. These weren't the halls of my own past, light and airy. These halls were dark—dim corridors with darkling light—not the bright luminescence of where I lived as a child. This was somewhere else.

Gray mists swirled around our feet as we cautiously walked forward, releasing a sweet scent, reminiscent of musky spice vanilla—oh holy hells—Adam. The mist smelled of Adam . . . or he smelled of the mist. The scent I associated with him was the scent of the world Below, the Unseelie Court. Niko seemed to realize it at the same time I did, his nostrils flaring. He glanced at Adam, yet remained in place, lips tight with anxiety, face set in determination. My brother walked beside us, ever wary, ever watchful. When we returned to Above, I needed to complete the bonding and Mark him—he would be a brilliant Protector, someone I could trust to be that close—Tucker, nearest to me in spirit, if not in age.

"Where should we head?" I asked as we eventually reached a spot where two corridors branched off from the one in which we stood. There was still no obvious source of light, nor of the underlying vibration that I could feel resonating in my bones. "Do you know, Adam?"

Adam reached for the wall, one hand taking my own, the other, palm flat against the dark glowing stone. "Feel this," he said.

Without even directly touching the wall, I felt the continuous rhythmic humming, the heartbeat of Faery, pulling, tugging. "That way," I said and with my other hand, pointed to the left-hand corridor.

"You know this?" Niko asked in puzzlement.

I nodded. "I felt the way."

"It calls, doesn't it?" Adam sounded almost . . . glad? I stared at him in surprise, but said nothing.

"Niko, Tucker, stay close," I said. "And don't forget, no food, no drink."

"It is true, then, the tales?" Niko's eyes widened. "About Faery?"

"Yes," Adam said harshly. "It would be like my father's people to want to keep us here. We can't partake of anything—not even blood."

I stifled a laugh. That hadn't actually occurred to me, but yeah, I supposed that would qualify as food if you were a blood drinker. "We won't stay long," I said. "Just find out what the hell is going on and then get out. I'll pull out the Gigi card if I have to."

"No need, Keira Kelly." The voice came from behind me. I jumped and turned to see a small person, one of the lesser fey from his gray-green skin and matching garb. "This way please. The king will see you now." The fey bowed to Tucker and Niko, a deeper bow for me, and for Adam, his brow touched the floor. "It is good to have you back home again, Aeddan."

"Only for a short time, Llwyd."

The wee man nodded, head bobbing quickly as he stood from his bow. "A time and then a time more. Follow me." With a scamper and another bow, he scurried up the left corridor. We followed, less with the scampering and more with the caution born of not trusting the fey.

"Was it me, or was his response as cryptic as it sounded?" I whispered to Adam.

"That's Llwyd," Adam replied, being as cryptic as the little man.

"Okay . . ." I began, but stopped as he continued.

"He is my father's Fool. No answer will be precise from that one."

"Hmm." The Court Fool. There'd been one at my mother's Court and her cousin's as well. I remembered only that he'd been, well, foolish and amusing. He'd treated me well, though. I remembered that.

"This can't be all there is to see of Faery," Tucker remarked as we walked down yet another featureless corridor, the small Fool gamboling ahead of us, turning and twirling and motioning us to follow. We larger, human-size folk kept moving cautiously, each of us still wary.

"It's not," Adam said. "For lack of a better word, they've cloaked a lot of the passageways."

"Hidden, then." Niko grimaced as he touched a wall. "They hide from us?"

"Mostly, yes." Adam looked at Niko as we walked, two by two, Adam and I ahead, Niko and Tucker taking our six. "They don't know what to expect from the two of you, so they hide."

"Us?" Niko didn't disguise his disdain. "We are the ones making them hide?"

"You are strangers. And for that, I am sorry. Nikolai, you are family to me and should be treated as such, just as yon wolf there is family to us both. It's—"

"They like to play games, Niko," I said, my voice weary. "It's in their nature. Head games, mind you, and they're damned good at it."

"So we are, dear lady, so we are."

A tall man stood at the bend in the corridor, the dark light that shone from the walls seeming to surround him. He wore dark shimmering clothing, tunic and trousers and highly polished boots. Long black hair swirled around his shoulder as he stood still, as if a hidden breeze moved about him. Was this the dark bard? Or someone else?

"Aeddan. Fancy that. You have come home?"

"As if you didn't know, Iolo," Adam answered, voice as neutral as Switzerland. "Were you the one Above then?"

"You knew about that?" The other man chuckled, no fey music accompanying his amusement. Instead, the dark swirl around him moved more quickly, in a new pattern.

"I'd surmised," Adam said. "I didn't know it was you, definitely."

"Ah well, then. Now you know."

Was this Iolo guy admitting to having been the one that killed the Sidhe bard? I opened my mouth to speak, but held back as Adam took my hand, giving it a squeeze as he addressed Iolo.

"My father?"

Iolo let his gaze rake over me first, then Niko and Tucker. With a slight bow, he motioned to his left. "After you, dear cousin, after you."

"I don't think so," I answered before Adam could. "We will follow you."

The bard studied me a moment with a wondering look. "You are heir to Branwen ferch Arianrhod; niece to High Queen Angharad?"

"I am." I stood my ground. What did my mother's heritage mean here at the Unseelie Court? Would I be treated as an equal, a visiting dignitary or simply an enemy? Or, almost worse, just Adam's girlfriend . . . his property?

"Welcome, Keira ap Huw ferch Branwen, you and your kin shall be as our kin."

With a wave and a motion of his hand, the walls shimmered, then faded. We were standing in a great hall,

all inky sheen and smooth polished stone, mixed with ebony wood and silver accents. I'd venture to guess it was pure silver in the decor. No steel in those pillars, no other base metals in the whorls of shine. Nothing to weaken or cause discomfort. In the center of the hall, a man sat on what could only be described as a throne. Upholstered in the richest black velvet, looking nothing like the elaborate white bone and silver chair that held my mother's cousin. I'd seen it only once . . . and once was enough to imprint the view for life. Even as a child, I could tell that chair hurt. This one, though, was the epitome of luxurious comfort.

"Father." Adam's voice was both smooth with diplomacy and rough with held-back emotion. What was he feeling? How long had it been?

"He who was once my son arrives." Drystan's voice was a twin to Adam's, a shade deeper and a hell of a lot more amused. "Still walking the night, I see."

"I am."

"And your companions—how droll. The other night-walker is yours?"

"I made him." At Adam's words, I saw Niko's arm tremble slightly, as if frightened. I glanced at his face. No, not fear—anger. Tucker grasped Niko's hand and with a caressing thumb, calmed the vampire. Niko's anger subsided and his lips held tight against the words I knew he forced back. "He is mine, but is also his." A slight nod indicated Tucker.

"Interesting." Drystan watched Tucker and Niko for a moment, a smile curling onto his lips. Egads. His mouth was so very much like Adam's. The family resemblance was strong and, to my very deepest regret, obviously extended to Gideon, who, I was now realizing, was stamped from this mold. How had I not noticed this before? Perhaps because Adam's nature, though darker by his very being, was so completely the opposite of Gideon's reckless abandon and need to dive into the dark. Adam, Gideon and their father were all tall, dark-haired and light-eyed. Adam's eyes were the deep green of the ocean; Gideon's the deep blue of midnight; Drystan's? Hard to tell at this distance, but I would bet on hazel.

"So you are the princess who captured the hearts of both my sons." Drystan, continuing his tack of amusement, rose from his chair and approached us.

"Not exactly planned," I said. "I guess I'm attracted to a certain type."

Tucker snorted behind me. Adam and Niko said nothing.

"A type, she says." Drystan grinned. "I like you."

"Goody." I let my sarcasm out again. "So, Drystan, what about the murders?"

A shock of murmuring sound ran through the hall, hidden Sidhe voices whispering. Even the walls have ears here, Keira, if they are walls at all—remember that. There may be no one visible, but they're all watching.

"The musician crossed boundaries," Drystan said with a dismissive wave of a beringed hand. "He disobeyed. We called him back and he would not return to us quietly."

"How can I believe that? He was stabbed, beaten—" I said evenly, trying to keep as calm as possible.

"After being drained of life—" Iolo interrupted his king, who gave him a royal glare. Iolo gave a slight nod and subsided.

"You killed humanely?" My words were bitter, a taste of foulness in my mouth.

"As humanely as you did with the man Pete Garza," Drystan declared. "You and your brother sentenced him to death."

"And you know this how?"

"We have our sources." The unseen crowd behind him tittered, an invisible Greek chorus. "You would do well to allow us our own ways here, Keira Kelly."

"And Above?" I ask. "Your ways do not—should not—reach there. Not to the city. Not to several human dead."

"Casualties." He lifted a shoulder, indifference visible in every gesture. "They were attuned to the fey. They dreamed themselves to death."

Well, damn. If he was telling the truth, this altered the picture considerably.

"Dreamed?" Niko's voice slid through, a mere whisper.

"Old men's dreams. They died happy," Iolo remarked. "In the old days, many chose to die that way."

"They were not murdered?" Tucker broke in.

"No," Iolo confessed. "I simply meant to find information in that place. The other, the bard had been there. The men were weak, already close to death."

I quickly sized up my companions' reactions. Niko still held a look of anger, but Tucker and Adam both seemed to be coming to the same conclusion I was.

Adam spoke on our behalf after a silent conversation with Niko, who sighed and nodded. "The humans, then, were only accidents—not outright murders. There was no retribution involved, no intent. Your action against your bard is a Sidhe affair."

"It could be your affair as well, son." Drystan approached Adam with a tilt to his head as if studying him. "You look well, Aeddan. How long has it been since you came Below?"

Adam regarded his father, his face giving away nothing as his face solidified into the now familiar to me vampire stone. "Measuring in years Above? Centuries."

"Ah, well then. Too long." The king then came to me, his hands open in greeting. "Your mother is my rival's cousin and heir presumptive. Welcome, daughter."

"Why do you call me daughter?" I asked. "Unless someone's really been pulling another fast one on me, my father is—"

"Huw Kelly of Clan Kelly. And you are heir to Minerva?"

"I am," I said, echoing Adam's earlier words. "You know a lot about me for someone who's not even related."

"I have watched you, Keira Kelly." Drystan's smile took on a feral quality. "You were with my son."

"And am still," I said too hotly, moving closer to Adam and taking his hand.

Shining laughter surrounded us, the sound of deep bells underlying the king's voice. "I meant my other son," he said. "The one like you."

"So, it really is true." I gripped Adam's hand tighter. Despite the plainly evident physical resemblance, I was still holding out hope that all this was purely really weird coincidence.

"Oh, very much so." The voice came from behind us . . . a voice I'd known as intimately as I'd ever known anyone's.

Gideon.

CHAPTER THIRTY

"NO AND NO and bloody hells, no freaking way are you here." I faced my former lover with hands on my hips. "Tell me this is not happening and that this is some secret brother y'all had squirreled away."

"'Fraid not, lover," Gideon drawled. "It's me."

I resisted the urge to move forward and slap his face. Tempting, but we were in Court; manners mattered. "Do not call me that, Gideon Kelly. What the hell are you doing here anyway? I thought you were—"

"Gideon ap Drystan, if you please and, as you can see, I'm no longer dying, dear cousin," Gideon interrupted with a sweeping gesture. "It was long past time to come visit my father. So here I am."

"Well, bully for you." I shot back at him. "What's this ap Drystan thing? Kelly no longer good enough for you?"

"Perhaps not," he said. "I find that there are many things about my father's Court that I find quite amenable."

"No doubt," I nearly spat. "I'm sure this is right up your very special dark alley. So you knew about him? How come you never said anything?"

A nonchalant shrug accompanied his answer. "Oh, I didn't actually know about my father before," he said. "But once I did, I wanted to find him. So here I am."

"Commendable, I suppose." I crossed my arms. "What about the coma and your impending death? I get a frantic visit from Isabel who tells me I have to come to BC, then

I get there and am told you are stable, no need to rush and now you aren't even at the enclave. You're *here* . . . in Faery." I gestured, indicating our surroundings. "Wherever here actually is."

"You mean you didn't know?" Gideon sounded legitimately surprised. "I'd assumed you came here because—"

I broke into laughter, cutting him off. "Oh. My. Gods and goddesses. You really thought I came down here because of *you*? That's some ego you have, Gideon Kelly, though I shouldn't be surprised. You always thought the world revolved around your shiny ass. Well, I have news, oh cousin and very former lover—it is so not all about you. In fact, it was never at all about you."

With a toss of his head and a vicious sneer, Gideon pushed past me, giving Adam an angry look. As he brushed by, a wave of dark energy hit me. My knees buckled. I grabbed onto Adam as I wavered, my balance fighting with the sense of power emanating from Gideon. My own shields responded, a moment too late, trying to shut out the energy. Dizzy, I held on to Adam's arm and shoulder, attempting to block what I could. Tendrils of energy still seeped inside. I could nearly see them, they vibrated so strongly, humming with a dark song, a melody that sounded vaguely familiar. Adam grabbed onto me, brow furrowed in a look of concern.

"What have you done?" He directed his anger at Gideon.

I broke free of Adam's grip and took a step toward my former lover.

Gideon paused when he saw my movement. He threw me an amused look, then continued to Drystan's side. He turned and then gave me the slow once-over, his smirk deepening, chest puffing out with self-importance. Oh, yeah, power play and loads of it . . . literally. The energy increased and pushed at me, the tendrils turning into thick ropes, weaving together, a multiheaded hydra attacking, looking for a way in.

I stood my ground, fists clenched. At my side, I heard Adam's quick breath. He took my left hand, forced my fist open and intertwined his fingers with mine.

"Let me help," he whispered so quietly that even I had trouble hearing him. What was he asking? I couldn't split my concentration now. Gideon's energy pulsed against my own reinforced shields. He pushed. I swallowed hard and tried to envision a smooth, reflective wall of glass and steel behind it—a mirror to reflect. Would it work?

Men could be so predictable. I should have expected this . . . revenge, was it? He'd been so angry when I left him. He'd never understood why I hadn't gleefully jumped into his plans.

My mind began to wander back to the day of my final argument with Gideon. Focus, Keira! Forcing my attention back to the present, I fought the sinuous energy as it wove around me, surrounding me, looking for a weak spot, a way in. I tensed, trembling with the effort. The room around me faded. Breathe, Keira. Breathe through this. You can—

Without warning, a surge of power breached my defenses, invisible hands touching me intimately, as I loved to be touched, as he'd well known once upon a time. "No," I gritted the word, clamping down on the power and unleashing my own. A second wave, dark green, the fresh scent of spice and vanilla bolstered by a musical chime of unearthly beauty, joined my own energy, merged with it, dancing, teasing. I tried to shake it off, then caught the flavor. Adam. I couldn't risk looking at him right now.

Resenting that I needed his help, but grateful for it, I stopped trying to shake him off.

Gideon's energy persisted: insistent, forcing, touching, a tendril up my side, across my breasts, on the insides of my thighs. The power clinging to him, the sheer energy of magick flowing in and around him—so heady, dark and extremely dangerous—so seductive, so . . . repellant. I didn't recognize this energy signature. It was so much more than he'd had back when we'd been a couple. He'd only had potential then, but this, this was the completed story; the denouement had come and Gideon, like me, had Changed—and apparently not for the better.

With a snarl, I fully accepted Adam's gift, weaving our power together, and with a twist and pull, tore Gideon's energy from us, pushing it away, rejecting it, thrusting it out, slinging it back toward its originator.

Gideon stumbled, hands out, grasping for support and, finding none, he sank to his knees, head bowed. His dark hair hid his expression, but I was willing to bet he was no longer smirking. Drystan, beside him, watched in amusement. Fucking Sidhe royalty.

"What in all the levels of all the hells was that? You've Changed—how?" I took a step forward, stopped only by Tucker, who immediately moved me to one side and stood in front of me, in instant bodyguard mode. On his other side, Niko took a similar stance, fangs bared and a subharmonic growl sliding past me. Adam remained at my side, hand gripping mine tightly. I shuddered as the tension rose in the room, a palpable sense of energy rising—thick and livid from Tucker and Niko; amused and tinged with darkness from Gideon, who'd recovered and stood.

I gritted my teeth and fought the renewed surge of energies, concentrating on bolstering my personal shields, wanting to stop it from affecting me. Was Gideon's power more than mine? Or was it that he'd never held himself to limits and was doing the power equivalent of flashing fang for a vampire? One deep breath, another and then—

"Enough!" Drystan held up a hand. "Gideon, that will do. The two of you, enough. Keira, he is no threat."

I'd have argued, but that was when a new surge hit me and I blacked out.

CHAPTER THIRTY-ONE

A WARM WETNESS slid across my face as I came to, gagging on raw power that, somehow, my body saved up and, at the same time, was trying to expel. Too little, too late, I thought as I turned on my side and took deep breaths. I had no intention of vomiting.

"Keira?" A woman's quiet voice came from my right. I blinked, taking in my surroundings. Wherever I was it was too dark to see well, unless I concentrated, and right now, my head felt as if someone had used it for a soccer ball. The soft light of a few lit candles overlaid the natural dark shine of the stone walls. I lay on some sort of chaise, the dark upholstery plush and soft under my skin. A small woman sat next to me, a cloth in her hand dampened with something that smelled faintly of lavender and other herbs, a bowl of water on a small table next to her infused with the same scent.

"May I?" she asked, her words soft. "It will help."

I nodded, my head protesting the movement. "How long?" I croaked as she bathed my forehead with the warm cloth. The lavender and other herbs smelled wonderful, soothing calming and restorative all at the same time. My skin tingled under her ministrations.

"Not long," she said. "An hour, perhaps."

She perched on some sort of ottoman. The lights in the room had dimmed . . . or was it me? I blinked again and the woman clucked as she placed a cool hand on my forehead.

"Stay still, child," she said. "You've had a power surge and need to restore yourself."

"A what?" Tucker growled, voice coming from behind me. I turned my aching head in his direction. He and Niko flanked the low chaise, standing in identical postures, still playing bodyguard. Huh. Was I going to have to Mark the vampire, too? It wasn't a bad idea . . . though as bad ideas went, what the ever-loving hells had my great-great-granny gotten us into? Two heirs? Two Changed Kelly heirs, both simultaneously half Sidhe and somehow interwoven in those lines of succession, too? Had she been hedging her bets? Or was this all some inane and extremely long-term plot to have the Kelly clan be the unifier of all the superteams . . . so to speak? In any case, the only one with the final multizillion-dollar answer wasn't in the room. I'd lay all sorts of bets that Drystan, like my mother, no doubt, had very little knowledge of the endgame.

"Power surge," the woman responded. "And be quiet. Keira will need quiet for a time."

"What's that?" I murmured, my body beginning to relax as she massaged my temples.

"It's to be expected from a newly empowered Sidhe. You've only come into your power recently, I take it?"

I nodded and immediately regretted the movement as my head decided to send another jolt of pain through my body. "Crap, that hurts," I whispered. "My head—"

"Is she going to be all right?" Tucker asked the woman.

"Yes, it's just a wee bit overwhelming right now. Everything for her is magnified."

"How'd this happen?" Tucker asked. "She was fine, then—"

"Then Gideon let unchecked power free—she reacted."

She scowled at the bowl of herb-scented water. "I am sorry for that, Keira. He should not have been—"

"There are a great many things he should not have been." Tucker gritted the words through his teeth. "Including that powerful. Has Drystan explained any of this?"

She shook her head. "He's said nothing, for all that I am his sister. Please, call me Glenys."

Adam's aunt. A family member from Adam's side of the family—his Sidhe side. Well, come to think on it, he was fully Sidhe, fully Unseelie Court, well, plus that whole vampire thing. Underneath the throbbing pain, I held on to my sanity with the tips of my mental fingernails, hoping that I wouldn't let myself fall into a gibbering heap.

She placed the cloth on my head. "Drystan keeps much from me, from the rest of the Court. None of us knew of Gideon until now."

"At all?" I croaked. "No one?"

"We knew of his existence, but since he was born Above, we thought he'd remain there." She smiled. "I suppose we should have known better. My brother is a tricksy one . . . with a long eye for the future."

I shifted on the chaise, my body aching, every muscle sore as if I'd been beaten by an expert. In a sense, perhaps I had been. How the fuck had *both* Gideon and I Changed? In everything I'd been taught, there could be only one heir at a time and those were few and far between. Many many centuries could pass before a new heir emerged. "I don't understand—"

Glenys's melodious voice soothed me, as if she felt my anxiety, a hand covering my eyes, soft scent of lavender filling my nostrils. "Hush, child, relax. Focus on your body, the channels of power. They're all twisted inside of you. You need to fix it." The words faded into one another as I let the words wash over me, muscles relaxing in the wake of her calm.

"Breathe deep, Keira," she instructed. "Focus on my voice, center your energy, stabilize it, balance . . ." She began to hum a low tune, soft and quiet as her words had been. "Breathe in, out. In. Out. Focus."

I complied, calling on training I'd had in meditation to help harness the potential talent in me, now realized and cut loose by my brush with Gideon. I caught my breath, losing the rhythm, but she shushed me again, still humming. Minutes, hours, days, time flowed into itself and back again as I sank deep into my own awareness, found the wild strands of power straining to escape. I corralled them, twisted them back to where they belonged, wove them back into the pattern of my body, my energy field. As the last strand fell back into place and merged with the rest, I let out a huge sigh and my body finally let go of the pain.

"Wow," I said in a near whisper. "You're good."

"Thank you," she said. "Aeddan has always been a favorite of mine. My brother's only son—at least, the only one he acknowledged. When he was first made vampire, I was there. I helped him. Those first few days of rebirth can be difficult."

I studied Glenys' countenance. She had one of those placid, serene faces often found in Renaissance portraits of women. Her dark auburn hair was dressed in two plaits, caught up behind her head at the nape of her neck. She wore a tunic and skirt, subdued dark colors complementing her pale Sidhe complexion.

"Thank you," I said. "For helping me. For helping Adam before."

Glenys gave me a quiet smile. "I am glad that I could be of service to you and to Aeddan. Your situation is unusual enough as it is."

"You said a mouthful, Glenys," I said as I sat up, my energy now back to normal. "What do you know of all of this?"

"Nothing more than you do, my dear. I apologize for not being able to enlighten you."

"Were you aware of Gideon's Change?" I asked her.

"In theory and in rumor, yes," she said. "I heard him discussing such with Drystan earlier this day. Am I to understand that he was once your lover?" Her gentle eyes blazed, a shrewdness and penetrating power now filling them.

"Afraid so," I said. "I had no idea, though—"

"Of any of it," Tucker interrupted. "I'm thinking Gigi has a load of 'splaining to do."

"I should think so," I said. "Where the hell is Adam, anyway? My vote is to get our carcasses out of Faery and back to Vancouver."

"That's just it," Tucker said. "After we brought you here to this room and Glenys arrived, Niko and I went back to the Great Hall. I wanted explanations and, frankly, I was ready to kick some Gideon Kelly ass. Everyone was gone from the hall."

"Gone where?"

"No idea," Tucker answered. "Niko and I searched around for a while, but all we saw were those blank corridors."

"They've taken Adam," Niko growled. "I can't feel him."

Startled, I instinctively reached out with my own

senses. I knew Adam's signature nearly as well as my own brother's. When he was anywhere near, it was there, a reassuring sensation. But now, Niko was right. It was gone.

"Fuck." I swung my legs around to stand. "We've got to go find him."

"I believe Drystan is in conference with both his sons," Glenys said. "I sent one of the servants to find Aeddan, but they were denied access to Drystan's rooms."

"Bloody brilliant." I gritted my teeth. "That's all we need—for Adam to get into it with his father and Gideon. After what he did to me . . ."

"What exactly *did* he do?" Niko asked. "All we could see were flashes of light, then you collapsed."

"He attacked me," I said bluntly. "Got inside my shields, touched me in ways not at all appropriate without permission and some simply not appropriate at all."

Tucker's growl merged with that of Niko. "He will pay for this, Keira."

"No, Tucker, don't." I rubbed my forehead. "I can handle Gideon. He took me by surprise. Daffyd was right: Gideon has Changed and, like me, he has all the Talents—the heirship."

"You mean . . . ?" Tucker closed the distance and sat next to me on the chaise, taking my hand. "Seriously, Keira, you mean Changed changed?"

I nodded. "I'm surprised you couldn't tell, Tucker. He's completely Talented, like me. Which is why he caught me out. I knew it was a possibility, but I guess I really wasn't expecting it to be true."

Niko joined us on the chaise, sitting next to Tucker. Glenys, a thoughtful look on her face, listened intently. "I thought you said there was only one heir at a time," Niko said.

"There is." Tucker was as confused as I was. "I have no idea what's going on."

"I think I do," Glenys put in.

The three of us looked at her as she continued. "Several decades ago, all of our people gathered—"

"Oh no, wait right there," I said. "The Summit. This was planned? Me, Gideon, both of us as possible heirs? I'm beginning to think that possible was more like probable." I turned to my brother. "How much you want to bet our fearless leader had this trick up her twisted sleeve all along?"

Tucker nodded. "Sounds like her type of machination."

"You mean she meant to have two heirs?" Niko looked astounded. "How could she know?"

"I have no freaking idea," I said. "But I'm damn well planning to find out. Our Gigi is no less ambitious than Attila the bloody Hun—just slightly more civilized in her attempts at taking over the world . . . our world."

"She meant for you and Gideon to be together," Tucker said. "Both of you, heirs to Kelly, connections to both the Seelie and Unseelie Courts."

"Then," Niko said, "Adam came into the picture."

Tucker nodded. "Heir to the High King—a better prospect, since he'd not actually been disinherited. Keira with Adam would give Gigi a greater possibility of aligning forces, creating the greater alliance. I've no doubt she's been scouring for a wer or other heir for Gideon to hook up with."

"Wait a damned minute, you two," I protested. "Theoretically, yeah, okay, this is totally just like Gigi. But—and a big but—I *chose* to be with Adam. Gigi had nothing to do with it."

Niko stared at me, a look of sorrow in his eyes. "He

pursued you, Keira. Desperately. He went to Texas for you. He contacted your leader as to your whereabouts when you left London."

"I know all of that," I retorted. "He told me. You can't mean to think this was at Gigi's behest?"

"Why could it not have been?" Niko argued. "Keira, I've known him for centuries. This singleminded pursuit of you was unlike him. We moved to Texas . . . to what, for us, was uncivilized country."

"Oh, please. Niko, do you not remember what we've found out about him? How he stalked you as a child and eventually rescued you? You can't tell me that obsessive behavior is outside the realm of Adam Walker's usual way of operating—it may be unusual, but not unheard of."

"She has a point, *cariad*," Tucker said, his voice gentle. "Perhaps he is selective about his focus."

"No less am I," Niko said fiercely and laid a sizzling kiss on Tucker's mouth. I watched in amusement for a long moment as the two men reaffirmed their commitment.

"Perhaps you and I should leave them to their privacy." Glenys, who'd kept silent throughout our discussion, said. "We can retire to my own rooms."

"I think not," I said. "Tucker, Niko, snap out of it. Plenty of time for snogging—or shagging—later. Let's go find Adam and get the hell out of Dodge."

CHAPTER THIRTY-TWO

"WHERE THE FUCK is he?" I asked Llwyd threateningly.

Niko, Tucker and I had spent what seemed like hours wandering corridors, searching for a sign of Adam, or even of Drystan or Gideon, before we'd run into the small fey, who'd then shown us back to the Great Hall. Like Tucker and Niko earlier, we'd found no one. Only Drystan's throne on a dais, two new throne-like chairs next to it and a few smaller stools and less-imposing chairs around those. "A seat for each son," Llwyd had said, and giggled.

One seat was *so* not likely to be used. Adam was coming back with us. Whether Gideon elected to stay, I neither knew nor cared.

"I cannot tell you, Keira Kelly." Llwyd cowered, covering his head with his small hands. "I would be forsworn."

Niko's eyes blazed, his fangs extended. "Forsworn or no, little man, you will take us to him. Now."

Llwyd hopped in place, agitation written all over his mobile face. "I cannot, I cannot."

"Stop, Niko." I put a hand up to hold the vampire back. "I think he's trying to say that he literally *can't* say . . . not won't."

"Is that true?" Niko addressed Llwyd.

The fey nodded happily. "Yes, yes, true. I cannot speak of this."

"Damntastic." I threw myself into one of the lesser chairs with a huff. "How the bloody hells are we going to find him?"

Llwyd winked at me, a sly smile crossing his face. "You could leave," he smirked. "Above, you could go. He could then follow."

I sat straight up. "Leave without Adam? No fucking way."

"Wait, Keira, Adam's bound to you now, isn't he?" Tucker reminded me. "A blood bond, just like he's bound to Niko."

I nodded. "Yes, but I can't sense him."

"And Gideon?" Niko asked. "Do you sense him?"

I thought a moment, closing my eyes. The scent of the Court hovered in the back of my nose, still smelling of Adam. A low murmur of music, familiar to me in a tantalizing way, teased the outer edges of my hearing. I concentrated, trying to identify it. Did it have something to do with Gideon? Or Adam?

A sudden turn of melody and I had it. It was the same music I'd heard in the taxicab. Iolo's Calling.

My eyes snapped open. "I don't feel either of them, but—the music. It's the same as I heard in the cab, and then later, as we searched for Daffyd."

"You hear it?" Llwyd's head tilted as he studied me, frowning. "Do the others of you hear it?"

Tucker and Niko shrugged. "We hear nothing," Tucker said. "But Keira's been hearing this on and off since we arrived in Vancouver."

"It's the song of the Court," Llwyd said. "It calls to kin. But you are not blood kin to us."

"Nor is Daffyd," I said. "My cousin on my mother's side. Seelie Court."

Another, deeper frown from the fey. "Only blood

should hear this. Only blood can Call." He took a few steps back. "I must . . . leave."

"No, wait—" I said as he scampered away, disappearing into one of the blank corridors.

I settled back into the seat. "Now what?" I threw up my hands. "Do either of you get the feeling that more things are rotten in Denmark than we've uncovered?"

"Yeah, we've uncovered enough rot to spread over all of Scandinavia, but there seems to be even more," Tucker said as he came to sit on a stool at my side. Niko came around to my other side but remained standing, one hand on the back of the chair. "I hate to say this, sis, but if only Unseelie can hear the music . . ."

"Do not go there, Tucker Kelly." I put my fingertips over his mouth before he could finish. "I know exactly the implication, and honestly, I have no more room for any more data right now. All I want is to find Adam. Then, once we're all back Above, back in our own turf, we'll figure this all out." And figure out how to close this door to Faery, I thought to myself.

"What about Gideon?"

"I'm all for him staying here if he wants. Let Gigi sort him out. For that matter, she can sort all of this out."

"I have a thought," Niko said. "What if we three returned Above—"

"Without Adam? I don't think so," I said, interrupting.

He put a hand on my shoulder. "Please, hear me out," he said. "I'm not saying we abandon him." I sat back, mollified.

"He is Sidhe, correct?" Niko looked at me as he spoke. I nodded. "As such, he can be Called, right?"

I frowned in confusion. Where was he going with this? "Yeah, sure, I guess, but what—"

"You hear the music," Niko explained. "The music that Called Daffyd from the taxicab. What's to prevent you, with your Sidhe heritage and your new Talents from Calling Adam once we reach the outside world? The Calling seems to work there as well as in Faery."

"Wow. That's . . ." I stood, paced a few steps forward, whirled and returned to face Niko. "What guarantee do we have that I can even do this?"

"None." Blue eyes steady on my own gray ones, a look of determination backed up by a sense of pleading, of need, kept me focused.

"You think I can?"

Niko nodded. "I believe that your power is great enough, yes."

"I'm no bard, no musician," I protested. "I play no instruments."

"You can hum," Niko stated. "Look, I know this is a long shot, Keira. But we could spend the rest of our existence wandering these featureless gray corridors and find nothing and no one. They have hidden from us. Whatever your powers are here, they cannot find Adam. I would wager they've been dampened somehow and that's why Gideon was able to affect you."

"Niko, you beautiful thing." Tucker got up and enveloped Niko in a bear hug, laying a smacking kiss on his mouth. "That's it, Keira," he said, turning to me. "I've been considering shifting, trying to find Adam that way, but every time I thought of it, I got distracted somehow, as if the thought slid away. This place restricts us."

Could he be right? I'd used Adam's power to block Gideon, but still had been laid low. I closed my eyes, trying to reach the part of myself that was wolf. I reached, turning my focus inside. There she was. I concentrated, calling her, but then as she came into my senses, she vanished, sliding away, like a dream fragment, only wisps of thought left. I tried again, fixing the image in my mind, but it was like trying to wrestle a greased pig on rain-wet caliche.

"You're right," I said with a grimace. "Niko, you are bloody marvelous. Here I was thinking we'd be stuck here forever, waiting until Drystan took it upon himself to communicate with us again."

"So we leave?" Niko asked. "And you will Call Adam?"

I nodded solemnly. "I'm not convinced it will work," I said. "But I know the entrance ritual now and if I can't call him to us, I have every intention of marshaling all the Kelly forces and convening my Seelie kin and Adam's vampires. I'll raise an army if I have to. We will not leave Adam here."

"You're willing to start a faery war?" Tucker looked at me in astonishment.

I nodded, purpose grim on my face. "If that's what it takes, brother. Drystan's got another think coming if he believes he can glamour his son away from me. I've no doubt that Adam is cooped up somewhere, trying to get free from his father."

Tucker nodded. "Then let's do this thing, sister . . . my liege."

I shot him an annoyed glance. "You may be my bondsman, brother mine, but stop with that liege shit." He started to protest but I raised a hand. "No, Tucker, I know, I know. It's technically true. Okay, completely true, but I don't intend to stand on any ceremony. Not with you." I regarded Niko. "Or you either, Nicholas. I've watched you guard me. It's not escaped me."

Niko bowed his head, a hand over his heart. "If you'll have me, Keira Kelly, my sister-companion, I pledge to guard you as your own kin." He knelt in front of me, sweeping his red hair from his neck.

As solemn as his oath, I stepped to him, lightly touching his nape. "I accept, Nicholas Marlowe, known as Niko."

Niko stood, and in an unexpected move, he embraced me, arms tight around me. "Thank you," he whispered in my ear. "Thank you for accepting me."

I hugged him back. How far we'd come in such a short time. I looked over at my brother, whose grin could have lit up the entire city of Vancouver.

"Well then, oh Protectors," I said as Niko stepped back. "Let's blow this pop stand."

CHAPTER THIRTY-THREE

"NO, THAT'S NOT quite it, damn it." I ran a hand through my windblown hair, no longer in its usual neat braid.

Niko, Tucker and I sat on the grassy hill of Victory Square, our exit from Faery less than spectacular and much too easy for my tastes. It was as if the place was glad to be rid of us.

The musicians we'd spoken to earlier, John and Rodney, were still there. Only a few minutes had passed in the outside world while we'd been Below. I'd argued with Tucker and Niko that we needed Daffyd—needed a Sidhe who could make music.

"But the two human musicians are here and they have no need of understanding your reasons," Niko had argued. "They have the old instruments. A guitar. A bodhrán. We have the flute. I am sure that with your help remembering the tune, we can do the calling."

"And how the hell am I supposed to explain it to them when Adam pops up out of nowhere?" I'd protested. "Let's go get Daffyd."

"I do not trust him." Niko had stood his ground. Stubborn vampire. Just as stubborn as his sire.

"Neither do I," Tucker had interjected. "What the hell, Keira, let's give it a try. If it works, you can vague them up."

Niko had shot Tucker a questioning look. "Vague them up?"

"Tamper with their memories," I'd explained. "Kelly Talent—which I guess I can do now. Though I have no idea how."

"I have faith in you," Tucker had said. "You'll figure it out."

I'd narrowed my eyes and scowled at my brother. "Glad you're so confident, brother." I'd sighed and shrugged. "Lead on, wolf. Let's to it."

Now I was trying to convey the tune to John. A Sidhe tune, that I, the non-musician, had heard vaguely and only in the back of my head. To his credit, he remained patient and didn't run away from this crazy woman and her two companions. On the other hand, I wondered how patient he'd have been if we hadn't paid them quite handsomely for their efforts.

"It's more like this." I closed my eyes, trying to conjure up the melody, the haunting refrain, the notes that wove in and out and beckoned to the blood. With a start, I flashed on Iolo, standing on a hill inside Faery, his lute in hand, strumming.

"What is it?" Tucker asked, worry in his voice. "You okay?"

I nodded. "Yeah, nothing. Never mind." I cleared my throat and began to hum again, focusing on the music. I let my mind bring forward the memory. Tucker sat close to me, his presence a comfort. I laid a hand on his arm, grounding myself, afraid to let myself get lost in the music again.

Behind me, Niko attempted to follow me on the flute, a talent I hadn't know he possessed. He'd explained he was but a dilettante; a brief flirtation with a musician some decades back led to his learning to play, but he'd not picked up the instrument in nearly as long. To John's left, Rodney softly beat the drum, trying to ascertain the beat. I continued to hum, Tucker taking up counterpoint, John strumming the strings softly. Slowly, we began to mesh, the faery melody becoming solid, real, harmony supporting it, the quiet beats of the bodhrán providing emphasis. The shivery hollow flute sound carried the sounds together, over the air, across the ground and into the very depths of our existence. I closed my eyes, the energies combining the five of us too strong for me to watch. We were creating a synergy, an unspoken spell, magick out of music. I continued to hum, zeroing in on my purpose—the Call. Without missing a beat, we each moved closer to the others.

The world Above fades around me as I follow the sound beyond and Below; my consciousness carries forth, targeting only one goal: Adam Walker. Here, the corridors are no longer dark-gray shining stone, but near transparent, shimmering colors chasing across the glassy surface. I see hordes of Sidhe folk, lesser fey, nymphs, dryads, fairies with gossamer wings flitting about. Some feasting, some fucking, some sitting and listening, entranced by Iolo's own bardic tales. Ignoring them all, I keep searching. In the far corner, I see a darkness out of the corner of my eye. A cloud, impenetrable by my vision, by my senses. There. Closer still, I see the cloud isn't completely opaque, just dense. Defenses laid thick by Gideon. I'd recognize that signature anywhere, despite its new flavor. Behind the curtain of dark gray, three men: Drystan, Gideon, Adam. Arguing, words silent to my hearing. Adam's fangs bare, something he never does outside of feeding. He is king, he cannot lose control.

Gideon struts along the back of the room, smirk now fixed on his face as a mask. Behind it, though, I see something else: jealousy, disappointment, want, perhaps?

Is it me he wants or power? Or power with me? I don't know and care even less. Gideon is less than nothing to me now. He fulfilled all his potential—the negative kind. Too bad for him.

Adam stops in his mute tirade, head tilted and eyes searching the richly appointed room. I barely notice the furnishings as my focus reaches Adam. He stills, his fangs retracting. Drystan moves into the periphery of my vision, but Adam bows to him, says something. Gideon springs forward, too late. Adam smiles and vanishes.

"He's coming," I said and sagged against Tucker's side.

"I'm here." Adam stepped out from behind us, and with a swift move, hauled me up into an embrace, burying his face in my hair.

"HOW DID you—?" Adam finally asked. "I was speaking to my father and then . . . I heard . . ." He stopped as he realized we had company.

John and Rodney, both of whom had stopped playing their instruments, regarded Adam with curiosity, but nothing more than could be expected of anyone meeting Adam for the first time. He did have a commanding presence—whether that was the vampire or the Sidhe prince, I had no idea, but in any case, most humans were usually impressed at first sight. Not to mention he'd appeared out of the thin night air.

"You're not the other guy," Rodney said with a sniff of dismissal. He bent back over his drum and fiddled with a fragment of leather.

"Other guy?" Adam asked, raising an eyebrow.

John ran a hand down the strings of the guitar. "The other musician guy," he said. "Who played this song a couple of days ago. Thought he might come back once we started playing. It was really cool, though," he added. "With the humming and the flute. Lots richer this time. Really great." He smiled, his love for the music shining in his face. "Thanks, yeah?"

"You are very welcome, John. We'd jam with you any time." I smiled broadly. "You all were brilliant." He had no idea how much.

"I'm afraid we must be going now," Adam said to the men. "Thank you for the music."

John studied the four of us. Niko, Tucker's arm wrapped around his shoulder. Me, my hand in Adam's. "You all take good care then, eh."

"That we will," I said. "And the same to you."

John nodded and turned back to his guitar, now picking out a new tune. One of the Child Ballads, I thought. I laughed as we walked away, recognizing the tune.

"What's so amusing?" Adam asked as we climbed the hill hand in hand toward the main street.

"I'm thinking yon musician knows a lot more than he let on," I said.

"What do you mean?" Tucker asked.

I smiled as I hailed a passing cab, unwilling as I was to walk the rest of the way to the condo. "Didn't you recognize the tune?" I asked.

"No," Adam said as he held the cab door open for Niko and I to enter the back.

I slid to the center seat and waited until everyone was settled and all doors shut and Tucker gave the driver the address of our building. "John was playing 'Tam Lin.'"

CHAPTER THIRTY-FOUR

I STEPPED INTO the condo, exhausted but exhilarated, the three men behind me. We'd spoken little on the short trip back. All I wanted to do now was spend the time relaxing for at least, oh, three years or so. I'd settle for a good day's sleep and then we'd tackle Daffyd. I intended to offer him the way into Faery if he'd go back and stay out of my affairs. True, this local door only led into the Unseelie lands, but I figured Daffyd could find his way from there. Then, I planned to consult with family to figure out how to seal this door for good. It wasn't safe having an avenue for the Sidhe to come into Vancouver. This was Kelly turf.

A figure, too small to be Rhys or Daffyd, sat in silhouette, perched on one of the armchairs in the darkened apartment, side-lit by a small lamp. Oh, bloody wonderful. This made my fucking day.

"Minerva." I remained standing in the entryway, reluctant to go any closer. Adam came up beside me, Tucker and Niko stopped behind.

"Not Gigi?" She grinned, white teeth flashing as I flipped a switch, illuminating the whole room with tasteful indirect lighting.

"A child's name for use by children." I met her steady gaze with an equally steady one. "Evidently, I'm not one anymore."

Her silvery laugh echoed in the room, bouncing off the walls as if we were in the Great Hall at Minas Tirith or

Edoras and not in a rather cozy living room in a glass-and-steel tower in the middle of a modern city.

"I missed you, child. You're like a breath of fresh air."

Yeah. Me and Hurricane Katrina.

"I hear you were Below," she said, keeping her amused tone. "Visiting."

"You could call it that, I suppose."

"Come, sit, dear one. Let's chat." She patted the arm of the chair. Yeah, right. Not even.

"I'll come sit," I said as I went in, heading for a spot across from her but not too close. "Adam, boys, shall we?"

The three men followed me into the living room. Tucker and Niko took up their now customary posts on either side of me.

Adam stepped toward Gigi and gave her a polite bow, one ruler to another. "Minerva."

"It's been too long, Aeddan," Gigi said with a smile.

"That's what my father said." Adam returned her smile. Neither of them let their smiles reach their eyes.

"How is Drystan?"

"The same."

"How droll." Gigi turned her attention to my brother. "Tucker, you look well."

"I am." He smiled, nodded, but didn't leave my side.

"And this must be Nicholas. A pleasure." Gigi extended a hand. Niko, ever the courtier, stepped forward, took it and bowed over it.

"The pleasure is mine, m'lady." He stood and returned to his place, guarding me.

My great-great-grandmother's eyes narrowed as she took in the scene. "Well, well . . . how . . . interesting. You seem to have garnered more than one champion, child."

"Seems that I have." I settled into an armchair across

from her. Adam perched on the arm of the chair, while Niko and Tucker flanked me. "So then, shall we talk?" Two could play this silly game, I thought.

My grandmother looked no different from when I last saw her: petite, dark of hair and eye, a society matron who would look no more out of place at a reception at Buckingham Palace than at Neiman Marcus. Her delicate feminine features hid a mind as sharp as a serpent's tooth and about as vicious. Family was her first and foremost obligation and focus, and woe betide he or she who crosses a Kelly. That said, she ruled her family with the proverbial velvet-gloved steel hand. She tolerated no fools, nor those who sought to harm the Kelly name.

"No entourage, Minerva?" I waved a hand, indicating the lack of bodyguards. "That's unusual." I briefly wondered how she'd gotten here. Surely Raine had not had time to fly north and fetch her back? For all I knew she'd flown here in a chariot drawn by winged dragons. Or had some Clan version of Scotty beam her down. But no need to waste brain cells cogitating on her travel arrangements. I had enough to deal with.

"Unusual circumstances, wouldn't you say, child?" She regarded me with amusement. "I came to rescue you or, perhaps, to keep you safe, since you didn't seem to be obeying my directive to come to me. Yet, you seem to need no rescuing."

I nodded. "I apologize for not leaving right away. I figured we"—I motioned to my companions—"could take on a rogue Sidhe. I didn't figure on the rest."

A raised eyebrow and another smile. "You bearded the lion in his den, then? How amusing. I take it you won."

"So to speak." I laid a hand on Adam's arm. "We all got out."

"Left Gideon there," Tucker put in. "Did you know about that? About him?"

Gigi's smile turned sour. "I did. Ungrateful child. He Changed, you know."

"Yeah, I kind of discovered that—the hard way." I spit out the words. "He attacked me, Gigi. I blacked out."

Her eyes widened, the only indication of surprise. "You seem to be fine."

"I am," I said, "thanks to one of Adam's relatives . . . and to Adam himself, who loaned me power. My cousin is dangerous, Gigi. I don't know what the freaking hell you were thinking with all of this, but of all the damned people—"

"He's as much heir as you are, Keira," she said. "Perhaps in more need of attention, but—"

"Attention, my ass." I sprang up and strode over to her chair. Crossing my arms, I stared down at her. "What exactly were you playing at, Minerva? Some half-baked breeding experiment trying to bond all the Other together? Was that it? If so, I think it's backfired . . . a lot."

She stood, her five-foot-and-a-smidgen stature no match for my own five foot ten. Despite that, I stepped back. She still overwhelmed me, power for power, and it was damned unmistakable. "Backfired? Oh no, my darling child. It's nowhere near a backfire. It's worked out much better than I ever thought."

"It's true, then." Adam crossed the room to join me, his voice as angry as mine. "All this was part of your manipulations, your machinations? Was it not bad enough that my own father had me made vampire? Now you're breeding between the various tribes of Other? Did you want the power that much?"

"You overstep your bounds, vampire," Gigi warned,

her power flaring. I put a hand on Adam's shoulder and with less effort than I expected, extended my shields while simultaneously increasing their resistance. Gigi stared at me, her eyes like steel. "You've learned much, Keira."

"I've had to." I slid my hand down to grasp Adam's hand. "Adam is mine, Minerva, and king in his own right. You had no business messing in our lives."

"Do not address things you know nothing of, child. There is more to this messing than you know." Gigi settled back into the chair, having once again attained her regal detachment. "Be assured your best interests are always at the heart of anything I do. You are my heir."

"And Gideon?" I countered. "He's the elder of the two of us. Wouldn't he be heir? I'm just the spare." I let go of Adam's hand and went back to my own chair. He followed after a curt bow in Gigi's direction.

"The existence of two heirs was more than I could have hoped for," she admitted. "It has no precedence. When you were both born, I saw the signs in each of you. I'd intended for you to remain with your mother, then come to us when it was time for the Change. You could have ruled your mother's Court, influenced her cousin's. Gideon was meant to be my heir here and, with his connection to Drystan, help influence the High King and his heir." She nodded, indicating Adam.

"But I hadn't anticipated the coldness of your mother's people toward you, Keira, so you joined us as a child. Later, when you were attracted to Gideon, I admit to seeing the interesting possibilities of your union, but I did not mess, as you say, in establishing your relationship."

I wasn't entirely sure I believed her.

"When Gideon demonstrated . . ." She paused a moment. "When he frightened you so with his experiments of the darker sort, I attributed it primarily to his youth and his Unseelie blood, but it also made me aware, for the first time, that you and Gideon were of quite different natures."

You got that right, granny, I thought to myself.

"Still, there were many alternatives and I continued in my campaign to unite all Other. I'd already convinced the wer's Fenrir to join us, to perhaps consider joining our families in a blood bond. I intended to eventually speak with yon vampire king." She nodded toward Adam. "Fate, it would seem, leant us her twisted hand in having him fall in love with you. Not necessarily a bad thing, mind you."

"Not at all." Adam placed his hand on my shoulder. "So all of this was part of that last summit, then? You admit, I was never part of those plans."

"No, you were not," Gigi said. "Your father and I thought it was best to keep our ideas to ourselves for the time being. There was no guarantee that our plan would work."

"What I still don't get," Tucker said, "is how you figured that breeding half Sidhe children would give you heirs. That's some genetic anomaly, right?"

Point to my brother, who asked the question that I hadn't even thought of. My great-great-granny was brilliant, conniving and beyond Machiavellian in her plotting, but there's no way to guarantee genetics, especially not nearly forty years ago . . . was there?

"I'd like to hear that answer, too," I found myself saying.

Gigi steepled her hands and brought them to her mouth, as if in thought. Was she pondering how to explain or how to, once again, prevaricate?

"What I say now, to you four, I only say because of your positions." Gigi had gone from amused to deadly serious—a tone I'd never before heard in her voice. "I only tell you, Keira, as my heir, and you, Aeddan ap Drystan, known as Adam Walker, as her partner and heir to the Unseelie Court. Tucker and Nicholas, you are Protectors and everything said in this room comes under privilege."

Whoa. Privilege. I've only *heard* of that, never been involved in a conversation where it was invoked. Privilege, to us, was as binding as the seal of the confessional, as client/attorney discussion, as the oath taken by healers to keep their patients' affairs secret.

I nodded, as did the men.

"Heirs are made, not born."

"What?" "How?" "That's impossible." Everyone began talking and arguing, each one speaking louder than the rest until it hurt to listen to the cacophony.

"Shut up, all of you," I demanded, the subharmonics returning. "I want to hear the explanation." All three men immediately quieted.

Gigi, back to amused, smiled at me. "Command voice, so soon."

"Enough from you, too," I said, trying to keep my temper. "Damn it, Gigi, you've kept me in the dark long enough. Explain yourself."

"Breeding is true," she said, "but if the genes are there, I can tell with a quick spell. Every child born in your generation as well as the one before yours was tested. You, Gideon and Marty each had the right genes."

"Marty? What the fuck?" This had now gone from the merely insane to the absolutely ridiculous. "Marty had no Talent, no power at all. He was a weird genetic glitch, a biological sport, one hundred percent human."

"He was, sadly enough," Gigi said. "When I discovered the genetic set you had, I and my companions—your father, Adam, and your mother, Keira, and Marty's father performed a ritual cleansing and Calling. The ritual is intended to wake the dormant genes, raise the Talent in you . . . to unlock the potential."

"Marty's had the opposite effect," Tucker stated, clueing in.

She nodded. "Not opposite, really, so much as the genes present were so blocked that no amount of Talent could manifest. His father was heartbroken. He and Marty's mother left our branch of the family and relocated somewhere in New Zealand."

"Well, I'll be—" I sank back into the comfort of the chair as I processed this new information. All these years, I believed—hell, all my family had always believed—that the Kelly heir was simply a crapshoot of genetics. Not so much. "You made us," I said. "Me, Gideon, and poor Marty."

"I'm afraid so," Gigi admitted. "Although, Marty would have been himself even if we hadn't performed the ritual."

Small comfort that. He'd died because I hadn't been vigilant enough. "What now, Gigi? You have two heirs. Gideon's Below with his father. I'm here, but I really prefer not to be."

"He and you have settled—quickly, I might add," Gigi said. "Normally, this takes weeks, sometimes even years, as you gather your strengths. Originally, I didn't want you here until I knew what would happen with Gideon."

"But then, why did you have Isabel come get me when he was in a coma?"

Gigi ducked her head, avoiding eye contact. Okay, that was new. She'd never done that before.

"Frankly, Keira, I was afraid I'd made a terrible mistake with him."

"How so?"

"He began to suspect he was the heir. I think he also learned who his father was. He'd come back to the Clan, not too long after we relocated. I believe he overheard some conversations he was never meant to hear or somehow obtained information intentionally kept from him."

"Gigi, please, of all people, you should have known better. Gideon is the consummate eavesdropper and shortcut taker."

"That's exactly why I sent for you."

"Sorry?"

"Gideon took a shortcut. He determined that he could force the Change by magick overload, forcing the near-death experience. I'm afraid he ended up in a coma. I wanted you to come, to help him along as Escort if this meant his death. And if he died, I wanted you to be here to be recognized as my heir. The reason for Gideon's death—that he thought himself heir and died trying to Change—might be guessed. It would be important to show there was an heir already. Besides, I wanted to have you in my territory."

"Texas is still your territory, Gigi," I reminded her. "As is all of the Americas. For that matter, you pretty much rule over all the Clan in the UK and parts of Switzerland—at least, the ones that aren't officially neutral."

"It's one thing to have you in Texas, my sweet, but another to have you nearby. Besides, your vampire rules there now."

"Over the vampires," I agreed. "Not us."

Gigi shrugged, a girlish gesture not at odds with her current appearance.

"Truth, but now that you are partnered with him . . ."

"My partnership, as you call it, does not include in any

way, shape or form, authority over his tribe, Gigi. Nor, for that matter, over the Unseelie Court."

"It could." Adam looked at me, then at Gigi. "I claimed Keira, as she has me," he said. "We have a blood bond, as I do with Niko and the rest of my tribe. She has as much authority with my people as Nikolai and I do. In my father's eyes, as my companion, she is heir alongside me."

CHAPTER THIRTY-FIVE

I GAPED AT the two of them, then looked over at Niko and Tucker, both of whom seemed to be struggling with this concept as well. "Seriously? You're not just saying this?"

"Why would I? I admit, I've enjoyed my solitude, my independence over the years, but if keeping you and yours safe means returning to my involvement with my father's court, I will do so. You would do the same for me and mine, would you not?" He amended the last. "In fact, you have. You risked your life for me, you've saved your friend Bea. You are a leader and a ruler in your very nature, Keira. Take this opportunity. If it means relocating to British Columbia, then so be it." He bowed to Gigi. "I will go where she goes."

Gigi's eyes locked with Adam's, both of them equals in many things, including power and damned stubbornness. I noticed Tucker had crossed his arms and pasted a "wait and see" expression on his face. Niko had dropped into vampire stillness.

For the first time since we'd returned, I wondered where Rhys and Daffyd were. Knowing Gigi, she'd had them go off on some fool's errand, aka, make yourselves scarce.

"You'd abandon your tribe?" Gigi finally asked, gaze never wavering.

Adam responded, "I would not. There is a great deal of land in British Columbia. Much wildlife. My tribe would do well here as in Texas, perhaps even better. There's not such heat here."

"And it rains a lot and is overcast," Tucker added. "Convenient."

"Keira." Gigi turned her attention to me. "Would you be content coming here to the Clan enclave? Learning to be my heir, living amongst the Kellys?"

"You're *asking* me?" Why was she all of a sudden asking and not telling? "What about Gideon?"

"Do not think of him. If he did not exist, would you want to come here? Live with family, be a part of the Clan and learn to become the Clan chief? Would you work with me to unite all the Other, become a power in the modern world?"

I shuddered. Politics. Damn. The last thing I ever wanted to think about. "Do I have a choice?" I asked. "Isn't this what being the Kelly heir is all about?"

Gigi studied me without answering. She stood and walked to me, looking down on my face, on my position. Without realizing it, I'd been gripping the arms of the chair as if it were about to take off into the air. Beside me, Adam still draped an arm over my shoulder. Tucker and Niko still stood to the side and slightly behind, each with a hand on the back of the chair.

"Look at you," she said quietly. "Already ruling. Already their leader. Adam may be king, but he rules with your well-being foremost in his mind. And you have a Protector from both Kelly and vampire clans already in your service. Whether you realize it or not, Keira, you are already uniting. In your small group of four, you've united both Sidhe Courts, our Clan and the vampires. You'll be a force to be reckoned with, child. Perhaps not now, but in time . . . in time." She bent and placed a kiss on the top of my head. A tingle of energy ran through me. She'd given me her blessing.

My great-great-grandmother returned to her seat. "I believe that, for now, I prefer you return to Texas. You and Adam can watch over the territory there. Gideon can remain Below for a while, reacquainting himself with his Sidhe heritage. He is also heir, but I intend to rule for a long time yet. We can readdress this sometime . . . later, I think." She settled into the comfortable chair. "You're going to need more family around, though. I believe I'll send Rhys and Ianto to you. Your father and Isabel will surely visit at some point. They were looking forward to seeing you while you were out here, but . . . well, the schedule didn't work out, did it?"

I studied her for a moment. "You had them go straight to the enclave because Gideon had disappeared, am I right? Woke up and scarpered. Figures."

My great-great-granny didn't even bother to address my remarks. She continued explaining her plans.

"I'll send the Sidhe Daffyd back to his own Court, but I will have perhaps one or two others join you, as you'll need some training." She looked at Adam. "There is room at that ranch of yours, is there not?"

Adam nodded, his face giving nothing away. Despite his lack of expression, I could feel the tension leaving his skin. I hadn't noticed how wound up he had been, probably because I was myself. I couldn't even look at Niko or Tucker, afraid to break out in hysterical laughter.

"Seriously?" I frowned at her. There had to be a catch. Surely she couldn't be letting me go like that? Not after everything? "You're going to let us go back to Texas, split up the family?"

"I'm not splitting up the family," Gigi said, a self-satisfied smile making me want to think she'd chased, killed and eaten something delectable. I wouldn't put it past her, actually. "Merely expanding my . . . our base of operations."

"Our?" I couldn't help the sarcasm that crept its way out of my mouth.

The canary-swallowed smile expanded. "Despite everything, darling, you are still one of my heirs."

Oh, for fuck's sake. I was getting my own Court. A retinue and all that came with this ridiculous position.

Rio Seco, Texas, was never going to be the same.

CODA

Aftermath

The song plays in the wind of the night, although there is no one there to hear it, no one to Call. Melody weaves into harmony, into the beat, beat, beat of the hearts pounding together in utter synchronicity. John picks up his guitar one more time, fingers straining to recapture that song, wondering why it's so elusive. Rodney prods him, ready to accompany him on the bodhrán.

"I can't remember it," John says. "It's gone."

"I do," Rodney says. "Here, let me."

He begins to hum.

After a moment, John's fingers find the notes.

Far below them, Underhill, a dark-haired bard picks up his lute and joins in.

TAKE A WALK ON THE DARK SIDE...